FANTASY ANGELS SERIES

THE FALL OF LILITH

VASHTI QUIROZ-VEGA

This book is dedicated to my husband JC Vega with love. What can I say about a man who doesn't read fiction, but tirelessly listened while I read this book again and again. And who after listening to the dark parts of the book continues to sleep next to me with the lights off.

To my parents, Rosa Maria and Rafael, my greatest heroes, thank you for instilling in me the love of reading.

To the bookworms, book nerds, and bibliophiles—this is for you.

THE FALL OF LILITH

BOOK I

HEAVEN

Chapter 1

IN THE BEGINNING

Before He created the universe, God was present. Alone and bored in Heaven, He decided to create angels—celestial beings to serve as companions. When God formed them, He made them perfect. He then endowed them with free will so they might choose their own way, making them somewhat unpredictable—and more interesting.

There are three realms of Heaven: Heaven Most High where God resides, Metá Heaven, and Floraison, the lowest realm of Heaven where God placed the angels. Different dimensions separate these realms and only God traveled between them as He pleased.

The angels were child-like when God first made them. A delicate brilliance emanated from within each one. They were formed with two small white wings, which carried them across the vast expanse of Floraison quickly and without much effort.

God clothed the angels because He desired to show distinction between the superior celestial beings and the other creatures that roamed the lowest realm of Heaven. There were many strict rules in God's system of law, as He held angels at higher standards than any other creature. The two most important vows of an angel were obedience and celibacy.

Although the young angels bore

many similarities early on, they developed distinct personalities and traits due to their free will. God also promised each angel one or more special ability, which in time they would develop and learn to control. What divine skill they would acquire and when was as individual as they were.

There was no need for a sun, moon, or stars to give Floraison light. God's splendor lit the lowest realm, and the skies were beautiful beyond compare. There was no true darkness where the angels lived. In Floraison's unit of time there was brillante, when the light was at its most intense and nightglow when at its dimmest.

There were many trees and meadows adorned with colorful flowers that emitted fragrances evoking happiness and vigor. Magnificent creatures abounded, large and small—perfect in every way and pleasing to the senses. Some of these creatures were prototypes for beings God created on different planets, and others were unique to Floraison.

The River of Life, a pure river with crystalline healing waters, flowed between realms and proceeded from God's throne room. The chamber was accessed through a portal that led to Metá Heaven where God's presence could be reached. Only by His expressed permission could one cross this portal. This hall was aglow with the most exquisite light ever seen, and it was in the throne room God passed laws and judgments.

There were fruit trees, root vegetables, bush berries, and many more edible delights in Floraison, but the angels did not require food. These delicacies existed to teach them self-discipline since these foods were delicious, producing energy and much pleasure. They were only allowed to partake of the food during celebrations and after strenuous workouts. It required God's consent. The young angels spent their early days getting to know one another and learning about God's laws, nature, animals, the cosmos, and themselves.

Lilith and Michael delighted in their home, for Floraison was exquisite and full of joy, most of the time.

"I accept rules because they establish guidelines for action and conduct," Michael said with a solemn expression. "Rules create stability, discipline, and promote safety. Could you imagine what Beelzebub would be like had he no rules to follow?" Lilith glanced at Michael, the corners of her lips fighting a smile, her eyebrows slightly raised. Michael's mouth twitched and soon they both burst into laughter.

"Beelzebub would be a complete mess without rules. I know that," Lilith said. "But still, I am not fond of the many rules set by God for our kind. You are an upholder while I am a questioner."

Michael puckered his brow. "How could one question God?"

Lilith ignored his question. "I cannot wait for the day I discover the divine talents He has promised. I hope my abilities are godlike." Perceiving the power of God, evident in all things, awakened in her mind an aspiration that consumed her. She was fired by the desire for divine power.

Michael looked at her sideways. "You have always told me that you longed to be close to God—to be first in his eyes. How do you expect to rise to Heaven Most High if you question God's laws?"

"God does not want us to follow his laws without question. That is why he gave us free will, so that we may follow our own path."

Michael gazed into her peculiar yet beautiful eyes, one blue iris and one brown iris. "Perhaps one day I shall come to understand you."

"Sooner rather than later—I hope." She gazed up at him through her long, dark lashes, giggled and grabbed his hand. "Come, let us go to Sonnoris." Lilith enjoyed the marvels in Floraison all the while imagining the day she would create wonders of her own.

Sonnoris was a scenic land densely populated in parts with many dwellings, but still open enough to allow for wide forested areas and marshes. There were green rolling hills, streams, and colorful gardens. The angels called Sonnoris home.

Many angels gathered at Sonnoris to discuss the day's events. They sat on grass, mossy ground, and flat rocks in a wooded area near a stream where towering weeping willows encircled them and formed a natural large, round chamber with a canopy overhead like a living gazebo. The angels took turn standing in the center of the gazebo and gave their accounts of the day.

One such day, Lilith stood in the center and addressed the others. "I have noticed that many of you have undergone changes. Yes, we have grown in the fourteen spans of our existence and our wings have grown with us, but I mean changes of another sort. I have yet to receive God's promised gift, but I am sure some of you already possess remarkable abilities. Come forth and tell us the gifts God has bestowed upon you." She scanned their faces. Some of the angels sitting around her squirmed and lowered their eyes, looking anxious under her unrelenting stare.

Hashmal jumped to his feet and tugged on Esar to stand with him. They moved to the center of the gazebo as Lilith sat by Michael. Lucifer glanced her way with a longing expression, but lowered his head when she caught his eye.

Hashmal cleared his throat as he often did when addressing a crowd. "I sat alone on the lush green grasses of Triumph Gardens. Instead of studying, I stared at my fingers, as I often did when in a fog." The surrounding angels laughed recognizing this to be so. "I was startled by a sound—a whimper I heard coming from nearby lilac bushes. I approached the thicket and saw a pair of enormous frog legs. I backed away but continued to stare at the large green ankles, soles, and webbed toes. Soft sobs emanated from the shrub, so I approached the intriguing lilac bushes once more to listen more closely. I knew frogs did not make sounds such as those.

"I held my breath and parted the branches. That's when I saw Esar sitting on the ground, holding his knees and rocking.

"Flanking his head on both sides were long fuzzy llama ears. They pointed straight up through his dark curly hair, stemming from where his ears should be. Large frog legs had replaced his own, but the rest of his body remained in his likeness. It was the first time I had ever witnessed Esar's bizarre shifting ability."

"How did you do that?" Lilith stared at Esar wild-eyed.

Esar lifted his deep-set dark eyes, wet with despair, and shrugged.

"Why do tears flow from your eyes? Does wearing frog and llama parts hurt?" Lilith asked.

Esar shook his head. "No, it does not hurt, but it frightens me. I hid because these strange changes shamed me."

Michael rose to his feet and approached Esar. "There is no need to fear your ability, for God granted you this power. Nor is there reason to be embarrassed, and certainly not hide." He touched foreheads with Esar, a sign of affection and returned to his place on the mossy grass next to Lilith.

"I am not clear how this happened to me." Esar said. "I saw a frog hop from lily pad to lily pad. Curious to know where it traveled to, I jumped into the pond after it, but the frog leaped rapidly, and I lost it. Soon afterward I spotted a llama, but by the time I reached the location where I had seen it, the creature had disappeared. This made me angry with myself for being so slow. Then llama ears sprang from my head, and my legs transformed into huge green ones." He shrugged and began to demonstrate how he hopped to and fro on frog legs. The angels burst into laughter.

Lilith stared at him as he hopped about, in awe of his strange litheness.

Once Esar stopped bouncing, Hashmal placed a hand on his shoulder. "Well, it is an impressive skill to be able to shift into other beings. You should be grateful. Pray God gives you control of it soon."

Esar looked at him sideways. "You think it is impressive to have furry ears and webbed feet?"

Hashmal chuckled. "Yes, you have a great talent."

Esar returned his smile and wiped his eyes. Hashmal put his arm over his shoulder and they sat.

Raphael got to his feet and stood before the others. "I accidently stepped on a small bird that had fallen out of its nest." His eyes were doleful. "It was dying. My heart ached with sorrow and guilt. When I lifted the bird, my hand took on a stellar glow. Words appeared in my mind's eye, and I was compelled to read them aloud. Soon the small bird's crushed body returned to its healthy form. Before long the small bird spread its wings and flew across the sky as if I had never injured it."

"You have the power to restore life?" Lilith's eyes were large round spheres.

"No, I have the gift of healing." Raphael walked away from the center and sat on a flat rock.

Lucifer jumped to his feet and swaggered toward the middle of the gazebo. "While training at Guidance Park I too discovered some of my abilities." He grinned at Lilith. "I possess enhanced physical and mental abilities."

"How so?" Lilith leaned forward staring at him.

Lucifer jutted his chin. "I am faster, stronger and overall superior to fellow members of our species."

"Are you saying there are no limits to your physical strength, speed or stamina?" Michael asked. He glanced at Lilith and saw her interest in Lucifer's words. She listened with her whole body.

"I am saying that I have yet to find my limits, and thus far I am more powerful than any other angel." Lucifer raised an eyebrow. "Furthermore, I discovered that I have the ability to track any of you using my mind, I can also create a mental map of an area."

"I believe we all have some capability to navigate intuitively." Michael crossed his arms.

"Not at the range that I can." Lucifer scowled at him and then turned away and gave the others a slight close-lipped smile.

"How do you know this?" Michael squinted his eyes and waited for his response.

"I just do." Lucifer's face turned an angry red.

There was an uncomfortable silence as Michael and Lucifer scrutinized one another.

Gabriel leapt from his seat. "Night glow is upon us. Perhaps we should get some rest for we know not what new trials the morrow shall bring."

"If it is God's plan to test us, will resting in our bungalows prepare us?" Lucifer stood straighter, jeering. "I shall go to Guidance Park and continue to fortify the gifts given to me. I suggest everyone do the same." He lumbered across the gazebo and headed toward the park.

Most of the angels followed him. Lilith got up to follow him also but Michael held her hand.

"Please wait. May I speak frankly with you?" He cupped her hand with his other hand.

"What is it?" Lilith looked into his green eyes and it was like diving into an emerald pool.

He moved closer to her. "I do not want you to be afraid of what is to come. I shall always look after you and protect you. I desire that we always be together for I am most at home by your side."

"I shall look after you as well." She leaned forward and touched her lips to his.

Michael jumped back. "What are you doing?"

Lilith gasped surprised by his reaction. "I only wanted to show affection."

"Show affection with words or by joining foreheads but not with actions such as that." Michael scowled. "Why do you insist on disobeying the laws established by God?"

"I question why we need such laws." Lilith clapped her hands on her hips. "I believe God made a mistake giving us free will. How could we go our own way if His laws impede our path?"

Michael stared at her in disbelief. "Why must you be so defiant? Do you not understand that we are a medium of God's power and wisdom?"

"If God were watching—"

"God is everywhere and sees everything, Lilith!"

"God cannot be everywhere at once—that's why he created us and that's why he needs us." She pulled her hand from his and flounced toward Guidance Park.

"Wait!" Michael clenched his jaw. "Do not be angry with me."

Lilith stopped and turned to him. "You told me we belonged together but cringe when I show the slightest affection."

A wary smile surfaced on Michael's lips. "If I hurt you it is not what I intended. We cannot be together in that way—remember the laws. Obedience and celibacy are binding oaths that we as angels made to God. There would be serious repercussions if these vows were broken. If we are to ascend together to Heaven Most High we must abide by the laws." He wrung his hands as she flounced away without a word.

He watched her until she was out of sight and hung his head. A tightening and burning sensation in his chest made him rub it without thinking. After a while he woke from his sorrowful fog and decided to join the others at Guidance Park.

When Michael arrived at the park Hashmal was wrestling with Beelzebub in the Performance Circle.

Beelzebub teased Hashmal without end. He pulled his strawberry-blond hair, which was not permitted. Hashmal's face became deep fire and he puffed as he tried to grab hold of him, but Beelzebub swerved and evaded his grasp. Too quick and agile for him he escaped every time and then jeered and teased him. Beelzebub turned his back on him to coax the other angels to clap and cheer for him. That is when Hashmal finally caught him and flung him to the ground.

Lying flat on the ground, Beelzebub was defenseless against Hashmal, who sat on top of him, one leg at each side. Beelzebub cackled. Hashmal pinned his arms to the ground and glared into his eyes. Beelzebub stopped his snickering and stared wide-eyed at his face.

"I do not hear mockeries coming from your mouth now!" As Hashmal yelled, red-orange flames shot from his mouth, singeing Beelzebub's eyebrows clean off. Hashmal's eyes were glowing red spheres. His scarlet strands of hair appeared to be pulled away from his head in every direction by a million tiny unseen hands.

Beelzebub wriggled and screamed. Hashmal released him and fell back on his rump. Beelzebub dragged himself across the ground, retreating. He trembled and tittered between sobs. His crimson face, scorched by Hashmal's fiery breath, began to form large blisters.

Hashmal tried to stand but plopped back to the ground. He dragged himself backward, his face ashen. His eyes shifted between Beelzebub, who lay on the ground moaning, and the spectators with shocked faces who had gathered around.

Lilith's mouth gaped and she approached the circle. "Why did you emit fire to injure Beelzebub?" Her wide eyes did not blink. "That is not part of wrestling."

Michael stepped forward and stood by her as she waited for an answer.

Hashmal appeared perplexed. He moved his mouth but words did not come, so he stared ahead and panted.

Beelzebub resembled a dark berry that had grown past the point of ripeness. Huge oozing blisters covered a greater part of his face. "My face, my face!" He slammed his eyes shut and groaned in pain.

"Perhaps h-he did not intend t-to do this." Esar walked over to Hashmal and put his arm around his shoulders. "Leave him be. Tend t-to your f-friend Beelzebub, for he suffers mm-much pain."

Lilith creased her brow, mystified by Esar's stuttering and Hashmal's ability to breathe fire. She helped Beelzebub to his feet.

Michael examined his injuries, as Beelzebub shrieked and groaned. "Raphael!" he called. "Perhaps you can help him."

Raphael approached. He placed a hand in front of Beelzebub's face. Beelzebub jerked and twitched. "Please be still," Raphael said. He closed his eyes and began to glow. The angels nearby flinched from the intensity of the light emanating from him. Many used their wings to shield their eyes, for he gleamed like a star.

He whispered words no other angel understood. A short time after, Beelzebub ceased his sniveling. The inflammation, darkness and blisters were gone, and his face was restored to a white blush.

Lilith gasped. "That was amazing!"

"Indeed it was," Michael said. "You are blessed to have such a gift."

Lilith turned to Hashmal and scowled. "Angels should never use their abilities to hurt our own!"

"It was not intentional." His eyes remained fixed to the ground and his voice was little more than a whisper.

Michael watched as he hung his head in shame.

"Was this the first time your ability to breathe fire manifested itself?" Michael's eyes held no judgment.

Hashmal nodded.

"Then the mishap was not your fault. You could not know this would happen." Michael patted him on shoulder.

"Do you see, my friend?" Esar placed a hand on his friend's shoulder and squeezed. "Do not be ashamed, for you have done no wrong."

Lilith's eyes flashed with fury. "He has nothing to feel shame for? If you had only seen what you looked like. Your eyes were glowing red like two globes on fire. An intense crimson glow radiated from your gullet. The red light shone through your skin as your neck expanded. Your hair seemed ablaze, standing upright on your head. Then you excreted fire from mouth like the monsters from Arathi, the land of fire on the planet Thanda-Garam!"

"Enough Lilith!" Michael took her arm gently but she wrested it from his hand.

Hashmal stared at her, trembling and pale. His face twisted in horror at her description. Michael saw how her words had affected him and frowned.

"I know the beasts of which you speak for I have seen them once during our study of the planet Thanda-Garam in the Atrium. Was I so terrible?" Hashmal's voice was brittle.

Esar shook his head wearing a stern expression. "You were intense. You demonstrated the power of God. Now that we both know what our abilities are we must work on mastering them before they take control of us.

"You are right, my friend." Hashmal took a deep breath.

Michael smiled at them and nodded in agreement.

Gabriel seemed to materialize out of thin air. Lilith gasped and jumped back. Others around recoiled. "I believe we all need to learn to control and develop the gifts we were given." Gabriel faced the crowd. "As I have demonstrated, I have the ability to take on a non-corporeal form. I can also move instantaneously from one location to another without occupying the space in between. I have the power to manipulate energy. Although, like Hashmal, I have much to learn about my abilities."

Lilith rolled her eyes. "Raphael, you have the ability to heal." She gestured to him and then turned to Gabriel. "You can change into spirit form and vanish like a mist in the wind. Esar has the ability to shift into different life forms and bend his body in unnatural ways and Hashmal breathes fire. Michael and Lucifer have the most impressive talents of all, but what about the rest of us? Does God not intend to bestow each of us with such gifts?"

"God promised that every angel shall develop abilities that are remarkable and astonishing—that includes you," Michael said with a sweet and gentle expression. "It may take longer for some to realize their gifts."

Lilith rolled her eyes skyward and heaved an exasperated sigh.

The angels continued to grow and further cultivated their characteristics and talents as they played, interacted with each other, and completed trials together.

Since the beginning every story has its dark side. Not all angels developed traits that were pure or righteous, and a hint of malevolence diffused little by little throughout Floraison.

Chapter 2

LILITH'S SECRET

The angels attended school each brillante in classrooms located throughout Floraison. Most of their lessons were taught in the Atrium, a vast salon where all the cosmos could be viewed. They were allowed to study and research planets and life forms outside the realm of Floraison, but they were prohibited from leaving and visiting these worlds.

This was one of many rules Lilith disliked. She took pleasure in observing the different planets and the species that inhabited them. She hoped that one brillante she would be able to visit them.

Her favorite planet was Thanda-Garam in the Black-Eye galaxy. The planet was divided into a frosted, bright segment, and a dark, fiery segment. The inhabitants of the planet were practical creatures who had adapted quite well to their environment. She enjoyed watching the inhabitants of both areas of the planet but was more intrigued by the side blanketed in snow and ice. They lived in ice caves and created many beautiful sculptures made of ice and snow to adorn their surroundings. Since it always snowed on their side, the sculptures would soon be buried, but that never stopped them from creating more.

Thanda-Garam could be observed from a small hidden room in the atrium. This was another reason she enjoyed observing the planet. Other angels rarely visited the area, and she knew she would not be disturbed.

She spent hours alone viewing the planet and its resilient inhabitants, all the while illicit thoughts whirled in her head. Thoughts of Michael, the gifts God had promised and freedom to do as she pleased. Lilith smiled and laughed while looking at the funny, busy little beings, for there was something she found truly inspiring and soothing about them. She often fell asleep in the process of watching and fantasizing. It was at such a moment that she experienced her first vision.

Lilith woke to screams. She stood in a dark forest, a place darker than any she had ever seen, unable to move or utter a sound. Her heart pounded as she watched two large, strong male beings chase a young female, whose burnt umber hair flowed in long waves behind her as she fled down a muddy trail. The young female ran as quickly as she could through the dark woods. In her arms she clutched a creature white as the snow on Thanda-Garam.

"Run, you witch!" one of the males yelled. "Both you and your familiar shall be dead before dawn!"

The young female panted. Her wide eyes darted in every direction as she tried to find a place to hide. Spotting a small cave, she headed toward it. She entered the cave and placed the albino feline on the ground.

"Phantom, you must stay here and be silent lest those witch-hunters find us and kill us," she whispered. The creature curled up into a ball of ghostly white fur and stared at her with lavender eyes full of fear.

"I shall conceal the cave," she said in a low voice. She stepped outside and began gathering branches, shrubs, and twigs to cover the opening of the cave, working as fast as she could.

Lilith heard the men approaching. She gasped and her pulse raced. Hurry, hide in the cave! She wanted to yell, but she was a silent witness. The female managed to cover three quarters of the cave from view before she crept back in. She lay down next to Phantom and waited.

"Oh, come out, come out wherever you are, little witch!" one of the hunters shouted.

"Why prolong the inevitable?" the other asked. "You shall be tied to a stake and roasting slowly before the sun rises."

The young female trembled. The feline meowed softly. She shook her head.

"Shhh. Please, Phantom, be quiet." Her teeth chattered and oceans of tears washed over her face as she heard the heavy tread of the men drawing near.

"You might as well come out of hiding, for we can smell the stench of a witch for miles!" They were right outside the cave now. The female placed both hands over her mouth, unable to contain her body-racking sobs.

Phantom jumped to his four paws, his amethyst eyes emitting a haunted glow. He began to tremble and meow. She picked him up and held him tightly against her throbbing bosom. She tried to get him to be quiet, but he was terrified. She felt his heart racing against her. She kissed the top of his head, and he finally became quiet, but it was too late.

A powerful arm reached in through the nest she had made and yanked her out by her messy dark hair. One hunter dragged her through the mud as the other man kicked her again and again. She wailed but never released her cherished companion.

"Let go of the cat, you witch!" the one kicking her yelled.

"No!" she screamed.

The hunter clutching her hair gestured to the other to stop kicking. "That is fine. Let her hold onto her cat—her familiar." He leered at her. "We're going to tie you and that fur ball together, just as you are now. You shall both burn slowly and painfully, beginning at the feet. Unless—you do something for us."

He exposed his male organs. She gasped and flinched twisting her face in disgust. "Go on, wrap those plump rosy lips around it. I'll pump it in and out of your mouth while you whirl your tongue around it. The more pleasure I feel, the less pain you and your familiar will feel. Then you can do my friend. If you pleasure us throughout the night, we'll give you a quick death. What say you?"

She sat on her legs and stared at him, her eyes flooded with hate. She nodded. The witch-hunter laughed and winked at his friend.

"Go on!" He held his engorged member. She rose to her knees, still holding Phantom close. Her chest heaved, as her face got closer to his genitals. The stench of urine and filth, accumulated after days without washing, wafted into her nose, making her stomach turn and she retched. The hunter inhaled a deep sigh and tilted his head back, eyes closed in anticipation.

Moving like the wind, she reached for his scrotum, opened her mouth wide, and clamped her teeth around the sac. Blood sprayed her face as the

15

hunter howled in pain. He yanked at her hair, trying to pry her loose, but she continued to bite down.

The other hunter kicked and punched her, but it only caused his companion more pain. She did not let go until she had torn his scrotum from his body. The hunter collapsed, howling as he tried to stop the jetting blood.

She spit the parts out of her mouth. When the other hunter saw his friend's scrotum mangled and bloodied on the ground, he pushed her down on her back and ran his blade through Phantom and into her heart. The cat died instantly, and with her last breath, she laughed. The hunter then realized he had spared her from a gruesome death by fire. He threw his head back and bellowed.

Lilith sat upright, gasping loudly, eyes large. Her heart thumped in her ears. She looked around relieved to see that she was still in the atrium.

What was that? Who were those beings? She got to her feet but the room spun and she collapsed to a seated position again. Those creatures physically resembled angels in almost every way. They were wingless, older and lacked their glow, but their similarity was uncanny. She had never seen beings such as these anywhere in the galaxies. Where were these creatures from? They must exist somewhere, or she would not have seen them. Why—how was she able to see this? It had seemed so real. Then she remembered the gift God promised—He gave her the gift of sight. She looked at her hands that were still trembling from the experience.

This has to be an oversight on God's part, for surely an angel was not meant to see such things. Part of her was excited; she was the only angel capable of seeing these beings and the things they did. She may be able to learn much from them. Another part of her dreaded these extremely realistic visions.

After this experience, Lilith continued to receive visions. She saw many episodes in the lives of the dark, wingless angels, as she began to call them. She sometimes had visions while awake, other times while asleep but she was always alone when they came. Sometimes she felt physically present in her vision, and other times she watched them unfold as if she was only observing. She received most of her visions in the small section of the atrium where she watched Thanda-Garam. Perhaps she had so many visions there because she was undisturbed and always felt calm and free.

She did not yet fully understand her visions or have control of when they came. She was still young. At some point these visions would serve a great purpose. In the meantime, she would continue learning from the dark, wingless angels, although much of what she would learn from these beings would be in direct violation to the laws of Floraison.

Chapter 3

QUEST FOR EXCITEMENT

Lilith's eyes glittered with mischief as she flitted throughout Floraison, searching for Gadreel. She had not had a vision in a while, and was bored and wanted a thrilling experience. Perhaps with a little help from a friend she could get what she craved—excitement.

She spotted Gadreel standing by a large bush bursting with pink and yellow peonies. To sniff them, Gadreel stuck her face into the flowers, which were bigger than her head, until she almost disappeared.

Lilith chuckled. "I was searching everywhere for you, and here you are with your face buried in flowers again."

Gadreel jumped. "The blooms are just opening, and their crisp and invigorating fragrance envelops me. It makes me float smiling throughout Floraison."

"Oh, Gadreel! You're standing before me, with feet firmly planted on the ground." She waved dismissingly. "I have a new game I would like us to—"

"I wish I owned a garment as beautiful as the petals on this flower, instead of this plain shapeless thing." She looked at her simple white garment and began to smooth it out with her hands. She stopped and met Lilith's gaze. Lilith's irises were two different colors: the right one was blue like the deepest part of the River of Life, and the left one a rich amber-brown. The angels had learned by now that when Lilith was annoyed she raised the brow over her blue eye. Seeing it now, Gadreel became silent, and her smile disappeared.

"Would you let me finish, or are you going to continue talking about these trivial flowers?" Lilith shook her leg.

"The flowers are not trivial," Gadreel muttered under her breath.

"What? Did you say something?" Lilith's eyebrows bumped together in a scowl.

Gadreel stood on tiptoe. "Apologies! I did not mean to interrupt. Please tell me about your new game."

Lilith rested a hand on her hip. "My new game involves hiding and seeking. I need you to help me find a large group of angels to try it out."

"Of course. I have a good idea where to find Samael. We can begin there."

"No! We shall find Michael first—then we shall look for Samael."

Gadreel lowered her large dark eyes and nodded. Even as a child Lilith was able to manipulate her friend with a mere glance. Lilith started on her way, fluttering her wings as she went to gain speed. Her simple one-piece garment made of a soft, white lightweight fabric flapped in the wind, and the flowers and bushes trembled as she passed them.

Gadreel hurried to follow, but she took a wrong step, tripped over her own feet, and landed hard on the muddy ground. Lilith laughed. Gadreel frowned.

Lilith stopped laughing when she realized Gadreel could have hurt herself. She would need her friend to organize the game, and she ran to help her.

"Are you alright?" Lilith asked in a honeyed tone.

Gadreel lifted her moist, imploring eyes and gazed at her.

Lilith extended her hand and pulled her friend to a standing position. Gadreel winced when she placed a foot on the ground. She lifted her leg, grabbed her aching ankle and rubbed it. Then she noticed how soiled her dress had gotten. She grimaced and tried to remove some of the mud but only succeeded in spreading the dirt further. Sensing Lilith's impatience, she searched her face.

"Stop looking at me that way," Lilith said.

"Apologies—I hate to delay you."

"You are constantly stumbling. We have only reached fifteen ages of life and have much growing to do. You shall not make it to maturity if you continue being so clumsy."

Gadreel avoided her gaze. "I shall be fine. Perhaps we should find the others." She put her foot down, clenching her teeth and wincing. She grabbed Lilith's hand and began hobbling beside her.

Lilith scowled at her. "Your hands are dirty!"

Gadreel gave her a toothy grin. Lilith giggled and returned her smile.

"I suspect we shall find Michael at Guidance Park," Lilith said as they strolled.

Guidance Park was a vast yard bordered on the north by Mount Verve. Dangerous forests enclosed the park on the east and west. The only permitted entry and exit was through two large, carved wooden doors located in the southern area of the yard. The smaller, but deadly, South Forest flanked the great wooden doors. The angels were forbidden to venture into any of the perilous woods edging Guidance Park.

Lilith was right—Michael was at the park sparring with Lucifer. They wrestled in the area of the park called Performance Circle. Each wore a piece of soft, lightweight white cloth, passed between the thighs and wound around the waist.

"Michael, Michael!" Lilith waved. "I have a new game I would like us all to play!"

Michael turned his deep viridian eyes her way. Lucifer took advantage of the distraction to knock him to the ground and straddle him. Lilith gasped. Biting her lip, Gadreel glanced at her. They gaped as Lucifer held Michael down.

Lilith observed Lucifer. He was a formidable opponent for Michael, even as a youngster he had broad-shoulders, hypnotic blue eyes, and long, thick dark hair like black garnet. His pure white wings grew larger and mightier with the passing of time, but even with his gifts, she believed he could not defeat Michael.

She turned her gaze to Michael. He was God's favorite—she was certain of it. Because of this she decided not to compete with him. Instead, she would make him her ally and catapult him to the greatest heights. Every angel would do all he commanded, and she would bend him to her will. As he was God's beloved, so would he be hers.

Grunting, Michael shoved Lucifer, who tumbled to the ground and rolled away. Gadreel stood on her tiptoes, nibbling her fingers. Lilith cheered as Michael jumped to his feet. His cropped blond hair shone like golden stardust in brillante light. He pounced on Lucifer, knocked him down, and pinned him to the ground. Lilith grinned, admiring Michael's power. She clapped and cheered for him, and Gadreel followed her lead.

"Great match, my brother. I learn something new from you every time we wrestle." Michael smiled, energetic green eyes earnest.

Lucifer sighed and placed his hand on his shoulder. "It pleases me that I can make you a better fighter, but I fear this shall be the last time you are one step ahead of me."

Michael smiled and nodded.

"Michael, you are the greatest warrior in Floraison!" Lilith twirled her long, dark hair around her fingers. Her eyes were a quiet storm and her heart beat fast with excitement. Michael thrilled her. God created him to be the best. She could learn much from him. She could become as powerful as he—if he would make it so. She would become vital to his very existence, and then once she was invaluable to him, he would make her his equal.

"You almost cost me the fight when you arrived." Michael scowled. "You must not distract me when in the middle of a bout."

Gadreel bit her quivering lower lip and glanced at Lilith.

Lilith grinned. "I apologize for diverting your attention. It was not my intention."

Michael smiled a faint smile and nodded. Gadreel stared at the ground. Lilith bit the inside of her lower lip and remained silent.

Lucifer had seen and heard everything and came forward. "Your game intrigues me."

Lilith grinned. She scanned the park and counted many other angels nearby: Jetrel and Raquel chatting, Dagon and Fornues racing around, Hashmal and Esar playing, and Beelzebub and Cam lying on the grass while listening to Gabriel's singing. She beckoned them all.

Beelzebub pranced to her. Hashmal and Esar strolled, but Esar did a cartwheel as he came near. Dagon and the others joined in, while Fornues clomped behind him, muttering under his breath.

Gadreel looked around for Samael, but could not find him. She gazed at the ground frowning, rocking on her feet.

"What goes on here?"

She raised her head and her face came to life when she realized Samael had asked the question. Her almond-shaped, russet eyes gleamed with delight. "Samael!" She ran to him, her wild, golden curls twirled and looped in the wind.

"We are going to play my new game." Lilith looked pleased with herself.

"Can I play too?" Samael asked.

"Of course." Gadreel interrupted their dialogue, looking giddy. Lilith scowled. Did Gadreel presume to take over her game? Only she decides who takes part in her activities.

Her friend gawped at her.

"Of course, Samael," Lilith said in a fawning voice. "You are one of the most nimble angels in Floraison. You would make my game all the more fun."

Samael licked his lips and smiled. Lucifer sucked his teeth and looked away.

"Go on, Lilith. Tell us how to play now," Fornues said, grumbling.

"Must we wait forevermore?" Beelzebub rolled his eyes and placed a hand on his hip.

"Just give me a—" Lilith began.

Esar began to perform weird tricks with his tongue. He stuck it out, folded it in half, and twisted it from side to side. Then he waved his tongue back and forth, so it undulated like the ripples on a lake.

The angels laughed and stared in amazement at his tongue.

"Why do you do such strange things, Esar?" Beelzebub opened his eyes in an exaggerated manner. "I often wonder if God made you merely as a joke to amuse the rest of us."

Lilith smirked. Oh Beelzebub, you're the amusement.

"If watching my stunts causes someone to smile, that pleases me,"

Esar said. Beelzebub's forehead puckered, he rolled his pale green eyes and retreated.

"Enough!" Lilith yelled. "The hour has come to play."

Michael turned and began to walk away.

"Michael?" Lilith frowned. "Why are you leaving? You shall not play my game?"

"Apologies, Lilith. I have important things to do. Playing is for children and I do not consider myself a child any longer." Michael looked at her with an apologetic expression and then turned and walked away.

Heat rose from the pit of Lilith's stomach and bloomed on her face. Her eyes narrowed to slits on her red face, her nostrils flared and her hands clenched. He was making a habit of rejecting her and she was beginning to feel differently toward him.

"Let us play then," Lucifer said with a grin.

Lilith took a deep breath and stood before them. "I shall choose one of you to be *it*." She pointed at them one by one. "*It* shall cover his or her eyes while the others hide. Then *it* shall try and find us."

"We shall play in this area," Lilith added, indicating the area bordered by Mount Verve, the River of Life, and the East and South Forests. She strutted to a large tree and beckoned everyone to gather round. "I choose Fornues to be *it*. He shall cover his eyes and wait while the rest of us hide."

"Me?" Fornues's large, heavy-lidded eyes opened wide. "Why me?"

Beelzebub sucked his teeth. "Obviously because you are far too large to find a suitable hiding place. It would be easier to hide the tree that stands before us."

Gadreel lowered her head and placed the back of her hand over her mouth to conceal her giggles.

Fornues' face grew bright pink, and he glowered at Beelzebub. Lilith grabbed a small section of his long, wavy auburn hair and yanked on it. He turned to face her. She let go of his hair, and he scowled as he rubbed his aching scalp.

"Pay attention," she told him. "You shall count to fifty against this tree while we hide. This tree shall also be home base. Stay alert, because as you are searching for us, we shall try to run to home base."

Fornues scrunched his brow, gazed downward, and scratched his head.

Dagon saw his confusion and went to assist. "Fornues, you go hide with the others. I shall be *it.*"

Raquel smiled at Dagon, and he returned her smile. Lilith watched their brief interaction and smirked.

"Very well, let us get underway!" Lilith yelled. "Count to fifty, Dagon. Then find and tap the hidden players. At the same time, try to tap the running players before they get to home base. The first player you tap shall be *it* in the game that follows."

Dagon nodded and turned to face the large tree. He covered his eyes with both hands. He began to count, and the young angels scurried in every direction.

There were plenty of trees, shrubs, and bushes at the perimeter of the game. The youths ran. Some climbed trees while others dove behind bushes and shrubs. They spooked many animals; small rodents with fuzzy tails dashed to and fro, tree animals swung from one branch to the next, and graceful felines leapt from trees and slunk away.

Lilith skittered to a flowering shrub and hid behind it. She saw Samael and waved him over. He squatted by her side.

"Gadreel, Fornues, come here!" Lilith called when she spotted them. They hurried and crowded next to her and Samael. "This bush shall not hide all of us. It is too small."

"Where should we hide?" Fornues looked bewildered.

"There are plenty of shrubs and trees. Look around and find your own location." Samael shoved him and shifted, showing his discomfort.

"Or—we can find a place where we can all hide together?" Lilith said.

"For what purpose?" Samael frowned.

"It would be more fun if we hid together," she said with an appealing grin.

"Indeed, let us find a suitable area." Gadreel jumped to her feet. Lilith pulled her back down.

"I know of a perfect place." Lilith's smile was devious. Finally, the excitement she craved.

Lilith led the others to the edge of the East Forest. Raquel and Jetrel hid within the branches of a nearby tree and watched the group pass them by.

"Where is Lilith taking the others?" Raquel asked Jetrel.

"I know not."

"I believe she leads them to the East Forest." Raquel seemed alarmed. "She means for them to enter."

"No, it cannot be so. Lilith knows we are forbidden to enter."

"Still, she moves toward its entrance, and the others follow," Raquel said.

Jetrel glanced at her with a concerned expression. When she observed Lilith and her group, her expression changed to a glower.

Lilith scanned the faces of those with her and smiled mischievously. There was no better time to test her ability to influence others to do her will. For the most part, she had always been able to influence other angels to do her bidding, but never something as big as this. If she succeeded, it would make her powerful in the eyes of the angels. She could exercise this talent, and no one shall be the wiser.

"Dagon would never find us in there," Lilith coaxed the others, pointing at the East Forest with her nose. Fornues stared at her, his big droopy eyes looking more awake than usual.

Gadreel's eyes opened wide. "Lilith, you know we should not enter the forests. It is prohibited."

"We are not going to enter the forest." Lilith smiled and caressed her face. "We shall simply step a few feet inside and remain within the outer edge. Surely that is not what God meant when He said not to enter the forest."

"Still, it feels wrong," Gadreel said. "We have no right to question God's rules."

"I agree," Samael said. "We should not venture past the bordering trees."

Lilith wore a jeering expression. "So, you do not trust yourselves to stay within the outer edge of the forest?" Lilith teased. "You are weak-minded and cannot control your actions?" If she could influence them to break God's rules, it would prove that she was quite influential. The consequences may prove exciting.

Samael seemed irresolute about whether to do as Lilith asks. He glanced at Gadreel and then at Fornues. They stared at him like turtle hatchlings waiting for their parent to show them the way to the river.

"I have no such weaknesses," he told Lilith.

"Prove it!" She mocked him. "Step beyond the bordering trees and remain within the edge of the forest, hidden behind a bush or rock, until the game ends."

He inhaled and stepped past the strip of trees along the border of the East Forest.

"No! Do not go any further." Gadreel ran after him. Fornues stomped in after Gadreel, and they both entered the forest. Lilith laughed, amused by her power over them. She continued to watch, narrowing her eyes as she waited to see if anything happened to them. When nothing did, she could not resist and walked in after them.

Fornues found a large moss-covered rock suitable to hide behind. Lilith squatted behind a large shrub. Gadreel crouched next to her. Samael hid behind a tall tree covered in vines. They waited.

Gadreel trembled and pressed her body against Lilith.

"Stop shaking so." Lilith bumped her.

"Why does the darkness rule here?" Gadreel's lips quivered.

"The trees cover us from Floraison's light," Lilith said. "Now, be quiet. Otherwise we shall be discovered."

Gadreel held tight to Lilith's arm and placed her head on her shoulder. Lilith rolled her eyes but rested her head on Gadreel's.

Samael reclined against the tree. He experienced a piercing pain almost immediately. He jumped forward and whisked around to stare at the tree. The vines climbing the trunk were covered in red spines as long as his fingers. Pairs of large, dark green leaves also grew along the length of the plant. The leaves were shaped like small angel wings—yet eerie and menacing. Samael had never seen anything like it. He looked around and noticed the vines covered almost everything, including the ground. They even entwined the tallest trees, forming a dense canopy.

The wing-like leaves began to flutter lifting the vines off the ground and trees, allowing them to hover above the angels. The vines began to move, flying hither and thither. Hundreds of leaves were beating at once, creating a loud, eerie flapping noise.

Gadreel covered her ears with her hands and closed her eyes. Lilith stared openmouthed as the vines came alive, whipping through the air and slithering on the ground. She jumped to her feet and scurried toward the edge of the forest. Gadreel gasped and tried to follow her but instead stumbled to the ground.

"Lilith, help me!" Gadreel reached for her as vines wrapped around her body, their red thorns pricking her skin. Lilith looked over her shoulder and saw her friend ensnared by the vines but did not stop. She escaped the forest.

Lilith encountered Raquel and Jetrel standing a few feet from the edge of the forest. Raquel was developing as the clever one, but for all her knowledge, could she have done what Lilith did? Jetrel was becoming a great warrior, yet she too could not have accomplished what she had done. Lilith had influenced three angels to break God's law with only a few well-chosen words. No doubt these two would try to judge her for it.

Lilith glowered at them as she tried to catch her breath.

"Where are the others?" Raquel's face was etched with concern.

"I tried to help them," Lilith said, gasping, "but I was too weak, so I escaped to get help."

"You should have never led them into those woods." Jetrel flung herself at her. Raquel held her back. "You know they are forbidden to us."

"It was not my plan to enter the forest." Lilith curled her lips with icy contempt. "Gadreel wished for us to hide together."

Jetrel's eyes narrowed into slits as she scrutinized her.

"What is happening?" Michael marched toward them. Raphael, Cam, Esar, Hashmal and Dagon were with him.

"Lilith, Gadreel, Samael, and Fornues ventured into the East Forest," Raquel told them, her voice thick with apprehension.

Michael raised his eyebrows and glanced at Raphael and Cam. Hashmal and Esar stared at each other struck dumb with wonder.

Dagon aimed his sights at the dark woods. "Lilith stands before me, but where are the others?"

"They remain within the darkness of the forest." Raquel's deep-set green eyes glistened like misted fern.

Dagon stepped toward the forest. Michael and Raphael swiftly held him back.

"Release me. I must help my friend!" Dagon struggled to get free. "Fornues shall not know what to do if he finds trouble."

Raquel crossed her hands over her mouth, moved by Dagon's concern for his friend.

"You must not make the same mistake our friends made." Michael stood between Dagon and the forest. "We are not allowed to enter. You know this."

Michael and Raphael released him. Dagon closed his eyes and hung his head.

"Our friends are in God's hands now." Raphael stared into the gloom beyond the bordering trees. "If God chooses to save them, then they shall be saved."

Raquel nodded and caressed Dagon's head with her hand. Dagon lifted his doleful eyes and smiled at her. "And if God chooses not to save our friends?" he asked in a brittle voice. Raquel frowned as she gazed at his pained face. Raphael shook his head and turned away.

Lilith lowered her head and bit her lower lip only now realizing the consequences of her actions.

"If God chooses not to save them, they shall forever become a part of the darkness they are now in," Jetrel said.

Lilith gasped and stared wide-eyed at her.

"No." Dagon groaned. Raquel clenched her jaw and stared at him with a heart-rending expression.

"Apologies." Jetrel's face turned the color of a sweet cherry. "It shames me to have been so rash and insensitive with my words."

Lilith slowly stepped away from them. Her hands trembled and she clasped them together to keep them from shaking. She stood by Michael and took his hand in hers only to have him wrest it away. She swallowed hard and glanced at his stolid expression. She needed him now but he refused to look at her.

Beelzebub pranced to the group with Gabriel at his side. "Has the game ended?"

No one spoke a word. He scanned the grim faces of the other angels and crinkled his brow.

"What has transpired?" Gabriel frowned when he saw the distraught look on Dagon's face.

"Somebody please tell us what has happened!" Beelzebub said in a shrill frantic cry.

"Gadreel, Samael, and Fornues have ventured into the East Forest," Raquel said.

Gabriel gasped. Beelzebub screeched, as his hands flew to his face.

"Lilith also disobeyed God and entered the forest." Jetrel glared at her. Lilith jumped at the mention of her name. "Yet here she stands, unharmed amongst us, while the others are still trapped in darkness."

Michael stared at Lilith, a dour look on his usually engaging face.

Beelzebub gawked at her. Gabriel looked at her curiously.

Lilith flounced to Jetrel and gazed into her vivid blue-violet eyes. "Perhaps God chose to save me." She stroked Jetrel's smooth, black hair. Jetrel grimaced and recoiled from her.

"You do not seem pleased with God's decision to save me." Lilith's cheeks flushed and she stared at the ground. "Perhaps you think your wisdom surpasses that of His?" Lilith believed God valued her. She was certain He knew she was powerful and would become even more so in time as she grew and developed her abilities.

"Enough!" Michael said. "No one knows God's mind. We must wait and see what He has decided."

"What God has decided about what?" Lucifer strolled toward the others. Lilith crossed her arms and dashed to his side.

"Three of our friends are trapped in the East Forest." Michael watched Lilith fidget and squirm.

"The East Forest?" Lucifer's voice was tight. "What are they doing in there in the first place? We all know it is against God's law to enter any of the forests that border Guidance Park."

"I wished to hide behind a flower bush with Samael." Lilith looked down unable to meet his eyes. "But Gadreel and Fornues insisted we look for a hiding place where all four of us could hide together. I tried to stop them."

Lucifer frowned. She kept her head down and tried to hide behind her thick long hair. He turned to Michael and Raphael. "What can we do to help them?"

"We can do naught," Michael said. "If we enter the forest, we too shall be disobeying God's orders, and we shall also run the risk of being trapped in shadows."

Lucifer sighed and stared at the banned woodland.

"I have already been inside the forest. Perhaps I should return and try to release the others." Lilith volunteered in a melodramatic fashion, knowing Lucifer and Michael would forbid it. She turned toward the forest taking deliberate steps.

"Certainly not, it would be futile." Lucifer grabbed her arm. "Your intentions are good Lilith, but you shall be defying God yet again. He saved you once. If you choose to disobey Him a second time, what makes you think He would show such mercy again?"

Lucifer was unknowingly becoming her redeemer. Lilith gazed at him. "You are right. You are always so wise." She believed everyone judged her. Loathed her. All except Lucifer and Beelzebub. She did not wish for Gadreel, Samael and Fornues to remain trapped in darkness for she would need them at some point to do her bidding. It was easy for her to manipulate them. She could no longer say the same for Raquel or Jetrel and certainly not Michael. She needed her allies freed.

Chapter 4

ORIGINAL PUNISHMENT

Samael lurched and stumbled as he attempted to free Gadreel from the vines.

"Help me Samael!" The vines tightened around Gadreel's body, immobilizing her on the ground. She writhed and groaned as the plant's long, sharp spines penetrated deeper into her flesh.

"The creeping plants are making it difficult for me to get to you." Samael could not move forward. The vines attacked him, whipping and coiling around his arms, torso, legs, and ankles. In addition to the spines, the dark leaves stung him with their prickles. Samael winced and howled in pain. "I need your assistance, Fornues!"

The vines had not captured Fornues yet. He crouched behind a mossy rock trying to make his body as small as possible. "What should I do?"

"Free me from these vines!" Samael grimaced and clenched his teeth as the red spines tormented him.

Fornues lumbered to him and began to rip vines off him, despite the injury to his hands as the crimson spines buried themselves in his palms. Samael finally broke free. Fornues fought the vines, stomping on creepers as they attempted to grab his friend yet again.

Samael trampled on the vines to get to Gadreel. He yanked and wrenched the plants coiled around her body until he freed her. He grabbed her by the hand. "Come, Fornues!"

Fornues continued fighting the vines to ensure they would escape.

Gadreel looked back and saw him still wrestling with the wild vegetation. "Fornues, you must come now!"

Samael pulled her by the arm and together they staggered out of the forest, leaving him behind.

Fornues fought as hard as he could. But he soon tired, and the trailing plants overran him. He collapsed, and the creeping vines slithered into and tangled in his long, wavy hair, pulling it away from his head. They twisted around his face, neck, and torso. The plants pinned his arms and legs together and tied him to the ground. Soon he was covered completely except for his heavy-lidded, hazel eyes, and tears dripped from their drooping outer corners.

When Gadreel and Samael tottered out of the forest and collapsed on the grass, the other angels ran to their aid. They were covered in scratches and red, inflamed rashes. Spines were buried deep in their skin. The all-consuming pain made them groan and writhe on the grass. Raquel and Jetrel tried to comfort Gadreel. Gabriel tried to remove the spines buried in Samael's body, but the attempts only made him howl in pain.

The young angels could not believe the condition their companions were in. They had never seen injuries like these.

Dagon continued to stare at the edge of the forest, expecting Fornues to appear at any moment. When he did not, he proceeded to Samael. "Where is Fornues?"

"He was overrun by ferocious vines," Samael told him in a low, raspy voice.

Dagon furrowed his brow and turned away. He panted as he moved toward the forest. He stopped and glanced over his shoulder. Seeing the others were occupied with Gadreel and Samael, he continued and crossed into the dark woods.

Lilith watched him enter the forest. She lowered her gaze and remained silent. Her lips curve upward into a faint smile. Soon the others would discover that Dagon has entered the forest in pursuit of Fornues. It was conceivable that someone would pursue him knowing he went in to save his friend. Perhaps Jetrel? She always tried to prove her courage. If she entered the dark woods, surely Michael would also venture in to save her, and then Raphael would follow. How wondrous it would be if they all went in—that way the focus would be removed from her and they would all be in the same predicament.

"What are we to do?" Gabriel frowned. "Nothing we have tried has helped them." His airy, pale blue eyes displayed distress.

"I have done all I could." Raphael placed a hand on Gabriel's shoulder. "It seems clear that we are not meant to heal them."

"We should pray for God to show mercy, for they suffer so." Raquel fell to her knees and closed her eyes in prayer.

"Perhaps God intended that suffering be the punishment for this disobedience." Jetrel wore a stern expression.

"I agree with Jetrel." Cam scrutinized Lilith, and his bouncing curls, tinged with red, bobbed as he nodded. "Gadreel and Samael disobeyed God. Now they must pay for their disobedience." Lilith scowled at him.

"Perhaps you are both right." Raphael approached Cam and Jetrel. "Still, we can pray for mercy."

"I shall go ask permission to enter the portal to cross into Metá Heaven and ask God what is His will." Michael stared at Lilith as he spoke. She fidgeted and tried to avoid the disappointed look on his face.

"Michael, the two of us shall go to God and speak on our brethren's behalf." Lucifer stood by him. "In the meantime, leave the injured be until such time as Michael and I return with Godly instructions."

"Hurry." Raquel looked at them with imploring eyes.

Lucifer and Michael flew away to seek God's guidance.

Raquel closed her eyes again and continued praying. Jetrel glowered at Lilith, who stood head down with her hair draped over her face. The others kept their eyes on the injured, which continued to wince and moan, except for Hashmal who stared at the edge of the forest.

"Why do you think God spared you the agony inflicted on Gadreel and Samael?" Jetrel asked Lilith.

"Perhaps because they entered the forest first."

"Yet I feel it was your influence which led them to the forest." Jetrel gritted her teeth.

"I might have mentioned the forest, but Samael entered first and Gadreel followed."

"What of Fornues?"

"He trailed Gadreel into the forest." Lilith inhaled a sharp breath.

Jetrel studied her face.

"It does not seem just that Gadreel and Samael are punished," Cam said, "and who knows what perils Fornues endures in the forest, while you, Lilith, stand before us unharmed."

Jetrel nodded in agreement.

Lilith puffed and frustration crinkled her eyes. "I was the last to enter the forest!"

"But you did go in!" Jetrel clapped her hands on her hips.

They glowered at each other.

"Do you mean to punish me on God's behalf?" Lilith asked Jetrel and Cam, in a scathing tone.

"Of course not." Cam pulled Jetrel away from her. "I simply state that God's ways are mysterious. When Michael and Lucifer return, we shall know what to do."

"Dagon has vanished from our midst." Hashmal moved closer to the edge of the forest.

Raquel's eyes snapped open and she jumped to her feet. "Oh, no! He must have gone in to save Fornues."

Raquel ran to Jetrel, and they embraced each other. They all stared at the darkness beyond the trees.

"Perhaps you should go after him." Lilith pointed at Jetrel. "You are so brave and strong. I have no doubt you can save him. Raquel would be most grateful."

Jetrel's charged indigo eyes glared at her.

"No," Raquel said. "Only God can save them. If it is His will, He shall lead them out."

Lilith rolled her eyes upward.

Moments later, Dagon staggered from the forest. He held Fornues, whose feet dragged. As soon as Dagon cleared the bordering trees, they both collapsed on the lush green grass of the Park. Once more, they gathered round the wounded, unable to help them. Both Dagon and Fornues were covered in spines, cuts and welts.

Raquel passed her fingers through Dagon's long, flaxen hair. His handsome face bore many scratches and deep cuts, yet he still smiled at her. It seemed the corners of her mouth were too heavy because she did not return his smile.

Dagon winced as he lifted his arm to caress her face. "Your eyes are like an emerald lake, flooding your exquisite face with sweet tears and your hair is glowing firelight that warms my soul. Admiring your beauty soothes me and lessens my pain."

Raquel did smile after hearing his dulcet words.

"What did this to you?" Beelzebub rubbed his cheek.

"Vines—monstrous creeping vines covered with long, sharp red spines," Dagon said in a gruff voice. "Their large leaves fluttered like wings, allowing the vines to soar through the air."

Beelzebub gasped. Raquel bit into her fist. The others stared wide-eyed. "The vines attacked us." Dagon cringed and groaned. "They restrained us and flayed us, gashing and stabbing with their spines and leaf prickles."

"It was by the grace of God you were able to escape," Raquel said.

"Those were the border guardians of the East Forest that you fought, Dagon," Michael approached them. Lucifer was by his side.

"We shall carry the wounded to their cottages at Sonnoris," Michael said.

"There, Samael and Gadreel shall remain for three days, suffering the effects of their wounds and the irritant the red spines inflicted on them. Fornues and Dagon shall remain in their rooms, but shall agonize one day only, for Fornues is easily influenced and Dagon's intentions were good when he entered the woods to save his friend. After the angels have suffered their corresponding fates, we are charged to take them to the River of Life, where they shall be healed."

"What of Lilith?" Jetrel looked at him with an intense expression.

Michael glanced at Lilith but quickly shifted his sight to Lucifer avoiding her anguished expression.

"Your punishment, Lilith, shall be the worst of all." Michael frowned and approached her but did not look into her eyes. "You are the reason the others entered the forest, yet at the first sign of trouble you ran, forsaking your brethren."

"Gadreel and Samael left Fornues behind too." Lilith rubbed the back of her neck and squirmed.

"God knows what occupies our minds and hearts, and he punishes us accordingly." Michael's eyes were stormy green seas as he focused them on her forehead. "You must suffer a worse fate than the others. You must enter the East Forest alone and remain within the dark woods until God instructs us to call you out."

Lilith's eyes widened, her mouth dropped open, and all color drained from her face.

"No! Gadreel, tell them!" She ran to her injured friend. "Tell them the truth—that it was all your doing. Tell them you and Samael entered the woods first."

"She speaks the truth. Samael and I entered the forest first. Please show leniency." Gadreel's red, puffy eyes implored Michael.

"We must fulfill God's orders." Michael gestured to Cam to come forward and help him. "We cannot question God's motives, for He knows everything." Together they grabbed Lilith by the arms and took her to the edge of the forest.

Lilith stared at him in shock. "You would do this to me?"

Michael continued to avoid her stare and tears began to meander down his cheeks. He swallowed hard. "This is not my doing. It is God's will and I must obey."

Lilith looked at him with a pleading expression. "Please, help me."

Large drops rolled off his face. He glanced at her and shook his head. "I cannot disobey God."

Lilith shrieked in frustration and tried to pull away, trembling with fear.

"You must not struggle so," Michael said. "Enter the forest God wills it!" She stared at him, her blue and brown eyes flashing with anger.

"We shall throw you in if we have to," Cam said.

Lilith looked once more at Michael, expecting him to save her. Their eyes met, but he turned away quickly.

"Wait, I know she must be punished for it is God's command but maybe I can accompany her." Lucifer rushed toward Michael and Cam.

Hashmal and Esar grabbed him before he could get any closer. "Let go! I want to go in with her." Lilith stared at him in awe.

Michael frowned. "What you are asking is not in accordance with God's command. You were there by my side. You know what must be done." He appeared perplexed by Lucifer's behavior. Lucifer lowered his head.

Lilith shifted her sight from Lucifer to the forest. Her heart pounded. She closed her eyes, took a deep breath and then snapped them open.

"Release me." Her tone was brusque. "I shall walk in of my own accord." She wrested her arm from Michael and glared at him. Cam stepped aside. They would not perceive her as weak. She would do this and prove that she was strong and brave. She did not believe God would destroy her. He simply required punishment for those who break his laws.

She glanced over her shoulder at the others and then looked to the forest again. Trembling she took another deep breath and inched her way inside the trees until she was enshrouded in darkness, and the others could no longer see her.

When she was out of sight Michael fell to one knee and pressed his face to his hands. He appeared inconsolable and the other angels surrounded him and tried to comfort him.

Once inside the forest, Lilith began to pant in fear. Her eyes flickered in every direction, searching for a safe place. She must remain calm.

A beam of light entered through a small opening in the canopy. She made her way there. The incandescent light illuminated a large rock and made it sparkle. That was it! That was where she would remain until she was summoned out of the forest. She plodded to the rock, stood before it, and allowed the radiance to wash over her.

She lifted her eyes to the source of the light. The hole looked large enough for her to fit through. She could fly beyond the forest through the opening above. She could remain above the canopy where she would be safe and nobody would see her.

Lilith climbed to the top of the boulder and tried to expand her wings, but they hung limp and heavy and did not budge. She made several attempts, but they would not move. She could not fly within the forest.

A gust of wind pushed her off the rock. She landed hard on the ground and winced. The vines that covered the forest floor began to slither toward her. She jumped to her feet.

Creeping plants twisted and looped around her ankles, anchoring her to the ground. She gasped at the flutter of wings as vines zipped through the air around her. Unable to move, she panted while creepers whipped around her wrists, twisting tightly. The plants held her arms and legs apart.

Lilith screamed, and a vine shoved leaves in her mouth to muffle her cries. Once the spiny vines bound her, the other plants settled down. Although her wrists and ankles burned and stung, she thought the worst was over. Her breathing slowed and then she saw something that stunned her: a plethora of insects. All manner of bugs flew, crawled, and scuttled toward her.

Lilith's eyes opened wide. She had never seen these ugly little life forms. The insects advanced, swarming. They climbed her legs. Some crawled under her garment, while others scurried over, gnawing at the thin cloth. They continued scuttling and landing over her. Never in her fifteen ages of existence had she experienced such fear.

Soon the pests covered every inch of her, until only a quivering mass of insects in her form remained. The leaves stuffed in her mouth muffled her wails as they crawled over her body, into her hair, and in and out of her nose and ears.

She shut her eyes. The sensation was maddening and the pain excruciating.

She suffered this agony for two days. Thoughts of Michael and Lucifer—her conviction that the others looked upon her with disdain tormented her. Michael had betrayed her and it was his fault she was there. Lucifer was willing to suffer the same fate to be with her. Feeling lonesome and abandoned she wept for the first time. The physical and mental pain from the punishment outweighed the pleasure she derived from her acts. This surprised her. She suffered great anguish wondering if she could endure long enough to make amends. Would this experience change who she was?

At the start of the third day, the flying insects took flight, leaving her body. The creepy-crawlies remained, but at least Lilith's eyes were uncovered. The vines came alive again, thrashing through the air, threatening to whip her, coming close, but never touching her.

Her heart thumped in her chest. She did not know how much more she could take. Her head spun with exhaustion. The vegetation in her mouth forced her jaws agape. Her saliva moistened the leaves, breaking them down. By the fourth day the bitter, rancid, and repugnant juices of the plants in her mouth oozed down her throat.

She gagged and retched until the bolus of leaves finally plopped out of her mouth. She gasped. She tried to scream but could not render a sound. Bugs invaded her mouth, as she swallowed some became lodged in her throat. She had a coughing fit and her eyes bulged in desperation. She wheezed and coughed until the bugs passed and she drew air in. She screamed with her lips wedged shut and wailed until every muscle in her face and neck ached and she was exhausted.

Suddenly, the vines twisting around her ankles unwound, releasing her legs. The vines around her wrists fell to the ground. Lilith did not move, afraid of the crawling life forms covering her face and body. After the vines released her, the insects abandoned her as well.

When all the insects had disappeared, she scanned her surroundings. The forest was silent, and the vines were still. She heard a familiar voice.

Lucifer called her out of the forest.

✣

The injured angels were taken to their rooms as God commanded. There they remained until their time had been served. At such time, Michael, Lucifer, and Cam came to get them, and they entered the River of Life to be healed. By the third day they were healed and suffered no more, but Lilith still remained in the East Forest.

Gadreel went to sit outside the golden double doors leading to God's throne room. She prayed that He would be merciful and release her friend from her punishment. She sang songs of praise to Him. In the afternoon, Gadreel and many other angels went to Guidance Park and sat near the edge of the East Forest to pray, sing, and play divine instruments, hoping Lilith could hear them.

On the fourth day Lucifer approached the edge of the forest and called

Lilith to come forth out of the darkness. She emerged from the woods and trudged her way into Guidance Park.

She was nude, pale, and her face was slack. A film of brown insect saliva covered her body and her usually lustrous, unsullied brown hair was a grotesque nest. She stared straight ahead as if in a trance. Scratches, cuts, and welts marred her ankles and wrists where the spines had been buried.

The angels around her cringed and stared in eerie wonder. Gadreel sprang to her feet and ran to embrace her, but when she got close she stopped, recoiled and puckered her face. The stench rising from her was suffocating and vile. Lilith turned her face to look at her.

"How is it that you have emerged from the East Forest with only injuries on your wrists and ankles?" Raquel asked. "And what happened to your garment?"

Lilith looked at her with vacant eyes. She opened her mouth to speak, but snapped it shut. She took a few steps forward and staggered. Despite her feelings of repulsion, Gadreel put her arm around her and helped her move ahead.

"Beelzebub, go and fetch a garment for her," Raquel said. "Make haste—our laws prohibit nakedness, and we do not want her punished any further."

Beelzebub sprang to his feet and hurried to Sonnoris to get clothes for Lilith.

"It pleases me that you are fine," Raquel told Lilith. "It intrigues me that the others were so injured when they emerged from the dark woods."

Lilith felt hot and dizzy. Everything around her began to spin, and she saw white spots. She lurched, but Gadreel held on to her. "Perhaps we should sit her on the grass."

Michael minced his way to her. Lilith's lips screwed into a disgusted grimace and she groaned gesturing with her arms for him to stay away. Michael's shoulders slumped. He looked broken.

"Please keep your distance, Michael. She does not want your help." Gadreel frowned with a sob in her throat, and beckoned Raphael to come help instead.

Raphael stepped forward. He turned his face away, wrinkling his nose and mouth as he helped Lilith to sit; her acrid smell was quite unpleasant.

Beelzebub arrived with a garment for her. Gadreel and Raquel helped her put it on and sat near her, anxious to hear what she would say about her experience. Raphael and other angels gathered round to listen too. Michael sat at a distance. He wanted to listen but did not want to upset her.

A flood of angels gathered to hear her words, her account. Lilith stared at them. Even as a youngster she was of interest to so many. She wiped her brow repeatedly and gulped.

"The vines—" she started in a raspy, low voice. She cleared her throat and tried to speak again. "Menacing vines tied my limbs to trees by my wrists and ankles, and threatened to tear me to shreds the entire time I was in there." Lilith's mind began to buzz. She showed the inflamed wounds around her wrists and ankles. Many of the angels stared, and some grimaced at the marks.

"The plants hovered in front of my face, always threatening. They crept around my feet, played with my hair, and intimidated me with their sharp, red spines." Lilith covered her face and hung her head. She peeked through her fingers and scanned the many faces enthralled by her words. She began to feel energized by the attention.

"All manner of tiny creatures—life forms never seen by any of you— swarmed around me," she said. "These small beasts covered my entire body." The others gasped and cringed. She saw how her mere words affected them. She lowered her head to hide a satisfied smile.

Gadreel rubbed her shoulders and back.

"Go on, Lilith!" Beelzebub rubbed his forehead and looked at her wide-eyed.

Gadreel stared at him, disapproving of his impatience. He shrugged his shoulders.

"I suffered maddening pricks as the small creatures ate my clothes. Bitter, pungent odors racked my senses. And there were horrible sounds!"

"You did not hear our singing and the music we played for you?" Gabriel asked.

"All I heard was the scuttling, rubbing, and slithering of the creatures in and around my ears, the eerie sounds of the vines' wing-shaped leaves beating furiously, and the thunderous crashing sounds of tree limbs giving way under the weight of the vigorous plants. They fell around me, and I thought at any moment, a large branch would fall and crush my body. The wind howled wretchedly through the heavy vegetation. The small creatures blinded me at first, but then the flying life forms that had scurried over my eyes took flight. When I opened my eyes, I saw the vines' long red spines pointing at me, ready to puncture my eyeballs at any moment. I could not move or even blink."

"How did you endure?" Esar's ears wiggled.

Beelzebub pointed at them and cackled.

"Quiet, Beelzebub! Let Lilith speak!" Gadreel reprimanded.

"At the beginning of this day, I believed I could take no more. The creatures had devoured my garment, and I was covered in this foul smelling goo. Vines loomed all around me, ready to strike. The wing-shaped leaves, with their sharp prickles, were flapping. Powerful odors continued to fill my nostrils—mingled with the stench of fear and pain. All my senses were bombarded with horrible sights, smells, and sounds. It was unbearable."

Gadreel's eyes glistened with sorrow for her friend. The angels stared openmouthed at Lilith.

She looked at their faces. So many of them suffered for her. One thing she learned through this experience was that her words were mighty and influential.

"Suddenly, the vines fell to the ground and scurried away from me," she said. "I heard Lucifer's voice calling me. A tunnel of light appeared before me, and I did not hesitate to walk through it. When I reached the edge of the tunnel, I had entered Guidance Park."

"Thus, the vines never flayed you, like they did me and the others," Gadreel said.

Lilith shook her head.

"God saw fit to punish you mentally rather than just physically," Raquel said.

"Why?" Beelzebub asked, looking bewildered.

"Perhaps a physical punishment alone would not have shown Lilith the lesson He wished her to learn," Raquel said. "We should not question His methods."

"What lesson did you learn, Lilith?" Esar asked.

"Physical and mental punishments are equally powerful," Lilith said. "I shall never disobey God's laws again." And she would never trust Michael again. She no longer carried him in her heart.

Gadreel smiled and hugged her despite the smelly slime that covered her. Beelzebub rushed to partake in the hug and scrunched his nose. Raquel laughed and embraced all three. Gabriel glanced at Esar, and they both joined the group hug.

Lilith chuckled, and the distress she endured began to melt away. Now that she figured out she had the power to manipulate the minds of others, she would use it to her advantage and grow powerful in the sight of God and the angels. She would make it so that the others found their existence lacking without her influence, and then they would do all that she asked. She supposed she should be wiser in executing her plans. She did not intend to get caught again.

Chapter 5

DEVELOPING ATTRACTIONS

God established principles and regulations applicable to every angel from the beginning. They knew that the two most important pledges of an angel were obedience and celibacy. The angels must be meek and totally devoted to God, and anything that interfered with their devotion was abolished.

Nothing was so powerful in drawing an angel away from God as the caresses of another. Carnal love was strictly forbidden. The selfish indulgence of such appetites was beneath the angels and would steer them away from their true calling, which was to serve, entertain, and worship God. Nudity in the presence of another angel was unlawful. Lascivious acts were punishable by imprisonment, expulsion from Floraison, or death, depending on the severity of the act.

The angels obeyed God's laws, but in time their bodies and minds began to develop. At seventeen spans of existence they were no longer children but not yet adults. With age and physical changes arose confusing awareness and temptations. As their bodies changed and matured, so did their emotions.

⚶

Raquel and Jetrel lay chatting on the

soft, green grass in Triumph Gardens, when Fornues and Dagon zoomed past them.

Raquel sat upright and watched as Dagon chased Fornues through the meadow. His long, flowing strands of corn-silk hair swayed rhythmically in the soft breeze. It mesmerized her. "Look!" She shoved Jetrel. "He keeps his wings tucked against his body, honoring the rules of the game." She rose to her knees and cheered when she saw him gaining on Fornues.

Fornues' auburn locks seemed ablaze in the glorious light of Floraison. His immense size made his body unwieldy and slow. He glanced behind him and saw that Dagon was about to tag him and win the game. Hence, he expanded his wings and used them to gain speed and propel himself ahead.

"No Fornues! You are breaking the rules of the game to gain advantage!" Raquel jumped to her feet and put her hands on her hips.

Dagon stopped and looked at her.

"If Fornues had not broken the rules, you would have won the race," Raquel told him.

"I am aware of this." Dagon chuckled, amused by her concern. "I allow him to use his wings on occasion. I know it gives him a slight advantage, but he needs it, for his height and large build make him sluggish."

"That is not fair," Raquel said. "Each one of us must make the best of what God has given us."

Jetrel nodded.

Dagon gazed at Raquel's face and stroked his chin. "Why do you fret about whether or not I let Fornues win?"

"Since you always allow him to attain victory, you never win. Once in a while, I would like to see you be the champion that you are meant to be."

A small smile played on his lips. "We must make the best of what God has given us. Are these not your words?"

Raquel nodded.

"When Fornues is content, I am happy. He is most pleased when he triumphs. So when he wins, does that not make me victorious as well?" He tilted his head to the side, making eye contact with her and wearing a coy, flirtatious smile.

"Yes, it does." She flushed a bright pink and stared at the ground.

He lifted her chin. "You should never stare at the ground, for God has given you the most striking green eyes I have ever seen. I envision the wonders of nature in them." The way he gazed into her eyes made her squirm.

"Dagon!" Fornues hollered from a distance, disrupting the moment. "Make haste! Lucifer requests our presence!"

"I shall be right with you, my friend!"

Dagon caressed Raquel's soft, rosy cheek. He moved closer and whispered goodbye against her ear. He took a few steps backward, never taking his eyes off her. Ultimately, he spun around and ran to Fornues.

Raquel quivered as her eyes followed him until he progressed beyond her sight.

Jetrel peered at her, looking at her sideways.

"Why do you stare at me thus?"

Jetrel released her wrinkled nose and crumpled brow and shrugged.

"I do not understand why my heart beats so swiftly, or why there is a warm tingling sensation circulating throughout my body," Raquel whispered under her breath. "Dagon—"

Jetrel came closer. "Did you say something?"

"No—nothing important." Raquel sighed.

"We should go and see what is happening," Jetrel said.

"Yes, good idea." Raquel nodded and grinned. Together they ran in the direction they saw their friends go, beyond the hill toward the running path.

Ahead on the path, Dagon met Fornues. Together they ran to Lucifer, who stood at the beginning of the open trail used for running exercises.

"What is taking place here?" Dagon noted Michael, Raphael, Esar, Hashmal, Beelzebub, and Gabriel all gathered around Lucifer.

"We are organizing a contest of speed," Michael said.

"I shall not be racing." Fornues kicked a pebble as he grumbled. "I have little chance of winning."

"I cannot say I blame you, brother. Mountains were not meant to sprint." Beelzebub snickered. The others laughed. Fornues was amongst the tallest and broadest of the angels.

"Stop your useless bantering, Beelzebub!" Fornues stomped his foot.

Beelzebub continued with his mockery. "Do not be angry, my friend, for I am pleased you are so big. I have more of you to tease."

Some of the other angels hid their giggles behind their hands.

Dagon scowled. "You are not amusing!"

"Clearly, I am. Judging by some of your brethren's reactions." Beelzebub extended his hand to demonstrate those who were laughing.

"Enough!" Hashmal emitted small flames from his mouth as he shouted. His irises became red coals, and his hair stood on end.

He jumped, still startled by his ability, since he yet held little control. "I do not understand why I am the only angel capable of breathing fire, but I remain faithful God gave me this gift for some great purpose and—"

"How do you begin an argument with a redhead?" Beelzebub dared to interrupt in his ongoing quest for attention.

"How?" Lilith swaggered toward the group.

Both Hashmal and Fornues were redheads. They glanced at each other and waited, displaying reluctance for the punch line.

"You simply say something!" Beelzebub and Lilith laughed.

Hashmal eyed Lucifer, letting him know he needed to take charge of Beelzebub. He was the only one who could stop him once he got on a roll.

"That is enough! It is time to begin the competition." As Lucifer spoke, Beelzebub stopped his mockery. He walked past Hashmal, giving him a vilifying glance. Lilith watched with admiration how Lucifer took command. He spoke and all listened.

"Who wishes to participate in this race?" Lucifer asked.

Michael, Raphael, and Gabriel offered to compete.

Jetrel and Raquel approached the group as Lucifer recruited racers. Jetrel saw that Michael was participating so she joined in too. Raquel smiled and patted her on the shoulder.

"I too shall race!" Dagon positioned himself with the group of competitors.

"As shall I!" Esar said.

"Why?" Beelzebub sneered. "You are but a hair smaller than Fornues! You could never win. You would need three pairs of wings just to get you going, and this is a leg race, but maybe you can—" Beelzebub met

Lucifer's gaze. The frosty blue eyes turned his core to ice and rendered him speechless.

"Anyone else?" Lucifer scanned the remaining angels. No one else volunteered.

"I too shall take part in this race," Lucifer said. "Lilith, you can give us the signal to start. Hashmal, you and Fornues can mark the finish line."

Everyone agreed to do their part. Hashmal and Fornues ran to mark the finish line. The racers positioned themselves at the starting line. Lilith placed herself in front of them to give them the signal to begin the race.

"What shall I do?" Beelzebub asked in a gentle manner.

"You can stand on the sidelines and cheer for your favorite." Lucifer grinned.

"But of course that would be you, Lucifer," Beelzebub uttered in a sing-song voice, all the while gazing at Gabriel with playful eyes. Gabriel smiled.

Lilith stood a few feet in front of the racers. She pivoted dramatically to face away from the runners and then lifted her arms, turned her head and glanced at Lucifer, batting her eyelashes.

"Go!" she yelled, as she dropped her arms to her sides. She zipped away from their path to join Beelzebub and Raquel on the sidelines.

"Behold, Lucifer runs like the wind!" Lilith cheered at the top of her voice.

Raquel cheered for Dagon in her mind.

"Lucifer is fast, and so are Michael and Jetrel, but none is more graceful than my Gabriel!" Beelzebub clapped while his eyes followed him along the track.

"Your Gabriel?" Lilith asked in an undertone. "I suggest you mind what you say."

Raquel glanced their way, but quickly turned away to focus on the race. Her eyes followed Dagon.

"Are you saying I cannot trust you, my dear friend?" Beelzebub's eyes were wide, and he pressed a hand against his chest, fingers spread.

"Shhhh!" Lilith indicated Raquel with her finger and whispered, "Have no doubts, my cherished one, your words are safe with me. It is in others you must not place your trust."

Beelzebub listened and stared.

"There are those among us who desire to be closer to God than anyone else," Lilith continued. "They are willing to become talebearers and get the rest of us in trouble. That is why you must be careful, and trust only those worthy of it."

Beelzebub nodded and smiled at her, and they resumed watching the race.

Hashmal and Fornues looked alert and excited as they waited for the winner to arrive at the finish line.

Lucifer was in the lead, with Jetrel close behind him. Michael was gaining on Jetrel. Gabriel, Raphael, and Dagon were a short distance away from her as well. Esar lagged behind. It was a good race, charged with driven competitors and the contest remained thrilling to the end, with the athletes running at wind speed, determined to overtake each other.

A few yards from the finish line, Jetrel began to sprint. She lengthened her lead on Michael and, like a stream of air she dashed past Lucifer to the finish line, winning the race.

Hashmal burst into a fit of laughter and clapped his hands. Lucifer, who came in second, bent at the waist, placed his hands on his knees, and expelled his breath in a puff.

Michael went to Jetrel at once to commend her on her triumph. Raphael, Gabriel, and Dagon also approached her in good sportsmanship and congratulated her. It took some time, but Lucifer finally approached her.

"Congratulations on winning the race. You used a good strategy." Lucifer sighed deeply.

"Thank you. It means a lot coming from you." Jetrel smiled. He returned her smile and slouched away.

Raquel strolled to Dagon.

"I really did lose this race," Dagon told her. "I did all I could to achieve victory."

"I know you did." Raquel grinned. "I saw you make a great effort, but your legs were probably tired from all the running around you did with Fornues prior to the race."

"Perhaps." Dagon beamed. He gazed at her and caught himself leaning his face toward hers. They stared at each other in awkward silence.

Beelzebub's shrieks roused them from their trance. He ran to Jetrel, hands extended forward.

"Jetrel, the champion!" He grinned and clapped.

He hugged her. He also embraced Lucifer for coming in second and Michael for reaching the finish line third. He offered Gabriel a consolation hug.

"You may not have won the speed contest, but you looked the best competing," Beelzebub whispered in his ear, making him blush. Gabriel pulled back from him and hurried away. Beelzebub ogled him as he fled.

Beelzebub strolled past Raphael, who stared at him sideways. Ignoring him, he pursed his lips, expressing insincere sympathy as he scrutinized Esar.

"Are there accolades for coming in last?" he asked Esar with a sardonic smile. "Maybe you should have turned into a rabbit and hopped all the way to the finish line. It might have been faster." Beelzebub giggled. Esar smiled.

"Oh, wait a minute," he continued. "If you had attempted to turn into a rabbit, you might have ended up with only a bushy tail. That would have been the only thing funnier than seeing you finish last. Watching you finally arrive at the finish line, in last place, with a rabbit's bushy tail sticking out from behind you, as evidence of your cheating!"

Beelzebub cocked his head and shook with laughter. Several angels standing around chortled with him, and he beamed at the attention.

Esar stared at him. He lifted one of his legs, bent it, and placed it behind his head, putting on a display. Others ran to see the fascinating bending and flexing stunts he did. He performed tongue tricks and wiggled his ears among other strange feats. The angels took no notice of Beelzebub as they passed him by. The crowd of spectators cheered and applauded Esar while Beelzebub huffed and sulked.

Close by, Lucifer kicked a stone lying on the ground. He stomped to and fro, frowning. "I could have done better if I had paced my steps until I was near the end and then sprinted to the finish line, similar to her strategy. She was more astute than I this time, but next time, I shall not be defeated," he muttered between his teeth.

Lilith observed him. From his demeanor, she deduced his ego was injured; thus, she hurried to his side to do what she did best.

"It was brilliant how you arranged for Jetrel to win that race." Lilith strolled toward him with an alluring smile.

He squinted and wrinkled his forehead, looking confused.

"You are aware of her lack of confidence." Lilith put her arms around his neck. "And how she is always trying to validate herself to the rest of us. So, you surrendered your pride, and gave her the victory—to make her feel worthy. You are the wisest and kindest of us."

With her flattery, Lilith convinced him to believe things happened as she described. He smiled and began to trust in his superiority once again.

"We should go to Lake Serena and celebrate." She lowered her head slightly and looked up at him.

Lucifer sighed and grinned. "Yes, you are right. We should celebrate."

Beelzebub spotted them as they sneaked away from the crowd gathering to watch Esar's spectacle. "Where are the two of you going?"

Lucifer spun around. "To Lake Serena!"

Lilith scowled. She desired to be alone with him.

"We should all go!" Beelzebub whisked around to try and convince everyone, especially Gabriel, to come along. Most of the angels were distracted by Esar's antics.

Beelzebub asked Michael to go. Michael glanced at Lilith's hand in Lucifer's and frowned. "I have training exercises and other matters arranged for the next few hours." He glowered at Lucifer and went on his way.

"Apologies, for I too have plans." Jetrel hurried off in pursuit of Michael.

"How about you, grumpy Fornues?" Beelzebub asked in playful tone, batting his eyelashes for a laugh.

"No. I have obtained my fill of you today." Fornues plodded away from the group.

Dagon and Hashmal wished to stay behind and continue to enjoy Esar's performance.

"I shall not be going to Lake Serena either, for I too have training exercises." Raphael turned to Gabriel, who he expected to leave without hesitation. "We should go to Guidance Park. We have many skills yet to master. It would be wise for us to train with Michael and Jetrel for a while."

"No, Gabriel, please." Beelzebub grabbed hold of his arm. "The lake is so beautiful and refreshing. You must come with us."

"Very well, I am inclined to go for a short while." Gabriel smiled.

Beelzebub grasped his chest. "Ah! I sense my heart shall burst from my chest with excitement." Gabriel chuckled.

Raphael's brow knitted in a frown and he ambled away.

Lilith and Lucifer wandered ahead as they conversed. Beelzebub and Gabriel lingered behind, admiring the beautiful, fragrant flowers in the meadow on the way to Lake Serena.

Beelzebub strolled alongside Gabriel and gazed at him in awe. "I appreciate your handsome, sweet face framed by your thick crop of soft, dark brown curls, and the way they rest on your strong shoulders." Beelzebub leered at Gabriel whose face turned bright pink. "I also enjoy your cheerful blue eyes, the color of little forget-me-not flowers." Beelzebub continued to stare. He ogled his delicate features and lean athletic build. Gabriel squirmed and moved further from him.

Beelzebub fidgeted and kept his eyes fixed on him. He knew he must gain control of his desires, for if his feelings for Gabriel were ever discovered, it would signify his end. God's laws prohibited any sexual relationship between angels, but carnal love between angels of the same sex was considered vile and a purely selfish act, and thus, a greater sin with harsher punishment. The thought of what that punishment might be made him shudder.

When the four angels reached Lake Serena, they stopped to admire the landscape around them. The beauty of the lake and its surroundings always took their breath away. Scores of graceful, flowering trees surrounded the lake, which reflected the colors of the blooms on its surface.

Lilith was the first to leap into the still waters, causing large ripples to break the glassy surface. "Jump in, the water is magnificent!"

The warm pebbles surrounding the lake crunched under Lucifer's feet as he moved closer to the edge. He watched Lilith enjoy herself as she made her way through the clear water, and dived in to join her.

Gabriel sprang into the lake, uniting with them.

"Come Beelzebub, get in!" Lilith yelled.

"I shall. Give me a moment to take it all in," Beelzebub responded in his melodramatic way. Before entering the lake, he watched Gabriel swim for a while.

After some time, he finally joined Lilith and the others. Together they splashed and frolicked in the water. Later, Lucifer tired and exited the water. He lay on the soft grass and took a nap. Gabriel and Beelzebub also left the lake. Lilith continued to swim.

Gabriel began to sing. Beelzebub was half sitting, half reclining on the grass. He gazed at him, who rested on his elbows and closed his eyes to make music with his beautiful voice.

The angels' white garments were wet, semitransparent and clinging to their bodies.

Beelzebub found it impossible to tear his eyes away from Gabriel's physique. He began to feel hot, flushed, and achy all over, but it was a delightful yearning. He trembled and could sense the rapid beating of his heart.

Hence, he jumped to his feet and stepped away to divert his eyes.

He took a deep breath to slow his breathing. He had to control these urges that drove him, but the longings were in every fiber of his being.

Lilith watched him hurry away from Gabriel. She left the water to find out what was happening. She approached him as he came across a delightful, sweet-smelling flower bush. "What is the matter, Beelzebub?" she asked, startling him. "Why do you look so flustered? And why did you leave Gabriel's side? It is not like you to do so. Did he ask you to leave?"

"No. I simply needed to get away for a moment to calm myself." Beelzebub continued to fidget and wring his hands.

"It does not look like your methods are working." Lilith looked at him with a mischievous expression. "Come with me." She took his hand. "I am going to show you something that shall put a smile on your face."

"Indeed?" Beelzebub beamed and followed. She took him to the atrium and then to a small hidden room.

"Why did you bring me here?" Beelzebub scrunched his brow and touched his cheek.

"This is where I come when I desire to be alone with my thoughts or when I wish to do something I want no other to see." Lilith wore an inscrutable expression.

Beelzebub shot her a coy glance.

"Come closer, I shall show you something I have learned," she said. "But you are not to tell anyone about this or come to this section of the atrium without my permission. Do you understand?"

Beelzebub nodded, his eyes round as moons.

"I want you to close your eyes."

Beelzebub obeyed.

"Imagine you are here, in this hidden, secluded place—with Gabriel."

He gasped and opened his eyes.

"Keep your eyes closed!" Lilith yelled.

He closed his eyes again.

"Pretend Gabriel is here with you. You are both comfortable, relaxed, and enjoying each other's company without interruption." Lilith paused, allowing her words to penetrate his mind. She chuckled at his contented expression. She leaned forward and kissed him on the lips. He snapped his eyes open. She kissed him again.

Beelzebub withdrew. "What are you doing?"

"Did you enjoy it?"

"Yes, but—"

"I am trying to teach you how to kiss."

"Kiss?" He blinked.

"God has given me the gift of sight. I have visions—this is something you must also keep secret," Lilith said with a solemn expression. Beelzebub bobbed his head. "In many of my visions I see beings very similar to us but without wings. I call them wingless angels and a kiss is something they do to show each other their love. Would you like to demonstrate your love to Gabriel?"

"Yes, but these acts are forbidden to us," Beelzebub said.

"Sometime in the future Floraison shall change—another supreme being shall rule, and all acts shall be allowed. You and Gabriel would be free to love each other without restraint."

His face glowed like a lotus petal.

"Now, would you like to learn to kiss, or not?"

Beelzebub nodded quickly.

"Very well, I shall teach you to show Gabriel love and affection while giving him pleasure, but you must do as I tell you and whisper a word of this to no one." Beelzebub nodded again, wide-eyed and mute.

Lilith kissed him on the lips again. Then she told him to part his lips. She inserted her tongue and taught him how to make his tongue dance with hers.

Afterward, Beelzebub's light green eyes shone with delight, and he wore a beatific grin. "I am excited to share this secret with you, and I'm pleased that now I know how to kiss. Someday I shall kiss my love, and Gabriel shall like it."

Lilith laughed and led him back to Lake Serena. "Be mindful that no one must know what we have done, or of my visions, and do not return to that area of the atrium without my permission."

"Yes, Lilith. I am heedful of your words." He looked toward where Gabriel sat, still singing. He picked some flowers and returned to him. Gabriel was finishing his song.

Lilith's lips screwed into an irritated smile as she watched him. She waved dismissively and returned to the water.

Beelzebub's eyes livened, and he looked overjoyed upon seeing Gabriel again. "I want to be by your side—always—to listen to your dulcet singing."

"Thank you, Beelzebub, but I sing only to praise God, not to seek admiration for myself."

"I am aware of that." Beelzebub's cheeks blushed pink. He presented him with the bouquet of fragrant blossoms. "Here, I picked these for you."

"Thank you again." Gabriel adjusted himself to receive the flowers. He sniffed them and placed them on the grass by his side. "Although I appreciate your gesture, the flowers would have been better served on their bush rather than torn apart from their stems."

"Apologies." Beelzebub rubbed his cheek and fidgeted. "I merely wished to present you with something delightful."

Gabriel placed a hand on his shoulder and smiled. "I understood your meaning, and your intent is appreciated. You are a good friend. I need no more than your presence to be delighted."

Beelzebub inhaled a long, deep breath. "Thank you for the kind words. They are like one of your songs—pleasing to my ears."

"It is so exquisite here in Floraison. We should be grateful God has chosen us to be here," Gabriel said between yawns. He lay on the grass once more and closed his eyes.

"I am especially appreciative of God's wonders," Beelzebub whispered to himself. In a sly manner, he placed his hand on Gabriel's knee.

Upon sensing Beelzebub's hand on his leg, his eyes sprang open. He glanced at his friend, who was casually gazing at the beautiful scenery. Gabriel scrunched his brow, shrugged and closed his eyes once more.

Beelzebub, who watched him from the corner of his eye, noticed his heavy eyelids close again. He took the opportunity to drag his hand further along his leg to his thigh.

Gabriel partly opened his eyes and stared at him, who again appeared to harmlessly admire the delightful flowers and trees. "Beelzebub."

"Yes?" Beelzebub raised his eyebrows high. He drummed the side of his opened mouth with the fingers of his free hand.

"Kindly remove your hand from my thigh."

"Apologies! I did not realize—"

"It is all right. I understand you were distracted by the splendor of this place."

"Indeed. That is what happened. I was distracted. I beg your pardon." Beelzebub rubbed his cheek.

"There is no need for regrets." Gabriel stared at Beelzebub's unsteady hands. He closed his eyes once more and this time fell into a deep slumber.

Beelzebub waited. His cheeks were red from rubbing. When he was certain Gabriel was sound asleep, he edged closer to him. He laid his head on his shoulder, arm on his chest. He watched it rise and fall with each breath. Moving his hand to his midsection, he passed his fingers across the peaks and valleys of his abdominal muscles. He continued sliding his hand downward.

Ruled by desire more powerful than his restraint, Beelzebub was compelled to do things forbidden. In doing so, he enjoyed a jolt of pleasure unlike anything he had ever experienced before.

Gabriel awoke to find Beelzebub clutching him. He blinked owlishly looking groggy and confused as he stared at him. His mouth moved to speak, but words did not form. In an instant, he became fully awake and leapt to his feet. He assumed spirit form—a shimmering, translucent fog in his likeness gliding like a gentle breeze.

"Apologies! Please forgive me, I know not what came over me," Beelzebub said between sobs and laughs. Gabriel glowered at him, his brows woven together in deliberation.

Beelzebub hopped to his feet and flitted about, touching his face. He reached for Gabriel's hand, but it was like immersing his hand in glacial water. Beelzebub rubbed his frozen hand and stared at him.

"You are never to place your hands on me, for any reason." Gabriel drifted away from him.

"I shall never lay hands on you. I swear this, please forgive me!" Beelzebub's wings quivered. He collapsed in a stupor.

Gabriel took pity on him. "I shall leave you now. Do not follow. I do not wish to look upon you for a long time." Like a mist, he faded into the air.

Beelzebub pulled his hair and screamed.

Lucifer awoke, eyes wide. "What is amiss?"

"I have done terrible things!" Beelzebub sobbed and rubbed his eyes.

"What have you done?" Lucifer watched Lilith emerge from the water from the corner of his eyes.

"My longings for Gabriel overwhelmed me. When I am close to him, I lose all restraint." Beelzebub convulsed with laughter, as tears fell from his eyes.

Lucifer looked confused and his eyes kept diverting to Lilith.

She strutted toward him, clad in the soaking wet, transparent garment that hugged her every curve. She led with her bosoms, her head held high, and shoulders relaxed. She wrung the lake water from her long, thick brown hair, while she swiveled her hips from side-to-side. Her rhythmic movements were a powerful distraction. Lilith noticed his entranced gaze and smiled, delighted to witness her control over him.

"What did you do?" Lilith asked with a coy grin.

"I touched him!" Beelzebub sobbed into his hands.

"What is your meaning?" Lucifer sucked his teeth and glanced to the side. "There is nothing wrong with touching someone."

Beelzebub burst into a fit of nervous laughter.

"Well—that would depend on where and how you touched him." Lilith smirked. "Where did you caress Gabriel, Beelzebub?"

"I seized his male organs. I stroked them, and I clutched them in my hands." Beelzebub rubbed his already bright red cheeks and avoided their stare.

Lucifer squinted, trying to make sense of what he had revealed.

Lilith tossed her head and laughed, to their amazed expressions. "How did he react to your fondling?"

"This is not amusing, Lilith!" Lucifer sighed and gestured to Beelzebub to answer her question.

Beelzebub lowered his head and stared at the ground while he spoke. "He was sleeping. I caressed his body but he only woke when I went too far. I groped his parts, and gripped him tightly. He took on spirit form and became as a dazzling mist and disappeared."

Lucifer gulped air and moved closer to him. "I have only seen Gabriel achieve this once, and even then, he did it by chance. Are you saying he can now take on spirit form at his bidding?"

"Yes. It would appear so. I wish to leave now." His voice had a low, raspy sound and his swollen, red eyes still aimed at the ground. "I intend to hide for a long while. It is Gabriel's wish. Farewell, my friends."

He trudged away with a bleak expression on his face.

"So long. If questions arise regarding this matter, I shall have words on your behalf." Lucifer looked troubled.

Lilith scowled at him. "You shall not. You are much too important to involve yourself in such trivial matters."

"This is not a trifling matter. If Michael and the others were to learn of what happened here, it would have disastrous consequences for Beelzebub. Lascivious behavior such as this is strictly forbidden, and the punishment is severe. Since it was done against Gabriel's will, Beelzebub may be destroyed."

"Beelzebub is close to Cam. Perhaps he would speak on his behalf," Lilith said in an undertone.

"No, Cam does not have the tolerance and patience needed for a situation such as this," Lucifer said. "He would have him go to the throne room, and confess his sins to God. And that would be the end of him."

Lilith closed her eyes and groaned.

"I advised that fool to stay away from Gabriel, but he did not heed my warnings." Lilith shook her leg as she often did when upset. "It has been obvious to me for quite some time that Beelzebub lusted after Gabriel, but I sensed he would never concede to his advances. I had warned him to resist the urge until the time was right."

Lucifer scratched the back of his head and sucked his teeth. "Clearly, it is too late now to worry about what he did or did not consider. I can only hope Gabriel chooses to forgive him and keeps Beelzebub's indiscretions to himself."

"Well, I no longer wish to concern myself with Beelzebub's lack of judgment. Besides, I always knew his reckless behavior would someday have consequences." Lilith's frown turned into a smile as she changed her demeanor. "We should go for a stroll."

She grabbed Lucifer by the hand and pulled him along the grassy field. He gazed into her eyes and at her enticing smile. Lilith held his gaze. Deep is your desire for me, Lucifer.

It served her purpose, for she had great aspirations for both of them. God had made him powerful, more powerful than any other angel. Yet she believed someday he would crumble at her feet, and he would offer her Floraison if she so desired. She would need only whisper.

Chapter 6

RIVALRY

In Guidance Park, Michael and Jetrel were geared for combat training. Every day, they trained hard, with many others, throwing the spear and wielding the sword for hours to keep their bodies healthy, strong and fit.

The angels' typical training consisted of running, calisthenics, and swimming to build physical strength and vitality. To gain combat skills, they fought with weapons shaped from heavy wood. They marched for miles with full battle gear to build stamina and endurance. They also sparred with one another.

The angelic beings had never stood in battle. They did not understand the reason for the intense training, but most of them knew better than to question God's purpose. Early on, they understood He knew all things past, present, and future. He was preparing them for something great, even if they did not yet comprehend what it was.

One of Michael's favorite places to spar was near the Divina Waterfall, which was the highest in Floraison. The falls' clear waters poured beyond the edge of a magnificent red mountain called Mount Verve. Fluffy white clouds gathered at the mountaintop, for it was thus high. The base of the falls fed into the River of Life, which advanced to the throne room.

The water possessed healing properties. Only with God's direct permission could the angels enter the river. However, there were no laws against standing near the torrents, thus Michael enjoyed the waterfall's refreshing and invigorating misty spray as he trained with his friends. He also enjoyed the falls' deafening roar, for it put him in a competitive disposition.

Michael's combat skills were clearly superior to Jetrel's, but he worked with her often to help her improve and refine them. He held great esteem for her. She was strong, fierce, and devoted to God's purpose.

She took pride in being devoted and tough. Standing six feet tall with a muscular, athletic build, she had the suppleness of a leopard and the speed of a cheetah—a force to be reckoned with. Michael was determined to make her one of his most ferocious warriors.

While he considered her a good friend and sparring partner, Jetrel regarded him as much more. In her mind and heart he was her lover, and she was his spiritual paramour. Her devotion to him was complete. Everything she did, she did for him. He was unaware of the depth of her commitment to him, and she realized it must remain so.

Lucifer and Lilith strolled into the park through the great wooden doors as Michael and Jetrel prepared to spar. Lilith always found their sparring sessions irritating, but not on this day. She and Lucifer sat on one of the flat rocks on the riverbank to watch.

Lilith stared at her with an expression full of scorn. Jetrel was strong, skillful, and yet she could not hide her feelings for Michael—at least not from her. Lilith enjoyed observing the raw attraction she tried to hide from him, the careful way in which she touched him, and how she gazed at him with those expressive indigo eyes that revealed so much desire.

They began to spar at a slow pace, as was their custom, increasing the pace a little at a time until their bodies heated, thus protecting their muscles from injury. When Michael considered his apprentice ready, it was time to really work. He pushed her as hard as he pushed himself. Jetrel gave him her all. She desired to let him and everyone present know how good a fighter she was.

She studied Michael's every move. He did not go easy on her, demonstrating his best technique and self-discipline. They both aimed to do their best, making their sparring sessions interesting to most. When they stopped to rest, Jetrel sat by Lilith on the bank of the River of Life.

"You did well." Lilith smiled.

"Yes, indeed, thank you. I have improved much. I owe it to Michael." Jetrel lifted her abundant black hair off her neck to cool off.

"Oh, I am certain you deserve some merits."

"Michael is an excellent teacher and sparring partner."

"Wouldn't it be wonderful if he could be partner to you in every way?" Lilith carefully tested her boundaries with her. She watched Jetrel's face twist awkwardly in angst.

"I do not think of such things. It is unlawful." Her face flushed bright pink.

"Oh, apologies. All this time, I thought it was all that occupied your mind. I have seen the way you ogle him when you think no one is looking." Lilith snickered at the haunted expression on her face.

Jetrel gasped.

"I also noticed you stand just a little too close to him. You search for any excuse to touch him, and you shadow him everywhere."

Jetrel's mouth fell open and her big blue-violet eyes widened in shock. Her chest began to heave and she glowered at her, the pink hue on her cheeks becoming a deep scarlet.

Lilith smirked. Could she use her knowledge of Jetrel's forbidden feelings to control her?

"Judging by your response it must be true."

Jetrel leapt to her feet and flitted away from her side. Lilith jeered and cackled as she fled. Jetrel made a dash for the park's wooden doors.

Michael observed Jetrel's abrupt departure. He detected distress on her face. He hurried after her. "Jetrel! Please wait a moment."

Lilith watched him chase after her. She frowned and pursed her lips.

Jetrel stopped, but did not turn to face him.

Michael stepped around her and looked into her eyes. She shed tears. He had never seen her so troubled or vulnerable. He stared at her, brows together, looking confused by her conduct. "What pains you? You did quite well in our fighting session. You gave me a rigorous workout."

"I admit I did well. I have a great teacher," she said.

Michael embraced her. She swooned. She seemed comfortable in his arms.

He took hold of her strong upper arms and moved her away gently.

"You know you may confide in me?" He brushed his hands up and down her arms. "Break words and unburden yourself if you must."

"I am aware your friendship is true. I am most grateful for you, Michael."

"Then reveal what is behind your sad eyes. Why do tears flow from them?"

"Lilith is cruel. She taunts me and upsets me so." Jetrel bit the inside of her lower lip.

"Whatever strife exists between you and Lilith must end now," Michael said in his usual mild manner. "You must be the one to lead by example, for you are able. She enjoys causing discord and manipulating the other angels. She has lost her way." Michael's face was etched in sorrow. "We must help her return to the right path, rather than become lost on the wrong one with her."

Jetrel nodded and swallowed hard. "I understand. I shall try my best."

"That is all I can ask." He placed his hands on her shoulders and pressed his forehead against hers.

She closed her eyes and her smile was tremulous.

"I must return to the Performance Circle. I spar with Lucifer next. Please choose to stay?" Michael gazed at her and grinned.

Jetrel bit her lip. She considered Michael's enthusiastic smile. "I'm almost convinced your bright smile contributes to Floraison's brilliance. Yes, I shall stay long enough to watch you spar with Lucifer."

Michael laughed and glowed bright red. He rushed back to the circle.

She returned to the riverbank but sat as far away as possible from Lilith, while still having a good view of where Michael would fight Lucifer.

They were the most skillful and entertaining fighters in Floraison. Michael had not been able to win a match in a very long time, but it had been a while since they last wrestled, and he had improved a considerable amount since their last bout. Yet, Lucifer devoted most of his time to Lilith.

Guidance Park was soon packed with angels who cheered and clapped while waiting for the sparring session to begin.

Michael and Lucifer faced each other in the Circle. They were dressed in short white one-piece garments. Over their garments they wore a battle skirt and cuirass made of a strong, heavyweight green material encrusted with bluish-green emeralds for added strength. Scaled guards made of gold shielded their arms and legs. They also wore layered gold neck and shoulder guards, and thick sandals studded on the bottom and attached to the foot with interlacing thongs.

They kept their knees bent, a technique developed by Lucifer that enabled them to move quickly and easily in any direction. Lucifer positioned himself with his hands by his temples, elbows tucked into his sides. Michael placed his hands by his cheeks; elbows also tucked into his sides, to more easily block his opponent's powerful blows to the head and body. Both appeared focused and ready.

Lucifer glanced at Lilith. He gave her a nod.

"Let the fight begin!" she yelled. The combat began to the roar of the angels.

Immediately, Lucifer threw punches at Michael's face. Michael blocked the blows, and stepped farther away from his two-inch reach advantage.

Lilith jumped to her feet and clapped. "That's it, Lucifer! You're the best fighter in Floraison!" Lucifer grinned. Michael frowned and glanced at Lilith with an agonized expression.

Michael's quick retreat assured Lucifer that he had struck him hard. Michael leaped off the ground, rolled in the air, and kicked him hard in the chest. Although Lucifer expected the kick, he was unable to block it and teetered off balance. He almost collapsed but regained his balance quickly. Lilith cheered. Lucifer lifted and jutted his strong chin with pride.

Michael's nostrils flared as he stepped closer and punched Lucifer in the torso. Lucifer tried to return the punch, overcome him and slam him to the ground in order to grapple. He did not succeed.

He threw an elbow at his face. It connected with Michael's jaw and rocked him. Pressing his advantage, Lucifer bashed him with his strong-as-iron wings, knocking him to the ground.

Lilith's cheers could be heard throughout the park. Jetrel sprung to her feet, eyebrows raised.

Lucifer leaped through the air to plunge on top of him. Michael rolled away and Lucifer crashed to the ground. The collision knocked the air from his lungs. He lay wheezing and gasping on the dirt. Michael glanced at Lilith, anger etched on his face. He pounced on Lucifer and delivered blow after blow to his body until he was incapacitated, winning Michael the fight.

Jetrel bounced and cheered along with many of the angels.

Lilith gawked at Lucifer, who lay beaten. "Rise, Lucifer!"

"The fight has ended, Lilith. Lucifer lost." Jetrel's lips curved into a gratified smile.

Lilith frowned. She sauntered to where Lucifer lay defeated, grunting and writhing in pain on the ground. She never thought she would see him conquered. His eyes, wide and imploring, gazed at her. She grimaced and did nothing to help him.

Was she wrong about him? Did she put her faith in the wrong angel? No. This was but one fight. It meant nothing. Lucifer was powerful and second only to God—at present.

Michael inched over to Lucifer. He did not make eye contact with Lilith. "Take my arm, Lucifer, I will help you to your feet." From the corner of his eye he saw Lilith glowering at him. Lucifer groaned as Michael helped him stand. Lilith looked away, scrunching her brow and nose.

Michael pulled at his neck guard and then crossed his arms while staring at the ground. "Apologies, for I confess I fought with excessive aggression. I vow it shall never happen again."

"Nonsense, you fought well." Lucifer sighed deeply.

Michael beamed. "I have been training quite hard of late."

"Your mentor taught you well." Lilith's tone was abrasive.

Michael bowed his head in a respectful manner. "Of course, sparring with you has taught me many lessons, but as of late, I have missed you in the Circle, my brother."

"You are right. I have not been training as hard as I should."

Michael glanced at Lilith. He raked her with freezing contempt and made it clear he held her responsible for Lucifer's lack of interest in training. Sensing his disapproval, she smirked and tossed her long, dark hair over her shoulder.

Michael managed a solemn expression and turned to Lucifer.

"This was but one fight. Do not get used to triumphing against me," Lucifer said.

"It shall prove difficult if I continue defeating you." Michael challenged him with a smile. Lucifer studied his face. After a pause, he laughed.

Lilith crossed her arms and scowled. He jested, but he had found a way to beat Lucifer. She gazed at Lucifer. Do not let your guard down or the pretender shall take all that is yours.

"I shall ask God for permission that you may enter the healing waters of the River of Life." Michael joined forehead with him and departed to make the request.

The remaining angels began to disperse. They had come to see an exciting fight and were not disappointed.

"Anyone can lose a fight once, and anyone can win one fight." Lilith approached Lucifer, having regained her wits. She helped him sit on the riverbank. He gazed at her face.

"You are disappointed." His usually strong voice fragmented like the seeds of a dandelion dispersing in the wind. "I hear the disdain in your voice."

"I am disappointed." Pouting, she stared at the grass, her lips lush as exotic flowers in deep bloom. "Disappointed at myself for diverting your attention. I have kept you from your rigorous training. For that I am regretful."

"It is not solely your fault," Lucifer said. "I am also to blame for being careless with my responsibilities, but I make this pledge to you: I shall never lose another fight again."

She wore an alluring smile and nodded. She was going to have to work harder. Things were not yet as she desired them to be. She must continue to exercise her powers of persuasion until Lucifer, Michael, and all the rest were eager to do her bidding. "No. You shall never lose another fight. Michael's win was a fluke. I shall remain by your side and ensure this never happens again."

Lucifer gazed at her in admiration. He grinned and nodded in agreement.

Lilith stared at him and laughed. Yes, this would be the beginning of her reign over him.

Lucifer, unsuspecting, joined her in laughter.

Chapter 7

MICHAEL'S REQUEST

Michael knelt before the golden doors leading to the anteroom, which gave access to the portal into Metá Heaven and the throne room. The combined strength of every angel in Floraison could not unlock these gilded doors. Only God was capable.

"Father, may I enter?"

Thou mayst enter, my son.

The golden doors opened, and he entered the anteroom. The anteroom was an area for cleansing and preparation. The small chamber had a crystal floor under which he saw the River of Life flowing.

A gentle breeze moved through his body. He became light-headed, giddy, and elated. Suddenly, he assumed spirit form. He stared at his ethereal hands.

Once he had transformed, a pair of full-length gates on the far side of the anteroom opened, allowing access to a courtyard shrouded in a fine mist. Michael moved across the enclosure, floating just above the river, which led him right to God's throne.

When Michael arrived in His awesome presence he fell before Him in reverence. He had been in the throne room once before but it was an experience one never got used to. God's love and mercy overwhelmed him. He covered his face with his wings.

Come hither, Michael, and do not fear, for thou art worthy to look upon me.

Upon hearing God's words, he uncovered his face and gazed at the throne. Such intense power emanated from it—more than enough to compel all things in Floraison and in all the galaxies to follow His will.

Yet God granted free will to all the angels so that they might find their own path. Michael was humbled by this recognition. It made him love Him even more.

God sat on his throne. Michael was in awe of his manifestation: a glorious light radiating power, love, and all things good. It was as close as his mind could come to a description.

The throne's overall appearance was one of unimaginable beauty, with hues defying those of the blooms in Triumph Gardens. It was encrusted with perfect rubies and diamonds, enhanced by a rainbow comprised of different shades of green, like a dazzling emerald catching the brilliance of Heaven. Clangs of thunder sounded and flashes of lightning rose from the seat.

Michael gaped at the splendor in front of him. However, he could not see beyond the throne: it was as though it was without limits —joined to infinity.

What is thy request?

"I have come to request that you permit Lucifer to step into the River of Life." Michael bowed his head.

Why hath Lucifer not come to beseech this for himself?

"I offered to do it for him, my Lord. I did not spar in good faith, for there was jealousy in my heart and I desired to hurt him." Michael pressed his face against his hands and wept like his face was melting.

Thou hast shown thy remorse. Hence, I shall grant thy request. However, only he is permitted to enter the waters of the River of Life at this time.

"Yes, my God."

Thou mayst leave my presence.

Michael floated backward above the river, so as not to turn his back on the Almighty. He kept his head hung low until he reached the anteroom, and the doors between him and the courtyard had closed before him. He returned to his natural form. He closed his eyes and took a deep breath to recover from his experience.

Michael followed the River of Life to Guidance Park. Lucifer yet rested, breathless and hunched, on the riverbank near the waterfall. Lilith sat by his side, running her fingers through his long, dark hair.

Michael closed his eyes. "Father, I bind that spirit of jealousy that attempts to consume my being. Remove it now, almighty God, along with the anger and fear that feed it." He opened his eyes and hurried to them. "I have returned."

"Well? Will God permit Lucifer to enter the River of Life, or not?" Lilith asked.

Michael looked at Lucifer. "Indeed, God has granted you passage into the waters."

Lilith helped Lucifer stand and assisted him across the rocks to the water.

"You must stop right there, Lilith!" Michael stepped forward.

She whipped her head around and glared at him. "I mean to help him into the river."

"Apologies, but you must not go any further. God's orders were that only Lucifer enter the water."

"But he is feeble and could collapse. I need to help him enter the water, for the path may be treacherous."

"Do not compel me to stop you, for if I must prevent your entering the water by force, I shall." Michael took another step forward. "If God means for him to enter the water unaided, surely he shall guide his steps and not allow him to fall."

Lucifer looked at Lilith, who gripped him. "You must let me go. I shall be fine."

She released him, keeping her arms extended in case he wobbled. He swayed, but regained his balance and entered the healing water. At once, healthy color returned to his cheeks, his swelling, redness, and bruising faded. Cuts and scrapes vanished.

Lilith and Michael watched the healing transformation in awe. Lucifer swam to and fro, submerged himself, leapt from the water and splashed around.

Lilith glowered at Michael. He was watching Lucifer and grinning. She rolled her eyes.

Michael turned to gaze at her. "We used to be inseparable, remember? Why have we grown apart?"

Lilith frowned. "I think you know why." She moved away from him.

Michael grabbed her arm. "Tell me, I implore you."

She stared at his hand clutching her arm until he let go. "You have reprimanded and rejected me once too often. Your only ambition is to earn your way to Heaven Most High to be at God's side. There is nothing left for me. Had I stayed by your side any longer I would have withered like a dried-out flower. I have flourished since I have been at Lucifer's side, and he too has benefitted from my company. We are good for each other and my affection for him is great."

Michael's chest heaved, his hands trembled and he blinked and stared at Lilith with a sorrowful grimace. He nodded and looked at the ground. "My chest burns and aches and everything around me is gray."

Lilith guffawed.

Michael stared with a stunned expression. "My anguish amuses you?"

She looked toward the river and laughed as she watched Lucifer splash about.

Michael continued to stare at her in amazement.

"I feel great!" Lucifer emerged from the water, seeming strong again. He hugged Lilith while yet drenched. She shuddered, an invigorating jolt shooting throughout her from the contact with his wet body.

Michael frowned and hastened out of the park.

The water from the River of Life was potent. If only she could enter the river whenever she desired, she would be formidable, indeed. Someday God's pointless rules would be no more, and the angels would be free to do as they please. But she would not get ahead of herself. There was still much work to be done before that could happen. She must first engage the angels with her power of suggestion. It may not be possible to persuade all the angels to align with her cause, but she was certain that most would join her. Michael, however, had proved to be quite a challenge, but she would not abandon hope yet. With Lucifer by her side, there was little she would not be able to do.

Chapter 8

GOD'S DECLARATION

The atrium was a vast, circular area the size of a small city. A high wall of blue gemstone encircled this space. Set within the wall were twelve gates made of carved pearl. Its foundations were garnished with a variety of precious stones.

The first foundation was decorated with fiery rubies. The second was embellished with blue sapphires. The rest of the foundations were enhanced with grayish-blue chalcedony, black onyx, orange carnelian, sparkling pale green peridot, violet amethysts, and citrines the color of burning stars.

Of the twelve gates, three were on the north side of the atrium, three on the east, three more on the south, and the last three were on the west side.

Inside the atrium, the pathways were pure gold, so fine it was translucent. The light in the atrium was magnificent, with the stars, planets, and all entities in the galaxies contributing to its brilliance.

It served as a classroom and conference room, where the angels gathered to learn about the various worlds and all matter and energy in the cosmos. At times God tested the angels spiritually, intellectually, and physically. The angels also gathered here to listen to declarations and other announcements pertaining to affairs of the celestial beings.

One brillante, God summoned

the angels to gather in the atrium. God never appeared to them, instead a window between Floraison and the realm of Metá Heaven opened and from this incandescent, ethereal opening in the atmosphere His voice was heard. When the angels were assembled, He proclaimed his intention to create a new life form, one with an appearance similar to their own and with intellect, marking the dawn of a new epoch in Heaven.

Many angels were not pleased with this announcement. Some were full of fear. Lilith seemed the most threatened by God's declaration. She was offended by the implication that she was not enough for Him. She had worked hard to get in His good graces. She was studious, scored high marks on tests and worshipped quite often, although her heart was not always in it. After finally reaching a level she was comfortable with, she feared she would have to compete for God's favor once again with the new race of beings He planned to create.

Lilith turned to Lucifer and Samael. She aimed to fill their heads with her fears. "Why would God need to create other beings when He already has us? Are we not enough for Him anymore? Does He mean to replace us?"

"We shall always come first in God's judgments. We are celestial beings and therefore His children." Lucifer leaned in and grinned.

"What makes you so certain? There is no assurance that when He creates these new creatures we shall not be forgotten."

Lucifer sighed deeply. "We are the closest to Him. Why would He prefer any other life form to us?"

"God shall create this new creature solely for His and our amusement." Samael interjected.

"Yes, but what if these creatures are to live amongst us? They, too, would become celestial beings such as us, would they not?"

They both furrowed their brows, considering her question.

"Surely they would try to compete for God's devotion." Lilith clenched her hands. "I, for one, do not want these beings residing with us. I hope you're right, but I don't know God's mind, and neither do you."

She departed, but not before she planted seeds of doubt in her friends' minds.

After God's revelation, a noisy disturbance arose, unlike anything ever witnessed in Floraison. Lilith dispersed her insecurities like an outbreak of disease. Doubts and fears spread amongst the angels, with sweeping influence. A myriad of angels needed reassurance. Many converged outside of the golden double doors—the portal to Metá Heaven. They wished to gain audiences with God. Lilith stood before them, knowing their agitated minds were like clay and could be easily shaped any way she desired.

"We are His celestial creations. We deserve to have a say about who resides with us in Floraison. These new beings have not earned the right to live amongst us. If these creatures reside with us, we shall lose many of our privileges. They shall compete with us for God's favor, and maybe they shall take it from us."

More angels assembled and listened to her words. They became noisy and boisterous.

Michael stepped forward and stood before them in a calm manner. "This is not the way to obtain an audience with God." Hashmal came and stood beside him.

Samael approached them with relaxed, confident strides. "Who are you to command us?"

Michael looked at him with an inscrutable expression but did not speak to him.

Hashmal stood before him. "We command nothing. However, this assembly does not please God, for there is no order. You cannot demand His presence." Lightning burst from Hashmal's mouth as he proclaimed God's will. Samael jolted and retreated a few steps.

Hashmal stepped forward and stood face-to-face with him. Samael tried to hide his trembling hands as he held his stance.

Lucifer hurried and stood between them. He placed a hand on Samael's shoulder and gazed into his eyes. "Hashmal is right."

He gestured with his eyes for Samael to retreat, and he obeyed without hesitation.

Lilith was impressed to see how the lightest touch from Lucifer caused him to obey without question. She had seen his power demonstrated on a plethora of angels many times before. Angels such as Beelzebub, Dagon, and Fornues, among many others, never wavered to do his bidding.

He was becoming more and more powerful, and this served her purpose well, for he also became more devoted to her, and more eager to please.

Lucifer was a remarkable ally to have on her side. He would help her achieve her goals. Whatever angels did not follow her would surely follow him. He awakened joy and excitement within her.

"We do not feel that the being God shall create is worthy of living in Floraison with us," Lilith said, as angels around her agreed. "We have earned our place here!"

"God and only God shall designate where these creatures shall dwell. He alone shall decide who is worthy." Hashmal's eyes blazed.

She flinched.

"You deem yourself worthier than the rest of us because you can breathe fire, but you are not superior." Full of defiance and without fear, she glared into his red eyes.

"Lucifer—" she said, extending both arms to point at him, "is second only to God. He is praiseworthy. You shall never be greater than he."

"Enough, Lilith please." Michael's voice was tender and dulcet, but Lilith glowered at him.

Raquel made her way through the spectators and stood between Michael and Hashmal. She scanned the crowd and saw the usual provocateurs: Beelzebub, Samael, and—not surprisingly—the queen agitator, Lilith, front and center. "Please remain calm."

"Calm, you say?" Lilith took a step forward. "We shall have peace of mind once we are certain the new beings shall not live amongst us."

Angels yelled in agreement and cheered.

"God shall reveal to us the answers we seek in good time," Raquel said. "Let us disperse for now. This assembly is not pleasing to God, and we shall not receive answers at this moment."

Lilith glared at her with venom in her large, almond-shaped eyes.

"I am leaving since I do not wish to be in your presence—not because you have ordered me to go." Lilith turned and shouted to the crowd, "Remember my words, my brethren! These beings shall replace us in time if they become celestial beings and live in Floraison."

Smiling, she swaggered away. Lucifer and Samael trailed behind her. Soon Gadreel, Fornues, and Beelzebub followed her as well.

"God deliver us from Lilith," Hashmal whispered, his throat glowing like a newly formed star. Raquel nodded. They exchanged anxious glances, as the crowd of protesting angels scattered to the four winds.

Michael's head hung low. Suddenly, above his head appeared a resplendent ring of light. He lifted his head and spoke to Hashmal and Raquel. "God is displeased by the irreverence and impertinence of the angels. He has always shown us love and never given us cause to feel insecure or fearful. I heard Him say in my mind, 'It is time for the angels to have a tangible purpose on Floraison.' Hashmal and Raquel were mesmerized by the divine radiance on his face and the glittering ethereal halo on his head as he spoke.

The angels had grown into impressive beings with great potential. God had always been proud of them all until now. The free will He had granted made them unique individuals. Many of them developed exceptional talents and incomparable abilities. Others chose to develop a perilous mindset.

God made the determination to divide the angels into ranks according to their strengths and talents. Through Hashmal, He summoned the angels to the atrium once more.

"Our time of idleness shall soon be at an end." Hashmal breathed fire with his words and commanded every angel's attention. "God shall divide us into groups according to our abilities and assign duties specific to our rankings. In three brillantes time God shall summon us to the atrium once more and at that time we shall learn where we rank in the hierarchy of angels"

The angels glanced at each other. Some were pleased, eager to prove themselves. Others were insecure and afraid.

"In three brillantes God shall determine every angel's strengths. This knowledge shall assist in establishing what duties are most suitable for each of us, and where we all belong in the ranks." Hashmal roared, forming a fireball before him.

Lilith watched him emanate flames with every word with lips fixed in a grim line. She would excel in these three brillantes as she had always done. She would prove her worth to God, as well as the other angels. She would also observe them, and the angels that surpass all others shall be primary targets for recruitment. Only the most intelligent, fastest, strongest, and most able could join her.

She would be vigilant.

Chapter 9

THE COSMOS AND NATURE INTERPRETATION TEST

Before the brillante of the ranking ceremony had arrived God chose seven angels to keep peace and order in Floraison: Michael, Raphael, Gabriel, Hashmal, Raquel, Esar, and Jetrel.

Lilith and Lucifer were upset by God's decision to exclude them but could do nothing but sulk. They resented those chosen.

"God prefers Michael, even above you, Lucifer," Lilith said.

Lucifer sighed, trying to conceal his disappointment. "God is all knowing. He has good reason for choosing Michael to lead."

"I believe you above all others deserved the honor." She enjoyed flattering him. It was the quickest way to make him susceptible to her suggestions. "You are the strongest, the fastest, and the most intelligent. You have the incredible ability to manipulate energy and to track the other angels. You are the most powerful being in Floraison. God can make mistakes and He has in choosing Michael over you. Prove Him wrong."

He glanced at her with a dim smile. "God is the most powerful being in all three realms of Heaven. Besides, I have yet to master my abilities."

"I am certain it shant be too long until you master your abilities, and when the time comes for you to take your rightful place you shall be ready." She smiled and walked away. Soon he would know her meaning.

She looked briefly over her shoulder at him. His eyes still focused on her. For now, excel and devastate the other angels—Michael, Raphael, and Gabriel—with your magnificence. Then they shall have no choice but to follow us.

Gabriel's strategy to keep the angels calm while waiting for God's ruling was to assess each angel's psychology, personality, and knowledge of the cosmos and nature.

Gabriel excelled above other angels in these areas during God's own catechism. Therefore, God granted him the opportunity to evaluate the angels, and he chose Esar to assist him. Esar was a strong and remarkable angel, and despite his greatness he was meek and fair. In Gabriel's eyes, he was a living symbol of God's justice and peace, which made him the perfect choice.

Gabriel developed the 'Cosmos and Nature Interpretation Test', to be conducted in the atrium. The great round, open hall served as a window that allowed the angels to view other worlds outside of Floraison. From this place they were able to observe every section of the different galaxies, stars, and planets.

The angels entered the large hall behind Gabriel and Esar. They always marveled at the immense beauty of the various worlds with their suns, moons, and stars, and at how each emanated or reflected its own colorful and dazzling luminosity.

Esar guided them to the main sitting area. The angels fell to their seats, fidgeting, chattering, and tapping their feet anticipating what the assessment would entail.

Gabriel stood before them. "The areas I shall test you on were covered in your lessons on the cosmos. One by one, you shall be called to come forward. You shall be shown a planet or a section of a galaxy or universe. After being given ample time to observe the region, I shall ask you to tell me a story involving the planet or the section of the cosmos you have seen."

Lilith observed the angels by her side, whose taut faces and clenched jaws betrayed their anxiety.

"Tell as intricate and dramatic a story as you are able." Gabriel handed Esar a list of the angels in the order he sought to assess them.

Esar became uneasy upon seeing the first name on the list: Lilith. She was the most beautiful and alluring being in Floraison, perhaps in all the galaxies. She was also intelligent and witty. As Esar pondered her charms, his knee joints began to bend backward.

Gabriel nudged him. "Esar, your legs."

Noticing his uncanny way of standing, Lilith and several other angels giggled.

Esar realized what he was doing and straightened his limbs. Several parts of his body were double-jointed and could bend and flex beyond the capacity of the other angels.

"Li-leeth!" Esar's voice cracked, and his face reddened. He cleared his throat and tried again. "Ll-lilith, p-please ca-come f-for-forr-ward!" He closed his eyes and took a breath. "Lilith, come forward please!"

Esar watched with an expression of admiration as she rose from her seat. Her walk was loose-hipped and relaxed, with a slight sway. She proceeded to him, beaming at him and Gabriel.

"I am ready to do what is asked of me." She gazed into Esar's dark brown eyes; like deep space, they twinkled with mystery and surprise. He shivered and began to wiggle his ears and pull his fingers far backward.

All of a sudden, his cranium shifted into the head of a lovebird. To the unrestrained laughter of the angels, he chirped a love song.

Once again, Esar's head morphed. This time, into the head of a koi fish boasting a heart-shaped mark on its forehead. Lilith backed away, her hand covering her mouth in amazement, but she could not help chuckling.

Gabriel grabbed Esar's forearm. He leaned and whispered in his ear, "Remain calm. Get a hold of yourself."

He closed his round fish eyes and took a deep breath. He changed once more, becoming himself again. His face turned bright red when he realized everyone was staring and laughing. He lowered his gaze as Lilith approached him. She passed her hand through his curly black hair.

"I find what you do amazing," Lilith whispered in his ear. "When you gain control of your shifting, no one shall find it amusing any longer. Everyone shall have to admit your ability is worthy of merit."

Esar was captivated by her words.

Gabriel took her by the hand and guided her to the center of the platform. "You may tell your story from here. Every angel in the atrium shall hear it."

"I thought only you would hear my tale." Lilith scanned the audience. There were so many. Michael was amongst them.

"No, we shall all listen. You have our undivided attention." Gabriel gestured with his arm to the audience.

So they wanted to hear a story, did they? Well, she would convey to them a tale they would never forget. Her narrative would awaken secret desires, and they would come to long for things they were missing. Doubts would bloom in their minds.

"Thanda-Garam is a small planet but an interesting one," Gabriel told her. "This is the planet you shall feature in your story. It is a terrestrial planet with extreme climatic regions. There are areas of extreme heat with many active volcanoes, and lava flows far and wide. There are areas of extreme cold where most things are covered in ice, and robust winds rush from icy mountain tops at hurricane speeds."

"I am familiar with this planet. It is one of my favorites." Lilith smiled. "I am most fond of the side blanketed by snow and ice—it is quite beautiful. I have observed the planet for long periods and have learned a lot from its inhabitants."

Gabriel raised an eyebrow at her last statement. What could Lilith wish to learn from the inhabitants of Thanda-Garam that she could not learn in Floraison from God?

"I would enjoy telling you a story about this planet," Lilith said.

"I am glad you find this planet fascinating. It shall make for an interesting narrative. I highly anticipate your story."

Lilith grinned and twirled her hair. How could she relate this story in the most traumatizing way possible, in order to sow seeds of doubt and rebellion against God's laws? Should she fret about what telling a provocative tale would reveal of her? What was Gabriel evaluating?

Gabriel, Cam, and Raquel and so many others would form a bad opinion of her despite the story she told. She shrugged. She would enjoy narrating her fable and implanting seeds of uncertainty and yearning in their self-righteous minds.

She had noticed the lingering gazes between Raquel and Dagon. Cam was far too fond of giving orders and governing the other angels. Esar stared at her when he thought she was not looking.

And Gabriel—ah, Gabriel—could Beelzebub be right about you? She would make them think of possibilities—things that could be if they rebelled against a God that imposes cruel rulings on His creations.

She nodded and Gabriel and Esar took their seats.

Lilith took a deep breath and smiled at the angels sitting before her and proceeded to narrate her story.

Chapter 10

STORYTELLING

Once upon a time on the planet Thanda-Garam, there were two kingdoms. The Kingdom of Kokin on the ice-covered side of the planet in the land of Nihar, and the Kingdom of Aag on the smoldering side of the planet in the land of Arathi. Separating these two kingdoms was a vast, roaring river called Jal. The only way to cross the river was to go over the Bandhutva Bridge. The forefathers of the present kings built the Bandhutva Bridge many centuries ago in an attempt to keep an alliance between the two kingdoms that had once been enemies. No one from the Kingdom of Kokin or the Kingdom of Aag had crossed the Bandhutva Bridge in a hundred years. The two nations preferred to remain on their own side of the Jal River.

The Arathians considered Nihar too cold and creepy a place, with its pink skies, icy castles, and endless snow. The Niharians deemed Arathi too menacing a place, with its huge lava-spewing volcanoes, fire-breathing animals, and magma lakes. Thus, the inhabitants of each kingdom remained isolated.

One day King Agnimukha of the Kingdom of Aag in Arathi summoned his faithful minister Rama to his royal chambers.

"How may I be of service to you, my king?" Rama asked.

"There is an important issue I need to discuss with both you and my son. Meet me here in an hour's time and be sure prince Kamal is with you."

Minister Rama bowed his head and departed, never showing the king his back.

An hour later, Minister Rama entered the king's chambers, accompanied by Prince Kamal. King Agnimukha sat on his bed. He was dying. The excessive volcanic ash and gas emissions had affected his health.

The land of Arathi was changing. The massive volcanoes were taking control of the land and atmosphere. The temperature was becoming too hot and the air toxic. Many of the older inhabitants of Arathi had fallen sick, and many more had perished. Minister Rama and the royal family were aware something must be done soon, or there would no longer be a Kingdom of Aag.

"We must venture to the land of Nihar to the Kingdom of Kokin," the king began. "I shall send a message to King Dhaval requesting an audience."

"No, Father, if he accepts, it could be to set a trap! Besides, you are far too sick to go on such a voyage. Why not invite him here instead?"

"It is far easier for us to survive their climate than it is for them to survive ours. King Dhaval would never come here. Besides, we do not wish for any Niharian to see the state of our once powerful kingdom," the king told his son between coughs.

"So why meet at all?" Prince Kamal wore an annoyed grimace. "Why should we risk our lives?"

"Be calm, my spirited son," King Agnimukha said. "You shall soon be king. It is time we traveled across the Bandhutva Bridge and saw with our own eyes what is transpiring in our neighboring kingdom. Perhaps we may learn something from those who were once our enemies."

He wheezed and coughed. Prince Kamal placed his hand on his father's shoulder and squeezed gently.

Minister Rama stepped forward, bowed, and lowered his head. "If I may, Your Majesty?"

"Please say what is on your mind, Minister. Your wise advice is always appreciated." King Agnimukha suffered a coughing fit. Prince Kamal handed his father a piece of cloth to wipe the blood he had just expelled.

"Thank you, Your Majesty," Rama said. "I have heard from my spies that soon Princess Manju shall take the crown as Queen of Kokin. It would be to our advantage if we created an alliance with her now. The land of Arathi is surely becoming a fiery wasteland, and soon no living thing shall be able to survive here. We need new lands to rule."

"And how do you suggest we take their lands?" Prince Kamal cocked his head.

"You, my prince, are the key." Rama smiled at the handsome young prince. "It is spoken that Princess Manju is beautiful and pure. And you, my prince, are quite handsome, charming, and experienced in the arts of desire."

Minister Rama and King Agnimukha exchanged devious smiles.

"Are you suggesting that I travel to the land of Nihar and seduce the Princess of Kokin?"

"You, my son, are a master of rhetoric and deception, as your mother once was." The King chuckled between gasps. "Surely it would not be too great a feat for you to entice an innocent—not with your vast experience with the female gender. With the Queen of Kokin devoted to you, my son, the Kingdom of Kokin shall be ours to rule."

"You have taken many to your bed, my prince," Minister Rama said. "Your sexual prowess is praised in all four corners of Arathi."

"No task is too great for my kingdom. I shall make myself ready for the journey." The prince beamed. "And with your permission, Father, I wish to take Minister Rama along as counsel."

"Yes, my son, take all that is needed."

"Minister, you shall make the arrangements for our journey."

"Yes, my prince, I shall begin at once."

❧

"Your Majesty, I have information from our neighboring kingdom," Minister Pratap said. "Arathian guards were seen marching across the Bandhutva Bridge headed our way."

"Truly?" King Dhaval asked with an incredulous expression. "After decades of silence, King Agnimukha chooses now to be provocative? Is he dying?"

The King's daughter who stood a few feet away giggled.

"I do not know, Your Highness." The minister snickered.

"Send my Elite Guards to intercept them before they cross the midway point of the bridge," King Dhaval ordered the minister. Princess Manju gasped and stared wide-eyed at her father.

The minister hurried to carry out the king's orders.

The princess rushed to the king, sat by his side, and held his arm.

"Do not fear, my sweet daughter. All shall be fine." The king caressed his daughter, his face etched with apprehension.

Minister Pratap gave the guards their orders. The young guards glanced at each other, their eyes glistening with trepidation. They had heard descriptions of the red and black lands of Arathi, with its lakes of fire and balls of lava erupting from the mouths of volcanoes. They also had heard accounts of Niharian soldiers who crossed the bridge to Arathi, only to be thrown into pits of molten fire to burn in slow agony. Despite their fears, the brave guards embarked on the nine-mile hike across the bridge to learn why Arathian soldiers marched toward Nihar.

As they neared the midpoint of the bridge, the guards began to experience the heat emitted from Arathi. Their bodies were soaked in sweat, and they began to feel faint and unsteady. A large cloud of smoke appeared before them. Afraid and unable to see past it, they halted.

As they stared at the gray fog, an intimidating Arathian dressed in a black and red hooded cloak stepped out of it. He was accompanied by a group of guards bearing weapons. The hooded cape worn by the chief Arathian cast eerie shadows on his bony face, frightening the young Niharian guards as he approached them.

"Do not come any closer!" The head Niharian guard yelled in a stern voice.

Minister Rama, his face hidden in the shadows of his cape, asked, "Do you mean to intercept our crossing of the Bandhutva Bridge?"

"We mean no harm or disrespect." The guard gulped and stared at the minister. "We are following orders to learn why you march toward our lands."

"I am Minister Rama. No one in the Kingdom of Aag is closer to King Agnimukha, with the exception of his son, Prince Kamal. I am here to deliver a message to King Dhaval from King Agnimukha."

The sentinel had heard countless tales of Minister Rama and his deeds. He stepped forward without displaying fear. "Very well, deliver it then, and I shall convey it to my king."

Minister Rama arched a sly brow, but he admired the young guard's courage. "Splendid, I shall deliver King Agnimukha's message to you then. My king would like an audience with your king. We shall return for King Dhaval's answer in two days' time."

"I shall deliver the message to King Dhaval. Now if that is all, I suggest you and your cohorts return to Arathi."

Minister Rama nodded, wearing a sinister smile that chilled the head guard's bones even in the intense heat. Then Rama gestured to his men to turn around and thus, they initiated their return to Arathi.

The Niharian guards watched as their rivals marched toward the Kingdom of Aag. When the Arathians were far enough away, they too filed away to the opposite side of the bridge toward Nihar.

Later that night, Minister Pratap returned to deliver the message from King Agnimukha to King Dhaval.

"It seems that King Agnimukha would like an audience with Your Highness." The minister raised his brow.

The king pondered the request. He was always curious about the fiery lands across the river Jal, but unlike his predecessors, he had never visited Arathi. When he inherited the throne, there was peace between the two lands, and there had been ever since. He never deemed it necessary to travel to the frightening land or meet King Agnimukha.

King Dhaval was now old. His beautiful daughter, Princess Manju, was his only heir and would soon succeed to the throne of Kokin. The king desired to ensure that when the princess became Queen of Kokin, the kingdom would be at peace and on good terms with the Kingdom of Aag, as it had been for centuries.

However, he suffered nightmares of a vicious war arising between the two realms, which robbed the king of peace of mind. The stories of bloody wars past, told to him as a child by the ancients, were terrible. He did not wish this upon his daughter.

King Dhaval trusted his Minister Pratap, a creature of dignity and distinction. "What do you think, Pratap? Should I accept a visit from King Agnimukha?"

"I believe it would be the wisest thing to do, Your Majesty." Pratap bowed his head.

King Dhaval nodded in agreement. "Yes, I do desire for peace to remain throughout my daughter's reign. I shall welcome the king with open arms. Send my response without delay and make preparations to receive our guests."

"Yes, Your Highness, I shall execute your commands without delay." The Minister bowed and left the king's presence.

In anticipation of the frosty weather in the Kingdom of Kokin, Minister Rama commissioned fine coats for himself and several others, including the prince, King Dhaval, his daughter, and his minister. The luxurious, warm coats were made of pelts of mala, large furry beasts dwelling near volcanoes. Mala fur was nearly indestructible, impermeable to both fire and ice. It was soft, rare, exquisite, and a suitable gift for royalty.

Soon Prince Kamal, the minister, and a handful of guards were on the Bandhutva Bridge on their way to the Kingdom of Kokin. A while after passing the midway point of the bridge, they began to tremble from the frosty air. They put on the mala fur coats and were instantly warmed.

At the end of the bridge, Minister Pratap and a dozen Niharian soldiers greeted them. An elegant carriage waited for them. Large, muscular, two-legged mammals with long iridescent white hair and sapphire eyes called Bāladāra Bhaloo drew it. Pratap invited Prince Kamal and Minister Rama to come onboard and ride to the Crystal Palace with him. The soldiers were to accompany the carriage on foot.

It was warm and comfortable inside the carriage, but Prince Kamal shifted in his seat, ill at ease sitting between the two ministers, who scrutinized each other.

"Prince Kamal, although it is a great honor to meet you," Minister Pratap said, "I am saddened your father, King Agnimukha, was unable to make it to Nihar. King Dhaval shall be disappointed."

"Yes, my father, too, was disappointed he could not meet King Dhaval, but he is much too old for such a journey. On the other hand, I am young, fit, and strong. My father's wisdom has been passed to me, and seeing as I shall soon be ruler of Arathi, it is only wise that I, the future King of Aag, and Princess Manju, the future Queen of Kokin, should meet at this time."

Minister Pratap jolted, stunned by the prince's vanity and pride.

When the carriage arrived at the Crystal Palace, Prince Kamal was the first to jump out. He was eager to meet the princess and get started with his deception. For a moment, the prince stopped to admire the enormous palace and surrounding country.

"The Crystal Palace is a masterpiece!" Minister Rama said. "Behold how it glitters in the light of day, reflecting the pink Niharian sky like a multicolored gemstone."

Prince Kamal nodded in agreement with a look of awe. Together they gaped at the palace and the countryside. It always snowed in Nihar, sometimes a light dusting, other times a heavy downpour. The crystal snowflakes reflected and refracted the light of its surroundings, making Nihar a sparkling paradise.

"This magnificent structure was carved from the mountain where it now sits. It is made of a powerful crystalline solid, which reflects light beautifully." Minister Pratap pointed to the castle as he boasted. "Let us enter the palace, for there are many wonders inside to delight you."

The visitors followed Pratap into the palace through massive white wooden doors. Once inside they smelled an enticing, smoky scent—one their noses had never detected before.

"What is the irresistible fragrance emanating from the entire castle?" The prince inhaled deeply.

"It is a native flower called Lahota.It is found only in the tallest, iciest peaks. Its alluring fragrance compels the king to send his finest soldiers to the treacherous summits every year when they are in bloom to collect them and bring them to the palace. We put them around all the fireplaces."

"It is an incredible scent that all together brings about feelings of excitement and relaxation." Prince Kamal closed his eyes and breathed it in.

"There is a perfume made from the Lahota flower. It is potent in its ability to influence the male gender. The fragrance adapts to the individual chemistry of the female wearing it, making her scent alluring." Minister Pratap grinned. "Few females are privy to this fragrance. Princess

Manju, her lady-in-waiting, and a select few noblewomen in court have small containers of the perfume. They wear the fragrance in moments of their choosing."

They strolled along a corridor with cold, white stone floors. The walls of the passageway were decorated with beautiful portraits of the princess and other royals carved in flat gemstones, above which were light fixtures to illuminate them at night.

The corridor led into a large open room with crystal walls. The walls appeared green-blue since they absorbed the light of the raging fires in the two huge fireplaces located on either side of an ample, spiraling staircase in the middle of the room.

Exquisite, colorful floor coverings masked most of the stone floors. Standing in a semicircle in front of the spiral staircase were the royal court and staff, waiting to greet the visitors.

"Prince Kamal, I am honored by your presence!" King Dhaval beamed as he waddled toward him with Princess Manju in hand. Princess Manju's lady-in-waiting remained by her side.

"The honor is all mine, Your Majesty." Prince Kamal bowed to the king. "I regret to inform you that my father, King Agnimukha, was unable to attend, for he is old, and the journey here would have been too taxing for him."

"I understand, for my bones are not what they used to be, and such treks are best left to you young people. I am, however, disappointed that I may never meet your father." King Dhaval frowned. He changed his manner to introduce his daughter. "Prince Kamal, I introduce to you my beautiful daughter, Princess Manju."

The princess stepped forward to greet the prince, as did her lady-in-waiting.

"Greetings, Prince Kamal. I hope your journey here was a pleasant one." Princess Manju's face flushed a bright pink.

The prince smiled at the princess, but when he caught sight of her lady-in-waiting, he leered at her.

The princess frowned. "You were saying, your highness?"

"I have longed to meet you, my princess. No journey would have been too long or strenuous." The prince took the princess's hand and kissed it.

The prince glanced at the princess's lady-in-waiting. What a striking creature.

I have never been in the presence of such an enticing being.

"I am certain you and your men are exhausted from your journey." The princess took her assistant's arm and yanked her forward. "My lady-in-waiting shall show you to your lodgings where you may rest and later prepare for our dinner celebration."

"Go now!" Princess Manju waved at her lady-in-waiting. "Make sure the prince is well accommodated."

"Yes, my princess." She curtsied and led the prince and his entourage up the spiral steps to their rooms.

"This is your room, Your Majesty. I hope it is to your fancy."

The prince gazed into her extraordinary eyes and smiled. "What is your name?"

"My name is Lily," she said in a smoky voice.

"Lily, return to my room once you have shown the other guests to their quarters."

"The princess shall be awaiting my return. I must help her prepare for tonight's event." She angled her head downward while turning her eyes toward the prince.

"The princess stated she wished for you to see me well accommodated, did she not?"

"Yes, my prince, she did voice it so." She smiled. "I shall return soon."

The princess's lady-in-waiting had instantly captured Prince Kamal's heart. He bathed and waited for her return. When she returned, she knocked on the door, waited for his official sanction to enter, and proceeded into the prince's room.

Prince Kamal stood in front of the fireplace in the nude. Lily gaped at him, never before having seen a naked male body.

"Come to me," he bid with bated breath.

She glided toward him, making the blood boil in his veins. The prince grabbed her. He kissed her in ways she never been kissed, and touched her in ways she had never been touched. She smiled and moaned with delight.

He removed every bit of clothing from her body until she was as naked as he and took her into his bed. He did things she had never imagined with his mouth, hands, and body, making her feel intense pleasure. When he proceeded to penetrate her, she trembled, but her eyes shimmered with excitement. "I have never been with a male this way."

"I vow I shall not hurt you." Prince Kamal took his time and was gentle.

When the deed was done, they held each other for a while, enjoying the culmination of the moment.

"I must soon depart, for Princess Manju must be missing me." Lily's eyes were doleful.

The prince kissed her forehead, the tip of her nose, her lips, and finally her neck.

"Go and wash my scent off your body. Return to the princess with a quiet tongue."

She left the bed. Before she exited the room, she glanced at him over her shoulder. He wore a satisfied smile, making her feel like she was floating on air.

She returned to the princess's chambers. Princess Manju wore a scowl.

"You have kept me waiting! Where have you been?"

"I apologize, but our guests required much attention." Lily looked at the floor and squirmed.

"Was Prince Kamal satisfied with his accommodations?"

Lily bit her lower lip to thwart a giggle. "Yes, Your Majesty, I believe he is well satisfied."

"Fine, help me get ready for the celebration dinner. I wish to look my best. I intend to steal the prince's heart tonight."

Lily frowned. She had fallen for the handsome prince.

Princess Manju is a daunting rival. She is quite fetching with smoldering russet eyes, and long, gleaming hair, dark as a raven's feathers and skin smooth and a beautiful shade of brown. In addition, she is a princess. How could I contend with that?

However, no other had ever looked at her the way the prince had, and the heart knows not of ranks and majesty. It only knows what it desires. She would not simply relinquish the prince to Princess Manju on a silver platter. She would fight to win his heart and mind. Once that was done, she, too, would be a princess in the Kingdom of Aag.

⤙

The Crystal Palace dining room was vast and elegant, adorned with marble columns and statues of Princess Manju and past princesses and queens. A long table in the center of the room was decorated with centerpieces of colorful and exotic flowers, which filled the room with intoxicating fragrances.

King Dhaval sat at the head of the table. Minister Pratap sat at the other end. Princess Manju took Prince Kamal by the hand and sat to the left of her father. Lily sat across from them, next to Minister Rama.

The princess wore a strapless, glossy silk gown the color of a frosted pomegranate. It featured a stunning bodice encrusted with jewels, and a gathered ball gown skirt with gemstone beading. On her head was a superb tiara of teardrop-shaped diamonds mounted on white gold. The jeweled coronet glinted, contrasting with her dark hair. Her cheeks were rosy with rouge and her lips a dewy cherry. Her warm eyes were outlined with kohl, giving them a sultry look.

Lily's dress was neither ornate nor luxurious but unadorned and color-less. She wore no make-up, for the princess forbade it, and she boasted no jewelry. However, when she strolled into the room, she caught everyone's eye, prominent as the sun at midday.

Many exquisite dishes were served. Everyone ate and drank their fill. Lily, however, found it difficult to swallow her food. The prince never laid eyes on her. Instead, he devoted all his attention to the princess.

When the celebratory dinner ended, the princess took the prince hand and led him outside where a carriage awaited. "I wish to show you the beauty of the land of Nihar at night."

The prince smiled and nodded and they entered the carriage.

"Have you been enjoying your stay in the Kingdom of Kokin, Your Highness?" Princess Manju batted her eyelashes.

"Yes, I have, and I believe you are the reason why." The prince gazed at her in his usual captivating way.

The princess returned his smile and shivered.

"You are cold. Let me warm you." He seized the moment and nestled close to her. He placed an arm around her shoulders and with the other caressed her face. He leaned his head toward hers, all the while gazing into her eyes. Princess Manju melted into his arms as he kissed her.

At the end of the night, they went their separate ways to their individual quarters. Princess Manju was enamored with the prince, and he wooed her for several days. However, he was unable to eliminate Lily's image from his mind and was eager to have her in his arms once more.

"Summon the princess's lady-in-waiting to my chambers," Prince Kamal ordered Minister Rama.

"What is your interest in the princess's lady-in-waiting?"

"Do not concern yourself with my pastimes. You have more serious issues to consider."

"Your activities are directly related to the outcome of our task here, so it concerns me that you are calling the princess's lady-in-waiting to your chambers. Everything is working flawlessly between you and Princess Manju. In no time, she shall throw herself at your feet. Why risk success for one night of pleasure?"

"I understand your concerns. Fear not, I shall not be reckless. Do as I ask, minister, and bring Lily to me, for I need her to carry on my deceit."

"As you wish, my prince." Minister Rama bowed his head.

He searched the castle for Lily. He finally spotted her as she left the princess's chambers. He lingered in a dark corner awhile to be certain she was alone.

"Lily," he called in a loud whisper.

She turned and gasped, startled by the dark figure appearing out of nowhere. "Minister Rama, how do you come to know my name?"

"The same way you came to know mine." He observed her with an inscrutable expression. "Prince Kamal would like the pleasure of your company in his chambers."

"Please inform the good prince I am unable to do his bidding at the moment, for I am fulfilling Princess Manju's requests." She continued on her way.

Minister Rama looked surprised by her boldness but understood at once what the prince found so appealing about her.

This Lily is dangerous. I must take strong measures to rid the prince of this untimely impediment. He returned to prince's quarters to deliver her reply.

"What do you mean, she refused me?!"

"She stated that she served Princess Manju, and she would not always be available to fulfill your wishes."

Prince Kamal's face flushed a deep scarlet and his chest heaved. He was unaccustomed to being rejected by the opposite sex. He stormed from his room to find her.

Minister Rama's mouth hung open, shocked by the prince's emotional outburst, he joined his eyebrows together in thought. "I must proceed with my plan before all is lost," he murmured under his breath.

He would put an end to Lily's hold on the prince.

The minister had learned that the Lahota flower was renowned for more than its seductive fragrance. Many of the guards sent to harvest the flowers, and numerous chemists who produced the perfume, had died horrible deaths in the process of handling the bright purple stem and leaves, which carried powerful toxins. Now Minister Rama set about procuring some for his purpose.

ᣖ

Prince Kamal found Lily in the Crystal Palace's dining room, overseeing the decoration of the salon for the night's dinner. He stormed across the room. Although his fists were balled tight, he spoke in a restrained voice.

"May I have a word with you?"

"Yes, my prince." She followed him to the outer hallway.

The moment they were alone, the prince grabbed her by the upper arms and pushed her against the wall. He pressed his body against hers.

"How dare you reject me?"

"It was not my intention to refuse you. Your Majesty, I serve another, and my time is not my own." Her glistening eyes stared into his.

The prince became docile as he gazed into them. He put his arms around her in a tight embrace and kissed her.

"Do you love the princess?" Lily asked in a brittle voice.

"I do not." He continued to gaze into her eyes.

"But you shall make her your wife, and when her father, King Dhaval, departs this life, you shall be king and she your queen?"

"Yes."

"Thus, I shall not love you, and you must release me." Her eyes expressed the pain of a broken heart.

"My kingdom is dying," he said. "As we speak, massive volcanoes are spewing their liquid fire across our lands, poisoning our water and crops and making our air toxic. We need a new kingdom; we need the Kingdom of Kokin!" Tears shone in Prince Kamal's eyes.

"As a consequence, you must marry Princess Manju in order to obtain this Kingdom," Lily said, finally understanding his plight.

"Naturally—but you are the one my heart desires. What can I do?" He caressed her face with his and whispered in her ear, "I risk losing all by divulging this to you. I hope it is proof enough of my devotion."

"Few people outside this palace have seen Princess Manju" Lily's eyes were wide and bright. "Many say there are countless similarities between the princess and me."

"What is your meaning?"

"I could replace the princess. I could stand in her place and be your wife!"

The prince puffed and took a step away. "That is not possible. The palace servants shall know the truth."

"Only a handful of servants have seen the princess. I have been often mistaken for her. Besides, once you have assumed command of the kingdom, they can be silenced."

The prince creased his brow and shook his head. "Surely King Dhaval would recognize his own daughter."

"He shall soon perish. I would not worry about him."

"Minister Pratap seems wise and powerful. I am certain he would not stand by while——"

"You say you love me, " Lily pushed him away, "but make a hundred pretexts not to be with me."

She pouted. The prince pulled her toward him again and kissed her head.

Once more, she gazed into the prince's eyes, making him weak with desire. "This plan can succeed. Simply command your minister to kill Minister Pratap. I shall take care of King Dhaval, and you shall end the princess' life."

Prince Kamal paled. He staggered away from her. His knees wavered, and he placed a hand against the wall for support.

She strolled to him and embraced him. "If you desire to reign as King of Kokin and spend your life with me, this is what must be done." She held his gaze while offering a small, sly smile.

He was soon convinced she was right, and agreed to execute her plan.

⌇

Minister Rama let himself into Princess Manju's room, which adjoined Lily's bedroom. In his hand, the minister carried a vial filled with a purple substance: the potent toxin derived from the stems and leaves of the Lahota flower.

Hearing an appealing voice singing nearby, Minister Rama hid behind a large wooden screen with delicate ornate carvings. He stole a glimpse and caught sight of Lily dressing herself. She had enjoyed a bath and sang as she clothed her naked body. Rama lost focus for a moment.

She opened a small, colorful bottle. A captivating fragrance traveled through the air, entering the minister's nostrils, causing his body to quiver. She dabbed the fragrance on various areas of her body. When she was done, she left the chamber.

Minister Rama hurried and entered her bedroom. Sitting on a small table was the colorful bottle of the Lahota flower's fragrance.

The minister opened the bottle, once more allowing the enticing fragrance to pirouette its way into his nose. He poured in the purple toxin, making sure none of the harmful substance fell on his skin.

One of the palace chemists had revealed another secret to Minister Rama: the Lahota flower alone was harmless, but if the toxin of its foliage were to be mixed with the flower's essence, the poison would be ten times more powerful.

Minister Rama imagined the consequences as he poured the poison into the perfume bottle. He heard the door to the princess's chambers open. He closed the flask as fast as possible and hid once more.

Princess Manju slipped into her room, excited about the night's festivities and thrilled to see the prince again. She took a bath and patted her skin dry. The princess remained nude as she sashayed to a table laden with beautiful bottles, carved jewelry boxes, and ornate jars. She searched the contents of the tabletop, but seemed unable to find what she was seeking.

Her calm and pleasant demeanor slowly changed. She grimaced in all-consuming anger; her nostrils flared and her hands clenched into tight fists.

"I have warned Lily a hundred times not to use my fragrance." The princess banged on the table as she muttered. She would reprimand her as soon as she set eyes on her. She would not be lenient for her servant had taken advantage of her tolerance and become quite a nuisance.

The princess stomped to Lily's room. She spotted the small, colorful bottle containing her fragrance.

As she approached Lily's table, the minister, who was hiding nearby, held his breath. He did not comprehend why the princess was strutting toward him. His body tensed and he watched in amazement as the princess grabbed the perfume vessel and opened it.

"Troublesome pest! I shall win Prince Kamal's heart tonight, and his eyes shall cease to wander in your direction. I shall make certain of it!" Princess Manju griped as she dabbed the inside of her ankles with the perfume.

Minister Rama jumped to his feet, but it was too late. The poison coursed through the princess's body to grotesque effect: her feet and ankles began to distend and turn a deep blackish purple. Where the toxin flowed, so did the hideous purple color. The princess groaned and clutched her aching extremities. She collapsed to the floor. Horror and agony were etched on her face. She wailed gaping at her swollen, purplish-black lower body.

Minister Rama's face dropped in remorse. He stood paralyzed and trembling with fear. "What have I done?" He ran to the princess and placed one of his large, bony hands upon her mouth to suppress her cries of torment. Her face, not yet attacked by the purple malice, was pale and her eyes were large with anguish.

As he crouched by the princess, the poison carried its malignancy to every tissue in her body, resembling violet tentacles sent out in every direction. The princess's entire body became the deep, blackish purple color. Her skin grew rough and bumpy. Her long, lustrous hair fell in clusters. Every muscle began to tighten and draw together simultaneously, causing her body to contort in disturbing ways. Her howls were reduced to quiet moans as her mandibles locked. Constant spasms of her facial muscles made her appear to have a heinous grin.

Minister Rama trembled and wept. Exhausted and sickened by what he beheld, he released her and watched the spasms spread to every muscle in her body.

Princess Manju underwent many convulsions. As the tremors progressed, they increased in intensity and frequency. The spasms became so violent, the minister heard several of her bones break.

Her mouth gaped and continued to open until the corners ripped. Thick dark colored blood gushed from the gashes. Her tongue, now the color of ripe mulberries, grew too large for her mouth and no longer fit. Her eyelids were stretched as far apart as possible, and her eyeballs bulged.

He turned away disgust twisted his features. She was no longer the young pretty princess with whom he was acquainted but a grotesque aberration.

"Die already—please perish before someone hears your cries." He wiped his eyes and covered his ears.

Princess Manju's backbone arched exaggeratedly many times, and she shrieked as more of her bones fractured.

"How could a body take so much suffering?" Minister Rama squeezed his eyes shut.

The princess's body became wet with perspiration. Purplish-black vomitus oozed out of her mouth, and it smelled sweet and fragrant like the Lahota flower.

Lily opened the door to the princess's chambers and proceeded to her room. She saw Minister Rama and stood at a halt.

"What are you doing in my bedchamber?"

The color drained from his face. His mouth moved but words did not come, there was no need, for Lily soon saw the horror before her.

Her hands sprang to her mouth to stifle a scream. She inched forward, her eyes becoming slits to avoid taking in the entire grotesque scene at once. She scrutinized the repulsive purple-black creature thrashing on the ground, producing unnatural sounds.

"What sort of creature is this?" Lily's eyes widened, and her lips parted. She raised her brows, realizing who the monstrosity before her was. "No, it cannot be." She took a closer look. "It is hard to believe that this hideous, broken creature was once a beautiful princess. How did this happen, Minister Rama?"

A powerful scent intruded upon her consciousness, and she swooned. The fragrance meant to lift her off the ground and carry her away. She stiffened, but the smell commanded attention. She covered her nostrils with the back of her hand and gained control of herself again. She noticed the small, colorful bottle of perfume lying near Princess Manju's body. A purple fluid ran from it and stained the floor covering.

"You must have poisoned her perfume!" She pointed at the minister. He trembled but remained silent. How had he known the perfume was property of the princess, and not hers, since it was on her table in her chamber? She gathered her brow in thought. Minister Rama thought the perfume belonged to her, since it was in her room. She was his intended victim!

Her hand gradually floated to cover her mouth. While she stared, the princess' convulsive tossing gradually ceased, she began to gasp for air; and in a few moments she died of asphyxiation.

Lily trembled, clenched her jaw and curled her hands into balls. She glared at the minister as he gaped at the princess's corpse. When the minister lifted his eyes, she changed her angry expression.

"Minister Rama, you have done Prince Kamal and me a great favor by extinguishing Princess Manju's life." She smiled. "Please, do tell me how you accomplished this deed?"

Minister Rama cleared his throat. "I used the toxic stems and leaves of the Lahota flower to formulate a poison. Later, I mixed it into the princess' fragrance and waited for the intended outcome."

"I see. Was this the conclusion you envisioned?" she asked to make him squirm.

"Of course! What other result could I have intended?" His voice trembled.

She nodded while searching his face. "You have many talents. The prince shall be most grateful to you."

"The prince knows I am devoted to him and his father King Dhaval."

She turned away from him and frowned. "Come, we must inform him of your good deed at once."

She took the minister's hand and pulled him toward the door, but he quickly released his hand from hers.

"What of Princess Manju's body?" He appeared tormented.

"No one enters this chamber other than me or the princess, so we can dispose of it later. We must leave this place at once—the scent is overwhelming."

They left the princess's chambers in search of the prince and found him sitting in the large open room with the spiral staircase and crystal walls, enjoying the warmth of the fireplace.

"Minister Rama, please wait here. Allow me to break the news to the prince." Lily smiled.

"Go on then." He dismissed her with a wave of a hand.

"I shall call you when the time comes," she said through clenched teeth.

She ran to the prince and told him everything. "The poison was meant for me. He intended for me to be the one writhing on the ground, deformed and in pain. Your minister wanted me to suffer a terrible death."

"And for that, he shall pay with his own life." The prince grabbed her by the shoulders. "If you had been the one to fall under his wicked poison, my life would have been forfeit, for I can no longer live without you." They kissed while Minister Rama watched from a distance wearing a sullen expression.

"Yes, my love, the minister must pay with his life, but not before ridding Minister Pratap and King Dhaval of theirs."

"That is brilliant!" Prince Kamal clapped his hands and chuckled. "Summon him."

Lily beckoned the minister to come, and Prince Kamal rose to greet him. "Minister Rama, I am grateful for what you have done for us. You shall be greatly rewarded."

The minister grinned with relief—his foolish blunder had transpired for the best. He bowed to the prince. "I have dedicated my life to you. I shall always be at your service."

The prince glanced at Lily, who smirked. "I am glad to hear you say those words, for I have two other tasks I need you to execute."

"Of course, Your Majesty. Anything you wish."

"As you know, I shall be king soon. Clearly, I have no need of two ministers."

Minister Rama's expression turned bleak.

"Since I prefer you to Minister Pratap, I suggest you get rid of him. I am certain he has already conceived of the means to replace you."

"You wish for me to end Pratap's life?"

Lily's face bloomed cerise with fury. "Surely you do not find what your prince asks to be too difficult a task? Princess Manju was young, beautiful, and innocent, yet you did not hesitate to bestow upon her a most heinous death."

Rama looked down and shuffled his feet. "I refuse my prince nothing he desires."

"Good, that is what I expected to hear." The prince placed a hand on his shoulder. "I shall also require you to take King Dhaval's life. After all, how long do you suppose you shall draw breath once the king discovers you brutally slaughtered his daughter?"

Rama lifted his pale face and stared wide-eyed at the prince. "I shall do all that Your Majesty asks."

"And for your deeds, you shall be rewarded." The prince smiled at Lily.

"Make haste," Lily said with a derisive grin. "Time is of the essence. Take Minister Pratap's life first. Afterward, you may slay King Dhaval. Be sure to notify us before and after each deed."

Minister Rama scowled at her and sulked.

"Do as Lily commands minister. Do not disappoint me," the prince said, in a brusque tone.

"I shall depart at once and execute your initial command. I shall notify you when Minister Pratap no longer draws breath." He bowed to the prince before taking leave.

As he walked away, he heard Lily's sniggering laughter. He gripped the jewel-encrusted hilt of his dagger as he dragged his feet along the long decorated corridor leading outside the Crystal Palace.

Outside it was snowing, but not too cold. Minister Rama wondered if the temperature was becoming milder in the land of Nihar. He needed to determine how he would achieve Prince Kamal's detestable orders. Then a thought occurred to him.

Minister Pratap had left to run errands for the king. There was only one road leading in and out of the palace. Perhaps if he waited along the road and convinced him to go for a stroll, he could make his move then.

The minister walked along the road and came across a small bench overlooking a frozen pond. He sat and waited for his victim's carriage to come. Lost in his thoughts, he stared at the snowflakes as they tumbled from the bright pink sky. He looked at the frozen pond and noticed peculiar little fish swimming underneath the pond's thin ice cap.

Soon the minister's carriage approached. He jumped to his feet and stood on the road, waving the carriage to stop. "Minister Pratap!"

Pratap craned his head outside the carriage window and saw the long, dark, sinewy figure of Minister Rama standing in the road waving his arms in the air. "What are you doing out here in the cold?"

"I needed the fresh air to clear my head, and I found this bench—" Rama extended his arm and indicated the bench.

"You shall freeze without your mala coat shielding you from the frigid bursts of wind. Come inside my carriage. I shall return you to the palace." Pratap beckoned him.

"It is a mild day and I prefer to return on foot, but thank you for the offer." Rama forced a smile. "I have been meaning to speak with you about Prince Kamal and Princess Manju for quite some time now. Perhaps you would like to walk with me for a while. Your mala coat shall keep you warm."

Come. Walk with me. You shall not feel the chill for long. If things go as planned, soon you shall feel nothing at all. Rama sneered.

Minister Pratap opened the carriage door and stepped into the cold.

"I shall accompany you." He gestured to the driver of the carriage to go. Rama watched the carriage roll away, taking with it all witnesses.

"I shall accept your company and enjoy it." Minister Rama flashed another lackluster smile. "Come have a seat with me. We have not had the time to become properly acquainted yet."

Pratap sat beside him on the bench. Rama tried to deflect his scrutiny.

"There are small fish swimming in the pond underneath the ice, but I cannot distinguish them well. Does the pond ever thaw completely?"

"No, this is actually the thinnest I have ever seen the ice. Overnight the temperatures shall plummet. The pond shall be frozen solid tomorrow, and you shall not be able to see the fish underneath at all," Minister Pratap explained while gazing at the pond.

"Shall the fish die as a result?"

"No. Perhaps you may catch a glimpse of them under the ice on another day, but the mild temperature today is a rare occurrence."

"The ice appears so fragile, as if it might crack if I toss a pebble at it." Rama smirked.

"Perhaps a large rock." Pratap smiled.

"Or a large corpse—"

Rama pulled his dagger from its covering and before the other man could react, plunged the nine-inch, serrated blade deep into his chest and twisted the weapon, causing irreparable damage. Pratap's eyes opened wide. His gaping mouth dripped with blood from the explosion of his heart.

Rama worked fast. He grabbed Pratap and pushed him into the frozen pond before his last gasp of air. The bloody corpse lay upon the ice for a while. Rama watched the road and then the pond. "Come on, come on— break—crack before someone comes!" Before long the thin ice shattered and gave way, plunging the body into the freezing depths.

Rama exhaled and stood overlooking the pond until Pratap's body sunk to the bottom and disappeared. Afterward, he marched to the Crystal Palace.

Prince Kamal and Lily were in the prince's chambers when a knock on the door interrupted their lovemaking. The door was bolted from the inside, so the prince left the warmth of his bed to open it.

The prince opened the door enough to wedge his face between it and doorframe without revealing his naked body. "Have you good tidings for me?"

"Minister Pratap no longer draws breath."

"Excellent. And what of the minister's body?"

"His corpse lies frozen at the bottom of a pond not two miles from here."

"You have completed marvelous deeds for our future, but there is yet much to be done. Soon it shall be nightfall. Guests shall begin to arrive for the night's festivities. King Dhaval must be deprived of life before this juncture."

"As you command. I shall bring to fruition what I have begun, and depart at once to the king's chambers. But first, I must borrow your dagger, for mine lies at the bottom of the pond in Pratap's chest."

"There shall be no need for daggers. The king is old, sick, and weak. Your hands shall suffice."

"Yes, my prince." Rama bowed his head and set forth to do the deed.

Lily hopped off the prince's bed, and together they began to clothe themselves for the night's festivities.

When Rama strolled into the king's chambers several servants were assisting him in preparing for the night. "Your Highness, if I may have a word with you?"

"Indeed, please break words freely."

"I shall need a moment alone with you. It is regarding Prince Kamal."

King Dhaval ordered his servants to leave his chambers and gave his utmost attention to the minister.

"Prince Kamal is in love with Princess Manju, and I believe she feels the same about him." Rama prowled the king's room as he spoke and crept behind him. "Both Minister Pratap and I feel the two youngsters shall—"

Rama placed his hands around King Dhaval's feeble neck. He squeezed with all his might. The king struggled, trying to pry the minister's bony hands from his throat.

When he could not remove the hands crushing his gullet he began to scratch at them, his eyes large with fear. Small ragged gasps escaped his throat.

The old man dug his nails into the minister's sinewy fingers. Rama winced, but continued to squeeze. Pressure began to build in the king's head. His eyes bulged.

Guards rushed into the king's chambers and saw Minister Rama strangulating the king. Rama released the old man's neck and gawped at the soldiers. They seized him.

Lily ran into the king's chamber, her face wet with tears. A flock of servants followed her in.

"Help the king! Take him to his bed!" Lily shouted.

The king's servants carried him to his bed and tended to him. She hurried to his bedside. Holding the king's hand, she glared at Minister Rama. She ordered the guards to remove him from the king's sight.

Rama's large eyes zipped in every direction. His face was ashen. He looked baffled and was unable to form words. The guards dragged him away to confinement where he would await his penalty.

"Your Majesty, I am so pleased you are fine." Lily kissed the king's hands. "I have long suspected Minister Rama was an evil being, thus, I kept close watch on him."

"You have done well. You saved my life. I have always loved you like a daughter, and now, even more so." King Dhaval tried to caress her face but was too weak to lift his arm.

"My king, oh my king, what sad truths I bring." Her eyes glistened. "My heart breaks at the thought of uttering these truths."

"My sweet child, why do you suffer so?"

"I was able to save your life, but I was too late to save the life of the princess."

King Dhaval's skin turned white as the snow covering the Niharian landscape.

"My daughter! Where is Princess Manju?"

"She is no longer in the land of the living." She stared at him. "The evil Rama poisoned her with the stems and leaves of the Lahota flower."

King Dhaval gripped his chest and grimaced. She saw how he struggled to live, so she tried to finish what the minister had begun.

"Princess Manju suffered a horrible death," She whispered in his ear. "At the end her naked body was twisted and deformed by the broken bones and contusions brought about by her violent and painful spasms."

The king's expansive eyes stared at her. He coughed and wheezed. His mouth moved, but words did not escape them.

Prince Kamal entered the king's chambers. He proceeded to Lily and stood by her. He regarded the king with furrowed brow. "Why does he yet live?"

"Princess—princess—" King Dhaval clutched his chest and groaned. His face twisted into a painful grimace. It appeared madness had defeated his mind, for he seemed unable to cope with the grief of having lost his daughter in such a cruel fashion.

"Listen, everyone!" Prince Kamal shouted. "King Dhaval has proclaimed Lily to be the new princess, and heir to his throne!"

The remaining guards and all the servants present directed their attention to King Dhaval.

"Princess—" The king tried to speak but only managed to croak. "Princess—my daughter—" He grasped Lily's arm.

Everyone in the room bowed to her.

"Princess Lily!" they exclaimed in unison.

Lily leaned over and kissed the king's forehead. "I shall be a far better queen than your daughter might have hoped to be," she whispered into his ear. She smiled as she pried his fingers from her arm. She stood tall and smiled at the guards and servants.

King Dhaval began to sweat and gasp for air. At last, the king drew his final breath.

There was a beautiful burial ceremony the next day for both King Dhaval and Princess Manju. Her casket remained closed. The following morning, Minister Rama was publicly executed for the murders of Princess Manju and Minister Pratap, and for the attempted murder of King Dhaval.

A week later, there was a huge coronation ceremony for Queen Lily. Citizens from the lands of Nihar and Arathi came to join in the celebration. A month later, Queen Lily wedded Prince Kamal. Together they ruled the Kingdom of Kokin.

The End

There was a long silence after Lilith's tale. Throughout her story, Gabriel and the other angels' faces had become ever more slack and ashen.

Disconcerted by her narrative, Gabriel could not form words. Her story revealed more about her soul than even he had anticipated.

Raquel glanced at him in a manner that suggested she was concealing emotions she hardly understood. The story perturbed her and yet in some ways, she wished to be the Lily in the story, so she could experience the love of the one most dear to her.

Esar wore a haunted expression. He carried feelings of guilt as he imagined over and over, quite vividly, certain elements of Lilith's story. Cam glowered at her, and gray smoke drifted out of Hashmal's nose. The angels were impacted by her story, and they had a lot to ponder.

Gabriel cleared his throat and finally addressed her.

"The beings you described do not inhabit the planet Thanda-Garam. There are no such life forms there."

"I spun a tale for you," Lilith said. "Were you not pleased?"

"I expected you would tell me about the creatures that live on the planet and how they survive in their habitat. I did not expect you to fabricate an entirely unique species and weave such a tale."

"Did I do well?" She relished the terrified look on his face. She peered at the angels around her. She saw from their faces that she had succeeded in awakening desires from deep in their minds. She saw doubt, uncertainty, and fear in their eyes.

"You did well in revealing your true nature." Gabriel's words emerged rough and barely audible. His characteristically soft blue eyes seemed hard. "You need to talk to God and ask him for direction, for you are on a path to damnation."

Lilith's story was meant to disturb him and make him think of possibilities, but she did not like his demeanor or the implications of his words.

Michael came forth and looked at her with an anguished expression. "Lilith—" He brooded. He took her hand. "Please, come with me. We can go to the golden doors and ask God for an audience. When you feel His presence—"

Lilith pulled her hand from his. "I knew these deceitful tests held an underlying purpose: for the elite to judge those they did not care for, so they could control and manipulate us."

"No Lilith, you are mistaken." She ignored his words and strutted past the other angels without so much as a glance in their direction and stormed out of the atrium.

Michael watched her leave. Many angels followed her. "This marks the end of the Lilith I knew and loved."

Gabriel approached him. "It is impossible to disregard the implications of Lilith's story. Her vanity, skills of deception, and ambition for power hold no bounds." He shuddered.

Hashmal, Esar and Raquel stood beside them. Raphael advanced to Michael and put his arm around him. Lucifer stared at them. He had a confused expression on his face.

"Come brother. You belong with us." Michael extended his arm.

Lucifer reached out to take his hand, stopped half way, regarded him with doleful eyes, and retracted his arm. He turned and flew after Lilith.

"Lucifer!" Michael called after him to no avail. "No."

Lilith smirked as she left the atrium and realized so many had followed her.

Her vision had served well as her story. She had simply placed the dark, wingless angels she had so often seen interacting in her dreams on the planet Thanda-Garam, and told Gabriel about one of the many visions she had had involving these mysterious beings—with a few embellishments, of course. She had thought it would make for a fascinating story. Apparently it had the effect she desired on him and the others.

Chapter 11

CELESTIAL HIERARCHIES

"**I** have an announcement from God," Michael shouted above the chatter of the angels congregated at Triumph Gardens. "There shall be a ceremony held in the atrium. God shall divide us into three Celestial Hierarchies according to our abilities."

The angels glanced at each other, excited and fearful. Michael, Cam, and Hashmal led them to the atrium.

"Let us fall to our seats," Michael said.

The angels sat, some excited, while others were apprehensive, concerned, and on edge.

Michael walked past Lilith, who sat between Lucifer and Samael as she often did. He stared as he walked by but she did not look his way.

She shifted in her seat and tapped her feet, her hands intertwining over and over.

"I grow weary of your restless moving about." Lucifer frowned. "What have you to fear?"

"I know not. There are stirrings within me that cause me great torment." She sat brooding.

Lucifer furrowed his brow, confused and concerned by her statement.

A brilliant opening appeared above them and all heard God's words.

Hashmal, come forth, for thou shall speaketh my words.

Hashmal hastened to the front and faced his brethren. He cleared his throat and spoke God's words.

"In the First Hierarchy, the highest order of angels are the Seraphim," he began. He called the Seraphs in ranking order.

"Michael, Raphael, Lucifer and Cam come forward and accept God's highest distinction."

Lilith gasped. She looked at the faces of the angels around her to see if they were as shocked as she was for not hearing her name called. Her heart pounded in her chest. She balled her hands into fists. How was this possible? She should have been up there with Lucifer. She was supposed to be a Seraph.

Beginning with Michael, the Seraphs transformed. They grew taller and brighter, and they sprouted four additional wings, so that each possessed six. They stood before their brethren as angels of the highest order—Seraphim.

"You may join your brethren." Hashmal bowed his head, humbled by their magnificent presence.

Lucifer strolled toward Lilith, and she could hardly contain her excitement and pride, for he yet gazed upon her with love and admiration. At the same time she pitied herself, for not having been chosen to be in the highest order of angels. Lucifer merited more than being merely second to God. He would be first and rule Floraison, and she would rule by his side.

"The second order of angels ranking after the Seraphim is the Cherubim." Hashmal emitted fire and lightning from his mouth.

"Lilith, Gadreel, and Beelzebub, you are among the ones God has chosen to serve as Cherubim. Come forth and accept your rank with reverence."

They also transformed, becoming more beautiful. An extra pair of wings sprang from them, so that they each displayed four.

"The last order of angels in the First Hierarchy is the Thrones. Esar is among those chosen by God to be a Throne angel. He shall be among the angels of pure humility, peace, and submission. Esar shall be a living symbol of God's justice."

The Second Hierarchy of angels included the Dominions, Virtues, and Powers. The angels chosen for these ranks would act as governors.

"Raquel and I were chosen by God to be Dominions, angels of leadership." Hashmal's irises were white with excitement. "We shall regulate the activities of all celestial beings and design tasks for angels in the lower orders."

"Raquel, you are assigned by God to watch over the good behavior of the other angels." "What?" Lilith rose to her feet. "How is this possible? Raquel is to keep watch on me? I rank higher than she, in the first hierarchy of angels!"

It had begun. This was what she had feared would happen. What good was it to be ranked in the first hierarchy of angels if a lesser angel could govern her?

"It is God's will, and He knows all things." Hashmal thundered.

"I did not hear God speak—only you." Lilith dropped on her seat.

"I was appointed to be God's mouthpiece. From this time forth, I shall make known His commands to all celestial beings!"

How convenient for you and your friends. Lilith gnashed her teeth.

As Hashmal roared, a terrible eruption of fire and lightning burst from him. The surrounding angels flinched and retreated, moving a good distance away.

Gabriel was classified as a Virtue. God granted him control of the elements and power to govern all nature. He was chosen to be the spirit of motion and commander of the seasons.

Jetrel was ranked a Power warrior angel, defending against all evil.

Michael, Raphael, Gabriel and Cam were also given this second designation of Power angel.

Samael, Dagon, and Fornues were positioned within the Third Hierarchy.

Samael and Dagon were ranked Principalities, divinely beautiful angels of the third-highest order whose physical beauty is powerful and beguiling. Lilith was also given this title. Michael, Raphael, and Gabriel were also among the order of Archangels. They would have a unique role as God's messengers when the time came.

Fornues was ranked in the lowest order simply called, Angels. He would have the capacity to access any and all angels at any time.

At the end of the ranking ceremony, all angels knew where they fit in the Celestial Hierarchy and what their specific duties were.

Lilith frowned. She approached Gadreel. "I am not satisfied with my ranking. I should have been a Seraph along with Lucifer. I'm also offended that other angels, whom I consider lesser than me, would have the ability to monitor me."

Gadreel's eyes remained fixed to the ground as Lilith spoke.

Lilith was confident that her abilities to manipulate and persuade the minds of her fellow angels, along with her incredible intelligence and intuition, would keep her always one step ahead. Besides, she also had her visions and the instruction of the dark, wingless angels, who had taught her many ways to succeed over her enemies.

Chapter 12

GOD'S TIDINGS

Some time after the angels were ranked and became settled in their new roles, God decided to address them once more.

Hashmal, thou shall summon thy brethren to the atrium for I have a new revelation.

Hashmal listened to God's words and did as commanded. He obtained the help of his friends Michael, Esar, Raphael, and Gabriel in order to expedite God's will. Gabriel played his horn, which was heard in all corners of Floraison and served to call together the angels.

They gathered in the atrium. Most were excited to hear God's tidings, while others were uneasy.

Michael proceeded to Lilith and Lucifer and nodded once with a half smile before taking his seat.

Lilith stared forward and did not acknowledge him. Lucifer greeted him but did not smile.

Michael sat a few rows behind them.

"Why do you think God summoned us to the atrium once more?" Gadreel asked Lilith.

"I do not claim to know God's mind but I did not benefit from the last few times we were here. So I do not look forward to being summoned again."

Hashmal stood before the angels. He waited for them to be seated and quiet.

"I stand humbly before you to make known the directives of God." His eyes were like blazing red-hot coals, and his straight, strawberry blonde locks stood upright and away from his face as if carried by gusts of wind.

Lilith sat by Lucifer in front—she did not wish to miss anything. She was certain these new tidings regarded the creature God meant to create. She hoped to comprehend the reason behind the conception of the new life form.

"The new being God is to create shall not live amongst us." Hashmal's statement was interrupted by an eruption of shouts and applause by a large group of the angels. He waited until they became calm once more. "God shall create a new world for these mortals to live in—a planet where they shall thrive and live in peace and harmony."

Lilith spun to face Lucifer with furrowed brow. He smiled and resumed listening to God's words through Hashmal. He stared at the fire-breathing angel with fascination.

"The happening shall be called Creation. This important event shall represent seven epochs, which shall cover the making of mankind. All shall be welcome, from the princely Seraphs to the angels of the lowest order, to witness this magnificent occasion." Flashes of lightning burst from his mouth as he concluded God's announcement.

The angels glanced at one another in wonderment.

"He took but a moment in time to create us, yet he is taking a significant period to create this new being." Lilith said aloud to Lucifer, hoping others in the vicinity would overhear. "Already God favors this creature above us."

"God is creating a new world for the life form to inhabit, since many of you did not desire them to reside with us." Michael stood to address her. "This is the reason this event shall take so long to be completed. And none of us know exactly how much time or energy God expended in making us."

Lilith pouted to find the surrounding angels nodding in agreement. She glared at Michael. He turned and left. The crowd began to disperse and go their separate ways.

"We should leave the atrium now," she told Lucifer. "We have much to discuss."

"I plan to go to Guidance Park and refine my fighting skills farther." Lucifer flapped his large wings. "My six wings have magnificent strength and abilities I have yet to master. I need much training, and I do not plan to spend my time discussing anything."

It was time to be wise. She would give him his space, and soon he would miss her attentions and come crawling to her once more.

"You're right. You do need much training." She smirked. "I'll leave you to it." With an enchanting smile, she left him behind. She glanced back at him, noting that his eyes followed her for a while, and then he sighed and shuffled away to Guidance Park.

You shall miss me more than you know for I am in your lifeblood and you cannot exist without me. I see how you long for me. I have you right where I desire you—in the palm of my hand.

Chapter 13

CREATION

All the angels assembled in the atrium, excited to witness God in action while he gave rise to the new life form and the world it would inhabit. The event Creation was set in motion, and every celestial creature observed in amazement as God began to fashion a brand new galaxy.

On the first day of Creation, an immense, resplendent rift appeared overhead. The dimensions and brilliance of this opening into the Metá realm was ineffable. God's voice was heard and with divine reason, He made the vast expanse of the galaxy. In this galaxy, he formed many planets; a small planet he named Earth was among them. God chose Earth for his new creatures to live on, but Earth was a dark and cold planet, as yet devoid of life.

Let there be light.

God spoke, and dim stars illuminated, brightly filling the galaxy and Earth with light.

Many angels clapped and cheered. Michael praised God, Gabriel played his trumpet, and Gadreel sang praises to Him for His incredible light show. Lilith glanced at Lucifer's excited face and frowned.

On the second day of Creation, God gazed at the well-lit Earth and decided to create air and sky to encompass the planet. He drew moisture from the enormous body of water occupying the Earth and formed clouds in the sky. When He finished, He was pleased.

The majority of angels applauded while they perceived the sights.

Lilith scowled. A myriad of angels were enthusiastic, but why? One might have believed they were going to inhabit this planet.

"Something is amiss." She touched Lucifer's shoulder, but he stared at the spectacle and disregarded her. She sulked and raked her hair with her fingers. Lucifer refused to see what was happening before his very eyes. God was creating wonders because his new life form would be a work of art. When He was done, He would no longer see the angels as His masterpieces. Then it would not be long before they were set aside and superseded.

She had to convince Lucifer and the others that this was so. They had to overthrow God and begin a new Floraison with new laws—their laws. Once they reigned in Floraison, they could destroy the new being God deemed fitting to dote on and with whom He planned to replace them.

On the third day of Creation, God commanded the waters covering the Earth to separate and allow dry ground to appear between them. Mountains rose from the seas toward the heavens, and valleys were formed. The angels watched as rolling hills formed in the boundless stretch of land. Volcanoes rose from the water and erupted to create islands.

God formed lakes and rivers across the land. The angels gasped at the magnificence of Creation.

Let the dry land bring forth plants of all kinds.

Great jungles and woodlands emerged. All manner of fruit trees came into being carrying seeds of their own kind. Tall and short grasses, bushes, and flowers covered the rolling hills and large areas of land. Soon, the Earth became an exquisite, fragrant, and colorful place. Most of the vegetation was different from what the angels had in Floraison but still quite lovely. God was pleased.

Gabriel sang and his apprentices played divine instruments conceived and made by him. Gadreel joined him in song.

Once again, Lilith was in Lucifer's ear. "It seems excessive, all the preparations for this new mortal. God bestows this being reward after reward, but has he earned them?"

Other angels heard her remarks and nodded.

"God is disappointed in us," Fornues said in his usual whiny way. "He no longer loves us, for we have conducted ourselves badly. We fight each other often. We constantly question His word. We have broken His rules more than once. We have disrupted the peace in Floraison on many occasions." His last three words dropped to a grumble.

"God has given us life," Michael said. "He has allowed us to reside near him in Floraison, and we have the opportunity to join Him in Heaven Most High in the future if we become worthy. This is the biggest gift of all."

"Let us sit and continue to gaze upon the miracle of Creation," Raquel said. "We must be grateful to God, for he has allowed us to witness this great event."

Michael and Raquel shifted their eyes to Earth and its transformation.

"Where is Beelzebub?" Lilith pulled on Lucifer's garment. "I have not seen him in so long. He would have supported me if he were here."

Lucifer looked at her sideways and frowned. "He is probably still in isolation in his quarters due to the incident with Gabriel. Now, be silent for I wish to watch the event in peace." He turned his face toward Earth. She rolled her eyes.

She saw Gadreel making music with Gabriel and she turned to consider Samael, who was staring in her direction. "You understood what I spoke, did you not?"

"Naturally, I agree with you." Samael's excessive blinking betrayed the lie.

"Have we become second best in God's eyes?" Fornues asked.

"I believe we soon shall be." Lilith nodded with a brooding expression.

On the fourth day of Creation, God divided every twenty-four hour period into day and night, using the sun and the moon to create the margin between them.

God assigned Gabriel, as the lead Virtue angel, the task of ensuring the sun would shine on the Earth during the daytime, creating brightness and warmth with its rays. At night, he would furnish the skies with gentle luminosity with the moon's reflective light and the stars.

Most angels enjoyed the beauty and marvels God crafted. But Lilith grew more and more perturbed with each new miracle, and her affliction was contagious. Many were soon aggravated by the entire concept of Creation, and they made comments, which pestered Lucifer and disrupted his peace of mind.

On the fifth day of Creation, God decided to produce other forms of life distinct from the trees and plants he had made. He filled the skies with all kinds of winged animals. Eagles, bats, bees, storks, and many more species flew through the air in various ways as the angels' eyes bounced and zigzagged, trying to follow them in flight.

Gadreel and Raquel jumped off their seats and ran to get a closer look at the birds swooping here and there. The flying creatures were unique to planet Earth and fascinating to the angels. Gadreel giggled with excitement as she watched the winged animals soar. Raquel threw her head back and laughed with glee, enjoying their liveliness.

Lilith glared at them with a sour expression. "We have flying creatures in Floraison. These species were different in many ways, but what is so exciting? Why are they enjoying this so much? Am I the only one capable of reason?"

"You must be the only one incapable of enjoying God's magnificence." Michael gazed at her. "Yes, we have flying creatures in Floraison but these are different and we did not have the opportunity to watch the creatures on Floraison being created by God!"

Lilith turned away from him and sulked. Michael frowned and watched her for a little while before focusing on Creation again.

God also created life forms to live in the vast bodies of water He called oceans. He spoke, and the Earth's waters were occupied with whales, dolphins, octopi, lobsters, starfish, and many other aquatic species. God blessed the sky and sea creatures and told them to be fruitful and multiply.

Most angels marveled at God's magnificence. Many formed ebullient choirs that sang lilt songs of praise. Dagon was fascinated with the sea creatures, especially the enormous variety of fish. He focused on the little gilled vertebrates swooshing around in the vast sea. Openmouthed, he watched dolphins erupt from the ocean and dance above it. He marveled at the sheer size of the whales and beamed when they spouted water from a hole on their heads.

Nearby, Lilith captivated a growing audience. "God must really hold these new creatures in high regard. Witness all the companions he has granted them. Yet we are not allowed companions."

Lucifer's attention shifted to Lilith upon hearing her last remarks. He nodded in agreement. Lilith beamed and continued her rhetoric.

"Why are we not worthy of having darlings?"

Raquel hurried toward Lilith and the attentive crowd. "God gave us free will and desires so that our virtue could be tested. Perhaps this is your proof that God does indeed hold us at a much higher standard than these new creatures."

Lucifer sighed deeply and leered at Lilith. Lilith possessed qualities that gave him great pleasure to look upon, and he longed for her company on countless occasions. But the kind of love he craved was forbidden to them in Floraison. He sucked his teeth and slumped in his seat. Raquel glanced at him, her prominent, hooded green eyes filled with concern.

Lilith also got Gadreel's attention; she believed her love for Samael ran deeper than the oceans she gazed upon with excitement.

Gadreel stole a glimpse of Samael and then glanced Lilith's way, biting the corner of her lip.

Raquel scanned the expressions on the surrounding angels' faces, and her eyes locked with Dagon's piercing gray-blue eyes. She quickly lowered her head and returned to her seat.

Raquel glanced at Michael. "As much as I hate to agree with any-thing that comes out of Lilith's mouth, I do sometimes think about what it would be like if angels were allowed companions." She lowered her head and stared at her shifting feet. Michael looked at her with a sympa-thetic expression.

Raquel looked toward Dagon again. He met her gaze and smiled as if he could read her mind. She turned away, and her cheeks flushed a bright pink.

God created all sorts of animals to fill the land. Some of the animals had similarities to the ones in Floraison, but others were unique to Earth. He made monkeys, which swung through the trees in the forests, causing the angels to point and laugh at their funny ways. Esar chortled and a long tail sprang from his rear. His head became the head of a monkey. He began to chatter and jump up and down, imitating the creature's behavior. The atrium shook with laughter.

God created massive elephants—which roamed the vast plains and left behind deep footprints—and lions, their golden manes flowing in the wind and their majestic roars heard for miles.

Reptiles and spiders crawled everywhere. Lilith was quite taken with the snakes, which slithered to and fro.

The angels spotted a group of mammals that displayed many angel-like behaviors and emotions. The gorillas were covered in hair, but they laughed, communicated with each other, walked on two legs, possessed hands similar to their own, and had small lively eyes set into hairless faces.

"Are these the new species we had anticipated?" Dagon asked, laughing. "I believe they are!" The angels erupted with cheers and praises to God for his incredible designs.

Lucifer sighed with relief and grinned at Lilith. However, they were mistaken, for God was not yet done.

In conclusion, I shall create the life form ye so awaited.

The celestial beings glanced at each other. Lucifer whisked his head in Lilith's direction, his face etched with trepidation.

God proceeded to make an extraordinary being, as only the finest and most unique artist in all of existence is capable. He formed out of the earth a beautiful new creature He called man.

The atrium grew silent. Not a creature budged—not even Lilith.

God breathed into the man and made a human being for the first time.

The angels gaped at the man as he rose from the ground and were awestruck upon the realization that God had made the human wingless in His own image.

Lilith gasped. The wingless angels she had seen in her visions for so long were human beings. Her hand flew to cover her mouth. She stood to get a better look at the new creature. She could not take her eyes off him. She licked her lips and grinned.

Lucifer watched her as she played with her hair, her interest in the man expanding. He glared at the human. God created this human in His own image. Lucifer clutched his heart and gasped for air. His pulse became so loud in his ears he no longer heard the cheering crowd. He plopped in his seat as if a massive load tied to his six wings pulled him down. He grabbed Lilith's hand. "I feel an enormous void in my heart—nothing shall ever be the same."

Lilith observed his reaction to the new creature. His eyes glinted with exasperation. She sensed his moment of weakness and pounced.

"He is a magnificent creature, this human." Her voice was alluring. "He is beautiful and makes my heart swell with fascination."

"We are God's beloved creations. We have always been near Him," Lucifer said in a hoarse voice. "Why would He shape another being in His own image, and not us? Are we not worthy?"

"I forewarned you!" Lilith pointed at him and others who sat nearby. "I cautioned all of you this would happen. He grows bored with us." She faced God's light. "God desires to replace us with the glorious human being He calls man, which He created wingless, in His own image."

Lucifer held his head in his hands and shook it.

Michael, Raquel, Hashmal, and Jetrel heard Lilith's ranting and hurried to intervene.

"Please be silent. Your every word offends God." Michael's face was bleak, as if he had lost all hope for her.

Hashmal's eyes glowed orange-red. "Listen to Michael."

Lilith dodged the flames spurting from his mouth. She expected Lucifer to come at once to her aid, but he still sat clutching his head. She glowered at Hashmal. "I have the right to speak my mind. Did we not receive the gift of free will, or are you authorized to take it away from me?"

Michael approached her and spoke gently but firmly. "Lilith, this is a great moment in time. Please do not degrade this occasion with your pessimism."

"The truth of this moment is cause for disdain." Lilith pointed at the crowd. "Many of you have wondered what my abilities are, or if in fact I had received any. I have the gift of sight and have visions that show me what is yet to come. I have seen the future of man, and I do not believe it is what God intended."

"Silence! What you speak is blasphemy." Jetrel took a step toward her but Michael was quick to stop his fierce friend from advancing any farther.

Jetrel's hands curved into fists. "I detest the way you always stir trouble between us." She glared at her, rocking her body.

Lilith noticed her closed fists and white knuckles and recoiled from her, for she was a Power angel and formidable warrior. She also dreaded Hashmal's fiery breath. Thus she returned to her seat beside Lucifer, who was still slumped forward head in hands. She did not utter another word, but simply stared forward, ignoring all of them.

She would choose her battles wisely. This was not the right moment, for she had yet a plethora of angels to convert to the idea of a new Floraison.

Michael, Jetrel, Hashmal, and Raquel watched her and after a short while, regained their seats.

As Raquel passed Dagon on the way to her chair, they exchanged longing glances. Lilith caught the exchange between them and left her seat to sit next to Dagon.

"I understand how you feel," Lilith whispered. "I have seen the way you look at Raquel."

"What is your meaning?" Dagon grew pale.

"Please do not deny it. I have seen that expression before, and I know what it means. I have also seen the way Raquel stares at you." Lilith sat back on her seat, back straight and spoke with confidence. Dagon lowered his head and sighed.

She swept behind his ear the strands of long, flaxen hair covering his face.

"You do not have to worry about me knowing this truth, for I too, share similar feelings with someone."

Dagon examined Lilith's misleadingly sweet and honest face. "I do have certain sentiments for Raquel that perhaps I should not have."

"Did you decide to have these feelings for Raquel?"

"No. One brillante these emotions flourished in my heart. I had no choice in the matter." He looked at the floor and squirmed in his seat.

"That is exactly my line of reasoning. These sentiments come naturally to us. We do not have a choice. So why should we be punished for having them?" She looked into his eyes. "I have affections for Lucifer. According to the laws of Floraison, these sensations are wrong and carry harsh punishments, but they come not by my choosing. Why allow us to have feelings and desires we cannot act upon? It is entirely cruel, in my opinion."

He continued to stare at the ground, grinding his teeth as he often did when anguished.

"Imagine a world where we can act upon our senses. A realm where we can love whosoever we choose in whatever way we desire to express it. Would this domain not be the perfect Floraison?"

"A dwelling where Raquel and I may express what we feel for one another would be a perfect home indeed." He chuckled and fidgeted.

"I described worlds I have observed from right here in the atrium. In the planet Thanda-Garam, every creature is allowed a companion. I have had visions of the future of this new life form God calls human being. They shall multiply and fill the Earth and they shall share their bodies and their emotions."

"How is such a thing possible?" Dagon seemed perplexed. "God has created one human being, and he shall be as we are, above companionship and carnal pleasures."

"God shall create more humans. You shall see. Even the animals on Earth have companions. We are the only beings not allowed by God to mate." Her resentment was evident by the glint in her eyes.

Dagon sighed.

"How would you consider a new Floraison where loving Raquel would be celebrated and not chastised?" Lilith grinned.

"It would be a home I would truly be happy in—a genuine paradise." Dagon looked confused and shrugged. "But it shall never be so. Floraison shall never be different than it is now."

"Floraison can change if there was a new Supreme Being to govern it." Lilith ran both hands through her hair, waiting a moment for her words to penetrate his mind. "Lucifer could be our new ruler."

Dagon stared at her, his eyes questioning.

She smiled and returned her attention to Creation, knowing her carefully chosen words would permeate his mind. There were many angels susceptible to her wiles. She would convince them with her powerful arguments and her suggestion of a new Floraison.

Creation continued and Lilith returned to her seat by Lucifer. God placed the man he created among the tigers, zebras, and bears and told him, *Thou art master over all the other creatures on Earth.*

Lucifer's eyes sprang open once more upon hearing this declaration.

"He makes man ruler of all his domain," Lilith whispered in Lucifer's ear. "What do you preside over?" He glanced at her with an offended expression.

"God made you a Seraph, second only to Him," she continued. "What has that title earned you? You should reign over all the angels in Floraison, but instead God put other angels of lesser ranks like Raquel and Hashmal to oversee you and me."

Lucifer clenched his jaw.

God did not wish the man to be alone but did not deem any other creature He created thus far suitable to be his partner. So once more, God decided to create another human being, a woman, to be the man's companion.

God called the first man Adam—meaning ground, from which He had created him. He allowed Adam to name the first woman, his wife, and he named her Eve—meaning life, since from her life would spring forth.

The woman God fashioned for Adam was exquisite in every way. Her oval-shaped face was adorned with dove-like eyes the color of mahogany.

Eve's high, wide cheekbones and rosy cheeks displayed a lingering smile. Her lips were full and plump, the color of pomegranates. Her smooth flawless skin glowed from within and her abundant long, beautiful hair glistened like golden honey reflecting sunshine. Eve was pleasing to all the senses.

God completed the act of Creation by establishing a home for Adam and Eve. He enclosed a vast land covered in lush green grasses, unique magnificent trees laden with fruit, flowering bushes, and countless exotic flowers and verdant plants. Refreshing ponds and sparkling lagoons were placed throughout. Four long rivers extended from a great lake near the center of the garden. These private grounds included all the beauty and miracles of nature in exclusive form, and it was a true paradise.

God placed Adam and Eve in their blissful home, and they were happy and excited. He observed what He prepared for them, and was delighted. God spoke to Adam and Eve.

Be ye fruitful and multiply.

Chapter 14

THE SEDUCTION OF LUCIFER

Lucifer sprang to his feet. "Eve is the most beautiful life form I have ever set eyes on. I do not comprehend why God considered it fitting to bestow her upon Adam." He looked at Lilith. She scowled at his words.

"God placed these mortals in paradise to be fruitful and multiply?" Lucifer appeared perplexed. "Perhaps you were right all along." He gazed at Lilith. "God has grown bored of us and means to replace us. He created us to worship Him and entertain Him, yet Creation seems like an act of pure love. God has given these humans everything He has always denied us." Lucifer frowned. He had witnessed enough of Creation.

He got to his feet, intending to leave the atrium. He appeared broken and defeated. His sense of security was fading; disgrace and confusion filled the void.

Lilith followed him and it was not long before Samael, shadowed by Gadreel, Dagon, and Fornues, did the same.

"Lucifer!" Lilith ran past the seated spectators. "Please wait for me!"

She reached him and grasped his arm. He stopped and turned to look at her.

"I know a place where we can speak in private. Away from the prying eyes and ears of the heavenly governors, and all those who think so much of themselves."

"What would we speak of in secret?" Lucifer asked with a black visage.

She led him into a small vacant hallway leading to the rearmost rooms, and the others followed. "We can discuss the truth—that your moment has arrived. You, princely Seraph, must take your rightful place in Heaven's reign."

The others stood by, they appeared to teem with interest and fear. Gadreel gnawed on her fingers while standing on her toes.

"What is your meaning? I have been bestowed the highest place among the ranks, second only to God, and my powers grow stronger every moment. I am a Seraph prince!" Lucifer lifted his chin with pride.

"Michael is a Seraph also and so is Raphael, Cam, and countless others."

Lucifer sucked his teeth, waved a hand, and began to shuffle away.

"Yes, you are the powerful Lucifer, Light Bearer, Morning Star." She chased after him. "No other angel can compete with your enhanced strength or combat ability. Your ability to track other angels and objects with your mind and create mental maps has no match. Your power to manipulate energy is astounding and when you master these—you will be mightier still." She caught up to him, and he stopped.

She turned him around with the tips of her fingers, and to be sure she had his attention, she gazed into his deep-set eyes.

"Why settle for second status, Almighty Lucifer?" Lilith asked to the gasp of the others standing around. She then directed her speech to all. "Lucifer is awe-inspiring even to God. Why would God not give him the throne to Floraison—if he earned it?"

"Enough! What you say is blasphemy." Lucifer scowled at her.

"Lilith speaks the truth. You are powerful and right for the purpose." Samael dared to step forward.

"I would serve with pleasure under your rule, Lucifer." Dagon bowed his head in reverence.

"I would follow you to the ends of the universe." Fornues' voice trembled. Gadreel stared at Lilith and then at the others. She swallowed hard and furrowed her brow.

"Do you see? You have many loyal followers." Lilith extended her hands to signal his devotees.

Samael bowed with great flare in front of Lucifer. "Rule Floraison, and I shall be your most loyal subject."

Gadreel placed the back of her fingers over her mouth and bit the knuckle on her middle finger.

Lucifer glanced at the small group. "You are but a fraction of the angels in Floraison, and the most powerful—Michael, Raphael, Gabriel, Cam, Raquel, Jetrel, Hashmal, and Esar—would never be convinced to follow me. This can never be."

He turned and walked away.

"Lilith, you must convince him of this. You are the only one who can." Samael licked his lips while ogling Gadreel.

"I shall discuss this further with him, but I need all of you to do your part." She bid Samael to confer with the female angels he believed he could turn, for he was popular among them. "Make whatever promises you have to, and sway them to come to our side."

He nodded and smirked.

"Gadreel, use your talents and charms to entice other angels to join our cause," Lilith said.

Gadreel nodded with a downward gaze. "I do not—"

Lilith drowned her words and stared at her. "This is too important for you to question. You are either with us or against us."

Gadreel jolted at Lilith's snarling voice. She glanced wide-eyed at Samael, who also waited for her answer. "Of course I am with you—"

"Then say no more and do what I have asked of you."

Gadreel indicated agreement. "I shall do all that you require."

Lilith told Dagon to begin filling Raquel's ears with thoughts of a new reign. "If Raquel could be convinced to side with us, we would have a powerful ally. Our chances of swaying Michael and Raphael into joining us would be much greater. However, you must choose your words carefully. Be wise in your ways."

Dagon nodded.

She instructed Fornues to observe the angels and report to her all those he found were unhappy or displeased with their new ranks and duties, angry with God, or disgruntled with the way things were. "We must seek out our dissatisfied and resentful brethren, for they shall be the easiest to persuade."

"What if I say the wrong things?" Fornues shuffled his feet.

"I did not ask you to speak, only to observe and report to me," Lilith said. "Do not say a single word to anyone about the rebellion. Simply be watchful."

"I can do that." Fornues puffed.

They all agreed to do Lilith's bidding and went their separate ways. She departed to find Lucifer again.

Once the atrium was cleared of angels, Lucifer returned there to be alone with his thoughts.

It was not simply about how he was second only to God, yet others seemed to have more power. It was about Creation, how God decided to create other beings and made these humans in His own image. It was about how Adam got to live in paradise with Eve by his side. Yet, despite his own high ranking, he still could not hold Lilith in his arms.

He slouched in his seat. His eyes burned with hatred as he stared at the new blue and green planet God called Earth.

Earth's rustic beauty—its majestic mountains, rolling green hills, golden deserts and large bodies of water—offended him. In the midst of all the Earth's magnificence, God created a secluded paradise for His humans, Adam and Eve.

Why would God give them so much? Why would He favor the humans more than His Celestial creations—more than me?

He peered farther into the home God provided the humans and saw Adam and Eve together in the Garden of Eden. They held hands and strolled through the beautiful botanical paradise and gazed into each other's eyes and kissed on the lips. They walked to a tree heavily laden with food.

The man reached for one of the delightful fruits and picked it from the tree. Without hesitation he handed it to his wife. She took a graceful bite and offered it to Adam, who in turn ate from it. Lucifer watched as they consumed the juicy fare and enjoyed every delicious morsel together.

Lucifer continued to track Adam as he lay on lush green grass, holding his spectacular woman in his arms. He caressed Eve's beautiful glowing skin and kissed her again and again. The man did things forbidden to angels in Floraison. Lucifer's throat contracted, and he was unable to draw breath or swallow as his frustration swelled.

"What are you staring at?" a sweet and seductive voice asked. He jolted, as he was caught unaware.

"Lilith," he said, breathless. "I am watching planet Earth and the new human creatures."

She glided to him, placed her hand on his shoulder, and squeezed. He experienced a strange but pleasant sensation when she did so.

"You should not have left me so abruptly." She frowned, her lips primed, demanding the fullest consideration. His mouth curved into a lackluster smile.

Despite her frown, she caressed his face in the same fashion Adam stroked Eve's and edged closer to him. She also nuzzled his cheeks with her lips. Pressing her mouth over his, she kissed him. A surge of pleasure coursed through his body. Bumps developed on the skin along his arms. His heart thumped, and heat spread throughout his body. He inhaled a sharp breath and exploded out of his chair.

"What are you doing?" He stared at her in disbelief. "How do you come to know such acts?"

"I have had many visions that show me the future of humans and how they interact with one another."

"You know these acts are prohibited to us." Lucifer lowered his head.

"When I lay my hands on your skin in forbidden ways, how did you feel?"

"I have never experienced anything finer."

"Why are these acts not permitted to us?"

Lucifer inhaled a deep breath and blew out slowly. "God sees us as above such acts."

"Why are they not prohibited to humans?" Lilith clutched Lucifer's face between her hands. "Why should they experience pleasures forbidden to us?"

Lucifer lowered her hands and wandered a small distance away, staring sightlessly. "God tests our righteousness at this very moment. We are superior to the humans, and He expects much more from us."

"Perhaps God is amused by our actions." Lilith smiled with scornful derision. "After all, He gave us free will so that we may choose our own course."

He whisked around and stared at her slack-mouthed. A smile dangled on the corner of her lips.

"Imagine a realm where we can express ourselves any way we desire. A place where we can experience such pleasures whenever we wish." She walked to him and guided him by the hand to his seat again. He sat and hung his head.

"Oh—such a world does exist!" Lilith nodded with a cynical look on her face. "The world God created for his humans is filled with pleasures beyond our imagination."

She watched him lift his head in recognition.

"We were meant to experience these things. Don't you feel it? Our bodies and minds demand this."

She saw a scintilla of acceptance in his eyes, as he contemplated her words.

"Brilliant Star, you could create a world such as this for us if you were in command." She caressed his face and whispered in his ear, "I can bring about in you incredible sensations if you would only permit me. What I achieved earlier was but a small taste of the pleasures I can bestow upon you if you were to reign in Floraison."

"I admire your astonishing beauty. You weaken me." Lucifer's chest heaved. "I want to believe every word that falls from your lips, but—I sense unfamiliar sensations occurring in my body that make me feel like I may lose control of myself." He sprung to his feet.

She pushed him back down and placed her hands strategically on his thighs. He drew a sharp breath and closed his eyes for a moment.

He gazed at her through partly closed eyes and took short, quick breaths. She came closer still and kissed his neck while running her fingers through his long, dark hair. He reclined his head. She felt the hairs on his neck stand upright.

"A powerful yearning overwhelms me," he said with bated breath. "Part of me wishes for you to be still, but a greater part of me craves for you to continue."

Lilith smiled. Before long, he gave in to her completely.

✺

Gadreel tried to find Samael to let him know she had located others who, like them, were unhappy with Floraison's current rule and aspired to be followers. She spotted Lilith and Lucifer in the atrium and decided to give them the news first.

She stopped short. "What is Lilith doing?" she whispered under her breath. Her mouth dropped open, and her eyes grew large with disbelief. She watched Lilith kiss Lucifer's lips, face, and neck. She passed her hands across his entire body, and he allowed her to do so. Gadreel gasped and covered her mouth with her hand.

They were violating one of the two most important pledges an angel makes. Gadreel bit her lower lip. "I should leave." She spun and took a few steps—she stopped and looked over her shoulder— "I cannot pull away." She hid behind a row of seats and gawked. She covered her mouth to restrain excited giggling as she watched them kiss and stroke each other.

Gadreel flinched when she heard a loud thunderous voice. "That's Cam's voice." She gasped and leapt to her feet and ran to warn her friends.

"Lilith!"

Lilith stopped her actions at once and tidied herself. Lucifer sat upright, arranged himself and crossed his arms.

"Apologies. I did not mean to interrupt you, but I heard Cam's voice nearby." She searched the ground, red faced.

"You did well to warn us, Gadreel. I am grateful," Lucifer said, without meeting her eyes.

Lilith glowered at her and exhaled a sharp breath.

Cam entered the atrium and approached them. "Have any of you seen Beelzebub?"

"I believe he is tucked away in his chambers," Lilith said, in a sour tone.

"I have not seen his face in quite a while." Cam scrutinized them. "Why would he isolate himself in his room for so long?"

"He claimed to require a period alone for reflection, but I am afraid that if you need know more, you'll have to ask Beelzebub himself." Lilith crossed her arms and lifted the eyebrow above her blue eye.

Cam peered at Lucifer, who gazed at the floor while shuffling his feet.

"All is right here?" Cam considered Lucifer's shrunk demeanor.

"What a strange question." Lilith smirked. "Why would anything be wrong here?" Her face was marked with disdain as Cam's bright green eyes focused on her.

"You are a most curious angel," Cam said in a calm manner. "Maybe one day you shall learn to be humble and reverent." He glanced at Lucifer in a prudent way and left, but before he could get too far, Lilith retorted.

"You, Cam, are a most vexing angel. Perhaps someday you'll learn to humble yourself in the presence of a supreme being."

Cam stopped and glanced over his shoulder at her, his eyebrows knit close together. Then without saying another word, he continued on his way.

Lilith blustered and looked at Lucifer. "How dare Cam address us in such a way? Do you see how they behave toward us?" She put her arms around his neck, rested her head on his large muscular chest, and played with his hair. He embraced her.

A short while later Lilith pushed away from Lucifer. She grabbed a handful of the black hair at the back of his head, tugged, and pressed her face against his while uttering with bated breath. "Perhaps you do not desire to feel my caress ever again?"

She knew her hot breath against his skin would cause pleasurable sensations in the area between his thighs. She kissed him on the lips once more and then let him go abruptly.

"Come, Gadreel, let us leave this place, for Lucifer has much to ponder."

"Yes, Lilith." Gadreel stared at her with incredulous eyes.

"Stop." Lucifer said. Lilith paused, wearing a wicked smile.

"Please do not leave." He rose from the chair and ogled her. "I desire your company. Now that I have experienced your lips caressing mine and your hands as they traced my body, I never wish to be without either again."

Lilith signaled Gadreel with her eyes to leave the atrium. Then, she proceeded to Lucifer. Her hips swayed as she walked. She provoked him and produced desires he had never known.

"I do not know how to control the emotions I am experiencing." Lucifer trembled and his breathing was quick and shallow.

"You do not have to try. This is about releasing control." Lilith smiled.

"I desire you more than anything. I am no longer concerned with losing everything, provided I have you." He held her close. "I never want to let you go."

"We must go to my secret place. The risk of exposure is too great here," she whispered in his ear making him shiver. She led him by the hand to her isolated corner. "There is only one planet visible from this remote area of the atrium—a lonely planet called Thanda-Garam. You may remember it from our earlier lessons on the cosmos. Few angels were interested in this little odd planet, so none ever comes here."

As she spoke, he ogled her.

Lilith licked her lips. "I have passed many hours in this exact place and have yet to be disturbed by anyone. I have had many visions of creatures I used to call dark wingless angels. I have come to know that these beings are in fact future Earthlings. These beings are similar to us in many ways. From the revelations I have had of these future humans, I have learned many ways to give you pleasure—all the while pretending to observe this planet."

Lucifer grabbed her and kissed her. They caressed each other with their lips and hands in ways he had never imagined. "I could never carry on without the pleasure of your touch again. I do not care what I have to do to ensure this."

Lilith guided his hands and body to do things she had learned from her visions. His moans of ecstasy filled the air in the small room. She grinned and closed her eyes. "Would you do all that I ask of you?"

He nodded and groaned. "I would rebel against God and Heaven if it meant that I would experience such pleasures always."

She guided his maleness inside her. They followed their natural instincts and copulated.

When the deed was done, they lay in each other's arms. Lucifer vowed, "I shall rule Floraison, and you shall be my Queen."

Chapter 15

BEELZEBUB'S OFFERING

Beelzebub wore a bleak expression, dragged his feet and remained out of sight after what happened between him and Gabriel. He often snuck out of his bungalow and went to his place of refuge, which was a cave in Mount Verve. It was situated at Guidance Park behind the Divina Waterfall and led to the opposite side of the mountain and out of the park. Few angels knew of this cave, for it was well hidden by the water of the falls and boulders that sat in front. Beelzebub had discovered it by accident a long time ago while playing Lilith's notorious game of hide-and-seek.

In the cave, he exhausted a great deal of time contemplating what he had done. He had groped another angel as he slept. "What a despicable act." Beelzebub shook his head as he murmured to himself. What if Gabriel had proceeded to Michael and divulged everything? "What would become of me?" His teeth chattered as he shook with fear. "If Gabriel had revealed the incident at Lake Serena, surely the Powers would have been looking for me by now." He sighed deeply and rubbed his cheek.

"I intend to do what Gabriel demanded of me." He would hide for a while.

Beelzebub put his hands together and closed his eyes. "Please forgive me, Gabriel and leave behind the memories of my vile act." He followed the cave out of Guidance Park, as he had done many times, and proceeded to his chamber at Sonnoris.

He looked around his room. "I shall endure a prolonged bout of loneliness here, but I deserve it."

When he finally left his room, he would present Gabriel with a gift. The offering must be one he would fashion with his hands. "Gabriel would appreciate the time and effort I put into something handmade." He searched every corner of his room to find materials to use for this task. He found bitumen stained bird bones he had collected in the cave in Mount Verve and some cane. It would have to do. "What does Gabriel enjoy most? Music! He loved music, so I shall make a musical instrument he could play at Triumph Gardens."

He made diligent use of his hands to piece the black bird bones into a hollow cylinder. He bore eight holes into the top of the pipe and blew into it. "No, it is not ready." He fashioned the cane into a mouthpiece and attached it to the instrument.

He blew into the bone flute and was satisfied with the sound it produced. When done he cheered and bounced like a click beetle. The project had taken him quite a while to finish.

Shaking with eagerness, he staggered out of his room and headed to Triumph Garden. It was Gabriel's favorite spot where he spent a lot of time playing music and composing songs.

When Beelzebub arrived at the gardens, he scanned the area and noticed him sitting by a small colorful lily pond playing a string instrument.

The music produced by the vibrating strings was colorful and dulcet, like butterflies fluttering above a pond. The sound was a source of felicity and affection. Gabriel held a kithara and it was well crafted. Its body was made of rosewood; Beelzebub followed its smooth curves and saw details of pure gold adorning its face.

He caught himself ogling Gabriel as he strummed his kithara and turned his face away, not trusting his eyes to behave. He rubbed his cheeks nonstop.

Beelzebub focused on Gabriel's resplendent, well-crafted kithara and then looked at his black bone flute. "My gift seems grotesque by comparison." Disgust twisted his features. He puffed and walked in circles with one hand clutching the flute, and the other playing with his long, wavy blond hair. His eyes glistened as he determined his love's gift was not yet ready to be presented. "I must first play it for Lilith and get her valued opinion," he said in an undertone.

He shuffled away from the gardens. "What if Gabriel never forgives me? I cannot stand the thought." The shoulders of his four wings shuddered. Leaving behind the awe-inspiring sounds of Gabriel's kithara, he made his way to the atrium where he expected to find Lilith.

He frolicked on the translucent golden pathways, admiring the exquisite blue gem walls surrounding the atrium. His morale was raised after seeing its splendor. He lifted his eyes and marveled at all the colorful, sparkling celestial bodies.

"Beelzebub?" Cam approached him.

Beelzebub spun around and held his breath.

"It is you. I have not seen you or heard any of your quips in quite a while." Cam grinned and hugged him. "I never thought I would miss your antics so much."

He looked toward Cam, exhaled and giggled, never making eye contact. Gabriel had not exposed him. If he had made known his vile act, Cam would have been amongst the first to have knowledge of it. If he knew what he had done, he would not be so pleasant.

"You are behaving unusually strange, my friend." Cam placed a hand on his shoulder and examined at his face. "Is there something wrong?"

"No-no, there is nothing wrong. Apologies—it was not my intention to give you that impression."

"No need to apologize." Cam tapped him on the upper arm. "I must be on my way, but we shall get together soon."

"Yes." He nodded and stared wide-eyed.

Cam moved away with his usual relaxed, confident stride, and Beelzebub hurried in the opposite direction. At last he found Lilith in her secret place.

Lucifer accompanied her and they were in an intimate moment. Beelzebub stared at them and everything else fell away. His lips quivered. He placed a hand over his mouth and ran away from the scene. He sat nearby on one of the chairs in the main hall, and began to play the bone flute he had crafted. The music it produced was sinister and horrid.

Lilith and Lucifer stopped their lovemaking. "What is that ugly sound?" Lilith covered her ears. "That noise penetrates my mind and I feel great woe, as if something beautiful and good in my existence is gone, and I am left alone in the dark."

Lucifer held her. "I experienced joy and pleasure by your side but once I heard this sound my wits have turned to darkness and confusion."

"What is that awful, pitiful sound?" Lilith rose to her feet and clothed herself.

"I know not where it comes from, but it sounds like death. It must be stopped at once. Such a sound should not be allowed in Floraison."

Lilith left the small room to seek out the source of the dispiriting dissonance, and Lucifer followed. In no time they came across Beelzebub blowing on his bone flute.

"Cease your blustering at once!" Lilith covered her ears.

He stopped playing his instrument and gawked at them. "What is wrong?"

"The sound of that thing perturbs the mind." Lucifer pointed at the flute. "What is it?"

Beelzebub presented his musical instrument. "I made this windpipe for Gabriel."

"Do you mean to kill him with it?" Lilith sneered.

Beelzebub's eyes broadened. "Of course not! I mean to present it to him as a gift."

She grabbed the black flute from him. She turned it in her hand and then showed it to Lucifer.

"It is a hideous contraption." She returned it with an expression of disgust. "I would not give it to Gabriel if I were you."

"The sound it makes can produce torment in even the most cheerful of beings." Lucifer scowled. "You must never play it outside your quarters."

Beelzebub hung his head. A lump in his throat made it hard for him to speak, and hot tears filled his eyes. Lucifer sighed, waved dismissively and walked away, holding Lilith's hand and pulling her toward the small room again.

"Save the device," Lilith said as she walked away, "and always keep it close to your heart as a reminder of how the undeserved laws inflicted on us keep you from Gabriel. Let the sound remind you of the grim fate awaiting us if we do not rebel against an unjust God."

Beelzebub nodded and hid the musical instrument in his garments. "I must join the rebellion against God in order to gain the freedom to indulge in my feelings for Gabriel, but what if I lose Gabriel for rebelling against God?"

He shuffled away without saying another word, a dull ache in his chest. It hurt him to breathe, swallow, and walk. Suddenly, all the brilliant colors in the atrium faded, and an aura of gray surrounded him.

Chapter 16

LILITH'S UPRISING

The mood in Floraison changed. Lilith enlisted many angels to join her rebellion with promises of a new Floraison and new laws. She also convinced those angels to recruit others to her cause.

Angels gathered together in corners throughout the atrium, crouched behind bushes and boulders within Triumph Gardens, huddled near the forbidden forests and Divina Falls at Guidance Park, conversing in secret about Lilith's ideas for a new kingdom where Lucifer would be supreme ruler. In this new Floraison, they would be free to go wherever their desires led them and do whatsoever they craved. Similar to the humans on Earth, they would be allowed to have companions and enjoy pleasures of the flesh.

Lilith's friends did a magnificent job of circulating her plan and recruiting angels they trusted and knew would be happy to be involved in the conquest. Subsequently, the new recruits enlisted other angels, and those converts in turn procured more allies to the uprising.

Each angel involved in the revolt was sworn to secrecy. Soon, one third of Floraison's angels had sided with Lilith and Lucifer to rebel against God.

Lilith was certain more would rebel. She needed time to reach them and work her powers of manipulation.

Using his charisma and splendor,

Samael obtained the support of many angels. He also made countless false promises such as the freedom to visit and rule other planets and indulge in carnal pleasures with any being they desired.

Dagon used his handsomeness and natural abilities to lure angels to their cause as well.

Beelzebub stared at Lilith. "What if I could convince Gabriel to join in the movement? I am certain I should at least try."

Lilith frowned. "No, Beelzebub."

He grabbed her arm with both hands and stared with a tight expression. "I am confident Gabriel would align with us."

Lilith waved her finger. "I forbid it. Even though Gabriel did not divulge the incident by the lake, I do not trust him, and neither does Lucifer or Samael. Do not speak to him of the rebellion for he shall no doubt go to Michael and Raphael."

Beelzebub's eyes shifted to the side and glistened with a layer of tears. He stood as still as a tree trunk and appeared lost in his thoughts. Gabriel would never betray me. He has proven himself by not divulging what occurred at Lake Serena to his Archangel brethren. He kept the incident to himself because he cares for me.

As he blinked, large drops fell from his eyelids. He clutched his chest. My heart is bursting with tender affections for Gabriel, and I believe my darling would join me in the rebellion.

Beelzebub searched for Gabriel at Triumph Gardens. He flitted about, peering into every corner of the atrium, but he was nowhere to be found. He hurried to Guidance Park where Michael and Jetrel were training in Michael's favorite place by the Divina Waterfall, but there was no sign of Gabriel.

He suffered an unbearable urgency to tell him everything. He was about to temporarily end his search when he caught a glimpse of Gabriel sitting on a small stone arch bridge. The little, elaborate structure spanned the River of Life, and led to the golden double doors that opened to the portal that led to God's throne room.

Gabriel sat near the golden doors, singing praises to God and in between, playing a wind instrument he had fabricated.

Beelzebub ogled him from afar for a while, playing with his light blond hair, and dragging sections between his fingers. He enjoyed his singing and the way his lips puckered and blew into the flute he played. He took a deep breath and finally approached him.

"Hello."

Gabriel stopped his singing and smiled. "Greetings, Beelzebub." He gestured for him to sit.

"I need to speak to you about something important." Beelzebub rubbed his forehead.

Gabriel searched his face. "Are you serious or jesting? I never know with you since you are such a prankster." Beelzebub remained earnest. "What could be so crucial as to wipe the smile off your face?"

Beelzebub glanced at the double doors and fidgeted. "I cannot speak of it in this place." He swallowed hard. "We must go someplace where we can talk in confidence."

Gabriel tilted his head to the side and scrutinized him for a while, his chin resting on his palm, looking uncertain.

"I do not understand. What is the nature of what you must reveal, which you refuse to disclose here and now?"

"Please trust me, Gabriel. I know you have no reason to, but look at the sincerity in my eyes. When you listen to my words, you shall understand why I am unable to speak of it in this place."

Gabriel tapped his fingers. "Very well." He climbed to his feet. "So where is it we need go to speak in private? Is there such a place in Floraison?"

"Yes! For I believe God does not mind us all the time. He grows bored of it. This is why he gave this duty to the governors and Power angels." Beelzebub held a lopsided smile and Gabriel looked at him sideways. "I know of a place where we can be alone and talk without interruption."

Gabriel remained stony-faced and chewed on his lower lip. He sighed and reluctantly followed his friend.

Beelzebub led him to the atrium, then ushered him to the small, isolated corner overlooking Thanda-Garam.

"What is so vital and so secretive you must disclose it to me hidden in this remote corner of the atrium?" Gabriel tugged on his ear.

"Please stop fiddling with your ears. You have made them the color of plum tomatoes." Beelzebub stared into his pale blue eyes and trembled, for he began to feel anxious about revealing the secret plans. "You know I love you, do you not?"

Gabriel never perceived him to be so genuine. "Yes, I know. I love you too, in the same way as I love all of God's children."

Beelzebub closed his eyes. "No—that is not what I intended to say." He smiled and caressed Gabriel's face, admiring his delicate features. "I mean I love everything about you. I love you in all ways, including the carnal way."

Gabriel stepped away.

"I love your smile. It makes me happy." Beelzebub moved toward him. "I cherish the way you glow when you play your instruments, and the way you close your eyes when you sing praises to God. I treasure the way your lips pucker just a little when you sleep, and even the sounds of your breathing are like music to my ears. That is how I love you!"

Gabriel gasped, and breathed quick and shallow openmouthed breaths. Beelzebub gently held his friend's face with both hands, brought him close, and kissed him on the lips. Gabriel stared at him, dazed by his words and acts.

"What are you doing?" Gabriel's face lost all its color. His soft blue eyes opened wider, and his lips parted.

"Please do not oppose this. Allow yourself the pleasure of freedom." Beelzebub leaned into him.

Gabriel pushed him away. "No! What you say is blasphemy, and God condemns your actions. We swore an oath of celibacy. We were created to worship Him."

Beelzebub's lower lip quivered as words crept their way out of his mouth. "Yes, but why should I be judged? I did not decide one brillante to love you this way. I did not have a choice—I do not have a choice."

Gabriel beheld his watery green eyes and hung his head.

Seeing empathy and love in Gabriel's face Beelzebub seized the moment and grabbed him by the arms, kissing him, as Lilith had taught him. Then he turned him to face away, embracing him from behind. Gabriel closed his eyes, giving in to his advances.

Beelzebub nipped the nape of Gabriel's neck and his shoulders, as though he were noshing on a scrumptious morsel. He passed his hands across his torso, cuddling, and fondling his chest.

Gabriel was in a daze and, for the moment, rendered helpless with intense, giddy pleasure. Beelzebub spun him around to face him again and kissed his neck, while clutching a handful of his bouncy dark curls. Gabriel gazed upward as pleasure grew inside him.

Beelzebub grabbed him and pushed him against the wall, while his hands worked their way to his lower body. He slid one hand around his torso and cupped a buttock. With the other he rubbed his groin. Gabriel was not prepared to guard himself against such forceful sensations of desire.

"There are so many pleasures we can explore together," he whispered, his mouth flush against Gabriel's ear. His warm breath causing small bumps to develop across his body. The hairs on Gabriel's arms and neck stood upright and he moaned as he experienced sensations and emotions he was never aware existed.

"I know you find pleasure in what I do to you." Beelzebub continued kissing and caressing him. "I sense it in the way your body responds to my touch."

"Yes, I experience much pleasure, but that does not make this right," Gabriel said, breathless. "I beg you, end these reckless acts, for I do not have the strength to do so."

Beelzebub did not stop. Instead, he reached under his garment and continued to stroke his organ faster and steadier, making Gabriel shudder and pant.

He pressed his mouth against his and kissed him over and over again. He caressed his face and neck with his lips and whispered promises of love and pleasure unimaginable. "In the new Floraison, we could be partners and lovers for all time. Think of all the enjoyment and exciting adventures we would have together."

He felt Gabriel's heart flutter like the wings of a hummingbird against his chest.

Spasms in the region between Gabriel's thighs introduced an intense sensation of pleasure. He began to undergo involuntary body movements, and jolts of pleasure continued to rake his being.

Moans and groans escaped Gabriel's mouth followed by a euphoric expression across his face. Reddish spots appeared on his abdomen, throat, and chest. His breathing began to slow, as he grew calm.

"Lucifer would be a great ruler. He would allow us to explore our feelings, and our bodies. He would—"

"What words do you speak?" Gabriel stirred from his dream-like state. He raked his fingers through his tousled hair and stared at Beelzebub through brooding, half-opened eyes.

"Lucifer is second only to God." Beelzebub's eyes were broad and bright, surprised by his abrupt change in demeanor. "With Lilith by his side and all the angels as his allies, he can become the Supreme Being in the new Floraison. Once Lucifer reigns here, all shall be different."

He held onto Gabriel's shoulders as he attempted to get away. If he could not convince him to join in the rebellion, all of Lilith and Lucifer's efforts to establish a new order would be worth nothing to him.

"All I desire is for us to be free to love each other. I cannot imagine a new Floraison without you by my side." He kissed Gabriel's cheeks and forehead. "We would have access to the River of Life whenever it suited us. The planets would be ours to visit or rule. Things we dare not even think about now would be made reality. Oh Gabriel, everything shall be so wonderful once Lucifer becomes our new god."

Gabriel covered his face with the palms of his hands.

"What is the matter?" Beelzebub continued to touch him and try to kiss him.

"You have been deceived!" Gabriel grabbed Beelzebub's busy hands and pushed them away from him. He wiped his face wet with tears and changed into spirit form and slipped from his grasp.

"Their plans are ludicrous and shall never come to pass. Lucifer can never be God! There is only one God, and he cannot be replaced." Gabriel hovered above the ground.

"But, Lucifer is powerful, akin to God."

"Lucifer is powerful because God made him so. God created us all, and He can destroy us with a single word if He so chooses. Lucifer is but a speck of dust in comparison to God." Gabriel clenched his fists. "I was weakened by you, and for that, I am ashamed and may never be forgiven.

But before we both suffer the consequences of our actions, you must disclose all of Lilith's plans to me."

Beelzebub rubbed his cheek while he gazed at the shimmering presence before him. He clenched his hands, rubbing his thumbs against each other. Then he began to pace, while Gabriel waited. He finally stopped and gazed at him.

"I shall reveal all that I know, for I long to demonstrate my love to you."

He made known to Gabriel all of the plans Lilith had formulated for the revolt. Upon revealing everything, he clutched his chest and grimaced in pain. "My whole world is falling apart." He dropped to his knees and wept in the bitter and hopeless way of children.

Gabriel gazed at him with a pitying expression. "I do not intend to force you to come with me to face God's judgment, but you know what you must do." He left Beelzebub crumpled on the ground and went forth to search for Michael and Raphael. He needed to convey this revelation to the Archangels and Powers.

≪

Gabriel found Michael and Raphael at Guidance Park, practicing their wrestling skills. He floated just above the ground toward them.

They stopped wrestling when they caught sight of him approaching them in spirit form. They rose to their feet and stared at him. They had seen Gabriel in spirit form twice before, but only for brief moments.

"My brothers, I have sinned, and I fear the fitting punishment for me is death." Returning to the flesh, he fell at their feet.

Michael and Raphael glanced at each other and appeared startled by his behavior. Gabriel lay on the ground, guilt and remorse contorted his features.

"Gabriel, you must reveal to us what has happened." Michael squatted to speak to him face to face. "I have only seen you brimming with joy, while you sang and played your musical instruments, taught other angels, and enjoyed nature with friends. I am concerned to see you this way."

"Yes, please enlighten us. Michael and I shall try to help you." Raphael stared at him.

"I am beyond your help." Gabriel's voice quavered between sobs. "These tears, which sting like bees, serve no purpose but to show my guilt."

"God is merciful. He shall forgive you if you are remorseful." Michael glanced at Raphael.

"We shall take you to God's throne room." Michael rose to his feet and extended his hand. "There you may confess your sins to God. He is all knowing, and if you are repentant, he shall recognize it and judge you accordingly."

Gabriel gasped and wheezed. When he clambered to his feet his legs faltered and he fell to his knees. Michael and Raphael helped him stand and stood on each side of him to offer support.

Gabriel kept hold of them. "This is the second time I permitted Beelzebub to touch me in ways forbidden. I am indeed remorseful for allowing him to have his way with me and for feeling carnal desires," he said under his breath.

Michael squeezed his brow and stared at his haunted face.

"My biggest fear is to be in God's presence. I am not worthy, but instead, too impure." Gabriel glanced at his friends through his tears, and divulged all that had taken place in the atrium, and also on the shores of Lake Serena. He also disclosed what Beelzebub had revealed to him about the plans to overthrow God so that Lucifer could rule Floraison as a god with Lilith as his goddess queen.

Michael stared before him for a long moment and then looked at Gabriel. "It is difficult to accept that Lucifer is involved in this foolish plan." His voice was soft, and a bit strained, like someone had punched him in the gut and he was still recovering. "I trust you in every respect, I am not sure I can trust Beelzebub. Lucifer would never turn against God. It is impossible."

They stared ahead, immobile for a while. Michael became ashen. "We must go now," Michael informed Gabriel after a short while. "You must confess all to God." He glanced at Raphael, whose harrowing expression conveyed that he, too, understood the repercussions if all Beelzebub had divulged to Gabriel was true. They flanked Gabriel as they began heading to God's throne room.

"God himself shall judge you," Michael said.

Chapter 17

BETRAYED BY LOVE

Lilith headed toward her favorite place in the atrium. When she arrived at her secret corner, she found Beelzebub there, curled into a ball, bawling.

"Beelzebub! What are you doing here? You know this is my favored place. Why are you—" She stopped yelling upon seeing his demeanor.

She moved closer to get a better look at him. He lifted his doleful eyes. Beelzebub's face was red and wet and his eyes were bloodshot and swollen.

Lilith's eyes, sparkling with energy, narrowed with suspicion. She began to tremble. Her jaw dropped and she gulped air.

"What did you do?" She grasped a handful of his hair and jerked his head. "Tell me—what have you done?"

"It is too late for all of us." Beelzebub wept in his hands. "Your plan to place Lucifer in control of Floraison has failed."

"What are you saying? Inform me at once." She clenched her jaw.

"I told Gabriel everything." Gloom etched his face as he confessed. Suddenly he giggled jarringly, making her jump.

Lilith glared and rushed him grabbing more of his hair. She yanked his head forward to meet her angry stare. He screamed.

"How could you do such a

thing?" Lilith had a wild expression in her eyes which made her look dangerous. "Why would you betray us?"

He dissolved in fits of uncontrollable nervous laughter. "I love him! I could not imagine a new Floraison without Gabriel by my side. I was certain he would fight with us and be mine forever."

"You fool!" She released his hair and threw his head backward in the process.

"You do not understand. I cannot control my feelings for him—the yearning for his kisses and touches. Even if my feelings for him are wicked, they are still there. They shall always be there!" Beelzebub rocked, and his wings vibrated. He tittered while tears erupted from his eyes.

Lilith glowered at him. She shrieked and grabbed a nearby chair and threw it against the wall. Her entire body trembled. A thick fog surrounded her, and she could not see her way through.

"I am still not convinced Gabriel shall not change his mind and join us," Beelzebub said, in a soft, frail voice. "He was affected by the things I told him. He never heard such words spoken by anyone before. I know he loves me. He did not betray me to Michael when I laid hand on him by Lake Serena. Gabriel shall not be disloyal to me."

Lilith stared at him in wonder. She clenched her hand and held it tight against her mouth and closed her eyes for a moment. "You are a ridiculous buffoon, and have condemned us all." She ran in search of Lucifer.

Beelzebub trembled and convulsed once more gasping and sobbing.

Lilith pierced the sky with her four wings. She knew she would find Lucifer at Triumph Gardens, for they had scheduled a meeting there. She had to inform him of Beelzebub's betrayal. Together they would determine what to do next. There was no doubt in her mind that Gabriel was at that moment confessing all to the Archangels. They had to prepare for what was to come.

Triumph Garden was a place for inspiration and meditation, with towering evergreens and majestic oaks. Assorted blossoms combined to create a vast palette of colors. Cheerful yellow daisies, exotic blue and pink orchids, and vivid tulips, among other flowers, created the perfect atmosphere for smiles to abound. The air was perfumed with their lingering fragrances. Scenic ponds decorated by buoyant water lilies reflected the colorful showy plants and graceful, blooming trees.

The scent of frangipani, sweet peas, and violets embraced the angels as they sat on the soft grass and discussed their lessons. Celestial musicians sat underneath magnolia trees to sing songs of praise and play their instruments.

The garden was one of Gabriel's favorite places in Floraison, ideal for learning about nature, from delicate buds to the most extraordinary plants. At present, Lucifer used this regal place of inspiration and education for scheming and enlisting rebel angels.

When Lilith found him, he was discussing conquest plans with Samael, Dagon, Fornues, and Gadreel, whom he had assigned as generals of their rebel army.

"It has begun!" Her face was pale and she clenched her teeth so tightly her jaw muscles visibly bulged.

"Lilith! What is the matter? What has begun?" Lucifer rushed to her.

"War is upon us." Lilith swallowed hard. "They know—Michael, Raphael, and Gabriel know our plans to revolt."

"Impossible!" Lucifer said.

"Misguided by lust, Beelzebub thought he could convince Gabriel to join us in the rebellion. He revealed everything to him. He was wrong in trusting him to hold his tongue, and I am certain Gabriel has already gone to Michael and told him of our plans," Lilith said. "By now, I have no doubt the others have been informed of our treachery, and soon the Power angels shall come for us."

Lucifer lowered his head, and paced, raking his fingers through his hair.

Some of the angels involved in the rebellion heard Lilith and burst into panicked chatter.

Gadreel took Lilith's hand and spoke in an undertone. "The angels are beginning to unravel, and look at Lucifer, he is crumbling. You must be strong and set things right. Otherwise, we are doomed."

Lilith closed her eyes and took a deep breath. "Moving forward is our best option." She looked at Gadreel. "If we surrender now, we would be judged and destroyed. There is yet hope for us to win. My words have always been a powerful influence on Lucifer. I shall use them now to convince him that our plans are irrefutable and we can win this war in spite of everything."

Gadreel smiled and exhaled in relief.

Lilith proceeded to Lucifer and whispered in his ear, "We must stay strong and focused. Only cowards are full of doubts. It is too late to change our direction now."

"We are not yet prepared," Lucifer said, avoiding her stare. "I knew eventually the Archangels and Powers would learn of our campaign, but it is too soon. We do not have enough rebels. We are not strong enough to go against Michael and the others yet. We need more time."

"Enough! Time is a convenience we no longer have. It is now or never." Frustrated by his vanquished attitude, she pulled him by the arm and took him away from the other angels, who gawped at them as they argued.

"You must show strength and leadership now more than ever." Lilith pointed at the generals. "The rebels are frightened. They look to us to give them courage."

Lucifer indicated agreement and took a deep, reinforcing breath. He strolled toward his officers with his head held high and his broad chest expanded.

He cleared his throat. "It is true that Michael gained knowledge of our plans sooner than expected, but this is something for which we have been preparing. The fact we were revealed earlier than anticipated means we have to work twice as fast and twice as hard to reach our goals, but it does not mean failure is imminent. We shall not fail!"

The angels surrounding him grinned and cheered. Gadreel bounced on her heels and smiled at Lilith.

Lilith stepped forward. "We must prepare to hit them hard with destructive force and fervor, such as they have never seen or imagined. We must stir fear into their hearts and weaken their spirits. That is how we shall win!"

The rebels cheered even louder. Lucifer gazed at her with admiration, and stood by her and leaned toward her ear. "How could I have doubted? With you by my side, victory is at hand."

Chapter 18

JUDGMENT DAY

On their way to the throne room, Michael and Raphael recruited Cam, Hashmal, Esar, Raquel, and Jetrel, and now they knelt beside Gabriel as they awaited God's response. They prayed the portal to Metá Heaven be opened so that they may gain entrance and be granted His divine presence. At last, God spoke in their minds.

Ye may enter, for I have been expecting thee.

Gabriel's knees faltered. Michael caught him and prevented his fall. "God's voice fills my heart with sorrow for having sinned against Him." Gabriel wept.

In the throne room, Gabriel kneeled before God's light and placed his chest and forehead on the ground. He hid his face in his hands. He trembled and between sobs confessed his sins to Him, in the presence of all his friends.

Gabriel revealed to them what Beelzebub had confided in him about the rebellion plotted by Lilith and led by Lucifer. The witnesses grew pallid, their jaws dropped as they gawked at each other.

Upon hearing Gabriel's words, Jetrel's face twisted in disgust. Raquel covered her gaping mouth. Esar's lips moved but he could not find words. Hashmal remained silent with his mouth shut tight, his gullet emanating an amber glow. Flame finally escaped his nostrils, while Cam clenched his jaw.

"My Father, what of Gabriel?" Michael waited, as did the others, to hear the fate of their dear friend.

I shall grant thee forgiveness, Gabriel, for thou art remorseful and thou art without malice. However, great was thy sin, and thou must suffer the consequences of thine acts.

As God spoke, the angels were motionless, and Gabriel held his breath awaiting his punishment.

Gabriel, thou shall remain a spirit for the rest of days. Thou shall no longer be able to take on physical form or experience the sensations of the flesh, since it weakens thee so. This shall be thy castigation.

After God imparted his judgment, He gave Michael and all present a list of the rebel angels. God embedded this list of names in their intellects so they might never forget those who defied Him and waged war against the lowest realm of Heaven and virtuousness.

He instructed Michael and his righteous brethren to gather all the holy angels in Guidance Park. There would be divinely consecrated battle gear in the park for each angel whose name did not appear on the list of rebels.

Once the holy angels were assembled in the park, the entrance would be sealed, and one by one, the angels would step into the River of Life to be prepared for battle.

Rise to thy feet, Gabriel, and position thyself by thine holy brethren.

God summoned the angels in the throne room, one after another, and they went forth. He gave them each an extraordinary weapon, divinely inspired and created for them.

He presented Michael with a golden spear, beautiful and lightweight, fast as lightning and impossible to dodge. A net made of an indestructible rope, which rendered the captive paralyzed when covered by it, God gave to Raphael. Cam received a sword. When drawn, the blade blazed with fire and could cut through anything—even rock and metal.

Jetrel obtained an unstoppable silver lance. When aimed and flung, the lance would not cease until it impaled the intended target. The Almighty granted Hashmal complete domination of his ability to emit fire from his mouth and also enhanced his talent. Like a fire-breathing giant, he would be able to annihilate multiple groups of the enemy.

Esar was given full command of his shifting abilities. God made it so Esar could shift into a fully formed, enormous mammal or into a small insect, at will. Raquel's intelligence and intuition were already powerful weapons, but God gave her a mace, a strong wooden shaft reinforced by metal with a round stone head. The slightest contact with the weapon's stone head would render an enemy confused, disoriented, and susceptible to her bidding.

Gabriel did not receive a weapon. In spirit form, he was able to become invisible to the eye and transcend physical barriers. God did, however, grant him something.

Gabriel since thou art the spirit of Truth, I shall grant one of thy instruments, thy horn, special powers, so that whosoever hears it shall have no option but to speak the truth.

He informed the holy angels in his midst, that in Guidance Park they would receive new green and gold uniforms to symbolize their unity.

Chapter 19

ENEMY SPY

In no time, Guidance Park began to fill with those who were not on God's list of corrupt angels. The large, carved wooden doors would soon be sealed so no one could enter or depart.

Michael, Raphael, Gabriel, and Jetrel were situated at different locations along the riverbank, and together they began to guide the faithful angels into the River of Life. The angels submerged in the pure water and were exhilarated and restored by its powers. One by one, the angels came forth from the river, drenched in its potent water, feeling strong, focused and ready for battle. Raquel, Hashmal, Esar, and Cam handed them their green and gold war garments to change into.

God appointed Michael supreme commander of His consecrated army. His role was to manage and command the entire army of holy angels. Michael appointed Raquel as his chief advisor and Raphael, Gabriel, Cam, Jetrel, Hashmal, and Esar as chief officers of their legions. They in turn appointed junior officers to help them organize and command the troops.

Together with Michael and Raquel, the six chief officers planned and directed strategies. The forces of holy angels were organized, well trained, equipped with holy weapons provided by God, and strengthened by the pure waters of the River of Life. Michael discussed war strategies with his chief officers, while the holy angels prepared themselves for battle.

Beelzebub was still shaken by the discord between him and Gabriel and his confrontation with Lilith. He was on his way to Guidance Park to hide in his place of refuge and think, when he noticed hordes of angels hurrying past him to enter the park.

Beelzebub stopped and peered at the groups of angels entering the park with a quizzical expression. As a rule, only a limited number of angels visited the park at one time. This ensured plenty of space for the angels there to spar and exercise. However, on this day it seemed all of Floraison's angels were gathering at the park, except for him and his friends.

Only on rare occasions had Beelzebub seen so many angels congregate in the park at once. "I have not heard Hashmal or Michael announce an assembly," he said in an undertone.

Beelzebub snuck into the park, he ran along the perimeter to avoid being seen by Michael or any of the other Archangels, Powers, or Dominions. He managed to creep past everyone, since the angels were near the center and directed to make their way into the River of Life. He made it to the Divina Waterfall. Once there, he blended with the plants growing wildly on either side of the waterfall and disappeared behind the cascades.

He slunk into the long, narrow cave in Mount Verve.

Once inside he grinned and exhaled. When he had found the cave long ago he placed more rocks in strategic places to cover the entrance. Since then, vines and other climbing plants had grown, wrapping themselves on the rocks and across the entrance, concealing it. Unless one knew the entrance was there, it would be impossible to find.

Beelzebub had never told anyone about the cave, not even Lilith. "Who knew that all the times I came here to daydream about Gabriel, to think, or to spy on unsuspecting angels who entered the park and sat by the falls, conversing without knowing I overheard their words was in preparation for this day?" He wore a scornful grin.

"Once more I shall use this place to spy on Michael and the others, for I am certain something of great importance shall be revealed in Guidance Park from which my friends and I were excluded."

He anticipated Michael would stand on the large rock next to Divina

Waterfall, since he had seen him use the same rock as a platform on many occasions to address large groups of angels. And indeed, Michael took his place on the large, flat rock and addressed all the legions now standing in formation in front of him.

"Michael is so predictable, and that is one of his weaknesses." He giggled.

Beelzebub scanned the park. "Michael's troops are well organized." He frowned. "They stand in tight formation, wearing green and gold armor as they wait for him to speak." He paid attention.

Michael beckoned his chief officers. "Hashmal, fire-breathing chief of the Dominions, come forth and stand beside me. Raphael, Seraph, Power, and Archangel with the power to heal; Gabriel, Virtue and Archangel, possessing the spirit of honesty with his Horn of Truth; Jetrel, fierce Power angel bearing her lance, which cannot miss; Esar the shifter, Throne angel and living symbol of God's justice; and Raquel, Dominion, an angel of leadership with her mace in hand—come forth. I ask that you stand beside me and before Floraison's army and serve as inspiration."

The chief officers climbed the rocky platform and stood on either side of Michael and faced the troops of holy angels.

"God has summoned you here to this unexpected gathering because we face an astonishing danger," Michael began to the wide-eyed stares of the holy angels. "Since the beginning, we have been training for combat, not knowing when or against whom we would battle. We all remained faithful that in the future we would come to understand the need for our intense training. On this brillante and on the eighteenth year of our existence you shall get the answers you seek."

Guidance Park became silent, as each angel hung on Michael's every word.

"A group of rebellious angels we once called friends have chosen to turn against God and his faithful followers." The troops huffed in disbelief.

Beelzebub gasped. "This could only mean one thing—Gabriel betrayed me! He must have informed Michael about everything." His legs faltered and he collapsed to his knees. He shook, gasping for air and sobbing. He rubbed his chest. "What is this fire that has ignited within my core?" Agony unlike anything he ever experienced before overwhelmed him.

"Lilith was right all along. Gabriel never loved me." He wiped his tears and continued to eavesdrop with conviction.

"I shall listen and observe all that comes to pass in Guidance Park. Then I shall deliver the information to Lilith. The rebels would have no choice but to forgive me for past wrongdoings, for the information I shall deliver would give them the advantage." He gulped and listened.

"God has given me and those standing by my side a list with the names of the rebel angels." Michael stepped forward. "We know that Lilith instigated the rebellion, and Lucifer, swayed by her wiles, has taken leadership of this campaign."

There was uproar in the park, and Michael paused and observed the reaction of the crowd. There were many shocked and confused faces, and he allowed them ample time to absorb the outrageous and distressing facts he had given them.

Many angels yelled and moaned in grief. Others ranted to one another, asking a multitude of questions. Some gasped for air and stood motionless, while others covered their mouths and their ears, shaking their heads in disbelief. A myriad of angels wept for the first time.

Michael beckoned Hashmal to come forth. "You must calm the troops, for you have a gift for handling dissent with a calm and logical mind."

Hashmal stepped forward. "This is not an occasion for disharmony." Bolts of lightning erupted from his mouth. The troops quickly returned to formation and became silent. They stared at the powerful angel. "We must listen to every word Michael voices, for he is proclaiming God's will."

He faced Michael and signaled him to continue his discourse. Michael smiled and gave him a nod of recognition as he stepped forward once more.

"We must come together and build unity in an era of upheaval," Michael said. "Time is the most limited asset we have available to us, so it must be used well. I understand the truths I have provided are astounding and upsetting to you, as they were to us, but we do not have time to lament. We must prepare and be strong in God's name."

The holy angels listened and contained their many emotions.

"I shall read the list God has provided us of the angels involved in the rebellion. Remember these names and embed them in your minds for all time."

Michael read the names on the list starting with Lilith and Lucifer. Each name astonished one angel or another.

Raquel's face paled upon hearing Dagon's name being called. "How could Dagon be involved in a rebellion against God?" Tears flooded her face.

Although Beelzebub knew it would be on the list, when he heard his name called aloud, he gripped his head, and swayed a moment before fainting. When he regained consciousness he sat balled on the ground, rubbing his temples with the thick part of his palms and wept.

Michael finished reading the list, and the park was still and quiet. He observed the motionless angels for a moment and then proceeded.

"Our mission is to capture the rebels named on God's list. We shall seek and find this enemy. They must come before God to be judged and punished. We have all we need to get this task done right here in Guidance Park. The chief officers you see standing by my side and I shall develop a course of action.

"In the meantime, each of you shall choose a weapon and become familiar with it. When I issue the order, we shall have battle drills and troop rehearsals. Afterward, you shall fall into battle formation and await further instructions. When everyone has selected their weapon of choice, the junior officers shall gather their troops and organize training exercises and sparring sessions to ensure all warriors master combat techniques with the weapons they have chosen. You may go procure your weapons."

The angels dispersed to choose their armaments.

Beelzebub pressed his cheeks between his hands. His eyes were wide. "I cannot believe it has come to this. Floraison's army prepares to wage war against us. It is time I warn the others." He jumped to his feet and ran along the cave's long passage to exit Guidance Park and warn Lilith and Lucifer of what was to come.

Chapter 20

PLAN OF ATTACK

Beelzebub hurried to the other opening of the cave that led out of Guidance Park. He flew to Triumph Gardens where Lucifer, his generals, and rebels often met. When he entered the garden, he searched for Lilith. He spotted Dagon and Fornues and ran to them.

"Dagon, Fornues." Beelzebub gasped and panted. "Where is Lilith?"

Dagon scowled at him. "How dare you show your face here?"

Fornues stepped forward, looking incredulous.

Beelzebub saw the look of hatred in their eyes, and he trembled and panted. "I know you think I have betrayed the cause, but it was not my intention. I have come now to make amends."

"How is it you plan to atone?" Dagon stomped toward him.

Fornues also drew near. Beelzebub retreated, bit by bit. He extended his arms before him.

"Surrender your life! It is the only way you shall ever make amends for your actions," a ferocious voice roared from the distance. Lucifer rushed toward him. Samael and Gadreel accompanied him.

Dagon charged Beelzebub, knocking him to the ground. He wrapped his large hands around his neck and squeezed.

"How could you ever atone for

condemning us to endless suffering?" Dagon squeezed harder. "Rebelling against God has a penalty worse than death!"

Beelzebub's mouth moved, but Dagon had a tight grip around his throat and he could only gurgle. Lucifer glowered at him as he watched Dagon attempt to take his life. Gadreel clenched her hands into fists.

"Release him," Lilith said. "We may need to hear what he has to say."

Dagon released his grip and withdrew grudgingly. He pointed at Beelzebub. "I shall finish this."

Beelzebub suffered a coughing fit. He wheezed and gasped. He cleared his throat and struggled to sit up.

"I have a secret place where I go to be alone with my thoughts, just as you do, Lilith." Beelzebub's voice was gruff as he fixed his eyes on her.

"How is this important to our cause?" Samael said. Lilith lifted her hand and silenced him.

"Go on, but remember we do not have much time." Lilith appeared composed.

"My secret place is a cave in Mount Verve, and it is located behind the Divina Waterfall in Guidance Park."

Lilith's gaze bore into Beelzebub's face. Lucifer raised an eyebrow. Dagon frowned. Samael listened. Fornues and Gadreel looked confused.

"What cave is this? And why don't I know of it?" Lilith moved forward.

"There is no such cave at the base of Mount Verve. He lies!" Samael sucked his teeth and kicked a pebble on the ground.

"That is of no importance now." Beelzebub stared at Lilith. She glared at him as he continued. "Today I watched as all of Floraison's angels, except the rebels, entered Guidance Park, summoned by Michael. Once there, I observed them being instructed to form lines and march into the River of Life."

Lilith kept eye contact.

"Michael stood on his usual platform rock in front of Divina Falls and read a list of names to all the angels present. God Himself gave this list to him, and my name was on it, as well as yours, Lilith and Lucifer's." Beelzebub gestured to them. "This list comprised the names of all the rebel angels. Michael's objectives are to capture us and place us before God for judgment."

Lilith and Lucifer glanced at each other, feigning valor. Gadreel caught her breath and used both hands to cover her mouth. Dagon closed his eyes looking pale. Samael tried to conceal his trembling hands.

"What were you expecting?" Lilith scowled at the surrounding angels. "This is what we have been preparing for!"

"We must get all rebels assembled here at once," Lucifer said.

"The majority of the rebel angels are already here. We must organize them and get them ready for combat," Lilith told him in an undertone.

They gathered the angels already in the garden. It did not take long for Samael, Dagon, Fornues, and Gadreel to return with the remaining rebels, for they knew time was of the essence.

Lilith found a large, flat rock she and Lucifer could use as a platform, as she had seen Michael do many times. She called Lucifer and his generals to stand with her on the platform. She stood to the right of Lucifer and Samael on his left. Gadreel positioned herself next to Samael, and Lilith called Beelzebub to stand next to her. Dagon and Fornues also took their places as generals on the dais.

"The event we have been preparing for has arrived. War in Floraison has begun." Lucifer's voice was controlled and pleasant. The impressive angel stood massive in size, his six large wings outstretched, and he glowed with stellar brightness. "Although the war has come sooner than anticipated, we are well prepared for battle. Michael hoped, with his army of holy angels, to hunt us like beasts and place us in God's presence to be judged and punished, but this shall not come to pass!"

The rebel angels cheered.

"We shall prevail, and cast those against us out of Floraison. We have new information that shall make this campaign a success." Lucifer grinned and gazed at Lilith.

She stepped forward and looked at the rebels. "We have a clear advantage over Michael's holy angels. Any laws established by the previous authority do not bind us. This means we can do anything we desire. We shall be cruel, vicious, and without mercy. We have the element of surprise. Let us take the battle to them and win Floraison for ourselves!" Lilith grinned as the crowd roared.

Her moment drew near. She would be Queen of Floraison. Lucifer shall be a god but a mere minion ruled by her charms. She would be goddess Queen, and have supremacy over Floraison.

Lucifer and his generals watched as the troops cheered and applauded, convinced they would be triumphant.

Lucifer spoke with his generals as rebel soldiers grabbed their weapons and prepared for battle. Weapons fashioned in secret had been hidden within thick bushes, underwater within the many ponds and lakes, and underground throughout the garden.

"Beelzebub, hand me the black bone flute you crafted." Lucifer extended his hand, knowing Beelzebub always carried it with him. Beelzebub reached into his garment and pulled out the flute and passed it to him with a mystified look on his face.

Lucifer held the device with both hands, placed his lips around the instrument's mouthpiece, and relaxed his fingers on the flute's openings. His cheeks puffed out a little and he blew into the simple apparatus, creating a dark and mournful sound.

Lilith and the others grimaced and cringed at the horrid music. Lucifer continued to blow into the black bony pipe while the rebels covered their ears and stared at him with confused expressions.

When Lucifer was done, he inspected the confounded faces and heaved a deep sigh.

Lucifer raised the bone flute for all to see. "The woeful sound this musical instrument produces has no equal and shall be my signal to attack once we are all in position."

Lilith exhaled with relief and chuckled. "There is always good reason behind your actions, no matter how peculiar they may seem at the time."

"Memorize the device's inharmonious sound, for upon hearing it, you are to attack at full force those who congregate in Guidance Park." Lucifer placed the bone flute in his mouth and played it again for a long moment.

The soldiers were divided into five fighting forces to be led by him and his generals. "By now, the large wooden doors that would give us access into Guidance Park have been sealed shut to prevent us from getting in."

"How shall we enter the park if the wooden doors are sealed?" Fornues asked with a tremulous voice. Lilith scowled at him for interrupting Lucifer.

Several rebels began to chatter amongst themselves. Some gawked, others rubbed their hands together, a few held their heads in their hands, and many fidgeted nonstop. They appeared to be frightened.

Lucifer sucked his teeth and raised a hand. "Silence! Be still!"

The angels became quiet, watching him as he continued to speak.

"Although the great wooden doors are shut, there are other ways to gain entrance into the park." Lucifer's azure eyes glinted with confidence. "We are familiar with the three jungles bordering the park, the East, West, and South Forests. We shall traverse these forests to enter Guidance Park."

"It is prohibited to enter the woodlands," a soldier said in a tremulous voice.

"We are no longer bound by the same rules. I determine what is forbidden now." Lucifer stood straighter, jutted his chin and scanned his troops.

The soldier who spoke out of turn lowered his eyes to the ground. Triumph Gardens became quiet once more and he continued.

"We can also enter the park by way of Mount Verve. There shall be no stopping us now. The War in Floraison has begun and we shall strike first."

Lucifer gave his generals their missions.

"The forbidden South Forest has the shortest distance, but it is alleged to be the most complex to get across. This is why I have assigned this task to you, Lilith, for I have total confidence in your strength and cunning. I know you shall lead your troops successfully through the perilous woods. When you reach the border between the woodland and Guidance Park, remain hidden until I give the order to charge with Beelzebub's bone flute."

As he spoke, he caressed her face.

"Please take care, for I cannot bear the thought of losing you," he whispered in her ear. She gently pushed away from him and smiled.

"I shall do as you ask." Lilith grinned. "I shall take my soldiers across the South Forest without harm."

Lucifer gave a nod and swaggered away and she departed the garden and advanced to the South Forest with her group.

"Samael, you shall lead your troops to the summit of Mount Verve."

Samael tittered, caught himself and turned as red as a sweet cherry. "The summit of Mount Verve has never been attained."

"That is because no celestial being has ever attempted such a task, but this day the crown of the mount shall be trodden by angel feet." Lucifer's solemn gaze met Samael's amber eyes. "We must surprise attack the holy army from all sides. They shall never expect a downpour of rebels from the mount and that is how we shall win—adding the element of surprise."

There was a somber note in his voice that was frightening. Samael knew he must stand firm. "Yes, my troops and I shall be the first to reach the summit."

A half smile bloomed on Lucifer's face. He placed his hand on Samael's shoulder.

"You and your troops shall remain on the mountain top in silence until you hear my signal to strike."

Samael bowed to him and stepped off the platform. He exited Triumph Gardens with his militia to begin the ascent of Mount Verve.

"Dagon," Lucifer commanded, "you and Fornues shall lead your troops through the East Forest into Guidance Park."

Fornues' droopy eyes opened wide, remembering the treacherous vines he encountered in the East Forest as a youth of fifteen years.

Dagon saw the fear on his friend's face. "We are no longer children, Fornues. We shall not be defeated by creeping vines." Fornues lowered his head.

"Remain hidden within the trees until everyone is in position and I give the indication to attack," Lucifer said.

Dagon and Fornues nodded in agreement and at once led their armies out of the garden and toward the forbidden East Forest.

Gadreel trembled and bit the tips of her fingers as she watched Dagon and Fornues, lead their troops out of the park.

Lucifer took her hand, pulled it from her mouth, and placed it by her side. "You shall make your way through the West Forest with your soldiers, Gadreel, and wait hidden within the trees at the edge of the forest. Listen for the bone flute's melancholy music to indicate attack."

Gadreel stared at him wearing a smile that did not reach her eyes.

Lucifer heaved a deep sigh. "I am counting on you to make me proud. Do not let me down."

Her demeanor changed and she raised her chin. "This brillante I shall exceed all expectations." A purposeful smile slid across her face.

With her head held high, she led her soldiers to the West Forest.

Hordes of rebel angels remained. They stared at Lucifer in silence, and waited with anxious expressions for his last instructions before heading to battle.

"Beelzebub, you shall lead me and the last unit through the cave in Mount Verve into Guidance Park."

Loud, nervous laughter erupted from Beelzebub in a high-pitched tone. He pressed the back of his hand against his mouth. He stared red-faced at Lucifer, who lowered his brow.

"I do not believe I am a leader. I have always been led," he whispered.

"You are Cherubim, ranked second highest in the hierarchies of celestial beings. Today you become a leader of angels."

Beelzebub gulped and then smiled with relief. "I am grateful to be able to atone for my mistakes. I shall do all that is required of me. I shall lead you and the last group of soldiers through my cave and unto victory."

Chapter 21

PERILS OF THE SOUTH FOREST

Lilith positioned her strongest warriors in front of the troop to slash a path through the dense forest with their swords. Flashbacks of the vicious vines, which taunted her in the East Forest years ago, clouded her mind. She trembled in fear.

She must be strong.

They encountered an enormous red plant, with an opening in the center like a mouth lined with dagger-like teeth. Crawling vines with finger-like leaf ends reached from the plant. The vines seized one of her soldiers and delivered him to the plant's mouth, where trapped in its fangs, he could not escape.

Lilith and the surrounding troops gawked in shock and horror while the vicious plant crushed and began to devour the captured soldier. Several troopers attempted to rescue the captive, but the plant devoured him too fast.

"Destroy the plant!" Lilith jumped away from the plant, shielding herself from the gripping vines with her quartet of powerful wings. She fluttered her wings, to fly away, but her wings had become useless. A supernatural force within the forest thwarted the angels' ability to fly.

Two brave soldiers stepped forward and hacked the plant to pieces with their swords but sustained injuries as the fierce tendrils lashed at their flesh.

"We must be vigilant, for the vegetation in this forest is ferocious." Lilith's eyes flicked through her surroundings.

They continued to hike through the gloomy woods, swords drawn and eyes watchful to detect danger. Soon the trees thinned, and they came to a field of huge gold and purple flowers. A cloying, nauseating stench wafted from the deceptively beautiful flowers and drifted into the troops' nostrils. At first the scent caused their noses to bleed, and then it caused madness.

The eyes of the soldiers closest to the flowers rolled to the back of their heads. They began to pull and scratch at their noses as they twitched and writhed about, staring sightlessly with the whites of their eyes and gesticulating wildly. Some shrieked and picked up rocks to beat their noses, smashing their facial bones. Others used their swords to cut their noses off and stab their faces. The affected soldiers did not stop until they lay faceless and dead on the ground.

Lilith's eyes widened. "Cover your nostrils! It's the scent—the flowers' rancid odor is lethal!" She pinched her nose and ran across the field. Her troops followed her lead. Her pulse beat in her ears. It deadened the wild shrieks of the soldiers who were too late covering their faces, for the poison had already invaded their nostrils and was ravaging their brains.

A short distance away, after they had escaped from the poisonous flowers, a swarm of insects flew toward them. Many of the rebels froze, astounded by the small creatures that seemed to have sharp swords for snouts.

Color drained from Lilith's face as she remembered the insects that had covered her body in the East Forest. The flying bugs attacked the soldiers again and again with their long stingers. They flew into their ears, noses, and mouths.

She shielded herself from the insects with her wings. She no longer controlled the shaking of her hands, but she took a deep breath and found courage for her troops.

"Use your wings as shields and strike the creatures down with them before they can get close enough to sting you!"

Some of the soldiers dropped to the ground after being stung hundreds of times. Others staggered about, covered in these creatures, their wails muffled by the insects teeming in their mouths. Lilith ran, swatting at the flying bugs with two of her four wings while protecting herself with the other two.

Her army continued evading carnivorous plants and swarming insects until they arrived at a dark river. The river rocks were mottled shades of black, green, and red, and were oddly shaped into twisted faces, which conveyed anguish and dread. Some of the soldiers trembled and were visibly shaken. Lilith looked at the daunting rocks and flinched, but remained strong.

"We must wade through the river," Lilith said to the muttered complaints of her troops. "With our wings useless for flying, I see no other way. We shall not condemn our brethren to failure because of some repulsive rocks."

The fearful soldiers lowered their heads, fidgeting and shuffling their feet. "You!" She pointed at a group of them. "Enter the river." Some of the rebels glanced at each other and gulped before stepping in. She trailed behind them and ordered the rest of the insurgents to follow. They surrounded her, safeguarding her from all sides.

Several of the soldiers in front collapsed in the murky water and began to wail and thrash. Others searched across the surface of the dark waters for something wicked. A few of them gasped and pulled at their garments.

"Remain calm and keep moving." Lilith's voice was thick with valor. She noticed a strong soldier by her side. He looked brave. His face was calm and resolute, and he appeared ready to defend her with his life.

"Carry me on your shoulders," she told him and without hesitation the brave soldier lifted her atop his broad shoulders. Wielding his sword, he waded across the river, carrying her.

Other soldiers continued to fall shrieking and floundering in the water, which was now waist high. Lilith finally spotted the calamity tormenting her soldiers.

"There!" She pointed to long, thin tubular-shaped creatures, which bore into the flesh of her soldiers. Hundreds attacked at once, attaching their mouths to their bodies. The victims sunk under the dark water.

Soldiers continued to be attacked, and the loud cries and bellowing persisted.

"You must move faster!" Lilith screamed to the angel carrying her.

"Yes, my queen," he said, but she struggled to hear him. When he finally got her across the river, he placed her with care on the riverbank and collapsed. She saw his legs and part of his torso were shrouded in the black, slimy creatures. They were buried deep in his flesh; only their tails remained visible outside his body, wriggling rapidly, trying to finish the horror they had begun. The areas of skin around the sunken wounds began to harden and turned a muted gray.

Lilith's face turned white and disgust twisted her features. She yanked the slippery fish from the warrior's body and tossed them into the river. The brave warrior squirmed and groaned all the while.

When she pulled the last slimy creature out of him, she held it before her and peered at it. "What manner of fish is this? It has no scales, and its large eyes sit on the top of its head." It had rows and rows of teeth in its sucking mouth. There were seven openings on each side of its head. She placed her hand upon these holes, and the creature began to thrash in her hand and then died. She grimaced and tossed the creature to the ground.

Many dead soldiers sprawled on the banks of the river. Their color had changed to that of stone, and their skin had solidified, and where the creatures had bored into them was hollow.

The snakefish creatures used their numerous sharp teeth to cut through the skin to extract body fluids and consume parts of their insides. They also released toxins, which caused the victims' tissues to dry and calcify.

"Push the corpses into the river." Lilith frowned and turned away. "I do not want to leave behind any mark of failure."

Rebels who had survived the river crossing pushed the desiccated bodies of their fallen comrades into the river. They watched with glistening eyes as the depleted corpses sank like stones to the riverbed.

Lilith regarded the angel who had valiantly carried her through the river.

"I have never suffered such physical anguish." The soldier looked at her with a brief smile that turned into a grimace of pain. "But I would put myself in harm's way once again if it meant your life would be spared, my queen."

"Do not die, my fierce warrior. Persevere a while longer, and when we enter Guidance Park, I promise I shall get you to the River of Life. Unlike this dark and lethal river, the River of Life shall make you whole again." Lilith's lower lip quivered and she held back tears but her face appeared confident.

Despite all they had been through, they would win this war. There could be no other outcome—they must triumph.

She commanded two strong soldiers to carry her sentinel the rest of the way. As the soldiers followed her command, she observed her remaining troops. They looked scared, tired, and many were hurt.

"I know we have been through much." Her soldiers turned their attention to her. "We are almost at the entrance to Guidance Park. Those who remain strong must help those who are injured. When we enter the park, we shall fight our way to the River of Life and partake of its healing powers. You shall be mended and restored!"

Her soldiers hailed with renewed vigor. They regrouped and began to trek through the forest once again, leaving the fearsome river behind.

On this side of the river, their single concern was the creeping vines with the red spikes and prickly leaves similar to the ones Lilith was familiar. The soldiers used their swords to eradicate them. When they reached the edge of the terrifying South Forest, Lilith ordered the soldiers to stand at ease.

"We must remain as still and quiet as the trees concealing us. We shall wait for Lucifer's signal to launch the attack." Lilith stared at the canopies overhead. "Stay watchful of your surroundings. I do not wish to lose another soldier to this hostile environment."

"We won this battle. Do you hear me, God?" She flared her nostrils and balled her fists. "Your invincible South Forest has been defeated. Yes, I lost many, but for every rebel angel I lost to this forest, I shall slay three holy angels."

She appeared the image of equanimity on the exterior, but inside she was a raging volcano. They would have victory. They could not be beaten. All they had suffered here, they would regain tenfold later when she became Queen of Floraison.

Chapter 22

THE CLIMB TO MOUNT VERVE'S SUMMIT

Samael and his troops flew halfway to Mount Verve's summit, but without warning, their wings became rigid and heavy, making it impossible to fly any farther.

Most of the rebel angels experienced a pulling sensation toward the ground when their wings began to stiffen, so they used the last bit of strength in their wings to hoist themselves onto the mountain's wall.

"Secure your weapons and hold on to the rock face with your limbs," Samael said. Still, many panicked as they scrambled to secure their swords in their sheaths and fell to their deaths.

"Grip unto the mountain side with your hands and feet, for we must climb the rest of the way using the strength of our arms and legs alone."

The remaining troops struggled to scale the mountain, but they made it to the summit. Once on the mount's crown, Samael glanced over the edge with a heavy heart, knowing many had fallen to their deaths. He saw only clouds as he stared downward, for the mountain was too high to allow a view of the ground.

He scanned the summit. On the crest of Mount Verve a raging river drained a beautiful lake with pink waters into the River of Life. As the water moved in the river, it lost its pink color, becoming crystalline before spilling over the mountain as the Divina Waterfall. There also grew many unusual trees loaded with small, round pink fruit.

"These trees are heavily laden with fruit." Samael licked his lips and sniffed the air. "We shall climb them, partake of the bounty, and regain our strength for battle. We must do this in silence and in small groups, so as not to be heard by our enemies in the park below."

A group of warriors hurried to climb the trees to get to the fruit. When their hands came in contact with the bark of the trees they became stuck. A viscid, adhesive matter covering the bark held them fast, and the trees drew them closer. Large blisters formed on their skin, beginning with the area attached to the tree trunks. The rest of their skin began to blister as the tree's poison made its way through their bodies. The soldiers howled in agony.

"Assist them!" Samael shouted. The other angels stood motionless, gaping at their comrades. "Pull them off the trees!"

The angels yanked at their brethren but could not release them. The trees began to absorb them; their bodies changed from solid to liquid, beginning with their skin, which melded with the bark. The process was slow, and the victims shrieked and groaned in torment. Samael was forced to make a dreadful decision as general.

"Slay them! Kill those in the trees' clutches! Silence their cries and put them out of their misery."

The soldiers hesitated for a brief moment, but soon followed Samael's orders, using their swords to silence the angels caught by the trees.

Samael watched his soldiers slash their friends' throats on his command. He was their leader, so he maintained a brave face, but a tear escaped his eye leaving a trace on his skin like the trace of a slug on a leaf. He wiped his face and heaved a deep sigh. After the deed was done, it became quiet once more.

He walked to the edge of the mountain, squatted, and focused his hearing to the ground below. He rose to his feet and addressed his troops. "We must remain calm, alert, close to the ground. We shall receive orders to attack soon. When we hear the sound of doom from Beelzebub's flute, we shall descend Mount Verve by hand and foot until midway. Thenceforth, we fly to the ground to defeat every holy angel that crosses our path."

He saw the look of apprehension on his soldiers' faces. "On our ascent we were able to fly to the mountain's midpoint before losing our ability, so it is safe to assume that when we descend to that point, we would be able to take flight once more."

The soldiers nodded in agreement.

"Glide your swords across the toxic secretions coating the trees. We shall take revenge on our enemies with the same poison that forced us to kill our brethren." Samael glared as he looked down at the park.

Chapter 23

GADREEL'S MISGIVINGS

Gadreel led her warriors through the dense vegetation of the West Forest, and the task proved most challenging. Like Lilith, she ordered several of her most resilient soldiers to run ahead and cut the stubborn vegetation blocking their path.

Some of the insurgents, depleted of energy, decided to replenish their bodies by eating fruit seeds off bushes along the way. The soldiers marched and ate bright red seeds. "These are sweet and scrumptious," one told another shoving handfuls of seeds in his mouth. Suddenly, he clutched his belly, grimaced and howled in pain.

Gadreel raised her hand. "Halt!" She hurried in the direction of the shrieks to witness the angel moaning and stooped in pain. He fell to his knees and began to salivate. Strange sounds derived from him, and he began to painfully expel the contents of his stomach. The angels around him retreated and winced, some covered their noses.

The afflicted soldier's face twisted into horrible shapes, and he had violent fits of uncontrollable shaking. Several of his comrades struggled to hold him down. Death followed within minutes.

Soon after his death, several others began exhibiting the same signs, until many lay dead on the busy forest floor. Gadreel stared at her fallen soldiers and a sense of dread crept upward from the pit of her stomach. The hairs rose on her neck and her mouth ran dry. She stood immobile and gawked ahead.

"What are your orders?" a soldier asked, trembling. "Please, we need to do something, or we shall perish here."

Gadreel stirred from her stupor. She gazed into the terrified eyes of the soldier. "No one is to consume or have any contact with any of the vegetation in this forest."

She led her troops forward for a short time before they came across colorful flowering shrubs. They were so numerous the soldiers had no choice but to walk near them. The shrubs' emitted an enticing, sweet fragrance that left the soldiers in a daze.

Spines discharged from the bushes with great force. The seven-inch spikes impaled scores of the soldiers. The body of one warrior fell before Gadreel.

Screaming, she recoiled, staring openmouthed at the corpse. It was difficult to see he was once an angel. The long, thick spines had ruptured his eyeballs, penetrated his forehead like horns, and stabbed his neck, chest—every part of him. Gadreel stared at his wounds. The spines carried poison. She gasped and pointed at the body. "Behold! Everywhere the spines pierced his body, the surrounding skin turned black, rough, and bumpy. They transmit poison!"

Spines split the air around her and angels ran in a frenzy wailing and shouting. Unable to move she stared, held her head and shrieked. She knew Lucifer had made a grave mistake choosing her to serve as general of his army. There were so many angels better suited for this task. "How many lives lost before battle had even begun?"

A soldier grabbed her and put her over his shoulder, using his wings to shield her body. As a consequence, he suffered the attacks of the spikes. He ran away from the lethal bushes as fast as he could. Many others were killed before they could escape.

They finally reached an open area, and she ordered her rescuer to stop and rest a moment. The soldier placed her on the ground and proceeded to remove the spines, which penetrated his wings. He winced and breathed hard as he did, and his face was void of color.

Gadreel watched his suffering with a grim expression. She held her hand out to caress him but pulled it back to her side. "I am most grateful to you, brave warrior. You saved my life, and Lucifer shall reward you."

The soldier smiled; pulled free a thick spike lodged in the rear of his head, and fell dead at her feet.

Her mouth opened, but no sound came forth. She retreated from his body. Her eyes rolled in every direction. The forest seemed to spin around her. What should she do now? She would command that they move forward. No. They should linger a while longer. But they could not fall behind. There were so many hurting. They had to keep moving but— When? How?

Soldiers were removing spines from their bodies. The ones who were uninjured or less injured helped others in more critical condition.

Gadreel turned an ashen color and pressed the palms of her hands into her eyes until she saw nothing but shiny spots. She took a few steps backward and almost stumbled. One of her soldiers grabbed her by the arm and kept her from falling. She held too many wild thoughts to form an intelligent idea.

The soldier watched her clutch her hair while turning her head in all directions with a terrified look on her face.

"Gadreel," he said in a strained voice, "you must tell us our next move." He grabbed her by the shoulders and shook her.

She opened her eyes wide and saw him. "Yes, we must move on." She wiped her face. "Have those less battered help those who may be of use to us in battle. Leave the rest."

Leaving behind the critically injured and the corpses of fallen warriors proved tough for her. But they must move on, and she could not lose control again. She was a general in Lucifer's military, and she needed to lead her troops to Guidance Park.

She took the lead and marched forward. Her soldiers followed, staying clear of the surrounding plants. When they reached the entrance to Guidance Park, she peered out from the cover of the forest and saw Michael standing on the large flat rock he often used as a platform. She heard the uninterrupted bubbling and roaring of the Divina Waterfall.

Gadreel scanned her troops. "Stay hidden in the darkness of the forest until the cacophony from Beelzebub's flute is heard by all."

She sat in a shadowy corner behind a bolder, closed her eyes and exhaled. They were almost out of this trap, but were they headed into a larger one? The warrior plants in this forest had killed many of her soldiers. How would they stand against God's holy warriors who outnumbered them two to one? Lucifer was powerful. Lilith said he was as powerful as God. Was he really? What would become of them?

Chapter 24

RETURN TO THE EAST FOREST

As Dagon and Fornues led their troops through the East Forest, they heard the loud, eerie flapping of a million wings. They came upon the vicious vines with the red spines and large wing-like leaves they had encountered long ago. The brutal creepers fought them every step of the way, obstructing their passage into the deep woods. Now armed with weapons they were able to fight them off and continue on their way.

They reached an expanse of giant, white flowers. The unusual blooms sprouted close to the ground, and their stems were hidden underground, so the angels could only see the heads of the flowers as they approached. From a distance, these blooms appeared beautiful and inviting.

As the rebel angels stepped closer to them, the foul, haunting stench of death wafted from the blossoms. Many angels were afraid to go any farther.

"Keep moving!" Fornues yelled as he shielded his nose with his arm.

"We must continue moving forward. It is our one option," Dagon said when he saw his soldiers dawdling. "Delaying the inevitable shall only make matters worse."

The soldiers followed him and Fornues, weapons drawn. They moved with care across the expanse of gigantic, white flowers, which covered the ground almost entirely.

As Dagon and the others slipped between the massive blooms, they noticed round openings in the middle of them. A strange viscous liquid bubbled within the cavities.

The flowers began to vibrate, making loud, piercing noises. As they moved by them, many winced and covered their ears. The dark, pungent fluid in the center of the flowers began to seethe and the sharp, putrid stench followed the angels and bombarded their nostrils.

Some soldiers began to cough and wheeze, while others gagged and retched. Many covered their nostrils. The soldiers became confused, unable to focus due to the loud piercing sounds and potent stench.

"Make haste!" Dagon yelled. "We must get through this field as quickly as possible." The flowers oscillated faster and faster and then began to discharged globs of the toxic fluid at the soldiers. The pelting liquid bored holes in the flesh wherever it made contact with the angels' bodies.

The flowers spewed their poison into numerous angels' eyes. Blind and disoriented, these soldiers shouted and flailed about in terror. Many of them tripped into the flowers and were caught in their toxic, liquid pools. The flowers then ingested them.

Some soldiers risked their lives trying to help their comrades. A warrior grabbed the legs of one who had fallen into the flower. He tried to pull his friend out while dodging globs of poison. He fell back hard on the ground, his hands still gripping the victim's half-dissolved severed legs. When he realized this, he howled and let go the limbs, only to have multiple globs hit his face and melt it away.

Dagon grimaced. "The soldiers in the flowers are beyond our help. Do not attempt to aid them in any way!" Many angels trembled and wept as they witnessed death for the first time, and their fearful eyes searched for Dagon and Fornues.

"Run! Use your wings to shield your eyes!" Dagon ran ahead.

"Keep moving," Fornues hollered above the terrible vibrations of the flowers and the tortured shrieking of the injured soldiers.

Dagon and Fornues ran with their wings safeguarding as much of their bodies as possible from the acid bombs the flowers were flinging. Their troops followed closely behind.

Many warriors remained behind, half consumed by the giant white flowers. Parts of their bodies not yet devoured still jutted from amid the petals.

Dagon, Fornues and the remaining soldiers finally got through the territory of the carnivorous flowers. Weary and shaken to the core many collapsed and crumbled on the ground, while others cradled their faces weeping and shaking their heads.

"I can hear the burble of the River of Life!" Fornues' face was etched with excitement.

"Quiet." Dagon tilted his head and focused his hearing. "If we can hear the sounds in the park, they can hear us. Guidance Park is beyond the trees and bushes ahead of us. We shall get close enough to see into the park, but we must remain out of sight. We must all wait in silence for Lucifer to give us the signal to attack. Stay alert, for we are not out of the woods yet."

Chapter 25

MOUNT VERVE'S LABYRINTH

Beelzebub led Lucifer and his legion of warriors into the cave. The cavern was not very wide, but three or four angels could pass through at a time. After a short while, he stopped, and several angels ran into each other.

"Why are we stopping?" Lucifer frowned.

Beelzebub trembled and giggled. He rubbed his cheeks nonstop.

Lucifer stepped toward him, and heaved a sigh. "Well? What is the matter?"

"This passage has changed." Beelzebub wore a confused expression.

"You were in this cave but a short while ago. It could not have changed in such an insignificant amount of time."

"Except it has." Beelzebub tittered. "The walls have been altered by some means and the passageway ceilings have lowered. I saw subtle variances when we first entered, but the changes have become more challenging."

The soldiers glanced at each other, their expressions marked with fear and confusion.

"More challenging? How so?" The muscles in Lucifer's face tensed.

"The tunnel before us was not here— it did not exist before." Beelzebub's wings quivered. "There is a menacing red glow emanating from it that I have never seen."

Lucifer sucked his teeth and looked at his troops. They stared back, looking stunned. "We must move on. Lead the way."

Beelzebub shifted closer. "The shaft seems to lead in the right direction toward Guidance Park, but I am afraid I am unable to guide you through it. I am weak-willed."

Lucifer glared at him. He squinted and scrunched his nose. "Remain close to me."

Was Beelzebub up to something? Perhaps Gabriel was able to convert him and now he led them to a trap? No. Beelzebub would not betray him. Then again, his love for Gabriel was great. Lucifer ordered two of his craftiest soldiers to lead them through the tunnel.

The two warriors got to their hands and knees and entered the low passage one at a time. Beelzebub followed after them, Lucifer followed him and behind him the rest of the angels crawled in a close line.

After a while, the tunnel expanded, allowing the rebels to stand. As they drew closer to the glowing red light, the temperature increased. The air became scarce, and many soldiers began to wheeze and breathe heavily.

One of the angels near the rear of the line panicked and attempted to exit the tunnel. Gasping for air, he pushed angels behind him against the walls and ran back the way they had come. As he crawled in the narrow area near the tunnel's exit, the others heard a rumble and saw rocks collapsed on him, burying him and sealing that end of the tunnel. The angels glanced at each other wide-eyed.

"There is no retreat!" Lucifer pointed at the rock pile. "Perhaps now this fact shall be embedded in your minds for all time. Keep moving onward!"

Upon hearing his command, the angel at the head of the procession continued forward.

The passage became smoky. "I am having a hard time seeing the path ahead through the smog," the lead angel told the angel behind him and Beelzebub. "My eyes sting." Beelzebub shrugged and waved his hand signaling him to continue. The lead angel and the angel following him coughed and wheezed. Beelzebub fanned the air before him.

A thick film of moisture covered the angels' bodies and their hair and garments were humid with perspiration. The lead angel's face began to singe from the intense heat emitted from the red glow ahead. Beelzebub watched great drops fall from his eyes, only to sizzle and evaporate on his cheeks.

The angel in front stopped. "The cave ends a few feet away. We must stop." A fissure interrupted the tunnel's pathway.

"Halt!" the lead angel cried, but the other angels kept pushing forward. Beelzebub panted as he rubbed his eyes and squinted. More angels began to wheeze and cough in the intense heat and smoke. They rammed into each other and pushed forward as panic began to spread through the group. They shoved the lead angel forward, closer to the edge of the deep crack.

"Stop, I implore you, stop advancing!" the angel in front shouted, to no avail. He tried to grip the rocky walls, breaking his fingernails against the surface. The angel directly behind him finally saw the pit, as did Beelzebub, but the mass of rebel angels kept moving forward.

They glanced at each other, openmouthed. Beelzebub tittered and rocked while the other angel shouted, "Stop! There is an opening!" He pointed to the ground, but the horde continued to move forward, shoving the lead angel, until he was forced off the edge of the crevasse and into a pit of molten fire. He shrieked all the while as he plummeted and then burst into flames.

Beelzebub tugged Lucifer's garments. "We must stop!" His red face looked horrified.

Lucifer saw the fear in his large, round eyes. "Halt!" All heard his sonorous voice and stopped just short of knocking the angel ahead of Beelzebub into the fissure. The angel collapsed to his knees, leaning away from the crack. His outstretched arms gripped the sides of the tunnel, while he panted.

"What do we do now?" Beelzebub gulped and caught his breath.

The angel ahead of him got to his feet. His skin singed, and smoke curls spiraled from his garments. Lucifer walked ahead to see for himself what hindered their progress. He observed the tunnel's vent and sighed.

A female angel moved ahead from the rear. "There is only a small separation between this part of the tunnel and the other side. We could fly across the fiery crevasse."

"Very well—go on. You fly across first." Lucifer stepped back and leaned against the wall.

Lucifer gestured to the angels to lean against the wall to give her room. The female angel went as far to the rear as she could to build momentum. She took a deep breath and ran toward the crevasse. As she did so, she tried to expand her wings to take flight, but she was unable to spread her wings fully, lifting herself only a little off the ground. Realizing this too late, she fell into the pit and burned. The troops stared motionless at Lucifer.

Lucifer stepped forward his face marked with stolid indifference. "There is not enough room to expand our wings in this narrow space. If we cannot expand our wings, we cannot fly."

"There must be a way to get across to the other side." Beelzebub rubbed his temples. "The crevasse is almost thirty feet across. We must cross this blazing pit before we burn alive."

Lucifer peered at the angel in the front who held onto the wall for dear life. "Leap across the fissure."

The soldier began to whimper, shaking his head. His eyes pleaded, first with Lucifer and then with Beelzebub. "S-she fell—she f-fell into the p-pit and b-burned." His teeth chattered.

Beelzebub turned away from his imploring gaze.

"Jump across to the other side!" Lucifer glared at him, but he did not move. Lucifer turned to Beelzebub. "Push him off the edge."

The other angel opened his eyes wide with disbelief. He opened his mouth to speak, but words did not come. He extended his arms in front of him and waggled his hands.

Without hesitation, Beelzebub shoved the angel into the fiery pit. The other soldiers stared with stunned and terrorized looks on their faces. Beelzebub tittered and then stopped. His trembling hand covered his mouth, but at Lucifer's glance his way, another giggle bubbled forth.

"Draw back as far as possible." Lucifer moved backward along with his soldiers, and pulled Beelzebub with him. He created a gap of a few feet between him and the crevasse.

"I shall create momentum and leap across the fissure to the other side," Lucifer said with confidence.

"After I get across," he told Beelzebub. "I want you to arrange the angels to do as I do and follow me to the other side, one by one, until they are all with me, at which instant, you shall take the leap and join us."

"As you command." Beelzebub bowed his head.

Lucifer moved back as far as he could. He ran to the edge, creating drive and without hesitation, he leapt across the fissure, making it easily to the opposite side. The soldiers clapped and cheered.

Beelzebub followed his orders, and one after another, the soldiers leapt across the crevice. Lucifer extended his hand to help the first soldier who jumped across, and then assigned him to help the others when they landed. He watched his courageous warriors soar above the fire pit to join him. A few angels did not make it across, but the majority did.

Now Beelzebub was the last angel standing on the opposite side of the fissure. He stared at the crevasse, gulped and rubbed his forehead and cheeks. "I am not as brave as the other soldiers. What if I waver and fall to a fiery death like several others did?" He paced.

"Go on Beelzebub, take the leap," Lucifer said.

"Apologies, my commander. My intellect advises me to jump, but my body does not respond."

"Lingering and burning alive is no better choice."

"Please do not leave me here to die!"

"Leap across now, or we shall continue without you." Lucifer scowled. "We have already wasted too much time."

Tears spilled from Beelzebub's eyes and evaporated in the heat of the tunnel. He moved off the sidewall, positioned himself in the center and faced Lucifer and the others. He placed the palms of his opened hands over his cheeks and pushed them in, making his lips poke out. He took a deep breath and looked over his shoulder to be sure he was as far back as he could be. Shrieking, he ran forward as fast as he could and leapt across, eyes closed.

He crashed against the ledge of the fissure. He opened his eyes to realize he had not yet made it across and gripped the edge of the crevice.

"Help me! I burn! Assist me, I implore you!" he screamed. The last soldier to cross before him reached his hand to hoist him onto the shelf.

Beelzebub took his hand. But the angel could not lift him. His feet were burning, and he shrieked in agony.

Lucifer sucked his teeth and made his way to the rim and leaned over the edge. He grabbed Beelzebub and pulled him onto the surface. Once more, the soldiers cheered.

"Move onward. We must leave this passageway at once." Frustration crept into Lucifer's voice.

The passage became narrow and low for a stretch, and his soldiers began to crawl again, until the shaft opened into a larger cavity in which the rebels were able to stand and walk once more. Once all the surviving soldiers were out of the tunnel, Lucifer commanded Beelzebub to lead them once more.

"I can see Floraison's light from here." Beelzebub trembled with excitement. "It is the light in Guidance Park."

"We must proceed with caution and be silent." Lucifer pushed him forward.

As they got closer to the light, they heard the roar of the Divina Waterfall. They began to hoot, laugh, and rush toward the familiar sound.

"Maintain formation." Lucifer glared at an angel guffawing. "If I have to silence you once more, I shall rip your throat out with my bare hands." The soldier and others became silent at once.

"We shall wait behind the waterfall until I sense all troops are ready for my signal. Then we shall attack with a force Floraison has never seen."

The soldiers nodded their approval.

Beelzebub had not betrayed them after all. They would storm out of this cave from behind the Divina Waterfall. As they made their way into Guidance Park, they would be soaked with the holy water, which plunges into the River of Life. Drenched in this healing water, Lucifer would be invincible. He would have his victory and rule Floraison with his queen, Lilith, by his side.

Chapter 26

SIGNAL TO SLAUGHTER

Lucifer stood behind the waterfall. He closed his eyes, sensing his generals and all his insurgents scattered around the perimeter of the park. By now, the generals would have discussed in detail a well-devised strategy of attack with their troops.

He felt their energy. They were waiting for his signal.

"Beelzebub, hand me your bone flute." Lucifer extended his hand.

Beelzebub searched throughout the front and sides of his garment, but could not find the instrument anywhere.

Lucifer frowned. "Where is it?" he asked under his breath.

"I—cannot—"He tittered, at a loss for words.

"Here it is," a soldier standing behind Beelzebub held the flute.

He stepped forward and handed it to Lucifer. "It was hanging off the back of Beelzebub's garment. Perhaps it had shifted from its original place when he leapt across the split in the tunnel."

Beelzebub exhaled with relief. Lucifer closed his eyes and heaved a deep sigh. Then he grinned, and faced his unit.

"The others are ready and waiting for my signal. Prepare yourselves. After I give the signal, we shall run through the opening behind the waterfall, immersing ourselves in the pure waters, and enter Guidance Park in full mental and physical capacity. We are fierce warriors. We shall slaughter Michael and his holy angels without mercy. Then Floraison shall be mine to govern, and you shall be free."

Lucifer's soldiers beamed, nodding and fidgeting as their leader brought the musical pipe to his lips and blew.

The sinister and gloomy disharmony, amplified by the Divina Waterfall, drifted from the cave into Guidance Park. Michael and all those in the park, as well as Lucifer's hordes standing by at the perimeter, heard the terrible music loud and clear.

Michael cocked his head and looked at his generals. "What is that?" His generals looked as confused as he. The holy angels covered their ears and cringed.

"What is producing that crippling sound?" Michael scanned the park.

His generals glanced at each other, disoriented by the sinister music, while their troops remained dazed and confused. Most continued covering their ears, many closing their eyes and yelling to muffle the unpleasant sound.

Cam leaned with his right ear, his eyes twitching now and again. The music sounded familiar. Where had he heard this devastating sound before? He placed a hand on his forehead, cocked his head left and rolled his eyes to the right. "I remember—" He lumbered across the platform to Michael. "I remember visiting Beelzebub in his chamber while he played a horrible bone flute. I left his bungalow in a hurry, unable to tolerate the depressing noise."

Michael inhaled a sharp breath and leaped into action feet hammering the flat rock podium. "Holy angels!" He stretched out his arms. "The enemy means to debilitate and distract us with this wicked disharmony. The sound comes from a device made by Beelzebub's treacherous hands! We must not focus on this instrument of deceit!"

The cacophony stopped.

Rebels rained down from Mount Verve, swarmed from the East, West and South, and emerged from the River of Life.

Michael and his generals leaped into action and stormed off the platform to fight.

Dark angels dashed in every direction. They stabbed, speared and gouged without mercy each holy angel they made contact with, and with ferocity never before witnessed in Floraison. The violence and depravity of the attacks stunned Michael's army. Despite their superior weapons, they were being annihilated.

Michael battled his way through the melee and climbed atop his platform rock once more. "We are God's Heavenly forces." Michael's silvery voice rang through the park. "The conflict between good and evil has begun. Wield your weapons without fear, holy angels, for we have the strength of God on our side."

Michael scanned Guidance Park and witnessed a myriad of his soldiers being cut to pieces. He slammed his eyes shut and opened them again. "Father, we need you!"

A mass of whirling air developed in the sky above him. The center of the vortex opened and a resplendent light poured over Michael.

His verdant eyes rolled skyward. An ethereal hand advanced through the opening and one finger touched the crown of his head. A shimmering, translucent chrysalis formed over his skin. Above Michael's head where God's finger touched him a brilliant, airy ring formed. "The strength of God courses within me. I am powerful, my senses are sharper, and I know that good shall triumph over evil." Michael declared in a booming voice. All angels were compelled to stop and listen.

"Holy angels, it was for this moment we were created! I do not need to tell you your duty. I do not have to inform you who you are. Lilith, Lucifer, and their dark forces have chosen to defy God and revolt against his followers, and for this, His wrath shall be terrible." Michael spoke with a faith and strength neither rebels nor righteous angels had ever heard, and his words gave the holy angels the might and assurance to succeed. "Show these rebellious angels no mercy, for you shall receive none!"

The consecrated angels were inspired and fought with conviction, defeating rebel after rebel, capturing many and detaining them for judgment. They secured the west side of the park and kept the captured in the West Forest with the help of the warrior vegetation. However, many rebels remained in the south and dominated the south portion of the

River of Life, creating a safe passage for injured comrades to enter the healing waters.

"We shall wield the hand of God and cut you down!" Michael pointed at the rebels still fighting.

Across the park, Lucifer set his sights on Michael and took long-legged strides in his direction, slashing with his short swords through groups of holy angels trying to stop him. He must put an end to Michael's rhetoric for it had motivated his troops too well.

Lucifer met Michael's unrelenting stare and continued to rush toward him. Michael's eyes narrowed to slits and flung his golden spear. The gilded weapon struck Lucifer in the chest, hurling him against a group of his rebel soldiers.

Lucifer felt an explosion in his core. Excruciating, vivid pain, unlike anything he had ever experienced, blinded him. The spear pierced his chest wall, missing his heart, exited his back, and pinned him to the ground. He stared dumbfounded at it, shaking his head. He attempted to pull it out, but howled and wailed instead. As rebel angels around him tried to help, holy angels who were waiting for Michael to claim his prize eliminated them at once.

Lucifer's eyes flashed wildly while he continued to shake his head in denial. He could not be defeated. He stared wide-eyed before him, as he lay sprawled on the ground, immobilized. The physical and mental anguish overwhelmed him. *Lilith, I have failed you.* He drooped his head and wept for the first time.

Michael lumbered across the park to Lucifer. He hovered over him like a threatening storm. Lucifer clenched his jaw at the sight of the manacles he held.

"You did this to yourself." Michael shackled him with ease.

Meanwhile, Lilith barged ahead searching for Lucifer. Battling her way through clusters of holy angels, slashing one after another with her sword. She skidded to an abrupt halt when she caught sight of him, crumpled on the ground, captured by Michael. She pivoted on her heel and ran, dragging her sword on the ground, to take cover behind a large tree nearby. Her chest heaved, and her eyes stung with gathering tears. She sagged against the tree, the color drained from her slack face. She peered around the trunk and stared wide-eyed at Lucifer.

Jetrel had been stalking her for a while, following her from the south to the north and watching her strike down many of her friends. Jetrel witnessed Michael's victory over Lucifer, and she desired a victory of her own. What could be worthier than capturing Lilith?

Lilith no longer wore an arrogant, self-satisfied expression; instead she appeared devastated, as if she were already captured. As she stared at Lucifer, Jetrel moved stealthily and crept her way up to her.

Jetrel grabbed her and Lilith struggled to get away. Raquel rushed over and struck Lilith's leg with her mace. Lilith became disoriented and completely susceptible to Raquel's bidding.

"Lilith, stand and surrender," Raquel said. "Proceed with Jetrel to face God's judgment."

Upon witnessing both Lucifer and Lilith captured, many rebels collapsed in stupor and captured, others dropped their swords and surrendered.

Soon Michael and his holy angels gained the upper hand. Hashmal annihilated large groups of rebels at once with his ability to emit fire. Fornues was caught in Raphael's indestructible net and was rendered paralyzed, allowing Raphael to bring him to justice.

Dagon flew over Cam's head and kicked him in the upper spine, rendering the Seraph breathless. He prepared to strike again, but Cam swung his blazing sword and sheared his wing. Dagon fell to the ground face down, his wing severed and burning. Cam leapt on him, tied his arms behind him, and detained him.

Hidden among a pile of rebel corpses not far from where Dagon was captured, Beelzebub peered in the direction of the Divina Waterfall. If only he could reach his once place of refuge, he could hide in the cave behind the falls until the conflict ended. He moved severed limbs, torsos, and heads until he was able to stand. He took a deep breath and ran.

A few steps from the entrance to his cavern, a vicious yank held him. Beelzebub struggled to get loose, agape, flailing his arms about, and flicking his eyes in every direction. An invisible force held him, preventing him from moving forward.

Raquel swooped upon him and clobbered him with her mace,

smashing his cheek against his teeth. Once the weapon's stone head made contact with his skin, Beelzebub surrendered to her will. Gabriel materialized before him, revealing himself as the powerful force that prevented his escape.

Across the park, Gadreel spun about several times searching for an escape. "We are defeated—how has this come to pass?" Her eyebrows bumped together in a scowl. She balled her hand and held it tight against her mouth so no sound would escape. Her eyes shifted to the River of Life. For a moment the roar of the river suppressed all other sounds.

She could disappear into the wide river. Gadreel panted and trembled. She would hide underneath the water letting the current take her, poking her nose and mouth above the water only when she must draw breath. Once she escaped Guidance Park, she could emerge from the river and hide until it was all finished.

She skulked past the edges of the troops and slid into the water submerging herself deeply in the River of Life. As she held her breath underwater, a feeling of dread crept over her. A cold wave passed through her and brillante turned to nightglow as an enormous dark figure loomed above her, blocking Floraison's luminosity. She opened her mouth to scream, but bubbles appeared instead.

The gigantic aquatic creature opened its mouth and she was being pulled into it. She clawed at the river's edge and flailed her four large wings, but the creature's open mouth kept dragging her toward it until the leviathan swallowed her whole.

Gadreel remained in the rear of the creature's mouth, holding on to one of its immense teeth. The creature emerged from the river and spewed her onto the bank. Sprawled on the side of the river, she inhaled a sharp breath. She lifted her hooded, brown eyes and stared imploringly at Hashmal, who stood before her. As she trembled and stared at Hashmal and the massive head of the creature, her lips set in a grim line, the leviathan transformed into Esar. She rose to her knees pressing her hands to her bosom and burst into convulsive sobs. Esar walked to her and offered his outstretched hand. He pulled her off the ground and prepared to take her to God's throne room where her fate would be determined.

Samael and his troops delivered a gruesome death to many holy angels with their swords coated in poison from the trees on Mount Verve's summit. At one point he was able to pause in fighting, and he scanned his surroundings. His shoulders slumped and his brows knitted in a frown when he saw countless of his troops lying on the ground dead or dying.

He wavered. "We are losing this battle." He looked stunned as he muttered. "How is this possible?" He looked toward the northwest and saw Michael's spear dive like a golden falcon and strike Lucifer down. He panted openmouthed and dropped his bloodied pike. He gawped as Michael grabbed Lucifer and restrained him effortlessly. His clouded eyes rolled about and settled on the South Forest.

He would escape through the dark woods, for all was lost now that Lucifer had been captured. Lilith was able to make it through, and so would he. He picked up his pike and a dead soldier's sword from the ground. Gripping both weapons, he stormed toward the dark woodland. He made it into the forest but soon afterward, he heard someone behind him—making a clicking noise in the back of his throat. His knees began to falter and he staggered as he recognized the sound. Without turning around he stopped and slammed his eyes shut.

Hashmal cleared his throat and expelled his fiery breath setting the vegetation surrounding Samael alight in vigorous flames. The heat emitted by the fire scorched Samael's skin. He pivoted on his heel and faced Hashmal with a gapping mouth stare and outstretched arms. "I shall not escape. Do not burn me I implore you." Fire and smoke enclosed him. He wheezed and coughed, and tottered unsteadily then collapsed.

As he lay crumpled on the ground, a disembodied arm reached to him through the heavy smoke and pulled him out of the forest and back into the Park. When Samael was done expelling hot, thick smoke from his lungs, he lifted his eyes and saw his captors.

Hashmal and Gabriel, in spirit form, stood before him. Hashmal glared at him with fierce red eyes and yanked him by the arm to his feet. "We shall take you before God for judgment." Once all the generals of the dark forces were detained, it was only a matter of time before all of the rebel angels were vanquished.

Lilith, and the remaining rebels were shackled and blindfolded before they were taken through the portal into Metá Heaven. Once inside the throne room their captors stood behind them and compelled them to their knees. Their blindfolds were removed and they were forced to recline on the ground in prostrate manner, eyes closed tight and face buried, lest they be blinded by God's presence—for they were marred by sin and no longer pure. They were lined up a short distance from each other, but they could not speak nor hear anything other than God's voice directed at them.

Lilith did not shed a tear as she lay face down in the presence of God. Her face was crimson with fury, nostrils flared, she curled her lips with icy contempt and gritted her teeth. She did not know what her fate or that of the others would be, but she would not show fear or weakness.

Then God spoke.

Lilith, thou hast always refused to abide by the existing rules in Floraison. Thou hast a rebellious heart, persistently craving more and not realizing thou already had all thy heart desired. Thou aspired to be Queen of Floraison. As the highest-ranking cherubim, thou wast royalty. Yet thine ambitions hath no bounds. Thou hast imparted thine own punishment.

God set his sights on Lucifer.

Lucifer, I loved thee. Thou wast my favorite. In thee, I created perfection with the most beautiful light. Thou shalt no longer be called Lucifer for thou art no longer the light bearer; darkness is what now resides in thee. From this moment forward thy name shall be Satan for thou hast become my adversary. Thou chose to follow a baleful creature, turning from the light and benighted by her desires. Thou hast disappointed me the most.

Lucifer inhaled a sharp breath. I did it for love. His body was racked with sobs.

God ordered the rebels be taken to the edge of Floraison to await sentencing.

Restrained by the Archangels and Powers, the rebels waited. They were not close enough to see each other, and only heard the voices of the angels restraining them and God's voice. They were not told that all the rebels had been dispersed along the edge of Floraison. Each thought he or she stood alone.

Thou hast sinned against me. For this, thou shalt be cast out of Floraison to live on planet Earth amongst the creatures thee thought so vile.

Lilith jutted her chin. God's words were like knives in her ears and the muscles in her face tightened. God commanded the rebels' garments be removed. Her body stiffened and she clamped her fingers into the tender flesh of her palms. Snarling she fought against the holy angels as her vestment was removed by force. She did not know how or when, but she would have her vengeance.

Thou shalt suffer many adversities, for thou wast ungrateful for the many gifts I bestowed upon thee.

Gadreel allowed the Powers to undress her without a struggle. She stood with slumped shoulders, stared at her feet and wept.

Thou shalt not remain in your likeness. As thou enter the Earth's atmosphere, thou shalt be transformed.

Lucifer slouched, his body racked with pain. He cringed and moaned as the Powers removed his garment. His pride was in equal pain. He thought about his humiliating defeat. How could he have failed? He sensed Lilith's presence. What must she think of him now? He lowered his head.

God sentenced all remaining rebels, with the exception of a few chosen ones, to live in exile on planet Earth.

Ye shalt be in exile, and planet Earth shalt not welcome ye— ye shall always be outcasts. Ye mayst seek redemption, but mayst never return to Floraison. Earth shall be thy prison for all time.

One by one, the angels of darkness were cast out to live amongst the creatures they despised. The fallen angels were never to set foot in Floraison again.

THE FALL OF LILITH

OF

LILITH

BOOK II

EARTH

Chapter 1

LILITH'S FATE

L ilith fell to Earth, crashing through trees, feeling the collision with every branch she broke along the way. She landed on moist ground and lost consciousness. When she awoke face down in the dark mud, she blinked owlishly at the dense vegetation surrounding her. Sunlight was barely able to filter through the massive trees.

She trembled as the forest absorbed her warmth. "I suffer an odd, distressing decrease in temperature I had never perceived in Floraison—not even in the forbidden forests." Her brows knitted in a frown. She passed her hands over her arms and touched her hair. "My skin and hair are wet, as if I had emerged from Lake Serena." Dark mud covered part of her arms, hands and chest. She brought her muddy hands to her nose, sniffed, gagged at the smell and wiped as much of it as possible against a rock.

"Everything about this place is eerie. The smells, the sounds—even the air feels dense like it's refusing to share its nutrients with me. It's hard to breathe." She looked around, eyes wide, forehead puckered. "Shall I survive this ominous atmosphere?" She lowered her head and heaved a deep breath.

Everything around her had a peculiar odor, different from anything she had sensed before. The damp leaves, wet moss, and vegetation combined to form a woody, musky, and slightly decaying odor. "The smells of decomposing plants, animal droppings, and wet creatures lurking about are horrid and repulsive!" She squirmed, her nose wrinkled at the smells and she gagged again. "I am not safe here."

"Where beams of light shine through the trees, strange shadows dance." She screwed up her face ready to cry. "This harsh planet evokes memories of the terrors I endured in the East and South Forests in Floraison, but I shall not cry." She clenched her dirty hands. With each new noise, her heart leapt to her throat. Branches creaking, leaves rustling, birds squawking, hostile screeches from unknown animals, the beat of paws against the ground—these sounds created a symphony of fear.

"I must remain calm," Lilith told herself in a low voice. "After all, this is Earth. I watched most of Creation, and I did not witness God create anything as menacing on this planet as in the forests in Floraison."

Still, she knew much had happened besides creation during Creation.

The trees loomed over her. They seemed to have eyes, which glowered at her with malice for breaking their limbs on her descent. The wind wailed through their distorted trunks causing an awful, lamenting clamor. Lilith's body stiffened.

In some ways, the noisy, wretched gusts reminded her of Fornues, who always whined or grumbled about one thing or another.

"Oh, Fornues, how I wish you were here. Even the company of a dim-witted ruffian such as you would be better than being alone." Her chest heaved, and her eyes burned with pooling tears. "I shall not weep!" She slammed her fist on the ground.

Where could she go? Was she imprisoned here? Was she doomed to die in this revolting forest alone?

"Lu–Lu," Lilith wished to scream his name, but could not pronounce it. She made another attempt.

"L-Lu-Lu–Satan." Lilith gasped. "Satan?" She cocked her head left and rolled her eyes to the right corner of the canopy. After a short moment, Satan was the only name she could remember calling him.

Above, an owl screeched. She flinched, then lifted her face to see it land to perch near another owl. The two began to hoot in harmony. She crossed her arms and with her hands cusped her upper arms and rubbed. "Satan—I need you more than ever." She heaved a deep sigh.

Where was he? Had he suffered the same fate as her? Was he far away—or close by, perhaps? "Please, give me a sign, and I shall come to you." Her voice was but a breath.

Yellow eyes glared at her from overgrown bushes. Her breathing became fast and shallow, and her heart pounded.

She made an awkward attempt to get off the ground but failed to rise. Using her arms to push herself off the wet soil, she tumbled face first into the mud again. "My legs must be bound together." She kicked and struggled to free her limbs, but when she finally set eyes on her lower body, the color drained from her face.

She dug her fingers into the ground and clutched handfuls of dirt crushing it in her fists and then flinging it at the trees. She shrieked, her face crimson with rage. For a lengthy period she sat on the cold, wet dirt with her face in her hands, shuddering, seized in utter grief. She cocked her head back and released a long, drawn out scream.

"Banishment was not enough?" Lilith glared upward. "You transform me into a lowly, revolting creature, requiring me to drag my body through the filth of the Earth for the rest of days?" She brandished her fists. "I shall have my vengeance!"

Lilith now possessed the naked torso of a woman, but the lower body of a snake. She examined herself further and discovered her four wings were no longer white, but black like the jungle. They were covered in eyes, some with brown irises, some with blue ones, resembling her own. Again she screamed in horror and shook her head, unable to accept the transformation.

With a sharp intake of breath, she scrambled to trace her eyes with her hand.

Yes, they were in their proper place.

She proceeded to explore the rest of her face with her fingers. She passed her hands over her head and clutched her hair. She touched her shoulders and chest and realized she was not changed above her waist. She took a deep breath, feeling ample relief.

She tittered. "I am but half a fiend. It is better than being a complete monstrosity." She slammed her eyes shut. "Things shall not always be as they are."

She wiped the tears and mud from her eyes and face. "I must leave this place." If she was exiled to this planet then there was a chance that the others were too. She must try to find them, for she no longer wished to be alone. She needed Satan and the others if she was to exact her revenge, and there was safety in numbers.

The forest was too dense so she did not try to fly, but she made another attempt to move. By undulating her tail and pushing it against rocks, twigs, and irregularities in the soil, she was finally able to advance. She slid along the jungle floor, not knowing where she was headed in the dark, only that she wished to exit the eerie place as soon as possible and find her friends.

Slinking ahead, she passed strange plants and twisted vines reminiscent of the South Forest. She shivered. Her head turned in several directions as she moved. It was never still.

She forced her way through the tangled vegetation until she heard crying in the distance. She halted and leaned with her right ear to determine where it came from. "That sound is familiar. Could it be one of my allies?" She proceeded in the direction of the weeping.

Lilith pressed the back of her hand over her nostrils. "The stench of the rotting wood and plants is overwhelming." She shuddered and focused on the beams of light fighting their way through the tall, dense trees. The radiance of the sun was dissimilar from the light in Floraison. She was fascinated by it and feared it at the same time.

She halted and stared ahead slack-mouthed. A tree's root grew around a huge rock, concealing it almost completely. Vines and other creeping plants devoured what remained. "If I stood still long enough, would the jungle consume me too?" She burst onward and made haste.

Lilith heard bubbling water nearby and smiled. "The thought of cleansing this filthy, black mud from my face and body is alluring." She followed the sound to a cascade, which emptied into a lake in the midst of the jungle.

The air at the waterfall was crisp and fresh. She heaved a deep breath. She crawled to the edge of the bank and peered into the water. "What menacing creatures lurk underneath these waters?" She recalled the snake-fish that mercilessly attacked her troops in a river in the South Forest.

"There is nothing like that here on Earth." She tittered and slid into the lake. She flailed at first but then realized she could move effortlessly in water. She positioned herself underneath the cascades, grinning as the water splashed on her shoulders and back, kneading her painful muscles.

Feeling clean and refreshed she resumed her trek to find the source of the wailing sounds. She slithered along, accidentally bumping her arm into a large, thorny bush.

Lilith howled and cringed in pain. The jungle whirled and she swayed. Peering at her limb with a painful grimace, she saw small barbs buried under her skin. She shook her arm to dislodge them, but this only caused her to stoop and moan.

With her fingernails, she pulled at one of the thorns and shrieked. Steeling herself, she pinched the exposed head of a thorn and was able to pull it out of her skin, though she winced all the while. Once the thorn was gone from her arm, the pain began to diminish. Sobbing and flinching she pulled out the thorns one by one. In the end, her arm was red, swollen, and continued to throb, but the pain was fading, so she proceeded.

She came across massive animal prints in the mud. "These marks were made by a creature that walks on two enormous feet." She jolted and scanned the area for any sign of the brute. Nothing. She proceeded in silence and remained alert.

A creature jumped out from behind a huge tree and stood a few steps in front of her. Lilith stared with wide eyes and stood motionless. The beast's body was covered in thick, brownish hair, and it appeared vaguely human. "I remember seeing a creature such as you near the end of creation." She observed it.

The creature's head was large with small brown eyes, which appeared to have knowledge behind them. Its arms were longer than its legs, and its large hands were shaped similarly to hers. The beast moved from side to side, beating its wide chest, and making grunting noises. Lilith tilted her head sideways, and squinted in a curious manner unsure what to make of the animal's display.

After a while, the animal advanced toward her, walking on its knuckles.

Her body stiffened and she leaned away from it, extended her arms before her and waggled her hands. "Do not harm me!" When the beast reached her, it rose to a two-legged stance and peered at her face, as if trying to understand what she was.

The mammal scrutinized her injured arm with its beady eyes and began to grunt and hoot, as if attempting to communicate with her. Lilith gagged at the animal's breath. "You are beginning to bore me beast." Frustration crinkled her eyes. Her tail began to rattle.

The animal gawked at her in a way that suggested it found her appealing. It reached for her hair, but she smacked its hand away. Her brow knitted in a frown.

"You dare touch me?" Her eyes burned with hatred. "I do not wish to be tainted by a creature as revolting as you!" She gritted her teeth. "The beasts on this planet do not know their place. I do not belong here. I am a celestial being." She stood straighter and jutted her chin with pride. After a short moment, her face wilted and she stared at the ground with slumped shoulders. Did God toss her unto this world to become merely another beast? "I shall never accept this."

"I am not an animal!" Lilith shouted to the Heavens, clenching her fists.

The gorilla growled and beat its chest. She flinched and stared. The creature grabbed her injured arm and yanked her toward it. A bolt of pain traveled through her arm, and she squealed.

The ape released her at once and retreated, its beady eyes wide. Lilith's tail whipped out, coiled around the gorilla's body, and began to thrash it violently. The animal's painful groans were terrible. Birds squawked, felines roared, and other mammals grunted, snorted, and growled in unison as if protesting her cruel act.

Enraged, Lilith ignored the jungle animals' pleas. She tightened her grip around the gorilla until she crushed its bones with the immense strength of her tail. She dropped the brute, deprived of existence, on the muddy ground.

Her eyes flashed with fury as she panted. The beings on this planet would receive the same mercy God had showed her when He cast her from Floraison to live among them as an animal.

Other creatures witnessed the torture and brutal slaughter. The terrified animals remained hidden within the dense vegetation until Lilith slithered out of sight. Many beasts that beheld the atrocity would remember and share what came to pass with others.

Lilith forged ahead in the direction of the weeping until she finally exited the jungle. As she entered the open savannah, her body was struck by the immense heat and radiance of the sun's rays. She paused to get a good reading on the relentless sobs then proceeded toward the source.

She staggered and swayed as she began to wither in the sun. God had bequeathed Gabriel the power to rule over the sun. She was now certain the cloudless sky and burning rays bearing down on her were his doing.

"I shall have my vengeance. I shall have my vengeance—" She repeated over and over. It helped her go on.

In search of relief from the powerful sun, she scanned her surroundings, becoming hopeful when she saw tall grasses, shrubs, and isolated trees scattered about. She hurried past a large herd of hoofed animals grazing on the grass, to a nearby tree. Although the tree's trunk was thick and rather wide, its branches were too few and too high to offer much protection from the sun.

Lilith spread her four dark wings and placed them together above her head. This shaded her face and body, but her black wings absorbed the sunlight and seemed ablaze.

She dragged herself over the new terrain. She was certain now that the sobs belonged to one of her allies. It was essential she find a friend. "I can not endure this desolate place alone."

Chapter 2

GADREEL'S BRUTAL ENCOUNTERS

Gadreel tumbled from Floraison, bawling all the while. As she fell, she trembled with fear and regret, but still she could not stop thinking about Samael.

Did he still draw breath? If he was yet alive, would she survive to be reunited with him on Earth?

She was still thinking of him when she collided with Earth and lost consciousness.

A pride of lions in the vicinity watched with curiosity as she fell out of the sky. They heard the impact of her arrival on the grasslands. A male lion decided to leave his pride to investigate.

As Gadreel lay lifeless, sprawled on the grass the lion approached her and peered for a long while at the strange winged creature, covered in sod, lying before him. Finally, he passed his coarse, wet tongue over her neck and face.

The sound of a lapping tongue woke Gadreel. Feeling woozy, she cradled her head in her hands and opened her eyes halfway. Little by little she sat upright. She winced and whimpered in pain and wiped saliva off her face with care. The curious beast gazed at her. She squinted in an inquisitive manner.

The lion roared. Her body shook with the tremor of the thunderous sound. She closed her eyes, shielding her ears with her hands, but she was not afraid. She intuited the creature meant her no harm.

The lion pranced away and jumped onto a large boulder. He swished his golden mane several times flaunting its length and thickness. She watched and giggled at his playfulness. She rustled her head of long golden curls at the beast. As the large feline sat upright on the rock, she gawked at his magnificence. He swayed his tail slowly from side to side with pride.

The sun beamed on him like a spotlight, he swiveled and shook his golden mane once more. Gadreel chortled and clapped. "Oh, you put on quite a show. I find you endearing." The lion jumped off the large rock and proceeded to her.

Its mane glinted in the sunshine, and the elegant and dashing creature fascinated her. She extended her hand to stroke his mane, and he lowered his head, permitting her to do so. She giggled as she caressed the lion's fur and gently tapped his wet, shiny nose.

Her face twisted in pain as she struggled to her feet. The lion watched her and tilted his head to the side with a curious expression. Full of play, she passed her hands across the cat's length and tickled her face with his tail. She moved toward his head and stared into his big, bright eyes.

"You are a beautiful and amusing beast." She put her arms around the its burly neck and cuddled the cat. The embrace was interrupted by a loud, angry growl from behind her.

Startled, she released the lion and turned to look. All the females in the pride were positioned before her, snarling. One large young female stepped forward. The lioness's face was creased, her small eyes focused on Gadreel. She bared her fangs.

Gadreel trembled and scuttled away from the lion's side. She fiddled with her hands and toddled toward the lioness, biting her lips.

"I meant no harm." Gadreel lowered her head. "I did not mean to invade your territory or take what is yours."

The lioness roared and growled at her. The animal twitched her tail and wiggled her hindquarters, signaling she was about to attack.

Gadreel sensed the lioness's intentions.

"No! I implore you!" She spun on her heel to flee, but the feline pounced on her, knocking her down face first. The lioness's claws dug deep into her flesh, Gadreel screamed in agony, as the immense weight of the cat pushed her into the ground. The lioness raised her paw, claws spread to rip Gadreel's wings apart, but the loud, dominant roar of the male lion immobilized her.

The lion flounced to the lioness, and they growled at each other, seeming to argue. Finally, the lioness padded away from Gadreel, roaring her rage. Without hesitation, the angel rose from the ground, ignoring the pain the lioness had inflicted on her body and ran. She made several attempts to fly, but the lioness had injured her wings.

She ran until she no longer heard the lions' roars. She sought refuge under a shady tree, and sagged against the trunk to the ground. It was cooler in the shade, away from the burning rays of the sun. Her chest heaved as she squeezed her arms and legs, wincing in pain. She lay down her head and closed her eyes.

Gadreel envisioned Samael's bright smile. The thought of his smoldering, amber eyes gazing into hers gave her comfort. Her daydream was intruded upon by a peculiar hissing sound.

When she opened her eyes she met the disconcerting stare of a slithering reptile hiding in the tree's trunk. She gasped and recoiled from the serpent. She observed how the strange, scaly creature moved with its long, limbless body.

The cobra slithered in her direction and lifted its head. The area by its head grew much wider than its body as it opened its hood. The reptile hissed, flicked its tongue, and flashed its sharp fangs. Beginning with its unblinking stare, the snake's entire aspect was menacing.

"Please do not cause me harm." Gadreel clambered to her feet and prepared to run away.

The spitting cobra shot venom into her eyes, rendering her temporarily blind. Thrown into darkness, she screamed and clutched at her stinging eyes. The snake launched forth and bit her on the neck.

Gadreel shrieked, staggering about in circles, her outstretched arms reaching in the blackness. She grasped her throat with both hands wheezing and gasping for air until she collapsed, unconscious.

After a while, she awoke kicking her feet and flailing her arms, as if fending off another attack from the legless reptile. In time, she realized the snake was gone. She crumpled in a heap on the grass, her eyes red, her neck swollen, and throbbing. "This planet is as hostile as the forests that surround Guidance Park. Is there no escape?" Her voice was hoarse with a horrified tone.

The day turned into night. Lilith had spoken of her experience with total darkness in Floraison when she was punished in the East Forest and the insects covered her eyes, but Gadreel had never experienced the darkness of night.

The grasslands came to life at night with unfamiliar noises. She heard a sharp, thrilling call overhead, the leaping and bounding of fleet-footed creatures avoiding predators on the ground, and all manner of growls, clicks, and hoots. An eerie, cold sensation crept into her bones.

She curled into a tight ball and trembled in the darkness. When the sun rose the following morning, she was astonished she had made it through the night.

The thought of remaining forever alone on this harsh planet made her blanch. She moaned and tears flowed from her painfully irritated eyes. Without any knowledge of what to do or where to go, she despaired.

Chapter 3

ALLIES REUNITE

L ilith followed the weeping noises for several long days and short
nights until she came to open grassland, where she found her friend
lying face down, wailing.

She rushed to her. "Do not lament. You are no longer alone."

Gadreel lifted her head and saw Lilith's face. She flipped over, propped
herself on her elbows and beamed—until she caught sight of her scaly tail.

Gadreel's face contorted with aversion and fear. Lilith scowled. "Stand
on your feet. Let me look at you."

Grimacing and moaning because her body still ached, Gadreel got to
her feet. Lilith inspected her from head to toe. Gadreel's delightful curvy
figure had not changed. Her clusters of long, untamed blonde curls still glistened in the light. Her heart-shaped face still carried the look of innocence:
rosy cheeks, small pouting mouth and big, hooded brown eyes. The only
apparent change was in her four wings, which were no longer
pure white—they were now comprised of areas both light and
dark.

Lilith raised the brow above her blue eye and scowled.

"Lilith, why do you stare at me thus?"

"You have not changed much since we were
exiled from Floraison. I merely wondered
why that is so, and what it may signify."

She received a streak of black across her wings. That is all. God had punished Lilith so severely, yet spared Gadreel the agony of being a monstrosity. Did she not rebel as Lilith did? Did Gadreel not disobey his laws too?

"What is your meaning?" Gadreel's lips closed in a grim line.

A lion roared in the distance, which made her jump. Lilith looked around, trying to decide what her next move should be. Gadreel pulled closer to her friend and remained by her side as she glided to and fro, inspecting the land. A large spotted creature hid in the tall grass. Its glittering eyes stared at them. They heard mews, hisses, and growls all around them.

Gadreel glanced through the area, wide-eyed. "Where are we?"

"We are on Earth. Where else would we be?" Lilith rolled her eyes.

"I meant to ask, where on Earth are we?"

Lilith cocked her head. "Quiet! I sensed a powerful disturbance underneath the deep ocean, a great distance from where we stand." She stared toward the west.

Gadreel nibbled her fingers as she watched Lilith, who seemed to be in a trance.

An earsplitting sound woke Lilith from her trance and caused both angels to shield their ears.

"What is that horrible sound?" Gadreel winced. "It conquers all other sounds and pains my head."

"I had a vision." Lilith stared ahead. "I saw a great being struggling in icy waters. I could not distinguish who it was."

Lilith slithered away in the direction of the sound, leading the way to the unknown.

Gadreel dusted off her naked body and chased after her. "Where are we going?"

Receiving no answer, she asked again in a determined voice, "Where are we headed, Lilith?"

Lilith turned and glared at her. Gadreel flinched. Perceiving the other angel's fear, Lilith wore a dull smile and explained. "I believe our allies have also been exiled on Earth. The disturbing shrill sound must come from one of our allies— perhaps Satan—we must follow it to its source. Thus, we are going on a journey to find the others."

Chapter 4

THE ANGRY MOUNTAIN

For many miles, over many long days and short nights, stopping only for rest, Lilith and Gadreel followed the penetrating, high-pitched sound through the grassland. Suddenly, it ceased.

Lilith skittered to and fro, breathing hard, and flattening the high grasses with her heavy tail. Her wide eyes flickered over the expansive plains and at the mountains in the distance.

"The shrill in my head has stopped. Do you hear it?"

"No, I too have ceased to hear it." Gadreel bit her lower lip and puckered her brow. "Without the shrill to guide us, we shall wander forevermore."

Lilith saw fear etched on Gadreel's face. She shut her eyes and inhaled a deep breath and blew out slowly. "You and I shall advance in the same direction until the sound returns. We shall rejoin the others for I shall have my vengeance against God, and I cannot do it alone."

"Perhaps we should not think in terms of revenge." Gadreel's voice was soft. "Let us join our friends and find a suitable place to settle and live in peace."

"Peace?" Lilith's nostrils flared. "You speak of peace when I am on a quest to destroy those who betrayed me."

"Betrayed you?" Gadreel's lips quivered. "We are the disloyal ones. We betrayed God and our brethren."

"They gave us no choice!" Lilith clenched her fists. "We had to rebel, for we were treated unfairly."

"Your anger and lust for power have already condemned us to this hostile planet. Please stop speaking of revenge and perhaps our fate shall change."

Lilith's eyes narrowed. "I am beginning to see why you were not transformed into a hideous creature as I was. You are an emissary for God and the holy angels!"

Lilith knocked her to the ground with her serpent's tail. Gadreel lay on her side, cringing and shaking in fear. She rubbed her torso with one hand and held her other arm in front of her head as a shield. "No, no! I am your friend and ally!"

"You are either with me or with them." She pointed to the sky. "You cannot have it both ways. If your allegiance is to God, then I shall leave you. From this day forth, you shall be my enemy, and my vengeance shall fall upon you, too!"

"No, please do not leave me. I shall not survive without you. I am sorry I have grieved you. I shall do all that you ask. My allegiance is to you."

"Stand!"

Gadreel stood as hastily as possible.

"Grieve me no more." Lilith slithered away.

Gadreel nodded and shuffled behind her, head hung low.

As they trudged on, sweltering heat enveloped them, and the sun's rays made their skin sizzle. Hours went by, and the nearby mountains appeared much closer.

Gadreel staggered and fell to her knees. "There was no sun in Floraison to torture us. We had brillantes, a time of divine light, which was like the warmth of God's smile. Here on earth, we have to endure days of glaring, fiery light, which stings our bodies and perturbs our minds. In Floraison, we had nightglows when light dimmed to a soft glow, which reminded us that God was still near. Here, we have night—the absence of light when we are left on our own. I miss our home." She wailed into her hands.

Lilith glared at her. "Floraison is no longer home to us. Earth is our home now and griping shall not change anything." Gadreel continued to weep. Lilith waved dismissingly. "I am too weary to argue with you." She coiled into a ball and covered herself with her wings to get some rest.

A thunderous blast jolted them. They sat upright and scanned the area. An enormous gray-black cloud of smoke and ash burst from a mountaintop. They gawked at the smoking mountain.

"Why does the mountain roar?" Gadreel asked in a tremulous voice, eyes open wide with fear.

"It seems the mountain dislikes our presence. Perhaps it desires us gone from this place. I know not where to go, since the shrill sound, which guided us, has ceased." Lilith stared at the mountain shoulders slumped.

The earth rumbled and shook. Gadreel tottered unsteadily and fell face down. The earth continued to quake and she screamed and clutched the tall grasses.

Lilith held her arms out to the sides to balance herself. "My heart thumps so hard against my chest, I am afraid it might burst." For a moment, she kept balance with her tail, but the earth trembled hard beneath her and soon she, too, tumbled to the ground. When the tremors lessened, she rose and helped Gadreel get to her feet.

Large rifts and fissures began to distort the landscape. Large trees quavered. Elephants, zebras, giraffes, and other creatures fled. The earth opened, swallowing animals and vegetation.

"We must get off the soft land and seek refuge on hard rock before the rifts swallow us as well!" Lilith's face looked grim. A short distance from them, the grassland began to crack.

"The Earth is opening underneath us! Death comes for us!" Gadreel exploded in a cascade of tears.

"Flap your wings with all your might!" Lilith flapped her black wings. "Rise from the ground!"

"I am unable to fly—the sun has weakened me so."

Lilith beat her wings and got off the ground. "If you do not act now, you shall surely perish."

Gadreel saw a fissure slither toward her. Gasping and sobbing, she agitated her wings again and again, with no effect. The gap continued to split in her direction. She extended her wings far apart and beat them furiously until she finally rose from the grass.

Lilith flew to a large, rocky hill nearby and watched Gadreel narrowly escape being devoured by the expanding fissure.

"Come to me!" She beckoned her, who flew only inches above the ground. "You must fly higher!"

"I am using all the power I can muster." Gadreel panted. When she arrived, she collapsed on the hillside. From their perch, they felt the ground continue to shake. Another explosion rocked the mountain, this one greater than the last. Flares stretched to the Heavens as lightning tore the sky apart. Gadreel dug her fingernails into the rocky ground and held on firmly with both hands.

Lilith watched in horror as the volcano erupted, spilling ash, smoke, and gasses. Bright red lava streamed down the mountain and spread across the plains, igniting everything it touched. Animals stampeded—lions, baboons, antelopes, and gazelles fleeing together from the flowing sea of molten fire.

Lilith stared wide-eyed at the animals. "Seeing the animals flee in such haste has filled me with foreboding. We must get further away from this angry mountain."

The sky glowed red now, like the skies she had seen so often on the smoldering side of Thanda-Garam. Ash shot miles upward, darkening the skies and turning day into night as it fell and blotted the sun. Gadreel lifted her head a little and peered at the darkness. She quickly lowered it again, trembling.

"What is that smell?" Lilith twisted her face in disgust. A pungent, sickly sweet odor filled the air. She wrinkled her nose and covered it with her arm.

There was a loud whistle, and the volcano ejected large globs of liquid fire through the air for miles in all directions. The lava bombs set ablaze everything they landed on: animals, trees, and even rocks.

"Behold the raining destruction!" Lilith yelled.

Gadreel lay face down, too afraid to lift her eyes again.

"Behold, Gadreel, you must." Lilith clutched a handful of her curls and lifted her head, forcing her to watch the erupting volcano.

Lava flooded the grasslands, fires broke out everywhere, and the intense heat was like an unwelcomed embrace. Gadreel wept nonstop.

Lilith pressed her lips together. "Enough! I grow weary of your constant lamenting. How did you lead our soldiers through the West Forest? Or did they lead you?"

Gadreel wept aloud with convulsive gasping. "I alone led those soldiers successfully through the treacherous forest. The war and the forest took all my physical and mental strength. I am now depleted. I cannot bear anymore, for I am weakened by this planet."

"You have done no more than I. Thus, you better find strength once again, since this is only the beginning." Lilith scrutinized her with freezing contempt. "I cannot endure any more of your whining. Cease your sniveling at once, or I shall toss you into the lake of fire and happily watch you dissolve."

Gadreel withered under her cold stare and wiped the tears from her eyes. "I have always wondered why God chose to make one of your eyes icy-blue and the other warm-brown—now I think I understand." Her lips quivered. "You possess a warm side, which I have enjoyed, but you also possess a callous side, which frightens me."

A large glob of lava struck inches from them, spurting molten magma on two of Gadreel's wings on one side of her body. Her wings burst into flames.

She squealed in pain. "I am burning!" She shook and floundered about, struggling to extinguish the fire. "Please, help me!"

Lilith puckered her brow and stared at Gadreel's wings. "You have never fought for anything. In Floraison I had to labor vigorously to earn God's good favor, but you always shone before him with your gift of song. I gathered the rebel forces—enduring the constant stress and fear of being caught—while you, were always so blithe, without care. Even now, on Earth, God punishes you by merely tainting your wings with a little darkness while he transforms me into a monster—you shall learn what it is to struggle."

Lilith watched her friend writhe and wail in pain while her lips curved in a satisfied smile.

The acrid, revolting stench of burning feathers wafted into her nostrils. She fanned the air in front of her nose and gagged.

"Lay still!" Lilith pinned Gadreel's burning wings to the ground with her tail and flung dirt on the flames.

Gadreel groaned and bit down on her lip. The flesh and feathers of her injured wings were almost completely consumed, exposing the charred bony frame, which would no longer be of any use to her.

She stifled a scream when her eyes met Lilith's and suffered in silence. "I now know what it is like to burn." She slammed her eyes shut. "I wish to never experience that kind of pain again." She pushed herself off the ground with her arms and clambered to her feet.

Lilith pulled her lips together in disdain.

"I am ready to go wherever you say we must, but I now have two fewer wings." Gadreel avoided Lilith's eyes.

Lilith smirked. "Let us leave this dreadful place."

The angels heard a loud rumbling noise and then an explosion. An instant later, there was another volcanic eruption. The ground beneath Lilith's feet shifted making her sway. She stretched out her arms to steady herself. The ground underneath her collapsed, and she tumbled into a sinkhole. Detached rocks bounced and rolled off the hill and into the cavity nearly burying her alive as heavy rocks and soil concealed three quarters of her body. The bones in her tail were crushed under the immense weight, and she screamed and squirmed in pain.

When the earth stopped shaking and the rocks stopped rolling, Gadreel, who had been pressed against the hillside, tiptoed to the edge of the hole and peered in.

"Lilith? Do you still draw breath?"

"Help me," Lilith said in a barely audible, deep grating voice.

"I am powerless to help you, for I am broken."

"All you have to do is make an attempt." Lilith groaned and squeezed her eyelids together in pain.

There was another booming eruption. More rocks and dirt tumbled on Lilith. She squealed in agony. Gadreel ran screaming to take cover. She clung to the hillside, covering her eyes and ears. When she uncovered her eyes, she gasped, for she caught sight of a terrifying phenomenon. She scrambled to the sinkhole once more. "Lilith, you must come out of there at once!"

Lilith frowned. "There is a reason I have been asking for your help." Frustration crinkled her eyes. "I am trapped!" She gnashed her teeth and moaned attempting to pull and squeeze her lower body out from under the pile of rocks.

Gadreel stared ahead. "There is an enormous cloud of fire, blazing stones, and ash, racing from the angry mountain's mouth at great speed. The black cloud glows red inside, lightning crisscrosses within it, and it destroys everything in its path." Gadreel panted. "It is headed this way!"

Lilith gripped the ground and yanked at her lower body trying to free herself from the rubble. She shrieked and wheezed, and twisted her body while thrashing her wings. "I am unable to free myself from the rocks."

The pyroclastic cloud was fast approaching with its noxious gasses, heating the air to such temperatures that birds fell from the sky, dead long before the black cloud touched them.

Gadreel gawked at the cloud. She pressed her hands to her cheeks and inched forward. Then she leaped into the pit, ignoring her own pain and pulled away rocks from the pile that ensnared her ally. Soon, Lilith was able to wriggle free, flapping her wings intensely. She snatched Gadreel by the arm and soared to the sky like a great, predatory bird with the other angel in her clutches.

The menacing current of hot gas and volcanic matter approached fast. The intense heat scorched their skin.

Lilith heard loud thunderclaps and glanced behind her to see bolts of lightning and volcanic fires amid the looming cloud of burning ash. The acrid odor emanating from it blew into their nostrils; toxic gasses seeped into their lungs, and drained them of energy. Lilith's tail hung limply as she raced across the skies. She flew over areas similar to the region she had found Gadreel in, and zoomed past land covered in short grass and woody plants, but barren of trees.

She looked over her shoulder again. This time the cloud was farther away and had begun to slow and dissipate. She searched the ground for refuge and saw sagebrush shrubs and then ergs, barren stone plateaus, and salt flats white as snow. The black cloud continued to expand and reduce speed, so Lilith was finally able to escape into the desert.

Chapter 5

CLOUDBURST

The cloud was no longer a threat, so Lilith scanned the surface for a place to land. She beheld large, shifting red dunes for miles. Her crushed tail and the blisters on her skin left by the desert sun debilitated her. She made a sweeping descent and released Gadreel on the desert floor from ten feet in the air.

Gadreel plopped on the crest of a dune and rolled to the bottom, landing on her stomach with her face in the sand. She turned over, eyes shut and mouth full of sand. She wheezed and coughed wiping the sand from her face.

When she opened her eyes, a large, hairy bug crawled in her direction. She jolted upright and gawped at the creature. Its eight legs propelled it across the desert surface, and it crawled up her leg while she remained immobile. She stiffened as the spider scurried toward her torso. Its body was decorated with radiating black bands, similar to the ones on her wings. There were claws at the end of each little leg, and the spider flashed its fangs.

Gadreel trembled, too terrified to move. The spider scuttled across her chest with its prickly feet and bit her on the breast. She shrieked and gathered enough strength to swat the spider away with a trembling hand. She writhed and moaned, grasping her breast, which was becoming red and twice the size.

The tarantula flew across the sand and landed upturned, but it flipped over quickly and scurried in her direction once again. It did not get far. Lilith crawled, arms dragging her limp tail like a crocodile, and slammed her fist on the spider.

"Revolting creature!" She rubbed her hand on the sand to remove the spider's parts, her face twisted in disgust. When she was done she glanced at Gadreel, who sat with her knees hugged against her chest. Her wild curls lay flattened by sand and ash.

Lilith extended her hand. "Rise. We must continue before more calamity befalls us."

Gadreel took her hand and pulled herself up, grasping her swollen breast with the other hand.

"We must be strong. We were exiled to this planet to suffer and be destroyed by it." Lilith was breathing hard. "The only way we shall survive is through resilience and by holding on to our desire for justice. My yearning to see harm befall God and those who pitched us out of Floraison motivates me."

Gadreel gazed at Lilith with an agonized expression. She squeezed her eyes shut and rubbed her breast. "I do not know what hurts more, the deep, burning pain of my bitten breast, my damaged wings or my broken heart," she said in a breath, as if speaking rather to her own soul than to Lilith. Her friend was going down a path she could not follow.

Lilith turned away and slithered ahead, using her arms and hands to advance. Gadreel noticed how her tail lagged behind, deformed, with areas that were uneven and lumpy and others that were smashed flat.

"You must be in much pain." Gadreel had a wary expression.

"Pain? Pain does not concern me. Look around you—there are a million ways to die here. This planet shall kill us if we let it."

"You are injured." Gadreel searched her face to find a hint of vulnerability. "Why not admit you are hurting and accept my help?"

"You wish to help me?" Lilith scoffed as she belly-crawled ahead. "You cannot even help yourself. We do not have a moment to whine, we must move on."

"Where shall we go?" Gadreel hastened onward. "We no longer have the shrill sound in our heads to guide us. We shall wander aimlessly in this desert until we wither away."

Lilith rolled her eyes upward. "The sound has returned. Initially it was faint with the noises around us, but now it is clear in my mind once more."

Gadreel stopped. She tilted and inclined her head. "I too hear the shrill sound!" She beamed with hope and resumed following Lilith.

Before long, she began to drag her feet in the sand. The throbbing pain in her breast gave her cold sweats, and she shivered. Her wings also ached terribly. She did not think she could go much further. As she lacked the courage to ask if they could stop and rest, she toiled away. Lilith was hurt and in great pain, but she had yet to complain and kept dragging herself onward.

Gadreel saw a cloud pass above her in the sky. She puckered her brow and stared as more clouds loomed above them. They grew darker, gathering in ominous grey mounds.

"Why are there so many large, dark clouds?" Gadreel braced herself for one of Lilith's outbursts but instead she gave her a half shrug and stared at the odd cloud formations too.

Lightning split the air, followed by a thunderclap. Lilith flinched. Gadreel cringed and covered her ears. Twin lightning bolts struck the ground a short distance away. They jolted and screamed as deafening growls, grumbles, and booms accompanied the lightning bolts.

As Lilith stared wide-eyed at the skies, a drop of water landed on her nose. She touched the spot and stared at her wet fingers. "Water falls from the sky, but why?" Another cool drop landed on her head, and one more on her shoulder.

Gadreel closed her eyes and tilted her head back letting the drops fall on her face. She noticed a sweet, pungent zing in her nostrils. A thousand questions floated around in her head, but judging from her friend's bewildered expression, she knew she would get no answers.

The drops increased, and refreshing rain soon splashed on their scorched skin. Gadreel opened her mouth, allowing rainwater to lubricate her parched throat. She watched Lilith close her eyes and smile, looking like she was enjoying the cooling sensation of the raindrops. The smells around them intensified as the falling water disturbed surface particles and carried them into the air.

"At last!" Lilith took a deep breath. "Nature is finally aiding us."

Gadreel stood on her toes, stretched her arms out wide and spun in circles, letting the heavy downpour wash the gritty sand off her bare body.

The clouds veiled the sun, and the temperature dropped. Before long, the fallen ones began to regain some of their strength and energy. Lilith lay propped on her elbows on the ground, wings widely spread, head reclined, eyes closed.

The heavy rain slammed the desert hard as it became a torrential downpour. Within minutes, small streams appeared around them. Water rose in every direction. Lilith skimmed the desert's surface, and her expression changed from blissful to an exasperated grimace.

Gadreel stopped spinning. She, too, noticed the overflowing. Her chest rose and fell with rapid breaths, she looked to Lilith.

Lilith's face contorted. She screamed, pounding the ground with her fists, the bulging blood vessels in her neck and forehead throbbing.

The rain from the sudden thunderstorm rushed down the hillsides and mountains, flooding the area. Lilith growled at the heavens, her angry tears mixing with the raindrops that splashed on her dour face.

Gadreel recoiled from her in fright, accidentally stumbling into the path of oncoming floodwaters, which hauled her away.

With renewed strength, Lilith took flight and hovered above Gadreel, who was seized anew by the undercurrent. She outstretched her arm. "Help me! Take my arm and lift me away."

"Use your wings and escape." Lilith watched her bob in the sandy water.

"You know I am unable to fly. My damaged wings are dragging me under."

Lilith gritted her teeth. "I grow weary of your pathetic frailty. Use your good pair of wings to save yourself."

Gadreel's wide eyes followed Lilith as she flew away to higher ground, abandoning her to drown in the desert. She clutched at the ground and attempted to stand but tumbled back again and again into the raging waters. Murky water gushed into her mouth, making her gag and cough. Her arms and legs floundered as she surged in the powerful flood. She opened her mouth to break words, slammed it closed, and gulped. Her voice was raspy, barely audible.

"Do not forsake me. We need each other to survive. I shall drown without your help." Gadreel lost consciousness.

Chapter 6

GREAT BIRD

Samael had been flying for many days and nights when he noticed two figures moving across a large expanse of desert. They were distinct from the other creatures; they looked somewhat like angels for they possessed wings. One dragged her feet, and he wondered if she might be a fallen comrade, but her companion slithered unnaturally across the golden sands. He decided it was safest to watch them from a distance for a while.

Flying became difficult for Samael. His wings were terribly singed, as though flames had engulfed them. Rain began to fall from the skies, initially offering some relief, but within minutes it turned into a torrential downpour, which pounded his wings and made them grow heavy. Lightning bolts streaked through the sky all around him. In the desert below, streams of rainwater became rivers.

Samael scanned the desert surface for a safe place to land. He watched, amazed, as the reptilian creature flew away, abandoning the other winged creature to be swept up by the floodwaters. He dove to rescue the drowning creature.

⚓

Through bleary, half-opened eyes, Gadreel saw a cloudy image of a great bird swoop down. It grasped her by the arm and hoisted her from the powerful current. She felt its hot breath as the creature leaned close to sniffed her, and she was certain the great bird would devour her. She coughed, retched, and lost consciousness once more.

Samael carried the angel to a cliff and set her down. He examined her body for injuries. Although she lay lifeless, he saw the gentle rise and fall of her breast, and knew she was alive. One of her breasts looked twice the size of the other and was red and shiny. Two of the creature's four wings were burned and disfigured. He stared at the injured being with a pitying expression.

Samael lowered his head and sniffed her. "I recognize this creature's scent; dulcet as the falling leaves of the Katsura tree in autumn or the fruit of the vanilla orchid in Floraison." He grinned and nodded. A clump of matted hair masked the being's face. When he parted it his smile grew wider.

"Gadreel!"

At the sound of the familiar voice, she slowly opened her eyes. Instead of a monstrous bird, she saw a handsome face close to hers.

"Samael?"

His rough hand caressed her cheek, leaving a spot of warmth wherever he touched. She inhaled a deep breath. "Thank God it is you, Samael. Now I am in safe hands." She exhaled and drifted into a deep sleep.

Lilith abandoned Gadreel to the roaring river and flew to a nearby hill. A moment later, she peered over her shoulder at her friend. Her face tightened. Although Gadreel was a whining nuisance, she was her only ally in this harsh new environment. "I shall pull her from the current." When she turned back she watched a black-winged figure carry Gadreel's limp body away. Lilith frowned and watched the creature land on the same mound where she stood, so she hurried to take cover on the other side of the hill.

Lilith's strong arms dragged her snake body over rough rocks and brush. She made her way up the back side of the hill. She skulked in the shadows of an overhang. She lifted her head and huffed. "I cannot allow this creature to devour my only ally." She spiraled to face the monster. She cringed and groaned in pain as she lifted her broken tail in the air, ready to attack.

"Samael!" She let her tail flop to the ground, grimaced and then grinned as she moved toward him, arms spread wide. His features twisted in disgust, he held out his arms and staggered away.

"What is wrong?" Lilith stopped and frowned. "Do you not recognize me? It is I, Lilith."

"Apologies, but your new form is—grotesque." Samael tensed. "What caused this cursed change upon you?"

"What is your meaning? Were you not transformed in some way when you landed on this forsaken planet?" She crawled around him, inspecting him. "Like Gadreel, it appears only your wings were altered. They are hideous." However, his handsome face, amber eyes, thick hair, and tall muscular body were intact. "You are desirable to me, yet you look upon me with disgust."

Samael dropped his eyes to the ground and avoided her hollow stare. He soon set his sights on Gadreel.

Gadreel shifted and opened her eyes. Samael knelt by her side, caressing her face.

"I am pleased you have awoken and delighted you were not transformed into a hideous creature." He cringed and glanced at Lilith shamefaced. She glared at him. He bit his lip and turned a vivid red.

"We were all transformed in one way or another." Gadreel glanced at Lilith who still glowered and then at Samael.

The rain continued to pour. The storm grew more violent, and lightning ripped through the sky. Gadreel jolted, and Samael held her.

Lilith stared at them, her lips curled with bitter indignation. "You gaze at her the way you once looked at me. You desire her."

Samael squirmed, looked down and licked his lips. Gadreel picked on her nails.

This must not be so, for it placed too much power in Gadreel's hands, but how could Lilith stop it? Gadreel still possessed her original form, while she was a monstrosity. Lilith clenched her jaw and slammed her eyes shut for a moment.

"Enough!" Lilith lowered her eyebrows. "We must leave! We've dawdled here long enough. We need to resume our journey to find the source of the shrill noise in our minds!"

"So both of you have heard the shrill sound?" Samael asked. Lilith and Gadreel nodded. "I have been following it also. It led me thus far."

"I am certain the sound is a distress call from one of the other fallen angels," Lilith said. "Satan may be in danger and calling for us. We must hurry. The sound originates in the great body of water God called Ocean. This is why we must go to the coast."

The storm dissipated, leaving behind a pleasant smell. Lilith and Samael took flight, each holding one of Gadreel's arms. They flew away from the flooded area to a different expanse of the desert, nearly expending the small amount of restored energy the rain provided them.

Chapter 7

SURVIVAL

Lilith, Gadreel and Samael arrived at another enchanting desert terrain. Lilith explored her surroundings. "Do not allow the beauty of this place to mislead you. This environment is harsh and hostile, and our survival has become extremely tenuous." The others nodded in agreement.

Samael and Gadreel dragged their feet in silence through the barren yet tranquil landscape. Lilith held her torso off the ground and continued to walk with her arms. She twisted from side to side, as she crawled and pushed the sand with her injured tail.

"We suffer from pain and exhaustion," Lilith said. "I have also found that we have developed new requirements for survival that we never needed in Floraison."

Samael cocked his head and Gadreel bit her lip and bobbed her head.

Lilith drew in a long breath and exhaled a harsh one. "We tire easier and faster than before, we are more fragile, and we suffer hunger and thirst. I feel less and less like an angel." She lowered her head and slumped her shoulders. "I am changing, and not merely in appearance, I sense the change in the essence of my being. The lingering effects of Floraison are diminishing. What would we become? What would we be if not angels?"

Gadreel's body drooped. "I am having trouble swallowing." She pressed a hand to her throat. "My mouth and throat are dry and painful."

Samael puckered his brow and looked at his belly. He rubbed it. "My insides burn. An intense pressure fills my middle and my body aches. Such things I never felt in Floraison."

Gadreel took a deep breath. "I am relieved I am not the only one experiencing these sensations. I, too, feel the burning and pressure inside me. It feels like something moves within me, getting under my ribs and my chest, causing me pain."

"It is a testament to our changed reality." Lilith wore a wry grin. "We yearn for sustenance. We are suffering the physical sensations of hunger. We have need for liquids as well, not unlike the humans God created."

"Impossible!" Samael's lower lip trembled and his voice had an urgent tone. "We are not human beings, we are angels, celestial beings, and we have no such needs to survive."

Lilith smirked. "Look around you—does this place resemble Floraison in any way?" She stared at him. "We are no longer celestial beings. And if I learned anything after landing on this planet, it is that nothing is impossible. We have been transformed more than we know. We may be losing our angelic powers. That is why it took many days to begin to perceive the distress of hunger and thirst. It must be another form of punishment, and yet another reason why we must retaliate against God. We have more in common now with human beings than we do with the angels."

Gadreel's face paled. "What are you saying? We are becoming human?"

Lilith rolled her eyes upward. "I have said no such thing. We are not human beings, but we have acquired some of their weaknesses since our arrival on this planet. We are not what we once were. That is beyond question. But what we are now, or what we shall become, is unknown to me."

Samael shoved his hair back away from his face and pressed a finger to his lips.

Lilith observed him. "You must accept the truth. Your life depends on it." He nodded once, never making eye contact.

Gadreel glanced at them. Her lips trembled and her arms clenched. "We understand the severity of our situation," she said in a flat tone.

Lilith kept a wary eye on her allies. "We must find water and nourishment before it is too late, for this state of exhaustion may precede death."

"You are right. My body is depleted, and I grow weaker by the day, but look around us." Gadreel indicated with her hand the barren region surrounding them. "This wilderness is arid and desolate. How are we to find food and water here?"

The others considered their environment for a moment.

"Indeed, there are not many plants but the animals we have seen manage to find food here. Are we not superior to them?" Lilith looked intentionally quizzical.

"Of course we are!" Samael scowled.

"We shall observe the animals. Behold where and how they find sustenance." Lilith began moving as soon as she had finished her sentence.

The fallen angels divided to cover more ground. They searched for a long while, finding nothing. Then Gadreel spotted a rabbit not far from where she stood. "Lilith! Samael! Come, I have found an animal."

They quickly arrived by her side, but the rabbit was swiftly burrowing into the sand.

"Grab it! Quick!" Lilith pointed at the little furry being as it briskly excavated its way under the desert.

Samael launched forth, but it was too late—the rabbit escaped below the surface of the sand. Chasing it had drained him of his last bit of energy. He lay on the sand, panting and holding his chest. The angels had nothing but their battered, scorched wings to shield them from the arid conditions and with each rising of the sun, their bodies grew weaker. The short night hours were not enough to fully restore them.

Lilith saw how frail her allies had become. She stood in a trance-like state, rubbing her neck deep in thought. Animals in the desert burrowed underground to survive the sun and heat, and to escape predators. They could do the same. They could use the sand as a shield against the burning rays of the sun.

"The sun must give way to the night, but I am not sure we can endure the extreme heat of the desert's surface. We must take shelter now, before it is too late." Lilith's low hoarse voice told of her fragility as well, but she would never acknowledge her vulnerability.

"Since we left the grasslands and landed on this desert, we have been unable to find shelter. How are we supposed to do so now?" Gadreel's entire body drooped.

"We shall do as the animals do in this harsh environment," Lilith told them. "We shall burrow underground until the sun sets."

Gadreel heaved a sharp breath. "I could never do that."

"We do not have a choice!" Lilith dragged her body toward her. "We are all capable, and we shall do it to survive." She grit her teeth. "I for one do not intend to allow this planet to defeat me. Not before I have quenched my thirst for vengeance."

She crept to a suitable area and began to dig a hole in the sand. She worked quickly, since it was tricky to keep the sand from sliding back into the hole. Samael moved a short distance away and began burrowing as well.

Gadreel watched wide-eyed as the two of them made their way into the desert floor. "I know I must do this." She could not stay under the sun alone. If they could do it, she should be able to do the same. She stared at the sand and rubbed her temples as a wary smile surfaced on her lips.

She dropped to the ground and scooped sand. The same golden-brown rabbit she had seen earlier appeared at her side, sniffing and twitching its little nose. She observed it as it began digging a trench. The rabbit stopped, placed one of its front feet on her arm, looked at her and then continued to burrow into the desert. Gadreel gave it a nod and began to dig like the long-eared creature.

"Thank you for helping me," Gadreel whispered, watching the little bushy tailed animal disappear into the sand.

"Flap your wings while you dig to bring air with you," Lilith yelled.

The others followed her instructions and swooped air in along with them as they dug their tunnels.

"When your burrow is deep enough, lie still to consume less air. I shall call you out at dusk." These were Lilith's final words before disappearing into her refuge.

In the tunnel, Gadreel lay on her side to avoid making contact with her throbbing, damaged wings. Despite the pain, she thought of Samael. He seemed so weary and feeble, unlike the Principatus she knew in Floraison. "Why do I devote so much time to thinking and fretting about him? Does he think of me as much? She sighed. "I do not imagine so, but at this moment, I desire nothing more than to lie by his side." She closed her eyes.

Samael lay motionless in his burrow. He closed his eyes and exhaled, relieved to be away from the sun's rays. Lilith's image rushed into his head—the Lilith he knew before she transformed into a hideous reptilian creature. Her beauty, before she changed, rivaled that of any creature. Now she was a beautiful woman whose lower body was devoured by a serpent. He shuddered as he thought of her crawling along with her hands, dragging her long, scaly tail behind like a crocodile.

Lilith lay still in her space below ground. She moaned and winced as she positioned her damaged tail with care. Her eyelids drooped and she curled into a ball. Her chest heaved, and her eyes stung with gathering tears.

"This is the farthest I've been from Floraison." She writhed and moaned. "I shall find a way to survive." She sensed a flutter in her chest and a pounding in her neck. Her breathing became shallow, so she calmed herself again. She closed her eyes. "I was once a beautiful and desirable being and I shall be that fetching angel once again. I do not know how, but it shall come to pass."

Lilith sensed the temperature on the surface was a few degrees cooler. She crawled out of her lair, rose from the ground. "I feel no pain." She gasped when she looked at her lower body and saw that she stood on her own two feet. "My snake tail is gone! I am myself again." She glanced at her four wings. They remained as black as the hole she crawled out of, and covered with fixed, expressionless eyes. She lifted her shoulder in a half shrug. "Why should I be concerned? I have legs!" She jumped and twirled and kicked her leg up in the air.

"Samael! Gadreel! You may surface now. Nightfall is almost upon us! Burrowing underground like the desert mammals was a great idea. As we lay inactive in our burrows, we recuperated and regained our strength."

Gadreel slinked from her hole and stared at Lilith in amazement. "Lilith, your legs have returned!"

"Have you noticed your wings are no longer damaged?" Lilith smiled.

"They stopped tormenting me." Gadreel glanced at the wings. "They are no longer charred, featherless, or hanging limp but whole once again!" She flapped them several times. She caught her breath with excitement and soared to the sky with her four wings outstretched, twirling high in midair and then landed on the desert's surface once more. She danced around on her toes, giggling, while her wings made swooshing sounds.

Like flames from the angry mountain, Samael burst out of the ground. His wavy hair hung around his handsome face. He seemed more striking than ever, standing tall, every muscle on his strong body outlined by the ambient light.

He gazed upon Lilith, who stood looking proud and beautiful on two legs. She posed on the peaceful dunes, her exquisite body shimmering in the colorful radiance of the setting sun. Her long hair moved rhythmically with the evening's pleasant, cool breeze. Her moist lips beckoned him without uttering a word. Gadreel observed with a look of horror, as he became Lilith's once more.

He stepped toward her in a trance. "You have become the beauty you once were. You are thus pleasing to the senses and worthy of desire once more, as you were in Floraison."

Lilith watched his chest rise and fall with rapid breaths. "I have not forgotten how you hurt me when you first laid eyes on me." She smirked and tossed her hair over her shoulder. Samael lowered his eyes and rubbed the back of his neck.

Lilith swaggered away from him and toward Gadreel. "Behold!" With a wide sweeping gesture of her arm she pointed to Gadreel. "Does she not look pleasing to you any longer? Is her long, curly hair not glowing golden in the evening light?" She stared at him with a sardonic grin.

Samael's neck flushed red. He shuffled his feet. "Indeed! Gadreel is pretty, but you must know there is no one who compares to you."

Gadreel's body sank and she lowered her doleful eyes to the sand.

Lilith stared at Samael awhile. The corners of her lips rose slowly to a sensual smile. She would use his desire to bend him to her will. He would serve her well, and in more ways than one, for she too had carnal desires to sate. "We have wasted enough time. We need to set forth to find the source of the shrill in our heads. Do you both hear it once again?"

"The shrill sound is in my mind, beckoning me." Gadreel gazed at Samael.

"I too hear it." Samael nodded.

"Good," Lilith said. "We must leave now and take advantage of our healthy state and hours of darkness."

"There is still the issue of sustenance for I still suffer the strange burning sensation in my middle. We need to eat and drink, otherwise the strength and vitality we are now experiencing shall soon be spent."

"Yes, we need nutrients to survive. We should continue following the sound while searching for food and water. Flying would consume much energy. We shall walk." Lilith led them on their arduous trek to the source of the shrill once more.

The sun was setting, and the golden sand glittered in the diffused sunlight. Swirls of pink and ginger mixed with yellows and gold appeared in the sky. As they watched the beauty of the sun setting the angels forgot, for a moment, about their hunger and thirst.

The sun disappeared in the place where Earth meets sky, it grew darker, and the desert came to life. Many animals emerged from their shelters to hunt for food. Owls hooted as they flew through the night sky, snakes slid from their burrows and slithered to and fro, hares gamboled about, and many other nocturnal animals became active.

Lilith and Gadreel observed the desert animals and the many brilliant stars lighting the sky, but Samael only set his sights on Lilith's beautiful form.

The females saw a hare. They ran after it to no avail. Samael laughed at their failure to catch the small animal and forged ahead.

"Wait for us!" Gadreel ran to catch up to him. He grinned and took a few more steps forward to taunt her. When he finally stopped, he began to fall through the ground. Realizing he was sinking into the desert, he shifted and shuffled his legs to release himself, but the movements only made him sink faster.

Lilith ran to him, but stopped short when she saw what was happening.

"Do not come any closer, otherwise you too shall be swallowed by the sand." Samael groaned as he struggled to loosen his body. He was buried up to his torso. He writhed and strained only to plunge deeper.

"The—sand—is—crushing—me." Samael gasped for air and wheezed as he continued to descend under the surface of the desert. He panted while simmering in the hot, liquid sand.

"Samael!" Gadreel stared wide-eyed and bounced on her toes, gnawing the tips of her fingers.

"Use your wings!" Lilith shouted in a desperate tone.

In his panic to release his legs, Samael did not think to use his wings, and now it was too late because they, too, were stuck in the quicksand. His eyes rolled to the back of his head.

Lilith scanned their surroundings. "We must find something—any-thing—a twig or vine—which could aid us in pulling Samael out of the sand."

Gadreel ran in circles her eyes flickering in every direction. "There is nothing but shallow plants." She pressed her hands to her cheeks.

Samael appeared dazed. They only saw his head, neck, and the upper part of his chest now. Lilith held her breath and clenched her hands. "If we do not act soon the sands shall consume him," she murmured under her breath.

She suffered a strange sensation in her legs and tumbled face first to the ground. When she glanced at her lower body her legs had been replaced by a snake's tail. Her shoulders slumped. She stared at Samael with woeful eyes but she did not have time for self-pity. She rose quickly, coiled her tail around him, and with a mighty tug, pulled him onto secure ground.

Samael was unconscious when Lilith laid him on dry sand. Gadreel ran to him wailing and lamenting.

Lilith closed her eyes. She willed her unsightly snake form to trans-form back into her beautiful lower half, and her long, shapely legs reap-peared. Thus, she became aware she possessed the power to choose which appearance to take at will. She was content that Samael was oblivious to her transformation into the snake creature.

Lilith strutted to him. She grabbed Gadreel by the arm and shoved her aside. "You must give him space to breathe and stop the sniveling at once. Are you not aware that I have saved him?"

Gadreel bobbed her head and wiped her eyes.

Samael opened his eyes and glanced at her. "How was I able to rise from the pit?" he asked with a raspy voice.

"You did not rise." Gadreel giggled. "Lilith pulled you out with her snake tail."

Lilith glared at her.

Samael lifted his head to glance at Lilith. "She no longer has a tail, Gadreel." He smiled and reclined his head on the ground.

"No, you see, Lilith did—" Gadreel met Lilith's glaring eyes and kept quiet.

"Rest here a moment." Lilith tucked a lock of hair behind Samael's ear. "I shall walk ahead to find a safe passage for us. There may be other such traps ahead. I must figure out the difference between this sand and the sand that bites and swallows. I shall be back soon. Gadreel, you stay with him."

"But, what if you do not return?" Gadreel frowned.

Lilith flaunted a smug smile. "Of course I shall return."

Gadreel was about to go after her, but Samael grabbed her arm and shook his head. He waited until Lilith was a short distance away and whispered, "Let her go. I have been waiting for a moment when we could be alone. I have something to share with you."

Gadreel opened her eyes wide in amazement. "Why not wait until Lilith returns and tell the two of us what is on your mind?"

"I am not sure this is the right moment to reveal it to her," Samael said.

Gadreel beamed. He had a secret he wanted to keep just between him and her?

Samael gazed into her eyes. "What I am about to tell you is of vital importance, but you are not to say a word of it to Lilith or anyone else we come in contact with later."

Gadreel stared at him.

"Do you understand?"

She gulped and nodded.

"I have been inside the Garden of Eden." He waited for her reaction. Gadreel gasped. "I have also seen Eve—I spoke to her."

"Eve understood your words? What was she like? Was the Garden of

Eden as beautiful as the Triumph Gardens in Floraison? How did you get in? Where was Adam?"

Samael chuckled. "I shall answer every one of your questions in time. For now, I simply wanted to tell someone."

"And you chose me." Her face was radiant with felicity.

"I do not think that now is a good moment to tell Lilith about my encounter with the humans in Eden." Samael's expression turned brooding and dark. "Her mind is focused on finding the others, which is what we all want. I believe she would change her focus if I told her that I have been to Eden. She would forget our current goal, and a new one would spring in its stead. I am convinced she would want to conquer Eden to take it for herself and destroy Adam and Eve in the process."

Gadreel pressed her fingers to her lips. "God's wrath would surely fall upon us then."

"I shall not allow her to destroy Eve. She is a magnificent creature," Samael said. Gadreel's face fell. He wished to protect the human woman.

"That is not all. I also saw Cam in the Garden. He threatened me with his flaming sword and marked me with it." He showed her a black heart-shaped mark on his chest. She passed her fingers over the slightly raised mar.

"If we are to return to the Garden of Eden, it should be with Satan and the others and with weapons." Samael gripped her shoulders. "It is the only way we shall have a chance to survive, and that is why I must wait to tell Lilith. She is impatient. She shall aspire to go to the Garden without delay, and if that comes to pass, we are as good as dead."

"I understand." Gadreel looked to the distance. "Do not fret, your secret is safe with me. Now be silent, for Lilith approaches." Samael let her go and reclined again.

Lilith proceeded to them and hovered over them. She was about to speak when she spotted a small creature near her feet. She peered at it. "This creature is black as night and carries a pair of grasping claws. This is not the same species that attacked you, Gadreel. This one possesses a threatening factor well beyond its size."

Lilith snatched the scorpion off the sand. The creature stung her hand with its venomous stinger. She howled in pain. Her face flushed crimson with fury, she bared her teeth and snared. She bit the creature in half and consumed it. She grimaced and gagged at the bitter taste. "The flavor is repulsive but I detect some satisfaction as it reaches my middle."

Gadreel stared at her in awe. Samael burst into laughter. Feeling better, he got off the ground. He got busy wiping the gritty, itchy sand embedded on his body.

Gadreel hurried to his side. "I can help you. I can brush off the areas of your body that are troublesome for you to reach."

She grabbed his male organ, gently passing her hand across the topside and underneath to eliminate the sand. She proceeded to kneel in front of him. She lifted his shaft and passed her hand softly around the sack beneath it.

Lilith twirled her hair and watched with eager curiosity, as an expression of delight lit up Samael's face. "You are sensing pleasure from Gadreel's touch, is this true?"

"I am. When she passes her hands across these areas, I feel a current of pleasure spread through my entire body."

Gadreel beamed.

"Your male organ is no longer lying dormant. It is rigid and larger than before." Gadreel smiled at him with a sidelong glance. "Is this a sign that you find my hands on your skin pleasing?"

"Yes, it is," Lilith interrupted. "The same happens to Satan when I stroke him there. It probably happens to all males." It was no wonder God feared carnal pleasures so, for it could be a powerful weapon. It was how she planned to control Satan and Samael to do her bidding. "It seems Gadreel is not without her charms."

Gadreel continued to brush the sand off him, relishing the look of pleasure on his face.

"That is plentiful, Gadreel! We have no time for you to amuse Samael. We must move on."

Gadreel stopped and jumped to her feet. She did not wish to rouse Lilith's fury.

Samael frowned and grabbed Lilith by the arm. "You offered such affections to Satan?" His tone was flat.

She wrested her arm from his grasp and ambled away with a smile dangling on the corner of her lips.

Chapter 8

WHITE NOURISHMENT

L ater, as they hiked under the starry sky, Samael spotted a large
creature with a similar but much smaller creature moving along
beside it.

"Behold!" He pointed at the animals.

Lilith looked in the direction he pointed and saw a humped creature
with long legs gliding across the sand without sinking, despite its size.

"We must go and inspect these animals. They may have something
to offer." She rushed toward the mammals, Samael ran close behind, and
Gadreel followed with a wary look on her face.

Lilith stopped a short distance from the camels. "Stop, do not come
any closer. We do not want to scare them away." She inched toward the
she-camel.

The large camel nuzzled the calf. Lilith smiled. The calf toddled to
the camel's lower body and reached under the camel's abdomen
with its muzzle, latched on to a teat, and began to suckle.

Samael raised his eyebrows and hurried to the long-
legged, hairy beast and squatted by her hind legs. His
eyes widened as he watched the calf slurp on one
of four teats hanging from the camel's belly.
He reached out and grabbed one of the
camel's teats and squeezed it. He

gasped when an opaque, white liquid squirted his face. He wiped his face and sniffed the milk on his fingers. The liquid had a sweet, creamy smell. He leaned his head toward the camel's teat and sniffed it also.

The calf seemed to enjoy the white liquid. Samael licked his lips and gulped. He reached for the teat with his mouth and did as the calf did. He drew the fluid into his mouth. The taste was mildly sweet and light, but warm and satisfying.

"What are you doing?" Lilith gawked at him. Gadreel moved closer as well, taking small, cautious steps.

The calf discontinued its suckling. It wobbled a few feet away to lie on the sand, evidently sated and ready to rest for the night.

Samael continued to suck on the camel's teat with voracity. He filled himself with as much milk as possible. He became overenthusiastic and pulled with brute force. The camel moaned, but he continued to draw hard until the camel kicked him away with one of her hind legs. He tumbled backward in the sand as milk streamed down the corners of his mouth. The females guffawed, which also prompted laughter from him.

"You both need to drink as I did." He wiped his face and chuckled. "The white liquid is both thirst-quencher and nourishment. You can both drink at once, as I drank with the small mammal." He pulled Lilith by the arm and placed her under one of the camel's teats.

She stared at the animal's udder. Crinkling her nose she wrapped her lips around one of them and sucked gently on it. Her mouth filled with the sweet, hot liquid. She swallowed, and it was good as it made its way into her hollow stomach. She closed her eyes and hummed as the milk began to extinguish her hunger and thirst.

Gadreel's gaze fluctuated between the camel and Lilith. The animal did not appear to suffer. She touched her cheek. "I cannot do this, Samael," she whispered. "What if the animal kicks me, as it did you?"

Samael took her hand. "Come, get on the side of the beast opposite Lilith." He guided her to the animal. "I shall hold both of the beast's hind legs firmly in my grasp. The animal shall not be able to kick either of you as you drink your fill."

Samael got behind the camel and held her two rear legs.

Gadreel dropped to her knees beside the camel. She outstretched her trembling hand and then withdrew it. Wide-eyed she stared at the teat arms crossed. "I am so hungry." She watched Lilith slurp on the animal's teat. She attempted to rise. "I have to do this or I shall die." She grimaced, leaned and draped her lips around the camel's teat and began to suckle. At once, warm liquid moistened her parched throat and filled her stomach, quieting it.

After they satisfied their hunger and thirst, they let the animal be. The camel walked to its calf and lay beside it to sleep.

Lilith watched the camels as they slept. She walked toward them, her feet sinking into the sand with each step. She sat against the large one and passed a hand across its thick coat.

Samael approached her with Gadreel trailing behind. "Perhaps we should continue our journey while it is still dark and we are well nourished."

"Yes, you are right, we should move on." Lilith rose to her feet. "What do you think shall happen the next time the sun shines brightly and weakens us? The night shall not last forever. By what means shall we feed when hunger attacks once more?"

"If we grow weak from the sun's menacing rays, we can burrow under the desert. The next time hunger takes hold of us, we could find another creature such as this one and drink from it." Samael held his chin high boasting a satisfied smile.

Gadreel giggled.

Lilith glanced at her and rolled her eyes, and then smirked. "How many such creatures have we encountered in this desolate land, Gadreel?"

"I have never seen this animal before," Gadreel said in a low voice.

"How many have you encountered thus far in your travels?" She looked at Samael, the brow above her blue eye arched high.

"This is the first time I have come across such a beast." He cleared his throat and looked at the ground.

"That is why we must take the beasts with us. The large one shall provide us with shade from the sun during the hot hours, so we do not waste time burrowing underground every day. We could drink from the animal before dawn and at night to maintain our strength."

Samael bobbed his hear.

"The animals are sleeping. How are we supposed to take them with us?" Gadreel fidgeted.

"We shall wake them." Samael glanced at Lilith.

"Do it quickly, we have squandered enough nighttime already."

Gadreel sulked when Lilith yelled orders at Samael, but he was always quick to do her bidding.

Samael woke the animals and pulled the large one to its feet. They resumed their quest to find the source of the shrill sound and their friends.

A full moon glowed over the landscape. The reflection of the moonlight on the sands was intense, and the beauty of the desert at night mesmerized the three. The brilliant stars shimmered upon the rolling red dunes. The shrill sound they followed for so long was alive in their heads and seemed closer.

Chapter 9

PILLAR OF SAND

Dawn approached and the sun began to rise, bringing the exquisite hues of nature along with it. The fallen angels moved in a steady trot and used the camel to shade them, but soon the midday sun would be directly above them, and there would be no escaping its rays.

Lilith lurched to an abrupt stop. "Behold! In the distance!" She pointed to a gigantic pillar of sand, which swirled with great force toward them.

"What is that?" Gadreel cowered behind Samael.

Lilith shrugged and let out a harsh breath. "I do not know, but I do know we should take notice. We must protect ourselves. This is yet another way God torments us." She clinched her jaw. "We have to remain calm. Our strength has returned, so we could fly away or burrow underground until it passes."

Samael shoved his hair back away from his face and crossed his arms. "Your words are wise as usual, but if we fly, we risk depleting our energy much faster. If we burrow underground, we risk losing our beast and our sustenance."

"We are almost gone from this arid land." Lilith pointed to the mountains in the distance. "We can fly until we are secure on highland. We can carry the beast with us."

"Lilith—" Gadreel's arms

remained clenched at her sides as she approached. "We are not strong enough to fly long distances, especially if we have to carry such a heavy load."

"We are stronger than you imagine." Lilith's eyes flashed with anger. "I am weary of your perpetual weakness."

Gadreel hung her head.

Lilith's snake tail reappeared. Samael flinched and gawked at her. She wrapped her long, powerful tail around the large camel and zoomed away toward the mountains.

Samael and Gadreel glanced at each other and then at the small camel. Samael lifted his shoulder in a half shrug and flew after Lilith.

"Samael—no, wait!" Gadreel stared at the approaching pillar of sand biting her lower lip. She spread her wings and then caught sight of the little camel again. From the corner of her eye, she saw the calf searching the skies for its mother, calling, "Baa, baa!" She snapped her eyes shut. "I shan't leave it to die."

She rushed to the small animal and tried to lift it. Her first attempt failed. "I can do this." The massive sand column rumbled onward. The wind raged around her, flinging sand at her, scraping and stinging her skin. "You are deceptively heavy," she told the calf.

Placing both arms around the calf's body from the top, she made another attempt to lift it. Flapping her four immense wings, she carried the little camel off the ground. The force of the cyclone dragged her and the camel, drawing them into its core. She flapped feverishly until she was able to fly away.

Gadreel looked over her shoulder at the desert she left behind. The tall, powerful column of air, sand and rocks blasted through the area where she and the others stood only moments before. She inhaled a deep breath and released it slowly. "I am happy I did not leave you behind." She smiled at the small camel. "You would have been torn apart by the vicious sand twister."

She flew in the direction she had seen the others go, toward the mountain ranges. Her eyebrows bumped together. "What new perils awaits us in this new terrain?"

Chapter 10

ICE CAVE

Lilith arrived first at the mountain range. She chose to land at the highest elevation. After placing the camel on the snowy rock face, she willed her legs to appear so she might land on her feet.

The temperature on the tall mountain was much cooler than the surrounding lowlands, and ice and snow covered the ground. She shuddered and wrapped her arms and wings around her body in an effort to keep warm. She watched Samael fly toward her, but Gadreel was nowhere in sight.

Samael landed a few feet from her. He sighed with relief and ogled her. "I am happy you are no longer the snake creature."

Lilith arched a sly brow. "You know, you might as well get used to the part of me you loathe. It is here to stay."

"You can turn into a snake creature at your pleasure?"

"I can, and there shall be moments when being a serpent shall be useful to me. I intend to transform whenever need be." Lilith gave him a subtle wink.

He smiled. "Becoming the legless reptile allowed you to save me from the sand trap. I am grateful to you for that."

Lilith gazed at him. He may be the desirable being through which she would work her objective. With his help she could influence Satan to do her bidding and then all would follow.

After some time, they spotted Gadreel flying in the distance, towing the calf. Her landing on the ice was tumultuous. Screaming the entire way, she landed too close to the edge of the cliff, slid, and nearly dropped the calf over the precipice.

Lilith rolled her eyes and gave a dismissive wave of her hand. "Maladroit."

Samael cocked his head back and guffawed.

Lilith ambled away. "I wish to explore the mountain and discover the closest route to the ocean."

Samael trailed behind her. He wrapped his arms around himself and used his wings to cover his body from the cold, as he saw her do. "My feet are numb from stepping on the ice-covered ground." He scooped a handful of the white, powdery substance. "It is light and fluffy in my hand." He brought it to his nose and sniffed. "It smells like fresh water." He shoved a handful in his mouth. He shuddered and shook his head. "The unnatural coldness made me jolt, but when I swallowed it satisfied my thirst."

Lilith continued walking and paid him no mind.

Once Gadreel set the small camel on the snow, it made a dash for its mother, slipping and sliding along the way. The large camel met her calf halfway and caressed the calf's head with her muzzle.

Gadreel hurried to catch up to the others. "Where are we going?" She shivered. "This weather is eerie and inexplicable. We have never experienced anything such as this. My wings are stiffened by the cold. What if this white substance is meant to congeal us into ice—or poison us?"

Samael gulped and gaped at Lilith since he had already eaten a few mouthfuls.

"It is not toxic, but it shall drain our heat until we are solid frost if we do not find shelter," Lilith said in a casual tone.

"Why stay here? Let us leave this mountain at once!" Gadreel's teeth chattered.

"At present, we cannot fly," Samael said. "We have exhausted our energy. Besides, our wings are painful and unyielding. We would plummet to our deaths if we tried."

"I would like to see how far we are from the ocean," Lilith said. "From this height, I am certain we could see the large body of saltwater."

The other two glanced at each other and then the three continued following the shrill sound in their heads, believing it would lead them toward the ocean and the others.

The mountain was vast. Unable to fly, they hiked for many days and nights in snowy conditions. Sunset was fast approaching once again. The night would bring bitterly cold winds.

Lilith shivered and rubbed her arms. "I Sense this night would be the coldest yet." She looked down at her feet and wiggled her plum colored toes. "I am not sure we could survive it without shelter."

They trudged forward, cold, weak, and hungry. They could not stop to feed in the open, for they would surely freeze. Their first taste of this icy cold weather proved an enormous challenge. They continued on, shivering and dragging their numb feet in the snow, trying to find a spot where they could nourish themselves again with the camel's milk. In time, they arrived at the entrance to a huge cave.

"We should take refuge in this cavern." Lilith pointed to the mouth of the cave.

Gadreel inched closer to peek inside. "It looks ever so cold in there. I am not sure we should enter. It appears we would freeze, and become fixtures in the void."

Samael stepped forward and glanced inside, shaking his head. "I detest disagreeing with you, Lilith, but I am of the same mind as Gadreel. There is an enormous amount of ice inside this hollow space and I believe we are capable of freezing."

A smile slid across Gadreel's face. Samael agreed with her.

Lilith scowled at them. "In Floraison, I spent many hours observing the inhabitants of the frozen side of the planet Thanda-Garam in the Black Eye galaxy. I have learned a great deal about their survival in the snow and ice. The creatures there used ice caves as shelter from the cold, and so shall we." She swaggered to them and stood before Gadreel. "In no universe would you be right where I was in the wrong."

Samael bowed his head. "I apologize. I should have known better than to doubt you."

Lilith stared at Gadreel, expecting an apology, but none came. "It seems you may be finally developing some fortitude. That is good—it serves my purpose, as long as you do not forget where your loyalties rest."

Lilith stepped into the cavern, followed by Samael pulling the large camel. Gadreel guided the calf into the cave. She minced her way up to Samael. "It is warmer in the cave. Lilith was right."

The cavity was large with many halls. "I shall search for a suitable area to settle for the night and feed."

As they hiked further in, they were mesmerized by the different ice formations decorating the cave. There were enormous monoliths and pillars of ice, dazzling ice waterfalls frozen in motion, and aqua-blue glaciers. Icicles dangled from the ceiling of the cavern like crystalline jewels. Intricate frost plumes lined some of the cave's walls.

They came across a huge, frozen pond adorned with ripples and swirls of aquamarine and cerulean, frozen in place. The body of water was suspended above them in the rear of the cave. Lilith rubbed her hands together and smiled an I–am–pleased–with–myself smile. "This is where I have decided we should camp for the night."

She beckoned Samael and Gadreel to come closer. "One thing I learned while observing Thanda-Garam: ice does not conduct heat well." Lilith passed her hand across the icy walls.

Gadreel squinted in confusion. "How is that beneficial to us?"

Lilith flounced to her and glared into her big, hooded brown eyes. "As a result, any heat generated inside the cave shall stay in the cave, with the ice not allowing its passage."

Lilith grabbed Gadreel's hair tightly around her fist, causing her to squeal and wince in pain. "Do not interrupt me as I express my thoughts." She released Gadreel's hair, roughly pushing her away.

Gadreel pursed her lips. "We were friends once. What has happened to us?"

"We no longer stand as such." Lilith's words were as cold as the wind outside the cave.

"Have I grieved you in any way?" Gadreel rubbed her scalp.

Lilith needed strong allies—not weak friends. Gadreel's lack of desire for revenge against God made her feeble and pitiful in her eyes. She would have her vengeance, and if Gadreel did not decide to join her soon, she would destroy her for her fickleness and treachery.

"There is no time for attachments now, only survival," Lilith said in a toneless voice. "We shall feed here." She gestured for Samael to bring forth the camel.

Gadreel guided the calf to the camel. The little mammal wobbled and stumbled on its way to its nurturer. Gadreel's lips trembled and tears welled in her eyes as she observed it. "I sense something is wrong with the calf." No one listened. She placed the calf near its mother's udder so it could have easy access to her teats, but the little calf stared blankly and tottered on its frail legs.

"What is amiss with the small one?" Lilith scrutinized the teetering calf.

"I am not certain—I believe it is dying." Gadreel's tears spilled down her cheeks and turned to soft ice. She wiped them away quickly before Lilith could see them.

"It cannot die!" Lilith yelled. Gadreel jolted. "If the little one dies, we shall receive no more nourishment."

"What is your meaning?" Samael narrowed his eyes and raked his fingers through his hair. "It is the large one that feeds us."

Lilith rolled her eyes upward. "This animal feeds us because we allow her to suckle her young, but if her calf dies, she shall no longer produce the white fluid that nourishes us."

"Than we shall take the nourishment by force!" Samael got on his knees upon the snow and grabbed the camel's teat with his teeth. He pulled hard, trying to draw the white liquid into his mouth, but no fluid came. The camel groaned and kicked.

Gadreel ran to him. "Samael, please stop! You are hurting her and she shall injure you in return." He did not listen to her. She approached the camel and passed her hand over the beast's face. "Be calm. I shall try—" The camel seemed confused and agitated. Gadreel continued caressing her and she bit her on the hand with her large, protruding teeth.

Blood gushed from the wound. Gadreel shrieked nonstop. "The soldiers—the soldiers died. I remember—the defeated soldiers who had lost blood from their bodies— perished." Her screams stopped Samael's efforts to suckle and he ran to her aid. Lilith followed.

Samael's jaw dropped and he buried his hands in his hair. Gadreel's hand appeared almost severed in half. She was losing a lot of blood.

Lilith approached Gadreel, who was now in hysterics, holding her hand while blood turned the snow red.

"Let me see the wound." Lilith wore a hardened expression. Gadreel's eyes opened wide with fear and she glanced at Samael.

"Go on, show her your hand," Samael said. "She may be able to help you. I know not what to do."

Gadreel closed her eyes and with care extended her trembling arm toward Lilith. Lilith grabbed her hand and examined it. Gadreel groaned and tightened her jaw. After manipulating her hand, Lilith pushed it flat against the icy wall of the cave. Gadreel wailed and struggled to loosen her hand, but Lilith continued to press it against the frost.

"Help me, Samael. The pain is unbearable. I shall die of anguish!" Gadreel's face was pale and etched with pain.

"Apologies. I am certain Lilith knows what she is doing, although her methods seem mystifying." Samael's body shook and he covered his eyes with a hand.

"Please let my hand go. It stings like bitter fire!" Gadreel cried but Lilith continued to press her hand against the frost, her face like stone.

Gadreel swayed. "I sense I am being drawn from this world. Black spots merge together in my vision, and soon I shall see only darkness." Her knees buckled, and she collapsed.

Lilith let go of her hand. "The wound is sealed and the bleeding has stopped."

Gadreel opened her eyes. The excruciating pain in her hand woke her from her stupor. She held her hand against her heaving chest. Tears ran from her swollen eyes, cold against her reddened cheeks.

Samael gazed at her with a pitying expression.

"She shall be fine now," Lilith told Samael. "Her vital life force no longer drains from her."

He stared at her with a mixture of admiration and dread. "Life force?"

"Yes." Lilith raised her chin. "Your blood is your life force. We know it exits our bodies when it is broken. We witnessed it in the forbidden forests and in battle. On Earth, we seem to lose a great deal more blood more easily than we ever did in Floraison. Lose enough of it, and your life shall come to an end. The wingless creatures in my visions, which I have come to know are future humans, also have such a fluid circulating through their bodies. It gives them life."

Samael blinked, looking confused.

Lilith sighed. "One is able to lose a certain amount of blood, and the body simply generates more to replace it. However, lose too much at one time, and the body would be unable to replace it fast enough, and you would perish like so many did in the war in Floraison."

"How is it you come to know so much?" he asked.

Lilith gazed into his eyes, the corners of her lips upstretched into a slow smile. She leaned in and nuzzled his neck, cheeks and lips with her face and parted lips. The warmth of her breath against his skin made him shudder with pleasure. She buried her fingers in his dark, wavy hair and pressed her soft, plump lips against his. He enjoyed a tingling, warming sensation throughout his body. He forgot the question he asked. He forgot he asked a question at all.

Lilith separated her lips further and slipped her tongue into his mouth, chasing his tongue with hers, then retrieving it and pressing her lips on his once more. As she withdrew from him, he caught her arms and pulled her near again. "Please remain by my side. I yearn for this moment to last a lifetime." His words were heavy breaths. She wrested her arms from him, and flashed a now-I-got-you-where-I-want-you smile. He ogled her. "I am captivated by your enticing ways."

From the ground, Gadreel observed Lilith seduce Samael, as she had Satan. Gadreel's eyes burned with hatred. Her sight blurred with stinging tears and her hands tightened into fists. She heaved a deep breath. "This negative energy is trying to unseal evil within me. I shall fight against it." She buried her face in her good hand.

Samael heard her cries and turned away from Lilith. He saw Gadreel crying and proceeded to her.

Lilith glared at them. "Perhaps Gadreel is not as foolish as I thought.

She exploits Samael's attentions. She may have plans of her own that require his alliance. I shall remain vigilant," Lilith said, in an undertone.

In the midst of these happenings, the little camel drew its last breath. No one seemed to notice. Later, the mother camel moaned and whimpered. When the fallen ones glanced her way, they saw the animal mourning her calf. The cries the camel uttered were the saddest sounds they ever heard.

Gadreel's body drooped and she hung her head. "Poor little creature." Her tone was flat and sad.

"We should consume it." Lilith licked her bottom lip.

Gadreel cocked her head, wide-eyed. "What? You cannot mean—" She raised her eyebrows in disbelief and pressed the back of a hand to her mouth.

Lilith clapped her hands on her hips. "We need nourishment to survive. The small animal's carcass can provide us with a substantial amount of food."

"But Lilith, consuming animal flesh is surely forbidden." Samael stared at her.

"Why?" Lilith asked, without hesitation. "The rules we lived by in Floraison no longer exist here on Earth. We are different creatures now, and we make our own rules."

"In Floraison we ate fruits and vegetables on occasion for the pleasure of it," Gadreel said. "I understand that on Earth we need sustenance to survive, but we were taught that animals should be cherished."

Lilith smiled. "We rule over these animals now and we shall do what we please with them."

She strutted to the small camel's carcass and lifted it from the ground. The large camel snapped at her several times, and finally latched onto one of her wings with its large teeth and held on tight.

Gadreel and Samael watched with horrified expressions as Lilith willed her serpent form and struck the animal with her tail until the camel surrendered and retreated.

Lilith placed the stiff calf on its back upon a flat surface of the cave. Her nails grew into sharp talons as they had in the jungle. She ripped the calf's soft underbelly open and began to gorge on its insides.

Samael rubbed his throat and inched toward her. He grimaced in disgust watching dark blood run along the sides of her mouth. Her neck and hands were coated in it too.

Gadreel turned her face away and gagged. "Are you enjoying that?"

Lilith raised her chin. "No. It is revolting, but it appeases my hunger, and strengthens me."

Samael knelt and pulled the calf's heart out of its small chest cavity. He lifted the organ to his nose and sniffed. The smell reminded him of his dead comrades in the war. He stuffed the structure in his mouth.

"Gadreel, you must eat." Samael spoke with a full mouth and a sour look on his face. "This planet is harsh, and we have yet to locate the others. We must still travel a ways to find the source of the shrill. Eating shall make you stronger and fit for the task."

Gadreel shook her head, her lips curled in disgust. She went to a small corner of the cave to lie down. Even with her four large wings wrapped around her body, she still trembled on the cold floor.

The camel hobbled to her and lay on the icy ground beside her. Gadreel flinched and her body tensed. "Please do not hurt me again." She almost sprang to her feet to get away, but the animal lay still against her and generated much warmth with its large body and thick coat. She relaxed and fell asleep.

The other two angels filled their bellies, leaving the carcass nearly void of edible material. Lilith peeled the skin and fur off the remains. She tore the hide into four pieces, two large and two small, and placed the skins flat on the cave's floor. Afterward, she was ready for some needed rest.

She and Samael searched for Gadreel. When they found her, their mouths fell open.

"She lies with the animal that almost bit her hand off!" Lilith clutched her full belly and guffawed. "Behold, she sleeps well."

Samael shrugged and watched Gadreel sleep.

"She is using the beast's body heat to keep warm," Lilith said. "In my visions, the humans huddled together in ice caves such as this one to share each other's warmth at night. You and I should do the same."

"I agree. I am tired and need my strength to resume our journey tomorrow. Come, I shall keep you warm." Samael lay down next to Gadreel and beckoned Lilith. He pulled her close. Lilith placed two of her wings underneath her to shield her from the snow and ice, and her other two wings rested over them. He lay on one of his large wings and wrapped the other over the two of them. Together, they created a cocoon of warmth.

"I sense we are much closer to the source of the shrill sound," she whispered. On the morrow, they would resume their journey to find their allies—to find Satan—and then she would be well on her way to having her vengeance on God.

Chapter 11

GADREEL'S SECRET

After several hours of sleep, they awoke looking well rested. "We should eat what remains of the carcass before we leave the cave." Lilith stretched and yawned.

Samael blinked owlishly and bobbed his head. "Gadreel, will you eat?"

Gadreel frowned and held up a palm. "I refuse to eat animal flesh." Her voice was weak and her legs shook from lack of nourishment.

The large camel got to its feet. It glanced at Gadreel, and then peeked at Samael and Lilith as they strolled away toward the small carcass to have their day's first meal.

Gadreel tried to move the beast along to follow them, but the camel would not budge.

She looked at the camel sideways. "Do you wish to remain in this ice cave by yourself?"

The camel nudged her on the back of the neck, almost knocking her to the ground. She was startled, but unexpectedly, unafraid. She rested a hand on her hip and squinted at the camel. The animal shoved her again and this time she fell to her knees.

Gadreel remained crouched on the ground. "Is this what you wish?" She blew out her cheeks and waited.

The camel positioned herself perpendicular to her and exposed her udder. Gadreel chortled. "Ah, I now realize your purpose." She straightened and tucked her curls behind her ears, placed her mouth around one of the teats and began to pull.

Before long, warm, sweet milk poured into her mouth. She was so hungry, her mouth quivered as she slurped.

After feeding to her heart's content, she got to her feet, and wiped her mouth. "This shall be our little secret," she whispered to the camel. The camel bobbed its head and followed her as she proceeded to find the others. She found them as they finished the last of the carcass. Lilith scooped snow off the ground to cleanse her face and hands. Samael mimicked her every move. Gadreel glowered at them.

"It is time we leave this icy cavern," Lilith said. "We shall need our strength today, for I intend to make it to the coast before we rest again."

"We have plenty of strength for that and more." Samael beamed and raked his fingers through his hair.

"We do, but Gadreel has not fed yet." Lilith scowled at her.

"Do not worry about me. I shall not linger." Gadreel raised her chin.

Lilith frowned and walked to her. "You look in good form and restored." She ambled around her. "Yet, you have not fed in quite a while." Was she growing stronger?

Gadreel inspected her fingernails. "Perhaps the rest did me well. I shall not dawdle, I promise."

"Perhaps you shall not delay us, but that large animal would certainly slow us." Lilith pointed to the camel that had not moved from Gadreel's side.

"No! The beast shall not lag behind either." She put her arm around the camel's neck.

Lilith pulled back, eyebrows lifted high. "I do not understand your attachment to this animal. You do remember that it nearly tore your hand in half?" She smiled the kind of smile that feels like a threat. "If the animal hinders us at any point, we shall leave it where it stands." The animal could still be of some use to them and perhaps serve as sustenance at some point. She would allow her to bring it with them. Besides, it would keep Gadreel busy and away from Samael.

"I agree," Samael said. "The beast is of no use to us anymore, since it does not allow us to drink of its nutritious fluid."

"Very well, if the animal slows us, I shall leave it." Gadreel crossed her arms.

Lilith proceeded to the skins she left lying on the ice overnight. She lifted one of the narrow sections, and wrapped it around her upper body. She tied the soft hide into a knot at the center, concealing her breasts. She then grabbed one of the larger pieces of the skin material, and secured it around her waist, creating a garment. The others watched with confused expressions. Afterward, she glanced at Gadreel and pointed to the remaining pieces of skin.

"Do as I did."

"I shall not!" Gadreel turned away, lips primed.

"In Floraison, we wore garments to cover our bodies. Those garments were removed from us when we were exiled. Do either of you know why?" Lilith raised an eyebrow and waited for a response.

Gadreel hung her head. Samael shrugged.

"The reason they stripped us bare before exiling us to this planet is because they expected us to live here like animals." Lilith peered into Samael's luminous amber eyes.

"That cannot be true," Samael said in a gruff voice. "We are superior to the animals."

"Not in God's eyes! Not anymore." Lilith pointed skyward. "That is why we must conceal our bodies—to defy Him who thinks so little of us."

Gadreel wrapped her arms around herself. "I understand now why we should cover our bodies, but I still cannot wear the small animal's skin. I shall find something else to use for garments soon enough."

"Very well, do what you must." Lilith marched toward the cave's exit.

Samael took the larger piece of camel skin and created a garment, which hung from his waist and hid his genitals. They strolled away from the ice cave with renewed vigor and strength. Outside the sun shone on the mountain, and for once its glaring, fiery light was welcomed.

The fallen angels and the camel moved on foot until they saw the ocean. Gadreel beamed as she watched the sun's rays frolic across the turquoise waters.

"We are close to Satan now. I can sense his presence." Lilith closed her eyes.

Samael sulked. She speaks of reuniting with Satan while he stood by her side, as if he were insignificant.

"We can fly to shore from here!" Lilith's eyes gleamed with enthusiasm.

"You must leave the mammal behind. Leave it and fly to shore," Samael said with a contemptuous toss of his head toward the edge of the mountain.

"No, I shall not leave it." Gadreel held on to the camel's neck. "What is wrong, Samael? Lilith's ebullience to join Satan put you in a foul mood?"

Lilith cocked her head and guffawed.

He threw his hands in the air. "Fine! I would like to see how you plan to fly to the coast carrying the beast."

"Lilith was able to carry the animal in flight to the mountaintop. Why would I not be able to do the same?" Gadreel climbed upon the camel, wrapped her arms around it, and began to flap her wings with vigor. She lifted the camel off the ground and proceeded to fly toward the coast.

Samael laughed and slapped a hand on his forehead. "She did it!"

The smile on Lilith's face did not change. It did not fade in the least. But the smile in her eyes, the authentic part of a smile, vanished.

Gadreel flew to the rim of the ocean. The temperature rose as she swooped to a red, rocky cliff, which gave way to a flat shoreline with beaches. She placed the camel on the rock and leapt down.

She gazed at the beautiful seashore and the vast, shimmering ocean. She caught sight of a large bird in the cloudless sky. It was elegant and agile in flight and she admired its full-feathered legs, large talons, powerful beak, and brown plumage combined with lustrous golden feathers on top of its head and neck. The bird was unlike any creature she had seen in Floraison.

Gadreel beckoned it. "Come to me, my feathered friend, so that I may take a better look at you." To her amazement the bird flew to her and perched on her left shoulder.

She laughed with excitement. She extended her left arm across her body, offering her limb as a perch. The large bird hopped onto her forearm, and she carried its weight. She bent her arm closer to her body. "Despite your size you are but a young raptor."

The eaglet stared into her eyes for a while and then it squealed and chirped. It seemed to be conversing with her, but the conversation was one-sided, since she did not understand its meaning. The eaglet screamed one more time and flew away. She followed the bird with her eyes as it soared across the sky until it was far beyond her sight. She was about to lower her eyes when she spotted Lilith and Samael in midair.

She watched them land on a great cliff across the beach from her. She placed her hand on the camel. "We must go meet them."

The camel sat on its hind legs. Gadreel pulled on her but the animal would not budge. Gadreel held the camel's face between her hands. "Please come with me."

The camel groaned and did not move.

"Come with me, I implore you. Do not leave me alone with Lilith and her minion." With a downward gaze, the camel stood on its hind legs and made a rumbling growl.

"I appreciate what you are doing for me." She smiled. It seemed she had been given a great gift. She could communicate with most animals, and they were responsive to her wishes and suggestions. However, a few species were hostile toward her. She must develop her talent further.

She caressed the beast's thick, woolly fur. Together, they made their way to the long strip of sand lapped by ocean waves.

On her way off the rocky surface, Gadreel came across many sizeable plants with large leaves. She collected long, wide leaves and vines, which she used to make a frock to cover her lower half, and a second garment to conceal her bosom.

The sun rose higher in the sky, creating a palette of hues on the water. She squinted at the sun. "Midday approaches, and the sun's powerful rays shall be sweltering and dangerous. My feet are red and painful, for the sand beneath them is hot. I thought the sun's warmth would have been a welcomed change from the ice and snow, but it is merely another form of torture." She glanced at the camel and smiled. "I wish I was as well provided as you are to cope with the sun's rays."

In the distance, she saw a tree with sizable shade beneath it. She hurried to rest on the shady patch of soft white sand. She gazed upward. The tree's crown of feather-shaped leaves held large clusters of round, nutty fruit. She reclined against the palm tree with the camel at her side.

She gazed at the camel and buried her hand in the curls on top of its head. "Lilith is set on retaliation against God for all that has gone wrong in Floraison and on Earth. She becomes more and more dangerous as thoughts of vengeance consume her." She pressed her lips together and stretched out her legs in front of her. The camel moaned softly. "What can I do? I am trapped. Lilith resents me more each day because I do not share her lust for revenge. I am terrified of what is to come. I must win over Samael, but how? I need him as an ally, but how could I compete with Lilith for his affections?" She rubbed her chin and tapped the air with her feet. "I am in constant fear for my life, but I must become brave or I shall not survive."

Chapter 12

SWEET NUTTY SUSTENANCE

L ilith and Samael dove to the fine white sands surrounded by mountains. They moved on foot toward Gadreel and met her under the coconut tree. The day grew hotter but they experienced some degree of comfort in the shade.

As they relaxed under the tree, the sound they followed became stronger in their minds.

"We must move closer to the ocean," Lilith told the others. "We are being summoned to the waters. Do you not hear it?"

"Yes, I hear it." Samael's tone was sarcastic and his lips pursed like he had been chewing on something sour.

Gadreel rose to her feet and stared at the water.

They drew closer to the ocean and spotted another coconut tree near the shoreline. Lilith and Samael sat in the shade. Gadreel stepped into the water and smiled. "The sensation of the water splashing against my legs is delightful." She slowly waded out farther and immersed herself in the salty ocean water. The gentle waves cradled her and swayed her to and fro. Soft sand swirled between her toes. She chortled and then inhaled and submerged herself.

There were many small fish underwater. The minute fish swam to her and softly pecked her on the nose, cheeks, forehead and chin, as if delivering little kisses. She watched them for a while, but realized she needed to come up for air. She surfaced and drew in a long, deep breath.

She sashayed toward the shoreline, water dripping from her hair and body. Her wet skin glistened in the sunlight. She glanced at Samael and smiled. He ogled her.

Lilith looked at Gadreel and then at him and scowled. "Do you desire her?"

He raised his eyebrows and shrugged. "She is fetching in a peculiar way, but you are beautiful beyond compare."

She grabbed his face and turned it toward her. When his eyes were fixed on hers, she kissed him.

Gadreel stopped and stared openmouthed. "What do we do now?" There was some bite in her tone.

"We wait," Lilith told her with a satisfied smile.

They lingered on the beach, staring out to sea. The coconut palm near the shoreline was smaller than the previous one and provided less shade. Meanwhile, the sun's rays beat on them. The camel helped block the sun for a little while, but it was not enough. Once more they began to lose strength and vigor.

The camel squirmed, shifted positions, and moaned. Gadreel observed the animal and stroked its fur. The camel stood and shuffled away behind the tree. The animal continued to move away from the others. Gadreel trailed behind it.

"Where are you and the beast going?" Lilith peered at her, having caught her slipping away.

"I believe the animal is hungry. It is trying to search for food." Gadreel bounced on her toes.

"Food? Maybe we should all follow the beast. It has been a long time since we last fed. We need sustenance as well."

"No!" Gadreel held up her palms. "I mean—do not expend your energy. If the beast finds food, I shall bring some for you both, or come get you and take you to the source. In the meantime, relax under the tree and conserve your energy." Gadreel hid her trembling hands behind her.

Lilith stared at her askance. There was a long, awkward silence. She appeared to be trying to read her intentions. "Splendid, go and follow your beast." She gave a dismissive wave of her hand. "We shall wait here for the food you shall provide for us." She glanced at Samael, who snickered with her.

"Gadreel the provider!" Samael mocked, resting his body against the tree.

Gadreel stormed away, following the camel to a small thicket of trees between immense rocks bordering the beach. Her face lost color as she stared at the small woodland. "This is not one of the forbidden forests in Floraison." She exhaled a rush of air and tiptoed amongst the trees. The camel ate plants and bushes, while she paced to and fro, wide eyes flitting in every direction, as she waited for the animal to get its fill of vegetation.

When the camel was done, it gestured for Gadreel to feed from it again. She scanned for signs of a threat. The camel nudged her once more, pushing her toward her hind legs. Once Gadreel's belly was full, she faced the camel. "Thank you for your generosity." She caressed the animal's face with the hand it had injured. The camel whimpered and licked her wound.

"Do not fret. My hand shall soon be healed. Lilith's bizarre methods do yield results. Besides, I know you were grief stricken and not yourself when you bit me. You were also frightened by Samael's brutish ways. I understand, and I am sorry for your loss."

Gadreel laughed as the camel caressed her head with its muzzle.

"We better return before those two come looking for us. It displeases me that I shan't be taking them food. They shall mock me for it."

On their way back, they passed several coconut palm trees. The camel stopped and kicked the trunk of one tree hard several times, and coconuts came crashing to the ground. One of the coconuts split open when it landed on a jagged rock, splashing Gadreel's face with its dulcet liquid.

She picked up one of the halves of the hard-shelled fruit and drank the rest of the opaque fluid. Her eyes opened wide. "It is delightful with a sweet and satisfying taste."

The camel began to tear the hard shell off the other coconut half, exposing a meaty white substance, and proceeded to eat it. Gadreel stared openmouthed. The beast tore off a piece of the coconut's white flesh and offered it to her.

"Oh! This is delicious!" Gadreel's mouth was full of coconut. "We can take some back to the others. I am sure they shan't think me useless after they have tasted this fruit."

She gathered several coconuts and walked in an uncoordinated way, heels raised, trying to balance them in her arms. The camel carried one in its mouth.

Samael and Lilith slept together, her head on his shoulder. Gadreel clenched her teeth and dropped the coconuts at their feet, giving them both a start.

"What is this?" Lilith gasped, jolted upright and pushed back against the tree in a startled motion and bumped her back and head.

Gadreel bit her lower lip to conceal a smile. "Here is the food I promised." She raised her chin, and stood taller.

Lilith glanced at the coconuts and then looked at her with disdain. "What are these things?"

"They are fruit. You can puncture a hole on the top, and drink its sweet nectar. The liquid shall quench your thirst. When you are done drinking, you can crack them open to expose the white flesh. Eat and satisfy your hunger." Gadreel's eyes glimmered with pride.

Samael lifted one of the coconuts and turned it in his hand. Gadreel found a jagged rock, placed it before him, and repeated her instructions in a singsong voice. He placed the coconut on the ground, lifted the sharp rock and struck the top of the fruit, puncturing a hole, spilling some of the liquid on the sand.

He sniffed the opening and grinned. "The fragrance resembles a mix of tropical flowers, with a hint of sweetness." He brought the fruit to his mouth and drank nearly all of the liquid. Lilith watched him, salivating. He then split the coconut into halves and handed her one. Together they sipped the remaining watery substance. He licked his lips. Lilith beamed.

Gadreel pried a piece of the white flesh off the outer brown shell and minced her way to him. She placed it in Samael's mouth in a coquettish manner. He chewed it slowly. "The taste is dulcet and has a flavor like that of nuts." He nodded and smiled.

They opened the remaining coconuts, drank the water and ate the meaty parts inside the shells. Soon, they lay satiated on the sand. They closed their eyes again.

Gadreel sulked. Lilith and Samael lay in each other's arms, happy and satisfied by the fruit she provided, yet they showed no gratitude. Did they think themselves king and queen of the planet? What would happen once they found Satan and the others? Satan would not be pleased to discover Lilith's treachery.

Chapter 13

THE SHRILL SOUND

Gadreel dragged her feet to the coastline and sat on the wet sand using her wings as shade. She meditated as the slow, steady waves moved ashore and covered her feet with foam. She hummed. The hum became a song. As she sang, the water slipped under her, pulling her farther into the ocean. The piercing sound in her head became louder. She stopped singing, for the shrill sound grew unbearable.

She pressed her hands over her ears and turned to stare at the others. It seemed the same unpleasant deafening sound had awakened them. She jumped to her feet and gaped at the ocean.

"Something is happening!" She trembled. The others ran to her side, their eyes also fixed on the now turbulent waters.

The camel ran to Gadreel and nudged her again and again. It emitted high-pitched moans and squeaks, but she could not hear the animal above the painful shrill tone. The animal lowered its head, bellowing and roaring. In spite of the camel's cautioning noises and nudges to her thigh, she did not take her eyes off the growing waves. After a while, the animal relinquished its efforts to carry her away to safety and galloped, unseen, to the forest in terror.

The fallen angels could not take their eyes off the tempestuous seas.

Massive waves formed and smashed onto shore. The shrill tone swelled in their minds, muffling the thunderous crash of the undulating swells. They took to the skies for fear of being struck and engulfed by the surfs. They flew to the top of a nearby cliff that towered above the sea. They watched wide-eyed and panting as the waters parted to reveal an enormous creature rising from the depths. The noxious stench of salt, fish, and seaweed overwhelmed them.

Streams of ocean water ran along the creature's body and poured off like waterfalls. Immense tentacles extended from the sea monster's body and reached toward the skies, almost making contact with the fallen ones on their high, rocky ledge.

The color drained from their faces. Gadreel screamed in horror. Lilith willed her snake form to appear and stood tall carrying her tail in a forward curve over her body like a scorpion.

Samael expanded his black spiny wings and gaped at the gigantic sea creature. "We were beguiled by this creature's shrill calls. It tricked us into finding it and now we shall become living nourishment for its consumption!"

The creature's head was black and shiny like polished onyx, and its eyes were the size of huge boulders. It had the torso of a powerful man, bluish-black in color and covered in a viscous slime. Wriggling and lashing at them were eight muscular appendages lined with multiple suction cups along its length. At the end of the tentacles were orbs of light. The angels' eyes hurt when the creature flashed the intense light of its orbs. Soon the sea monster stopped emerging from the water and headed toward them.

Lilith veered her tail in front of her to defend against the beast. "We must stand strong against it!"

"No! We must flee for our lives!" Gadreel gasped and pulled Samael's arm. "We cannot triumph against such a creature any more than we can prevail over a lava spewing volcano!"

"We must not permit any other species to claim what is ours," Lilith said. "We are the new rulers of this planet, and any other creature who wishes to reign stands in our way and must be destroyed!"

Gadreel stared at her with an incredulous expression.

Samael panted and his body shook but he straightened and glared at the leviathan.

The sea monster stood before them and observed them with large, expressive eyes. It opened its mouth to display long, blade-like fangs and emitted the loud piercing sound they all recognized. At such close range, it was unbearable.

Gadreel wailed in pain as blood flowed from her ears. Samael caught sight of this, and took flight, charging the beast.

"Stop that shrill noise at once!" Samael ordered the water giant, forgetting his fear and the pain in his head. Upon his command the beast instantly fell silent. Samael's eyebrows rose high and he stared at the creature slack-mouthed.

Lilith flew to the monster's head and attacked it with her vicious tail. She flew around to clobber its eyes, in order to render it sightless. The creature secreted a black liquid, which quickly bloomed over the surface of the water tainting it in gloom.

"I sense the creature's fear!" Lilith shouted to Samael. "We need to finish him now!"

"No, please!" a familiar voice pleaded in their minds. "Why do you persist in harming me? Stop, I implore you."

"Wait!" Gadreel yelled. "The creature's voice––it is familiar." She flew closer and gazed into the sea giant's eyes. She gasped. "I believe this creature to be Fornues." She covered her mouth with both hands.

"Fornues? Impossible!" Samael shook his head.

"Look at his eyes." She pointed.

Lilith scrutinized the beast's large bloodshot eyes. They were heavy-lidded, hazel eyes with drooping outer corners. "It is he."

"Fornues, why were you trying to hurt us?" Gadreel stared at him, eyebrows joined in a frown, blood still oozing from her ears.

"I am sorry. It was not my intention to hurt any of you. I have yet to acquire the skills to control this new bulk I have been cursed with." Fornues communicated without speaking.

"Are you able to utter words?" Samael asked.

"I have come to realize that I should only communicate in your minds."

If I open my mouth to speak, the loud shrill sound that hurt you shall be all you hear."

Lilith's bleak expression told of her disappointment. "I was certain the shrill sound had originated from Satan. Instead, it was you, Fornues, in your monstrous form who had summoned us."

Lilith put her hands on her hips and lowered her head. "Where are the others? Where is Satan?"

Before Fornues answered, she heard above her an unexpected, but welcomed, voice.

Chapter 14

TRANSFORMATIONS

"I am here, my treasured one."

Lilith beamed, lifted her eyes to the sky and saw a creature hovering above her. She recoiled. The being with Satan's voice did not appear to be him at all.

The creature's skin was the color of blood. Huge curved horns extended from his hairless head. His wings were hideous: black as night, fleshy and featherless, with a claw at the end of each section. He also possessed a long, massive tail with a spiky end.

The fiend landed in front of her. She inhaled a sharp breath and shuddered.

Satan held out his arms. Disgust distorted her face and she withdrew. He frowned and let his arms drop to his sides and his shoulders slumped. "I know I do not appear as I once did, but please do not fear me. After all, you too have gone through a transformation."

Lilith remained motionless before him in her snake form. She looked stunned. She could not gaze into his dark blue eyes, for black pits had replaced them. She could no longer caress his smooth, pale skin. She shook her head, squeezed her eyes shut and hugged herself.

He reached out to caress her, but

at the slightest touch her eyes sprung open. She cringed and recoiled, as Samael had done when he first saw her snake creature form.

"You are not the beautiful angel you once were. Your touch shall no longer be warm or inviting. This is the worst punishment of all." She hung her head. "My thirst for vengeance has doubled since God has taken my love from me."

Satan clutched his chest and his body drooped. He reached for her. She jerked away.

Without further delay, she transformed herself into her appealing angel form.

Satan's jaw dropped. "How were you able to transform to your angel form?"

"I just desired it, and it was so." She stared at the ground to avoid the sight of him.

Satan's breaths quickened and he moved closer. She flinched. "Do not touch me with your clawed hands." He sucked his teeth and stomped away from her.

Halting several steps away, he closed his eyes, and thought of himself the way he used to be. He pictured his dark hair, blue eyes and tall, muscular body in his mind. He willed his angel form to return, and it was so. When he opened his eyes he examined his hands, his skin. He threaded his hand through his long, thick hair and grinned. He turned and gazed at Lilith.

Now he stood before her, appearing as he did in Floraison, with the exception of his wings, which remained pitch black and leathery with claw-like spikes.

Lilith ran to him and embraced him. This was the beautiful and powerful angel she knew and loved. She held on to him. "I hope you could forgive me for the way I behaved." She should have been cleverer.

"I am disappointed you could not accept me the way I first presented myself. I had no knowledge that I could transform into my angel form. Your rejection wounded me more than Michael's golden spear." He did not enfold her in his arms, instead he pulled her off him and turned away. She remained motionless as her eyes trailed him.

Satan strolled to Gadreel and grinned. She returned his smile, proceeded to him, and held him in a welcoming embrace. Lilith glowered at her. Satan moved to Samael and hugged him as well.

"It is good to see you are all well." Satan smiled. He stood straight, shoulders back. "I am feeling myself again."

Lilith hung her head and stared at her shuffling feet.

"It pleases me to have found you at last, my friend," Samael looked away from Satan to glance at Fornues. "For a moment, I thought we were beguiled by a monster whose sole purpose was to have us for nourishment." Samael and Satan chuckled. Samael added, "No offense, Fornues."

"None taken."

"We have traveled for many miles, mostly on foot," Gadreel said. "For many days and nights, we followed Fornues' shrilling sound. Lilith was certain we would find you at its source." Gadreel glanced at Lilith. Grudgingly, Lilith smiled at her for saying so.

"We have suffered many hardships, but the thought of finding you gave us strength to continue." Lilith gazed into his eyes and moved toward him rolling and undulating her hips. She caressed his face and kissed him on the lips. "Apologies, my prince. I did not respond well to your vulgar red appearance. It was disgraceful of me."

She kept eye contact and spoke with a seductive tone. "Naturally, I would devote myself to you in any form. I merely needed a small measure of time to adjust. Please understand my predicament."

He drew in a long breath. "Yes, I grasp your meaning. You are exonerated." He pulled her close and held her tight as he kissed her neck, face and lips.

Samael walked a short distance away and sulked.

"Could I return to my original shape?" asked another familiar voice from the waters below them.

Satan looked toward the water. "Fornues, raise our friend from the sea."

The others hurried to the edge of the cliff to see who would be taken from the waters.

Fornues wrapped one of his tentacles around Dagon's torso, and lifted him from the water so the others could see him. Lilith's eyes opened wide and Samael stood openmouthed.

Gadreel gasped. "Dagon! You are a water creature."

Dagon's ruggedly handsome face, long flaxen hair, and penetrating gray-blue eyes were as everyone remembered. His strong, masculine torso had also not changed, but he no longer had wings and his lower body was that of a fish.

"Place him on this rock." Satan pointed at the rocky surface under his feet.

Fornues lowered Dagon, who sat on the cliff, his flailing fish tail flinging water everywhere. The others stepped away, wiping saltwater off their faces and rubbing their eyes.

"If I wish to be my former self, shall it be so?" Dagon looked to Satan for an answer.

"You shall not know unless you try," Satan said.

Dagon closed his eyes and imagined himself as he once was in Floraison. When he opened his eyes he was astonished to see the fish tail was gone. He jumped to his feet, ran around, leapt and guffawed. The others proceeded to him, wrapping him in a collective embrace.

"It is good to be all together again!" Dagon shouted.

"One of us is still missing," Satan said. "I have not seen Beelzebub since I was cast from Floraison."

"Gadreel and I have not come across Beelzebub in our travels." Lilith glanced at Gadreel while shaking her head.

"We must find him," Satan said. "I fear he needs our help. I can sense his presence on Earth, as I detected all of you. He is far from this place. Mayhem besieges him."

"Thus, we must depart at once. We should find our friend Beelzebub." Lilith feigned concern. Beelzebub served her well in Floraison. He would be a good ally on Earth. Satan smiled and put his arms around her.

"What of me?" Fornues said. "Perhaps I, too, can switch into my previous form?"

"Carry on then, make an attempt." Lilith's eyes rolled upward.

Like Dagon and Satan before him, Fornues closed his eyes and imagined the angel he used to be in Floraison: eight feet tall with alabaster skin and long, wavy auburn hair. Fornues saw himself standing on two legs on the high cliff, ready to embrace the others with his long, muscular arms, just as Dagon did.

Fornues opened his eyes. To his and everyone's disappointment, he was still the large, ferocious-looking creature who stirred the ocean. He closed his eyes again. He wished with all his might he could change to his essential makeup. Once more he opened his eyes to find he was still imprisoned in his new form as a monster of the deep. Giant drops fell from his eyes, hitting the rocks jutting out of the ocean like the explosion of a star. He produced a horrible lament, filling his friends' ears and psyches with intolerable tumult.

The fallen angels plugged their ears, but the sound penetrated their minds, nerves, and entire beings. Satan, Samael, and Dagon experienced painful vibrations in all their muscles. Gadreel and Lilith's ears bled.

"Cease sobbing at once!" Lilith screamed. "Otherwise, you shall kill us all with your lamentations!"

"There is no need for you to change to your previous form," Satan said in a stern, convincing voice. "You shall be of great value to me as a large, fierce sea creature."

Fornues stopped his wailing. They all collapsed to the ground, trembling and moaning.

"Yes, master," Fornues said, in a flat tone.

"We shall rest until nightfall. When we rise, we shall begin our journey to locate Beelzebub." Satan rubbed his arm and leg muscles. "Once we have found Beelzebub, we shall search for a place where we can live together in peace."

Lilith cocked her head and stared at him. Peace? There shall be no peace until she had finished what she began. She would convince them of this, and she would have her vengeance.

"We shall need all of our strength to cross the desert for a second time." Lilith rose to her feet as she cautioned them. "We shall also need plenty of nourishment before we embark on this task."

She caught a glimpse of Gadreel pointing toward the coconut trees at the beach.

"There is plenty to eat here," Lilith blurted, before Gadreel could open her mouth. "The trees on the sand strip are heavily laden with fruit, which contain liquid to quench your thirst and fleshy white substance to satisfy your hunger. Come, I shall show you."

She took Satan by the hand and glided off the rocky cliff to a coconut tree. Samael swaggered off the edge of the cliff, floating gracefully all the way to the sand.

Dagon asked Fornues to place him on the beach since he no longer had wings and could not fly. He trailed behind Lilith and Satan, having also experienced the empty, burning sensation in his belly.

Dagon and Fornues had been underwater, and Satan had spent many days in the darkness of a great cave. Therefore, they did not have as much exposure to the sun as Lilith, Gadreel, and Samael. This seemed to have extended the lingering effects of Floraison and their angel powers, staving off the need to feed—until now.

Gadreel's large, brown eyes glittered with loathing for Lilith. She pitched herself off the cliff and landed roughly on the sand. She rose and followed the others to the coconut palms.

Lilith once again changed herself into the snake creature, pounding on the tree's trunk until coconuts began to fall. She cracked one against a rock, offering half to Satan, and the other half to Dagon.

They drank the dulcet nectar of the coconut. She showed them how to pry out chunks of the white edible substance. Satan and Dagon devoured the coconut flesh.

Gadreel hurried away to the forest to find her camel, figuring the clever mammal might have gone there to hide and feed, but she did not find the beast. She dragged her feet as she left the woodland and returned to where the others still gorged on coconuts.

She strolled to the shoreline and sat with her feet in the water. "I miss Floraison." Fornues' mysterious energy drew her. She wiped her eyes with the back of her hand and entered the water. A large wave advanced in her direction. She prepared to fly away.

"Please do not be frightened. It is only I, Fornues." As he emerged from the water, it grew dark, for he obscured the sun. He gazed at her with his large hazel-green eyes.

"You frightened me. I truly know not how much more I can endure. I have already been through so much on this planet."

"Do not despair. Satan shall lead us to a wonderful place where we can dwell together in peace."

"You mean Lilith, do you not?" Gadreel used a sarcastic tone.

"What are you insinuating? I do not comprehend."

"Lilith influences every action involving Satan. Wherever she desires to go is where we shall live. Besides, you are confined to the deep waters. You shall not be able to reside with the rest of us, for we cannot survive under the sea." Gadreel slapped a hand over her mouth.

"I do not wish to dwell in the dark seas as a lonely, pathetic monster." A large teardrop fell on Gadreel's head drenching her wild curls and flattening them against her scalp.

"Please do not weep. I did not mean we would abandon you. I am certain we shall live near a shore somewhere close to you. We shall always see each other and spend time together. It is what Satan desires most of all: for the fallen angels to come together."

"Is that what we are? Fallen angels?"

"We are angels who fell from grace." Gadreel smiled, but there was no joy behind her smile.

"I do not feel like an angel." He extended one of his tentacles and caressed Gadreel's head and body. Although he soaked her with saltwater dripping from his appendage, she appreciated his show of affection.

"You shall never be alone, Fornues. You must not fret." Gadreel patted his tentacle. "I am curious to know what the others are doing at this moment. I shall leave you now. When the sun sets, we shall begin our journey."

"I am most grateful to you." Fornues withdrew his tentacle. "I shall remain in the shallows near the shore, but I shall be able to hear all that is spoken, for my hearing distance reaches many miles. I can also communicate with all of you. It shall be as if I were right there."

Gadreel nodded and left to rejoin the others who were seated under a group of coconut palms farther up the beach. Lilith was bragging about her bravery during their trek through the desert.

Lilith caught sight of Gadreel approaching and when she was within earshot she continued her boasting. "I rescued Gadreel several times. She was a great burden; her weakness and incompetence nearly killed us on many occasions."

Gadreel frowned. "I recall saving you on at least one occasion." She sat on the ground.

"We have not heard your story, Satan." Lilith ignored Gadreel and gazed at him. "Where did you land? How did you come to find Fornues and Dagon?" She tilted her head to one side to listen.

Satan smiled and recounted what he underwent after his fall.

Chapter 15

LUCIFER'S FALL

"I was renamed Satan, for I am now the adversary of God and the holy angels. When I fell from Floraison, the mutation—which had begun with the injury inflicted to my chest by Michael's golden spear—continued to evolve. A burning sensation throughout my entire body caused me much grief.

"Four of my wings fused together to create two large ones, which became dark, leathery, and hideous as the white plumage burned away. The third pair of wings was ripped from my backbone, and I howled in anguish and pain."

Samael sucked air through his teeth and winced.

"Intense pain boomed in my skull," Satan continued. "My hands flew to the throbbing areas on my head, and I felt two sharp projections protruding through my scalp!"

Lilith narrowed her eyes and shuddered.

"The lower part of my spine pulsated," he said. "The pain was hard to bear. I yelled for mercy but knew no one would hear me. I attempted to examine my rear, but it was difficult to see the area causing so much agony. Reaching toward the pain I finally understood what was happening to me. I had sprouted a tail.

"I hit the ground with an explosion, creating a huge crater and dust cloud. I was weakened by the fall, the injury to my chest, and the excruciating and shameful alterations to my body. The pain consumed me. I was in and out of consciousness for several days and nights."

The fallen angels around him stared as he continued to tell his harrowing account. Except Lilith, she looked down and away, her shoulders slumped.

She rubbed her bosom. In Floraison he was a Seraph, a prince—second only to God. He lost everything for her ambitions. She tightened her fists and trembled. She would not be consumed by what she did, or obsess over her shamefulness. She did what was needed. They had ornate titles, but they were mere slaves to unjust laws. She would not allow this fitful fever to destroy her. What was done was done. It was time to press forward. She would bury this useless sentiment deep in the dark crevices of her psyche, never again to cause remorse.

"When I became conscious, I was horrified and ashamed." Satan lowered his eyes. "I lay exposed and vulnerable, covered in soil. The sun's brilliance hurt my eyes, reducing them to mere slits and attacked my new, strange red skin and black wings. It drained me of vital energy.

"I scanned the area around me, trying to identify where I landed. I plodded around. Every step, twitch or shift sent a surge of pain throughout my body, but I refused to remain still any longer.

"I saw mountains covered in vegetation and tall trees on all sides. I stood in a flourishing valley with opulent green growth, but could not get relief from Gabriel's brilliant star, whose emissions assaulted me."

Satan lowered his head and closed his eyes. Lilith glanced at him and her lips trembled but remained composed. Gadreel and Dagon exchanged anxious glances. Samael placed a hand on his shoulder, urging him to continue.

"I thought of Lilith." Satan raised his head and gazed at her. "By the end of the war, there was only chaos for the rebel angels. I was defeated by Michael and procured for judgment. I lost sight of her and my other generals. After my capture, it was all a blur, and the next thing I knew, I was pitched out of paradise. I thought only, what has become of my Lilith?

I assumed she must have suffered the same fate as I, and I was determined to find her on this new planet, but first, I understood, I must survive."

Lilith's eyes flashed with seduction as she smiled at him. Samael sulked.

"I decided to make my way to the mountains," Satan said. 'It was quite a long distance, and I struggled in my weakened state. I had to rest often. I wished to shout, but I could not fetch enough air into my lungs. My chest was a fiery desert. I endured, and fought my way through overgrown vegetation and across steep rocks. I struggled, dragging my feet as I progressed through the jungle, scraping and tearing my sore skin along the way.

"I came to a large circular opening in the ground and stopped short of falling in. I heard a whistling sound coming from the hollow. A loud, fearsome blowing sound followed. I retreated a few steps and waited for some terrible creature to arise from the underground void. I wondered how I would battle such a beast in my pathetic state. Nothing surfaced.

"I stepped toward the edge of the cavity and peered in. What I saw appealed to me. It was an area shielded from the fierce rays of the sun. I was determined to progress into the hole. I flapped my two large wings, but it only caused me pain. I learned it would be some time before I could fly, for my wings were damaged and weakened by the fall and the sun's powerful rays.

"I lowered myself into the large chamber. Once at the bottom I noticed another opening, which led into a cave beneath the Earth's surface. In the main passage of the cave, it was a few degrees cooler, and the sun's rays did not invade it fully. The beauty inside captivated me. Again, I thought of Lilith and how she would have enjoyed what I saw."

Lilith clutched his hand. Samael looked at her and then at their interlaced hands and scowled.

Gadreel looked panicked as she stared at Samael. His behavior was odd. Was he jealous? Was he so blinded by his lust for Lilith? She shifted on the ground and looked at Satan attempting to focus on his words. Even so, there were flickers of pain and disappointment in her eyes.

"The walls of the cave appeared as though someone or something had carved artistic designs into them," Satan went on. "Distinctive cone-shaped formations hung from the ceiling of the cave, like giant icicles of rock. Towers of funnel-shaped stones on the cave's floor stretched upward.

Some formed hands whose fingers reached to the sky from underground. Small windows created by collapsed areas in the roof allowed some light in, but the cave remained cool and dim.

"I began to heal in this subterranean world. Already stronger, I wandered farther into the huge cavern and came across a large, fast-flowing river. I realized that the roar and gurgle of the river echoed in the cave and was the menacing sound I had heard when I stood above ground. It was a beautiful sight. I imagined when I found Lilith, we could settle there."

At these words, Samael's expression darkened, and he gave an almost inaudible whimper.

"I saw that the mighty, noisy underground river traveled far into the cave," Satan said. "I decided it would be best to continue following it to see where it led me. I hiked for miles. I came upon a tight passage that descended steeply. I fell and slid fast down the dark watery tunnel, howling the entire way." Satan's neck flushed red and he chuckled as he looked at the ground.

Dagon laughed to himself. Smiling, Gadreel glanced at Samael, who gazed at Lilith. Satan and Lilith exchanged affectionate smiles and he continued.

"The passage was long but eventually opened into a wide domed room. I spouted out and rolled a few times before finally stopping. I lay flat on the ground, gasping. My heart pounded. Rays of light forced through openings in the ceiling of the cave. I was amazed the gleam of Gabriel's star reached so far. The beams of light shimmered on the sculptured rocks, giving them the appearance of being set ablaze.

"An animal I had detected earlier lurking nearby revealed itself to me and proceeded in my direction. I wondered if the animal had been tracking me all the while. The large beast was covered in thick, black fur. It stood on its hind legs and stared at me from a few feet away. The beast had a large, round head, with ears set far apart on its crown, and long, curved, pointed claws. However, I experienced no fear.

"The animal came closer. I stood my ground and permitted the beast to get within reach. I was as curious about it as it was about me. There was a white crescent-moon shape on the beast's chest. I thought perhaps I should have a marking such as this, unique to me, so as to never be confused with any other creature.

"The animal came close enough to smell me. Still, I remained motionless and observed it, eager to know more about it. The large, hairy creature did not seem threatening. It sniffed me and licked my face.

"The animal whimpered and staggered backward as if displeased by the taste of my flesh. The beast moved further away, pawing at its mouth as though putting out a fire on its tongue. It appeared to be trying to remove the taste left in its mouth by my blood-colored skin.

"I sensed the beast's fear and repulsion and became infuriated by it." Satan clenched his fists and flared his nostrils. "I underwent a strange sensation in my fingers. When I examined my hands I saw my nails growing at alarming speed. They became like the creature's claws—sharp, powerful, black, and curved.

"The process was painful, and my breathing became erratic and fast. I glowered at the beast, my menacing horns targeting it. My chest heaved with rage. The animal growled and stumbled backward. I was offended by it's loathing of me."

Lilith's face flushed with shame for she had offended him in the same way the beast did.

"I crouched forward, claws spread. The beast snapped its jaws several times and swatted the ground with its front paw while blowing and snorting in an attempt to intimidate me.

"Gnashing my newly pointed teeth, I lifted my gruesome talons and lashed at the animal's face and neck, causing large, bloody gashes. The animal began salivating, roaring, and circling. I bashed the creature's arms and shoulders with my powerful tail, to show that I was in command. I charged and rammed my horns into its chest. The beast fell to the ground, rolled and then hobbled away in terror, whimpering in agony, its face, neck, and upper body a bloody mess.

"I realized I was quite strong and held power I did not comprehend fully. I understood I must learn to uncover these strengths. Thus I, and not God's humans, could subsequently reign over the animals on Earth. I vowed to teach them all—including Adam—who is truly master of this realm.

"I carried on with my inspection of the cave, feeling robust and more powerful with each step I took, having learned already I could thrive in darkness. I scanned the area and once more turned my attention toward the river with its roaring and whistling sounds that reverberated off the cave's walls and ceilings.

"I was fascinated by this underground world and wished I could share it with Lilith. She had been on my mind since I crashed to Earth and after seeing this magnificent underworld, I missed her even more."

Lilith leaned her head and rested it on his shoulder. She lifted his hand to her lips and kissed it. Samael clenched his jaw. Dagon saw her act of affection and glanced at Gadreel with a how-about-you-and-me smile. She twirled her hair several times and tucked it behind her ear.

Satan continued, "I summoned Lilith saying, 'Lilith, where are you? Come to me, my beloved, find a way to get to me.' My heart thumped." He faced her. "Did you receive my thoughts?"

She smiled. "I did sense you were summoning me, my love, on several occasions."

"It is true, for she told Samael and me of this." Gadreel nodded. Satan kissed Lilith's forehead and continued his account.

"I resolved to enter the river. Wading across it, I noticed the water was quite warm. A short distance in, I was amazed when the river's force knocked me off my feet and transported me above the rushing waters, like a leaf carried away by the current of a steam. The river lugged me through dark tunnels and passages, eventually dropping me in a cascade, which poured into a large underground lake, far below the Earth's surface, where the sun barely penetrated.

"I rode the waterfall and plunged into the deep lake, and the waters enveloped me in intense heat. Holding my breath, I sank deeper toward a bright, red glow below me. The water became hotter as I dropped closer to the burning radiance. Then I heard a loud, piercing sound, which alarmed me.

"I gasped underwater, and my lungs began to flood. I looked to the surface, now so far away. I flapped my wings and ascended. When my head emerged above water, I coughed and wheezed, finally inhaling long and deep. I climbed out of the lake, and stood immobile on its bank.

"I honed in on the sound I had heard in the depths of the lake. I still heard it, though not as clear as when I was deep underwater. The penetrating shrill sound was strangely familiar—although I did not understand how, since I did not recall ever hearing anything like it before—but the image of Fornues' eyes appeared in my mind. I trusted the sound would lead me to my brethren and eventually to Lilith.

"It was difficult to leave my new subterranean domain, but the vibrating sound in my head persisted and beckoned me to follow it to its source. I committed to follow it, wherever it led. I departed the cave fully restored and was able to take flight. I flapped my wings at great speeds, and they accelerated me through the skies toward an unknown destination, where I was convinced I would find some, if not all, of my allies.

"After a lengthy period of stifling sunlight hours and well-received nights, I arrived at the freezing upper atmosphere of the arctic. The sound became louder and more intense, pinpointing the location of the source. As the shrill noise became clearer, I recognized a distinct quality about it. It was a cry for help, and I knew who did the beseeching.

"I came to rest on a small glacier, and summoned my friend. 'Fornues, show your face, come to the surface where I may look upon you.' He shot from the water with tremendous force, causing great waves around him. An immense wave crashed into the small glacier where I stood and knocked me off my feet. As the water drained away from the ice mass, it dragged me into the freezing sea.

"Once more, I was sinking. I had never experienced cold such as this; it penetrated my very essence. Immediately ice crystals began to form on my wings. I began to beat them fast and exploded out of the icy waters. From the sky, I scanned the area and spotted another glacier much larger than the previous one. This glacier's surface rose above the water and stretched sky-high, similar to an ice mountain.

"I perched on the towering glacier and finally got a good look at Fornues. I stared at his monstrous form in amazement.

"Then I heard his voice in my head.

'Is it you, Satan?'

I assured him it was.

'I am an inept monstrosity. Look upon me. It would have been best if God had decided to end my life in Floraison!'

"I told him it was hard to believe he was my friend. Were it not for his distinctive hazel-green eyes with their drooping outer corners and voice, I would not have believed it. I assured him that useless he was not. I knew his appearance and strength would be especially beneficial to my purpose.

"He was relieved to know that his monstrous form would be of assistance to me. He told me he desired to continue to serve me on Earth as he did in Floraison. I was pleased to hear of his loyalty, and I vowed I would make good use of him.

"From below, another familiar voice asked, 'Would you have use for me as well?' I looked down from my perch on the iceberg and saw another being in the water. 'Is that you, Dagon?' I asked, noticing he had transformed into a half-man, half-fish sea creature.

"Dagon had also heard the sounds emitted by Fornues. I requested that Fornues continue his shrill sounds in the hopes that the others, too, would hear it. I sensed all of you, and I wanted us to be reunited. We are stronger in numbers.

"I took flight once more and led Fornues and Dagon in the direction where I intuited the rest of you were. I flew through the air, while they followed closely behind in the waters below. Thus, we travelled for many dawns and moonrises until today, at last, we found you."

Chapter 16

FORNUES' CURSE

"I have learned much from Satan's account of his fall," Lilith said. "Perhaps we should all tell our stories. It may prove enlightening."

"That is a great idea." Samael puffed himself up to tell his story next.

Gadreel glared at him, still hurt by his display of jealousy earlier. "It is a wonderful idea. Dagon, perhaps you should give your account next. I am certain we are all curious to learn how you came to be transformed into a merman."

Samael muttered under his breath.

Dagon smiled at her. "I think it may be more interesting if Fornues told his story first."

Samael frowned and huffed.

"Indeed, I am rather curious about how Fornues entered this world and how he came to be as he is," Lilith said.

"How can the monster tell his story when he cannot break words?" Samael said in a sarcastic tone.

"He is not a monster!" Gadreel frowned and her hands squeezed into fists. "He is our friend and he can communicate to us in our minds as he has done since we came together." She rolled her eyes at him and turned to Dagon again, touching her hair.

"Shall we move closer to shore, Satan?" Lilith asked.

Fornues interjected, "There is no need, for I can hear all your words clearly—even yours, Samael." He dropped the last three words to a grumble.

"Apologies, Fornues, I meant no harm." Samael shrugged.

"Go on, Fornues, reveal your story in our minds," Satan said.

"I looked down from the edge of Floraison and saw the dark, icy waters of a vast frozen sea," Fornues began. "Every fiber of my body trembled in fear of the unknown. As I plunged toward Earth, I thought of only doom. I was void of hope. If there was a future to be had at all, I saw only blackness."

Fornues became more and more emotional as he unintentionally transferred the feelings and experiences he described to the other angels. They suffered the despair and physical agony he communicated.

"I crashed through solid ice into freezing waters. The pain that swathed me was indescribable. I did not believe I could survive. I suffered a million sharp spears stabbing me simultaneously over my entire body, again and again. I wailed in despair, for who could hear me?"

So real was his description in their minds that the others howled in pain, as though their bodies were crashing through the congealed surface of the frigid sea.

Gadreel's limp body lay sprawled on the ground, as if damaged and immersed in freezing water. Dagon hollered as the excruciating pain of freezing body tissues gripped him.

"I struggled as ice water filled my lungs paralyzing them," Fornues continued. "I flapped my wings, flailed my arms, and thrashed my legs. It seemed the more I struggled, the faster I sank. I experienced crushing pressure, blows to my abdomen, and small explosions in my eyes. I longed for the light above me whose distance grew further out of my reach."

Lilith screamed and writhed in agony as her body underwent cold, piercing jabs. Satan tried to assist her, but he, too, suffered the physical torments Fornues described. Samael convulsed as he experienced drowning in the frozen waters.

"I began to undergo a massive transformation, which began with my wings growing heavy. They began to tingle and blister as the freezing water destroyed underlying tissues. My wings congealed and became as ice. They became so painful I wanted to rip them off. My body grew and expanded in every direction. All the while, I shrieked and groaned, believing my body was being torn apart."

Satan howled, clutching and tugging at his wings, for the pain they yielded was unbearable.

Fornues stopped communicating. His friends moaned, contorted, and juddered on the ground.

"What is happening?" he asked.

"You have drawn us into your rendering, and we have suffered all you have described thus far," Lilith said, breathless and wincing.

Fornues realized for the first time that he had the ability to project his feelings and physical torments onto others if he did not control his emotions. "Apologies. I was not aware I had such capacity. Perhaps I should not render my account."

"Nonsense!" Dagon winced as he rubbed his chest and arms. "Simply control your projected feelings. We have all been through much suffering, but this is in our past. Tell us what happened to you, knowing in your heart that you have already overcome all you described and are the better for it."

Samael threw his hands in the air. "He shall be the death of us all."

Dagon and Gadreel glowered at him.

"What say you, my prince?" Lilith directed her sight on Satan.

"Pay no mind to Samael and continue your story, but heed Dagon's counsel and project your feelings inward and not at us," Satan said.

Samael clenched his jaw and lowered his head.

Fornues continued his story. "I no longer possessed the form of an angel, but had become the monster you see now. My wings were gone. I do not know why, but I mourn my wings the most.

"I realized I could no longer break words. When I opened my mouth to cry out for help, the sound I produced was a terrible shrill. I continued uttering the jarring sounds as I struggled in the frozen waters, hoping one of my friends would hear my call and somehow recognize it was I. My metamorphosis caused me intense pain, and I was afraid."

Dagon hung his head.

"I was aware I was all alone and cursed," Fornues continued. "I struggled against the changes, but only caused myself more pain and suffering. Still, I panicked and lamented, 'Please, someone help me! I am all alone and in so much trouble.' I hoped against hope that one of my allies would hear me and come to my rescue."

"That was uncharacteristically optimistic of you, Fornues," Lilith said, mocking him.

"His optimism served him and us well since we were able to find each other because of his hopeful cries," Gadreel said. "Dagon, please tell us your story. I am certain—"

"What of Beelzebub?" Lilith glanced at Gadreel with a sneering smirk. "Does anyone know what became of him?"

"I believe I was the last of us to see Beelzebub in Floraison," Dagon said. "We were to share the same fate."

"Tell us!" Lilith leaned forward and stared into his gray-blue eyes. "What became of Beelzebub?"

Chapter 17

BEELZEBUB DESTINY

"Beelzebub writhed and screamed." Dagon closed his eyes and stroked his chin. "While Cam, whom he once called best friend, held him against his will. He was pale. His eyes, wide with grief, shifted in every direction. I could not believe it had come to this moment, which was surreal in its degree of horror.

"Esar, accompanied by Hashmal and Jetrel, marched toward Cam and Beelzebub, carrying an immense metal chain. The chain was so heavy it took the combined strength of all three to carry it.

"Beelzebub's body trembled. When he caught sight of the chain he shook his head in a frantic manner and shrieked. He struggled against Cam, trying to break free from his tight grip, but his small frame was no match for him.

"It appeared Beelzebub reached exhaustion for he ended his struggles and looked about. He saw me and other fallen angels in the same struggle. Our eyes locked, and he yelled, 'All has gone amiss! Where are Lilith and Satan? Have they been captured as well, or have they forsaken us?'"

Dagon paused his narrative, leaned back and looked at the sky. Lilith lowered her head and Satan looked down and away from the others.

Dagon resumed his account. "Cam constrained him with his powerful arms. Even the one he loved, Gabriel, had a hand in his capture and now stood against him.

"Beelzebub watched as Raphael and Gabriel restrained me, for I was to be bound as well. I made efforts to escape, but as strong as I am, I was no match for the combined might of the two archangels.

"Raquel came across my path. She saw my struggle and hurried to us. 'Where are you taking him?' She exuded anguish with each word. She stared at the injury Cam had inflicted on my wing during the war, and shuddered.

"Raphael said, 'He shall be bound until judgment day comes.' Raquel gasped and tears began to flow from her eyes. 'That shall be an eternity. He shall suffer greatly. I cannot bear the thought of this.'

"'Apologies, my sister, but it is what we must do.' Raphael's face was etched with sorrow. It was clear to me that he did not find joy in what he did."

Lilith raised an eyebrow and smiled a slight close-lipped smile, like she knew something Dagon did not.

"Raquel questioned why I should be bound for eternity. She pleaded for me, asking Raphael and Gabriel to release me. Her bright green eyes were flooded with tears. 'Why not allow him the same fate God bestowed upon the wicked Lilith and Satan? Exile him to Earth.'"

Dagon gazed at Gadreel through sight made hazy by tears. With a meaningful expression, she touched him on the arm. Samael crossed his arms and watched them with narrowed eyes.

"Raquel stared at me. 'You must release him. Let him fall to Earth as the rest, I implore you.'

"I fought hard to free myself. A jolt of pain from my damaged wing accompanied my every move, but it did not stop me from struggling. I looked toward Beelzebub, and his eyes were fixed in my direction. He glared at Raquel as she pleaded for my release. He had random fits of cackling and weeping. He shouted, 'Hope is gone!' as he continued to stare my way.

Gadreel covered her face with her hands and shook with sobs. Lilith rolled her eyes at her.

"Michael approached Gabriel and Raphael," Dagon continued. "He gestured for them to release me. They left my chains behind and walked me to the edge of Floraison.

"'No you cannot do that!' Beelzebub shouted. 'You cannot free him whilst I still linger in chains! Raquel intervenes, and you release him?' He snarled and growled in between fits of senseless laughter. Raphael and Gabriel ignored him and continued guiding me to my fate.

"Raquel and I said our farewells without breaking words. My eyes told her more than I could have ever said past my lips, and she kissed me by way of her own eyes."

Gadreel sat up straight and stared at him with furrowed brow.

"Now will you tell us what happened to you when you fell?" She ran her hand through his sleek, pale blond hair. Dagon wiped his eyes with the back of his hands and nodded.

Chapter 18

DAGON'S PLUNGE FROM GRACE

"I plunged into the cosmos with my eyes closed, picturing Raquel's green eyes gleaming like jewels," Dagon began. "They overflowed with tears for me. I imagined running my hands through her long red waves of hair. I reached for her, and an abrupt pain in my back woke me from my stupor.

"I was stunned by the cruel nature of my physical torment—my eyes sprung open in shock. I looked over my shoulder to see what was happening to me. A powerful force had ripped my wings off my frame. I howled and winced as I tumbled to Earth. I shouted, clenched my hands, and gnashed my teeth trying to endure the pain.

"I plunged into an iridescent sea. The crash took my breath away. I flailed my arms and legs as I sank deeper into the colorful depths. I gagged and choked as briny water forced its way into my lungs.

"My legs withered and then I experienced a tightening sensation in my lower body, as though an enormous vise held my legs together in a constricting grip.

"I groaned and grimaced, suffering great distress. I shook my lower body in violent ways, attempting to release myself from the vise's grasp, and instead managed to swim. Moving through the water became easier, although I continued to endure unpleasant physical sensations for quite a while.

"I glanced at the basis of my grief and saw that my lower body had been changed into a fish tail, I was stunned. In my amazement, I also realized I was capable of breathing underwater. I had transformed into an aquatic creature half angel, half fish. I am the first of my kind for I have never seen anything that resembles me.

"At once I began to swim and explore my new environment, content to be a new species and to have survived my fall from grace. I observed the many sea creatures around me with the curiosity of a child. The ocean's creatures remained vigilant of me too, perhaps trying to figure out what I was.

"From a short distance, I examined sea turtles, eels, and many species of sea life I had only seen during Creation. I made attempts to approach them, but every time I tried to get closer, the creatures scattered. It did not take me long to conclude I was the superior being.

"'I shall preside over you,' I spoke to the creatures surrounding me. Fish, mollusks, crustaceans, and other living things in the vicinity quickly hid from view. I threw my head back and laughed."

Dagon's face and neck reddened with embarrassment and he bowed his head.

"My guffaws echoed in the deep sea, but they were interrupted by a blaring, high-pitched noise. The shrill sound filled my head. My hands rushed to cover my ears to prevent the harsh sound from penetrating them, but it was no use, for the sound grew louder in my mind.

"Although the vibrations overwhelmed my senses, a familiarity in the sound compelled me to follow it to its origin. Thus, I began to swim as fast as I could, headed toward the shrill sound's source and darker, colder waters.

"I swam and listened for the sound waves guiding me to their origin. Somehow, I knew in my heart the sound would lead me to my friends. I did not desire to be alone on the watery planet, no matter how fascinating I learnt it to be. I needed companionship.

"I cried, 'Where are you? Have you all suffered my fate?'

"I traced the unpleasant noise to a frightening aquatic environment. The water was dark and freezing cold. It was quite different from the warm, bright waters I fell into upon arriving on this planet.

"A luminescence in the distance caught my eye. I swam toward a multicolored glow to investigate and discovered a bloom of giant jellyfish was providing the radiance. I swam to the large, colorful creatures and stared at them in awe. The skin of the jellyfish was thin and transparent, and their long fringe-like expansions frolicked and shimmered in the blue-black waters.

Overcome by curiosity, I neared one of the creatures and grabbed a handful of its tentacles. The jellyfish recoiled and scampered away, leaving a few of its tentacles behind in my clutches.

"It was not my intention to yank the creature's parts off. I shook the tentacles off my hand, unable to hide my revulsion, and they floated away. I had wounded the jellyfish, and feared retaliation.

"The sea animal returned and charged me. It grabbed me by the arm with its remaining tentacles and with its appendages wrapped around me, it released spiky lances, which pierced my skin. I was stung again and again. I groaned and wrestled with the giant creature. I managed to get the aggressor off of me, only to be attacked by the swarm of jellyfish surrounding me."

Gadreel gasped and covered her mouth. The others leaned forward and squirmed.

"Tentacles wrapped around every part of my body, stinging me again and again," Dagon continued. "My arms floundered and I writhed in agony as I fought to free myself.

"My physical suffering continued when a large, hard projection broke through my skull and jutted out of my forehead. I traced the growth with trembling webbed fingers and realized it was a bony horn. I did not understand what was happening to me. Unable to stand the pain any longer I attacked the giants with my new tusk, and liberated myself from the swarm's grasp at last.

"Once free I made haste and got away. When I was far enough from the light they emitted I stopped, drained and ailing. I examined myself and found raised, red welts of different sizes on my bare torso, arms, and neck. The wounds inflicted by the jellyfish caused intense stinging and itching. I touched one of the marks and winced for the simplest contact with the swollen areas caused me pain."

Gadreel placed a hand on his thigh and looked up through her lashes. Dagon held eye contact and touched her hair. Samael watched them with clenched teeth.

"I wondered if I would recover," Dagon said, turning his sight on the others. "I thought I would die a slow, painful death by poison. 'Shall I remain at the bottom of the ocean, until the very creatures I expected to rule pick me apart?'

"Having no choice, I endured and continued my voyage to find the basis of the sound, which beckoned me. As I neared the shrill sound, the waters became blacker and icier. I was forced to slow down.

"My pulse slowed and I shook nonstop. My fishtail grew heavy, and harder to control as it became covered with frost. I gnashed my teeth and persisted to swim ahead, uncertain I would survive. I thought only of my friends."

Gadreel squeezed his thigh. Satan smiled and nodded. Samael stared at the ground, sulking.

"I encountered numerous ice masses, which bore distinct shapes like frozen, inverted mountains. Their bulk partly floated on the surface, while the greater part plunged to great depths in the ocean. Visibility became somewhat better since these ice masses reflected light from the surface. They emitted an aqua-blue glow that colored the water.

"However, the surging glaciers still created great obstacles as I tried to avoid getting crushed between them. I began to feel numb. I was afraid if I stopped for a moment, I would turn to ice.

"My ability to see was diminished once more when I came upon an area where an enormous cloud of dust was lifted from the ocean floor. When I approached the cloud, I noticed something massive moved within it. In addition, I became aware the high-pitched sound I followed was produced by whatever was in the fog of sea dirt. I was terrified—a feeling I had become quite familiar with since I was exiled from Floraison.

"I swam through the wall of disturbed silt. I was compelled to see what was on the other side, causing the painful sound. I began to blink incessantly as seabed particles irritated my eyes. I closed my eyes and continued to swim across the freezing, murky waters.

"When the small particles no longer crashed against my face, I opened my eyes. I quickly wished I had kept them closed, for what I saw made my heart thump and my throat constrict in fear. A ferocious looking colossus floated but a short distance from me. I opened my mouth to yell, but released only bubbles and gurgling sounds. I was immobilized at the sight of the massive creature and gaped in total disbelief as it swam toward me in silence."

Gadreel grabbed his hand while he spoke, her attention fixed on him. Samael engrossed in his own darkly teeming emotions scowled at her and Dagon, and kicked a stone that lay at his feet. Dagon narrowed his eyes at him, but continued his account.

"The sea giant lowered its head to get a better look at me. I stood my ground, trembling all the while. The creature's eyes met mine. I wondered why the eyes appeared so familiar.

"I heard a well-known voice in my mind. 'Dagon, it is I, Fornues, your friend.'

"Did the monster swallow my friend, I wondered."

Lilith laughed and slapped her thigh.

"'No, Dagon! I am Fornues, and I am also the monster you see before you.'

I looked at the sea monster and after observing its sleepy, hazel-green eyes, I knew it was my friend returning my stare.

"'Look upon me. Behold the grotesque creature I have become,' Fornues said without breaking words.

"I complained that I, too, had been transformed, since I held no wings, but instead possessed a fish tail, fins, gills, and scales.

"'Nonetheless,' he said, 'you are still a semblance of what you once were. I recognized you. I have turned into a hideous monster of the sea. There is nothing left of who I was. I have been cursed worse of all.' Fornues dropped the last three words to a grumble.

"I consoled him, telling him he could count on me, as well as the others, to always be his friends despite his appearance. I urged him to continue emitting the high-pitched sound, for its familiarity led me to him. I thought perhaps the others had heard it as well, and would follow it to us. I was right. I did request he emit it not quite as loudly, for I feared he would render me deaf."

Dagon chuckled.

"You are a good friend and ally." Gadreel's lips parted and she arched her back. "Fornues is right—you do look as handsome as you did in Floraison." Gadreel glanced at Samael. He glared at both of them. Dagon, in turn, clenched his jaw and glowered at him.

Chapter 19

SORROW AND DESIRE

Lilith caught sight of the rising tension between Dagon and Samael, and she rose to her feet. "I think we have heard enough accounts of our fall from God's favor for the time being."

"I have not yet told my story." Samael frowned.

"There shall be plenty of time for that later," Lilith said. "Let us partake of the abundant fruit available to us."

Samael crossed his arms over his chest and nodded.

"Despite all we have endured, at least we are now free to enjoy what was forbidden in Floraison." Lilith ogled at Satan. He smiled.

Dagon and Gadreel exchanged grins. Samael forced a lackluster smile.

The angels satiated their bellies with coconut. Desiring time alone with Satan, Lilith guided him away from the others. She invited him to sit with her under another coconut tree.

Beneath the tree she caressed his body, kissed his chest and neck, and touched him in places designed to bring him great pleasure. She whispered in his ear, "It is wonderful to be free, is it not? Foolish laws no longer bind us. You think you know pleasure? I shall show you pleasures beyond your wildest dreams."

Satan drew quick, shallow breaths, and it was not long before he was fully aroused.

From a nearby tree Samael observed Lilith seduce Satan as she had seduced him in the ice cave. He narrowed his eyes and tightened his lips, but he could do nothing. She belonged to him.

Gadreel watched Samael and proceeded to him. She placed her hand on his shoulder. He jolted at her touch. She gazed into his eyes and smiled the kind of smile only expressed by true desire.

Samael chuckled and fidgeted then turned to watch Lilith with Satan again. Gadreel gently turned his face toward her. He squinted and when she leaned forward to kiss him he stepped back, turned his face away once more to watch the lovers.

Gadreel's lips quivered. She pressed her hand on her bosom as if in severe pain. She walked away dragging her feet, wilted. She wrapped her arms around herself. "You have inflicted a deep wound in my heart, Samael. Even after Lilith clearly chose Satan over you, you still choose her over me." She covered her face with her hands. What more could she do to show him how much she loved him? She glanced over her shoulder. He was still mesmerized and unaware she had left his side. If Satan discovered what Lilith and Samael had done in his absence—she slammed her eyes shut.

"I must demonstrate to Samael that I am not without my wiles," she said under her breath. She had learned much from watching Lilith. She would do as she does, since it has worked so well for her. She would see Samael seethe with jealousy when he saw the pleasures she could provide.

Gadreel sashayed toward Dagon, who lay sprawled under a coconut tree. He watched her practiced sensual stroll and sat upright. He ogled her. She sat by his side and edged closer to him gazing into his intense gray-blue eyes.

She kissed his neck and passed her hands across his chest. His eyes were half closed. "I have never experienced such sensations."

She continued to kiss his face as her hands traveled down his body. His breaths quickened. When she touched him there, his eyes snapped opened. Panting, he glanced below. His male organ was stiff and stood upright, pointing to the sky. Gadreel gasped.

She pressed her lips against his and wrapped her hand around his erection. He jolted. "Heat rushes through my body to culminate there."

Gadreel pressed a finger to his lips. "Quiet." His body quivered deep inside. He panted and grinned. He touched her hair and caressed her face.

Gadreel lay on the ground, legs apart, and drew him upon her. She guided him into her. Dagon followed his natural instincts and pushed. He threw his head back and groaned as he entered her.

She arched her neck and moaned with pleasure and pain as he penetrated her. He leaned in and kissed her lips and neck. She frowned and crinkled her nose. "What is that pungent odor that assaults my nose?" She pushed him away. He withdrew from her.

"What is the matter?" Dagon appeared confused. Red-faced she looked to the side and shook her head. He plunged deep into her once more. He panted and groaned as he continued to do this again and again.

Along with pleasure, he began to feel excruciating pain in his head. However, he could not stop. He continued to drive himself in and out of her. As his pleasure and excitement grew, so did a pointy projection, which surged between his brows and jutted from his forehead. It expanded until it developed into a great tusk, as it had in the deep sea. The tusk was large and menacing. In his eagerness, he did not realize that the tusk came dangerously close to Gadreel, threatening to gouge her. He closed his eyes and continued to thrust as she screamed and flinched.

She shoved him but it was like trying to stop a raging bull.

Samael heard her cries and followed them to find Dagon on top of her. Heat bloomed in his face. His nostrils flared and he closed his hands into tight fists.

Gadreel spotted him approaching. She judged the expression on his face and interpreted his intent. "No, Samael! Do not come any closer. Go away and leave us be!"

He stopped, flabbergasted. "Is this what you desire?"

Dagon roared and pointed his tusk at him in a menacing way, but at no moment did he cede his actions with regard to Gadreel.

Samael stepped back at the sight of the projection on his forehead.

"Yes, I desire this," Gadreel said with shallow breath. She stared at him with partly closed, shimmering eyes.

Samael shuffled away, staring at the ground. What was happening to him? The sight of Dagon and Gadreel intertwined perturbed him. He did not know why, but seeing them together and knowing she desired to be with him upset him. He huffed and kicked a coconut lying in his way.

Dagon carried on with his sexual activity until he reached climax. Thunderous sounds escaped his mouth, whilst tides of pleasure coursed through his entire body. When he was done, he pulled out from within her and lay depleted on the sand. He winced as the horn retracted into his head once more and fell asleep with a contented expression on his face.

Gadreel lay motionless on the ground next to him, staring at the night sky with tears meandering over flushed cheeks. She longed for him to be gone. His fishy smell was upon her. She suffered due to his brutish ways. Her actions had originated in spite, and a sense of loss overwhelmed her. She wiped away her tears and lay sulking—wishing every decision she had made thus far had been different.

Satan made love to Lilith, and they were both enjoying the sex act when his form began to change. She squinted when she saw a red spot appear on his forehead. The color spread quickly in every direction, turning his pale skin a bloody red. Her eyes widened when his lush dark hair blew off his head like dandelion seeds in the wind and disappeared into thin air. Horns sprang from his skull. She shrieked and beat on his chest. "Stop! Get off me at once!"

Satan furrowed his brow. "What is wrong?"

She stared at him with wide eyes and raised eyebrows. "How is it possible you do not detect your own transformation? Look at yourself! You have become the appalling red creature." She grimaced in repulsion.

Satan gaped at his arms and chest, hardly believing his eyes. "This occurred against my will." He stared at his clawed hands with a shocked expression. "I changed into the horned fiend in the midst of making love to you. How is this possible?"

He squeezed his eyelids together. "I wish to switch to my original state." He opened his eyes but there was no change. He made additional efforts to power the transformation, but nothing occurred.

"Why are you still this monstrosity? Are you chastising me?" Lilith peered at him from between her fingers.

"Like Fornues, I am trapped in this hideous body." His body drooped and he gazed at her downcast. "I believe I understand what is happening."

"What do you mean?" Lilith clenched her hands until her knuckles turned white. "Get away from me! You discuss me!" She kicked her legs and pounded on his chest.

Satan lowered his eyebrow, slammed his fist on the ground by her head and growled. "I grow weary of your rejections and demands!" He jutted his chin and puffed his chest then grabbed her by the neck and rammed her head against the ground. The black pits he had for eyes stared at her with unblinking focus.

Lilith clutched at the enormous, clawed hand squeezing her windpipe. She watched the throbbing veins in his neck as she writhed and winced underneath him while he resumed his brutal sexual assault. She opened her mouth, but his grip on her throat was too tight, and she was not able to produce audible sounds. When she turned purple and her eyes began to roll to the back of her head, he released her. She wheezed, gasping for air.

The others heard her cries and whimpering. They ran to where she was and were horrified to witness the red beast ravage her time after time.

Lilith tried to transform into the snake creature to defend herself, but as long as Satan was inside her, her efforts were in vain. She shrieked and fought, but he persisted until his act reached its conclusion. When it was done, he rolled off of her and at once turned into his angel form.

Lilith gasped. "He could not change while he was engaged in sex with me, but the moment he stopped, he transformed to his angel form almost instantly. What did this mean?" She murmured under her breath. She covered her mouth with her hand and raised her eyebrows high. The sex act with Satan shall only be possible under the condition he be transformed into the red monstrosity—yet another punishment from above. She turned away from him, curled into a fetal position, and shook with sobs.

Satan lay on the ground immobile, listening to her cries. He slammed his eyes shut and clutched his chest. He, too, grasped the meaning behind what happened. Whenever he attempted to mate with her he would transform into the red fiend against his will. He would never again make love to her in the form of an angel.

Satan rose to his knees, tightened his hands into fists and spread out his arms. He leaned back and cocked his head skyward, and a deafening roar escaped his mouth. Expanding his massive wings he growled his rage to the Heavens. His maniacal groans made the others flinch.

He yanked his hair in clumps from his scalp as his large horns projected from his head once more, and his skin became the color of fury. Sharp, curved claws grew from his thick, large fingers. His tail slithered from him, its pointy arrowhead aimed at Heaven. He foamed at the mouth, and saliva ran down his chin as he exposed his fangs. He was a gruesome sight, and the others paled and shook in fear.

Lilith wrapped her arms around herself, rocked side to side and screamed on the ground beside him.

Terrified, Gadreel leapt into Dagon's arms. Lilith crept away from Satan, clambered to her feet and scurried to Samael. He held her.

In a fit of rage, Satan rammed the palm tree under which he had copulated with Lilith. He struck it many times with his massive horns until he knocked it to the ground. He inflicted large gashes in the trunk by thrashing it with his massive tail.

Satan pivoted toward the others. He glowered at Samael who held Lilith. Seething, his chest rose and fell with might. Samael let go and pulled away from Lilith. He lifted his hands and shrank from Satan's black eye sockets. Lilith frowned at Samael.

Lilith crossed her arms and dragged her feet toward Satan. Samael held her arm and shook his head. She jerked her arm away and approached the beast. She stood before him as fear nibbled at her making her knees shudder. With a trembling hand she caressed his face. She had to calm him and convince him that everything was still good between them, before all was lost. She needed him in order to accomplish her goals.

"I shall learn to love you as you are now," she said. "Together, we shall exact vengeance on God for what he has done to us. These things I vow to you." Her eyes flashed with promise and seduction. "Am I still your treasure? I desire to be."

From this moment forward she would say the things he wished to hear, but they would all be lies. She would do whatever she had to do to get what she needed. Her lips curved to a slow, sensual smile.

Satan's breathing slowed. The muscles in his face eased. He gazed at her for a long moment.

"You shall always be my treasure." He took her hand and kissed it. The color of his face became golden ivory, thick black hair sprouted from his scalp, and the looped horns retracted into his skull. Once again, Satan became his former self. Lilith inhaled a deep breath and blew it out slowly: beauty had tamed the savage beast.

"Let us get some rest before sundown," Satan said. "The plan is to fly past the mountains and proceed east until the heat of the sun compels us to take refuge in the shade."

Lilith guided Satan to another tree, since he had destroyed the previous one. They lay in the shade together and slept. There was a pleasant, cool breeze coming off the ocean. Samael waited until the lovers fell asleep, and then lay down next to Lilith.

Dagon grabbed Gadreel's hand, she wrested it away and hurried toward the beach. Dagon furrowed his brow as he watched her run away from him. He lowered his sight to the ground, and dragged his feet to his tree where he slept alone.

Gadreel jolted and froze when she detected an unusual stirring inside of her. "What is this strange physical sensation? I have never experienced anything like it before." She tilted her head and pressed her lips. When she didn't feel it again she gave a half shrug strolled to the edge of the beach, dug a small trench in the wet sand, and slept by the water.

"Sleep well," she heard Fornues say softly in her mind.

"You get some rest also, Fornues."

Chapter 20

BEELZEBUB'S CURSED LOVE

L ilith awakened in the night. Realizing Samael lay next to her, she pulled his arm around her waist. She hoped to make the best of things by continuing her affair with Samael as compensation for Satan's monstrous form. She closed her eyes, her mind began to drift, and her thoughts about Dagon's story of Beelzebub bound in chains became a dream, and then a vision. Soon she was witnessing the story unfold through Beelzebub's eyes.

In Heaven I watched Raquel plead for Dagon's release, and then I saw Gabriel and Raphael let loose the chains that bound him.

I was painfully perplexed. Why was Dagon set free, while I remained in the clutches of Cam?

I began to tussle again, only to have Cam tighten his hold on me. I realized all my resisting was to no avail, so I thought of another strategy.

"We were once friends, were we not?" I asked Cam, using my most submissive tone.

"Yes, prior to your betrayal. We no longer stand as such," Cam replied in his usual stern voice. He was determined not to exhibit any sentiments, but I knew there was a fire burning painfully in his chest. I saw it in his eyes he grieved for me.

"Please have mercy on me now, brother."

"We stopped being brothers the moment you decided to turn against God." Cam tightened his grip once more. "The sins you have committed are unforgivable."

I implored him with my gaze. "Unforgivable? No, I would not deem it so."

He looked away. "You must suffer the consequences of your actions."

"Why am I the only one to suffer in chains? Are my sins uniquely vile?"

"Look to your left, Beelzebub. Three other rebels share your fate. You shall not be alone—be grateful for that."

I froze and stared wide-eyed at him. "Grateful? I should give thanks to be bound in chains until the end of days?" I shook my head in disbelief and tittered. "Where is Lilith, the mastermind of this conflict, and her accomplice Satan? Running free on Earth?" At the sight of the three unholy angels, bound in chains, gagged and blindfolded, I began to wail.

Cam's lip quivered, he moved to gag me but then stopped and signaled Jetrel to gag me instead.

I watched him slump and his face contort with grief. "What is the matter, my friend? You cannot stand to hear my arguments any longer?" Jetrel rushed forward and stuffed cloth into my mouth, wrapping material across it and around my head to keep me from breaking words.

I yelled and shook my head furiously, trying to avoid being muzzled, but she was strong and managed to silence me.

"Be still, agitator!" Hashmal said, emitting flames and lightning from his mouth with each word he uttered.

His fiery breath made contact with my face, singeing my skin like he did so long ago when we were children wrestling in Guidance Park. Unable to do otherwise, I suffered the pain. Briny tears ran from my eyes and further stung my blistering skin.

Cam no longer wore his stoic and rough exterior but he restrained me while Jetrel bound my hands and feet.

Then Hashmal and Esar beckoned Jetrel so she could help them carry the chain to bind me. It was quite a burden on them, so Esar shifted to twice his size and carried the chain the remainder of the way. He threw part of the chain upon his shoulder, and the weight of it wobbled his legs. He pushed the chain off, and it got caught in his long, curly hair. I cackled through my gag. Under different circumstances, the others might have thought it funny, but not on this day. They gawped at me brows bumped together as I guffawed, while tears inundated my face.

When Esar got the chain close enough to me, he began to wind it around my body. I shivered when the icy metal touched my skin, and my knees buckled under its weight. I released a hoarse, braying laugh, which startled the others, except Cam, for he knew I had the tendency to laugh in moments of extreme stress.

Esar's lack of control over the heavy chain as he entwined it, caused unintentional injuries to my body. He often glanced at me with apologetic eyes during this process, but I was not in less pain for it.

The chain's connecting metal links pinched and bit my skin and pulled wads of hair from my scalp. I winced, shuddered, and screamed, but my cries went unheard, silenced by the gag forced upon me.

I caught sight of Gabriel. He watched me from a short distance. Did it pain him most of all to see me, his former lover, one who had caused so many smiles to appear on his face in the past, standing before him, bound in chains, bloody, bruised, and suffering because I loved him? Certainly, he suffered knowing this was only the beginning, for I was to be imprisoned for all eternity.

"Why did you fail to listen to us when we warned you about Lilith?" Jetrel paced from side to side. She glared at me callously. "Now you must suffer what you have earned with your treachery."

Always impatient with imperfection, Jetrel refused to accept feebleness. She was cruel. I glowered at her with hatred.

During the time Esar shackled me, his gentle brown eyes avoided mine. When the last of the chain was secured around me, he uttered in a voice thick with sorrow, "It is done."

"Beelzebub shall never escape these chains on his own," Hashmal informed the others. "It is made of the strongest metal in existence and forged together by my fiery breath."

Jetrel saw that the three other rebels were also ready to be taken away. "Where are the rebels to be imprisoned? I cocked my head and pointed an ear toward Michael for I, too, desired to know this.

Michael beckoned the holy angels in charge of this arduous task to gather together. "It is to be our burden to deliver these lost souls to their prisons."

"Shall their prisons be here—in one of the forbidden forests, perhaps?" Jetrel chewed the inside of her cheek and rocked lightly, no doubt hoping our confinement would not be in Floraison.

Michael pointed at me and the three other bound angels and said, "Floraison is too holy a place to keep vile creatures such as these in our midst. Even the plant life in the forbidden forests would protest such a thing."

"Floraison is a place of love, peace, and light. Dark forces do not belong here!" Gabriel cast me a fleeting, cold glance. My heart grew heavy with sorrow.

I could not understand what was so terrible about my actions. If Floraison is about love, why is my love for Gabriel so cursed? Still, I searched for his eyes—the color of a blue icy mist—and saw Heaven in them, despite the fact I was now doomed for simply loving him.

My mind tried to escape by daydreaming of a time when all was right in Floraison, a time when I could stroll to Gabriel, place my hand on his shoulder, caress his smooth face, or play with his soft, dark-brown curls. I reminisced about the many instances when I sat on the lush grasses of Triumph Gardens and listened to his beautiful, soothing voice singing praises to God, or times I lay my head on his lap as he played his trumpet and other instruments for long periods. I cherished these memories, and I was determined to hold onto them during my long imprisonment. Otherwise, I might go mad.

Michael addressed the holy angels as if we were not present. "There is a river on Earth we shall call Euphrates. It is the deepest river on the planet and derives from the Garden of Eden, the paradise God created for Mankind. The river is one of the four heads branching from the split of the main river in Eden. The four deepest points of the Euphrates River shall be prisons for the bound ones, until the end of days. This is God's will."

"So be it," the surrounding holy angels shouted in unison.

Michael's words rang cold in my ears. A sudden chill bloomed across my being, and the hairs on my body stood on end. My heart pounded. My nostrils flared as I gasped through my nose, unable to use my mouth. My upper eyelids stretched upward. Jetrel approached me again and blindfolded me, avoiding my terrified gaze.

I trembled but did not panic as a pair of strong hands grabbed me and moved me along. I knew it would not be long before I met my destiny. I wished to cry out Gabriel's name one last time, but the gag prevented me.

I was cast out of Floraison, and as I plunged toward Earth, I pictured Gabriel, as he was the last time we were alone together. The way his lips parted and received my tongue, his languorous movements, and the way he arched his back and moaned when I kissed him or touched him. My lovely thoughts were interrupted when the chains around me became blistering hot. I wailed in agony as the scorching metal links seared into my skin. I howled in intense pain, but the shroud covering my mouth concealed my cries. The chains continued to eat away at my flesh, and the pain was intolerable.

I splashed into a cold waterway. Many of my bones shattered when I collided with the water. I was rendered unconscious. Before long, the saltwater seeped into my wounds and roused me unmercifully. I woke immersed in black waters.

As I sank deeper into the river, water rushed forcibly into my nostrils. I tried to take in air, but murky water filled my lungs instead. The heavy chains dragged me rapidly into the abyss. The pressure squeezed my lungs, my throat stung with trapped air, and I heard my heart thudding in my ears.

Instinctively, I tried to move my arms and legs, but the tightly wound chains gnawed at my flesh and made movement impossible.

I heard the roar of the river. I was disoriented, unable to determine which way was up. I struggled to survive. Although the chains hurt me, I flailed and twisted my shackled body.

Pressure built in my head as I plummeted deeper into the Euphrates. A great force pressed against my eyes from inside my head. My eyeballs burst out of their sockets and smashed against the blindfold Jetrel had placed over them.

No memory of Gabriel or his mellifluous songs could mask the severe, throbbing pain I endured. I opened my mouth to wail, allowing water to filter through the cloth and enter my respiratory organs. My lungs began to swell with the muddy water. I no longer heard the rumbling of the river, for my consciousness was slipping away.

When I awoke, I was lying at the bottom of the Euphrates, the weight of the water crushing down on me. Unable to move, I was able to hear the sounds of the river and feel the loathsome, maddening pecking of small fish.

How did I survive the fall from Floraison? I thought it had been divine *intervention. Perhaps someone there still cared for me. Somehow, despite what I had endured, I still desired to live—but my desire was ephemeral.*

I lay immobile and powerless on the riverbed. Many days and nights slipped by. Thoughts were my only companion. Thus, I tried to fill my moments with joyful recollections I had in some of my favorite places in Floraison, Sonnoris, the Atrium, Guidance Park, Serena Lake, Triumph Gardens, and my cave in Mount Verve.

Lilith jolted upright, panting and shivering. She touched her face and hair, and looked around her. Realizing she was sitting between Satan and Samael who slept, she relaxed and exhaled.

She tilted her head back and saw pink, orange, and yellow hues mixing with the blue of the sky as the sun commenced its downward journey. She stared at her hands, still trembling. By way of her vision, she saw Beelzebub's fall, as if through his own eyes. Perhaps this was a strength she could hone, for such knowledge could be beneficial.

She reclined between Satan and Samael once more to get additional repose before nightfall.

Chapter 21

JEALOUSY

The sun dropped. The temperature became much cooler. Samael awoke and saw Lilith sleeping in Satan's arms. He frowned and poked her several times until she opened her eyes half way and glanced at him.

"What is the matter?" She yawned.

"It is night." Samael rolled his eyes.

"Yes, you are right." Lilith ignored Samael's scowling displeasure and turned her back on him to wake Satan.

Samael got to his feet and stormed to the shoreline. On his way, he encountered Dagon, sleeping under a palm. He kicked him hard on his side. Dagon awoke, rubbed his side and glowered at him.

"It is time to leave this place." Samael pressed his lips together.

"There was no need to——" An excruciating pain in his legs interrupted Dagon's words. Wincing, he glanced at his lower body. His lower limbs were wedged together as if by an invisible vise. Their shape began to change before his eyes. Scales developed to replace his skin. Vents opened on both sides of his neck. Webbing formed between his fingers. He squeezed his eyelids together.

Samael watched him through narrowed eyes.

Dagon writhed and floundered on the ground, for the pain was intense. When he opened his eyes, he was a merman. He wheezed and gasped for air. The gills on his neck opened and closed attempting to capture oxygen from the atmosphere.

"Help me, Samael." Dagon reached out for him.

Samael stepped out of reach. "Why?"

"I must get to the water, or I shall perish." Dagon struggled for breath. Samael remained motionless, staring at him with a sullen expression.

Fornues heard his friend plead for help. He emerged from the depths and rose above the water.

Gadreel slept on the sand near the water fifty feet from where Dagon slept. She was awakened by Fornues' voice in her head.

"Rise! Please awaken! Dagon needs your help!"

Gadreel sat upright and blinked owlishly out to sea. "Fornues? What has happened?"

"Apologies, I did not mean to rattle you, but my friend needs your help. Please go to Dagon!"

Without hesitation, Gadreel hurried to the area where she last saw him.

As she drew nearer, she saw him writhing on the ground in merman form, his arms extended toward Samael. He appeared to be requesting help, but Samael stood before him and offered no assistance. She ran to them.

"What is happening?"

"I need—to—water—please," Dagon said, breathless. She scowled at Samael.

"It is quite amusing." Samael chuckled. "You see, your lover turned into a merman when the sun hid in the horizon. He was unable to stop the transformation." He shrugged. Gadreel stared at him in disbelief.

"Come, I shall help you move to the water. Give me your hand," Gadreel said in a calm voice, pretending her heart was not in her throat.

Samael guffawed and slapped his thigh. "He can hardly lift his eyes, much less his limbs."

Her eyebrows bumped together in a scowl. She grabbed both his arms and pulled him toward the ocean. Grunting with effort, she dragged him over the sand. He continued to gasp for air.

"Samael, he is suffocating! Please help me."

"You seem to be doing fine on your own." He lifted his shoulder in a half shrug.

"I implore you!" Her lips trembled. "He is going to die if he is not immersed in sea water soon."

He waved his hands at her in a short motion with fingers down. "You best be on your way. Go on, lug your lover to the ocean." Samael smirked and swaggered away.

Gadreel's eyes opened wide as she watched him abandon them. Dagon was no longer conscious. She hauled him as fast as she could. When she got closer to the shoreline, she appealed to Fornues for help.

"Help Fornues!"

"You are still much too far for my reach," he communicated.

"Try or your friend shall surely die."

He extended his tentacles as far inland as possible, but his closest appendage was still several feet away. Gadreel flapped her wings and dragged Dagon toward his tentacle. When he was within reach, Fornues coiled a tentacle around his body, and carried him into the sea.

Gadreel collapsed sprawled out on the sand. She let out a harsh breath and wiped her damp eyes.

Fornues swam far and deep, where the waters were darkest. He waited by his friend's side, hoping he would regain consciousness. After a while, Dagon awoke and began to thrash in the water. His eyes bulged as he flailed uncontrollably. His body twitched a few times, and then he stopped moving and became lifeless, sinking deeper into the ocean.

Fornues turned from a deep purplish-black to a ghastly white. "Dagon, do not die. The thought of losing you and remaining alone in the deep is intolerable." He expelled a deafening squirt of black ink.

Then, without warning, Dagon came to life again. At first he appeared confused and flustered, but then he became himself and swam to Fornues.

"My friend! Are you well?" Fornues stared.

"Yes, I am myself again." Dagon creased his brow. "Why have you lost your color?"

"I was frightened I had lost you. You appeared to have drowned. It was awful to witness." Color began to bloom and disperse over Fornues.

"Since we joined the others, I have learned three important things."

Dagon hung his head. "One, I can only transform into my angel form during the light of day. At sundown, I become a sea creature once again, and I cannot survive out of the water for long. Two, I must suffer the drowning process every time I return to the ocean. And three, Samael is no friend of mine. I lay asphyxiating on the sand before him, and he did nothing to help me."

"And he shall pay a high price for it!"

"No, Fornues! He is Satan's right hand," Dagon said. "For now, we must keep the peace with him."

Meanwhile, back at the beach Samael conversed with Lilith and Satan as if nothing had occurred.

Gadreel glared at him from a distance and rubbed her chin. "Everything I desire to express I shall have to keep to myself until the moment is right," she whispered to herself. "Samael has strong allies. With both Lilith and Satan by his side, he is untouchable. He has been cruel to me. He has rejected me and yet my foolish heart still yearns for him. I could retaliate by telling Satan everything I know: his sexual encounters with Lilith, and the secret he hides about having been to Eden and seeing the humans. Divulging this shall make both Satan and Lilith his enemies. Still, I do not desire harm to befall him." She bit her lower lip and proceeded to them.

"Where is Dagon?" Lilith asked her.

"Samael did not tell you?" Gadreel looked at him. "Dagon turned into his fish form, and nearly suffocated on the sand. I dragged him to sea so he would not perish."

"Why did he not wait to turn into the sea creature once he was in the water?" Satan asked, perplexed.

Gadreel turned to Samael. He rolled his eyes and gave an exasperated sigh. "He spontaneously transformed into his aquatic form upon nightfall."

"Dagon can only walk on two legs during the day?" Satan furrowed his brow.

"Yes, it would seem so."

"So now we must worry about being near water come nightfall?" Lilith crossed her arms and frowned.

"Dagon shall have to worry about his own surroundings." Samael looked at Gadreel, sneering.

"We shall follow the coast to the east, for that is where I sense we shall find Beelzebub," Lucifer said. "It is best for us as well, for there is plenty of food along the shoreline, and it is much cooler. This way Fornues and Dagon can follow us. They are our allies. We may need them both at some point in our journey."

Gadreel grinned. Samael sulked.

"Let us go to the beach and notify them of our plans so we can be on our way." Satan pointed to the shoreline.

Lilith kissed Satan on the cheek. "We should feed first, my prince."

"Yes, you are right. We should feed first." He followed her.

Gadreel pursed her lips and shook her head.

At the seashore, Satan called for Fornues and Dagon.

Gadreel paced on tiptoes with her fingertips in her mouth. Did Dagon survive?

Fornues rose above the sea. Dagon's head and shoulders emerged from the water, and he waved at Gadreel. She chortled and waved in return. He glared at Samael.

"I am glad you are well, Dagon." Satan stood tall and clasped arms behind him.

"I was close to death," Dagon said. "I give merits to Gadreel and Fornues. They are the reason I am still among the living and ready to follow your plans."

Satan gazed at Gadreel and gave a nod. "We shall feed first and then begin our journey. We shall fly past the mountains, and proceed close to the coast so you and Fornues are able to follow us."

"We shall feed as well," Dagon said, "and be ready to follow you by sea."

"Would you like for me to bring food to the water?" Gadreel leaned forward and kept steady eye contact with Dagon.

"No, thank you. We shall find suitable food in the sea." Dagon disappeared under the water with Fornues.

"Good, let us eat and waste no more nighttime." Lilith transformed into the snake creature to use her viper's tail to gather coconuts.

Satan, too, changed into the red fiend to help knock fruit off the trees with his horns and tail.

Chapter 22

ADVENTURES OF THE DEEP

Dagon and Fornues departed to search for their meal in the ocean. They glided near the top of the water, scanning for possible food sources. Fornues had not eaten since his fall and was starving.

In the distance, he noticed a great black shadow moving through the water. His keen eyesight apprehended a group of over fifty large black sea creatures, and he stopped, his color fading once more.

Dagon stopped alongside his friend, as dark liquid encircled him. "What is it that you see?"

"There is a large group of sea mammals a short span ahead." Fornues extended one of his tentacles to point at the whales. His voice quivered even though he communicated psychically.

"Are you afraid?"

"I am!" Once more, Fornues squirted thick, black ink in a large cloud accompanied by a loud rumbling sound. He lowered his eyes and looked away.

"Why do you tint the water around us in gloom?" Dagon pressed his palm on his forehead, undulated his fish tail, pivoting to and fro.

"When I experience fear the dark liquid is excreted from me—sometimes with a disgusting, loud squirting sound." Fornues lowered his head. "I have no control of its release."

"Why do you fear that which cannot hurt you?" Dagon puckered his forehead. "You are the largest and most ferocious appearing creature I have seen in these waters. Thus, you should not fear any creature that crosses your path."

Fornues tilted his head and stroked his chin with a tentacle. "You are right. I am a mighty creature."

"Indeed, you are! The ocean is your territory, and any creature that enters it must answer to you."

The black whales dove to the ocean depths. Fornues submerged to observe the creatures in action. One of the whales attempted to capture prey with a high-speed burst. "Did you see the swiftness of the large water mammal?" Fornues looked wide-eyed at Dagon and laughed. "I had no idea one so large could move so fast. Although, I suppose we are all small in the expanse of this great ocean."

The largest whale of the pod set its sights on Dagon. The mammal's large bulbous head broke through the water as it swam toward him at high speed. Dagon recoiled and held up his hands.

The whale opened its mouth, displaying rows of enormous teeth. At the instant the whale darted to make its kill, one of Fornues' tentacles knocked the whale, sending it rolling through the water into its pod.

Dagon emitted a short burst of bubbles. "Thank you. You saved my life again."

Fornues stared as the other whales examined their injured pod member. He heard them communicate with each other using whistles and pulsed sounds. They swam to the surface and set forth, carrying away their injured ally.

Dagon pointed to the fleeing pod of whales. "Are you convinced now? You have dominance over all the other creatures in the sea. They fear you!"

"Indeed. I am beginning to understand the extent of my power in this realm. I also appreciate why Satan prefers me in this form."

They continued to drift along in the deep ocean currents. Dagon consumed crustaceans along the way and shared them with his friend. "It is difficult for me to see clearly at such depths." Dagon squinted in the dark.

Fornues used the lights on his head and at the end of his tentacles to illuminate the way.

Fornues opened his mouth and swam through a large school of colorful, luminescent fish. "I have ingested a myriad of fish, but my hunger pangs persists."

"I realize you need a lot of energy to power your massive body. Small fish, lobsters, shrimps, and crabs do not provide enough meat for you. There has to be some creature in the vast expanse of the ocean that could serve as satisfying meal for you." Dagon's lips formed a grim line.

Slowly cruising the ocean, they came to a steep drop-off. There, they encountered an immense, aggressive-looking fish with amazing maneuverability. Its broad, strong, bronze-colored body glided at high speeds.

The predator spotted Dagon with the hollow black globes it used for eyes and made a sharp turn with its long, wing-like fins. Dagon crouched forward, preparing to defend himself.

A pounding in his skull threw his head back. Despite the pain, he swung his head forward and trained his eyes on his fierce rival. He roared in pain as his tusk broke through bone, muscle and skin. When his massive forehead tusk emerged, the pain ceased. Once again, he set his sights on the fish as it circled, taunting him.

He mimicked the shark's moves and maintained eye contact as it approached him. It appeared ready to attack when the opportunity presented itself.

Dagon groaned and cringed experiencing an agonizing stinging sensation in his lower body. He looked and saw a large bite mark on his tail. The water around him became stained with his blood.

He searched for Fornues, who had left him behind while seeking nourishment. Before he could form a word, he perceived another torturous assault to his flank. He jolted and jerked, unable to control what was happening to his body. More attacks came, too many to be from one creature. Dagon was betrayed by his own blood, which swathed him, making it impossible for him to see his attackers.

He wailed in agony as a shiver of sharks attacked him mercilessly. Fornues heard the cries and returned to witness his friend receive bite after bite from multiple frenzied sharks. Dagon drifted, gushing blood from open wounds.

Enraged, Fornues turned a bright purple color. He sliced through the water, emitting blinding flashes of light at the sharks to disorient them. He wrapped his tentacles around them. The ferocious fish struggled in his tight grasp. They opened their mouths to display large, triangular teeth with serrated edges, but they were no matches for Fornues' long, sharp fangs.

Fornues tasted the sharks' flesh as the suction cups lining his tentacles came in contact with their skin. He injected his prey with paralyzing saliva, rendering them immobile. Dagon watched slack-jawed as Fornues dismembered the sharks, then rotated his hinged skull upward and swallowed. "I have found gratification in this feast; my hunger was satisfied."

"Help me." Dagon sank further into the deep, unable to move his body.

"I am coming, my friend." Energized, he rushed to him with a surprising burst of speed. He grasped his friend gently with one of his tentacles. He took him deeper into the lightless, suffocating depths of the sea and deposited his limp body on a flat rock. The pressure, darkness, and coolness of the deep waters had curative properties for sea creatures, and Dagon's wounds began to heal quickly.

Fornues obtained fish for him to consume once he revived. After some time, Dagon opened his eyes to find his friend by his side.

"Once again, I owe my life to you."

"Do not be so appreciative." Fornues handed him a fish. "My motives for rescuing you are to some extent selfish, for I cannot imagine a life in these cold waters without you."

Dagon sat upright. "The curative effects of the deep have revitalized me, but since there is little oxygen, we shall soon have to swim to shallower depths."

He gorged on the bounty of fish Fornues provided. He reclined on his elbows and tilted his head back. "The view of the ocean from below is spectacular. From this perspective, the deep sea resembles the Earth's sky at twilight. It seems all the creatures of the deep emit some kind of light, including you, Fornues. The luminescent creatures simulate shooting meteors, flickering stars, rolling comets with tails, and colorful nebulas."

"We must return to shore," Fornues said. "Satan summons us once more."

Dagon nodded. "I am ready to return."

They swam upward to shallow waters and proceeded to the coastline to find their friends.

Chapter 23

SAMAEL'S STORY
OF PARADISE

Gadreel sang a mellifluous melody, sitting on the beach watching the calm black sea. Satan stood on a rocky cliff overlooking the ocean accompanied by Lilith and Samael.

"Fornues, Dagon, arise from the sea," Satan called in a booming voice. "I summon you!"

"Is it possible they cannot hear you, my prince?" Lilith paced back and forth.

Satan heaved a deep sigh. "Of course they hear me."

"Why have they not returned?" Frustration creased her eyes.

"Perhaps they swam far, and now it shall take them some time to return." Samael tucked his chin slightly and held up his palms.

"Why would they go far if we told them we would be leaving shortly?" Lilith rolled her eyes and continued to pace on the rock.

"Fare in these dark waters may not be easy to find, and I suppose it would take plenty of food to satisfy a sea giant like Fornues. It is also their first time hunting at sea. We should be patient, my love." Satan placed a hand on his cheek and walked to the edge of the cliff. He looked over the ocean with gathered brow.

Lilith brooded.

Gadreel lay flat on her back, knees bent, and toes digging into the wet sand of the shoreline, waiting for the return of Fornues and Dagon.

"Every star is displayed and shining in full brilliance tonight," she sang. She rubbed her belly. She had consumed twice what she normally ate and was quite satiated.

The stars appeared near each other, so she began connecting groups of stars with her finger to form patterns. In one cluster of stars, she formed an image of Gabriel blowing on his horn of truth, while in another ensemble she drew an outline of Michael standing upon his rock pedestal. Elsewhere, Hashmal emitted fire from his mouth. "I am able to see all the holy angels I once called friends in the starry sky. However, I do not recognize myself or any of my fallen companions in the stars." She covered her face with her arms. After a long moment, she rose to seek the others and found Lilith and Satan focusing all their attention on Samael.

⚘

"What I am about to reveal occurred in my travels," Samael said. "I think it would be of great interest to you."

Gadreel gasped. He plans to tell them about Eden. He must be convinced that Lilith would not harm Eve, because Satan was around. However, Gadreel believed if Lilith desired it, no one could stop her. Yet, she supposed Samael could not keep his encounter with the humans a secret forever.

"Tell us what you have encountered in your long, difficult journey, Samael," Satan said.

"I have been in The Garden Of Eden," he said to the shocked gasps of those around him.

"What?" Lilith's face contorted with anger. "Why did you wait so long to tell us? We spent many moons together, and you never mentioned having been in Eden. Why?"

Samael gulped, and looked down. "I thought it best to wait until we found Satan and we were together before revealing this information."

Lilith's nose flared. "Speak now. Tell us what you have seen."

"Be silent, Lilith!" Satan lifted his chin and puffed out his chest. "I shall be the only one to make demands here!"

"Apologies." Lilith lowered her head while clenching her jaw.

She looked at Samael sideways and sat close to him. Satan sat beside her, and Gadreel tiptoed to them and also sat nearby.

"Samael, you did well to delay this revelation until you were in my presence." Satan glimpsed at Lilith. "Tell us everything."

"After I was cast out of Floraison, I awoke lying upon sand in an arid region. I lay bare and weak. I howled in pain as I clambered to my feet. There was sand embedded in my skin, but my attempts to wipe off the tiny particles caused stinging and burning, so I left it alone.

"I scanned my surroundings through partly closed eyes not yet accustomed to the eerie brightness. I saw reddish hills of sand and valleys with windblown designs, which looked like wavy ripples on an ocean.

"My surroundings were beautiful, but also mysterious and frightening. The heat swathed my body like flames. The powerful star above scorched my vulnerable skin and made my head throb. I realized I must depart the exquisite, but deadly, place at once. However, there was only sand in every direction as far as the eye could see. I could not determine where to go.

"I closed my eyes and tried to think of a plan, but the sweltering sun beating on me made it impossible to concentrate. It seemed at any moment my hair would burst into flames and my cranium would explode. I was too weak to fly, so I lifted my wings above my head, using them as a shield.

"Out of nowhere, a high-pitched shrill sound penetrated my already aching head. Shielding my ears did not stop the pain. Although I had never heard anything like it before, I believed it was familiar somehow. I decided to follow this shrill tone to its source, hoping it would lead me to one of my friends. In any case, it was far better than wandering aimlessly in circles following the ever-changing landscape. The mysterious, yet familiar, noise oriented me in the direction I must go, and I began my journey to find its origin.

"Dragging my feet across the desert and climbing the high dunes proved almost too great a burden. I kept my scorched wings raised above my head to protect my face and body from the sun's fiery attacks.

"At one point, a black feather fell in my path, and then another. As one floated downward, I caught it and brought it to my nose. It had a pungent sulfurous smell. My stomach turned. The feather fell from my fingers, but more tumbled to the ground around me. My mouth fell open when I realized they had fallen from my own wings!

"I swung my wings forward and scrutinized them for the first time since I descended from Floraison. They were no longer brilliant white, but were black as a raven's wings. Featherless areas exposed sharp, spiny projections. I stared at them in awe. Dread surged from the pit of my stomach and I gagged and retched. My wings were revolting. What was I becoming? Would the rest of me change as well?

"After seeing what had become of me, my chest burned and ached. Knowing there was no turning back, acknowledging I was no longer the creature I once was, I suffered a moment of regret." His shoulders slumped and he buried his face in his hands.

Gadreel looked down.

Lilith pursed her lips and rolled her eyes away. Regret? She would make him regret not divulging his secret about Eden to her. From now on, she would make sure his allegiance to her came first.

"A loud, drawn-out, wavering howl emerged in the distance," Samael continued. "Looking toward the horizon, I identified a wall of brown air stretching high, but I was unable to comprehend the phenomenon. It was difficult to judge how far it was, but the ominous wall of sand was headed in my direction. The high-pitched sounds it produced became louder, obliterating all else. The sand mass was gaining energy and magnitude, devouring everything in its path. My eyes searched for refuge.

"I scrambled behind a large rock. I heard the sand wave advancing. My heart beat hard against my chest, and it was difficult to catch my breath. I lifted my nose and smelled the thunderous sand wave draw near. I wrapped my large wings around myself.

"Before long, the violent winds attacked me. Stones began to fly around, beating me without mercy. Clouds of sand and dust whipped through the air, producing terrible screeching and hissing sounds. I trembled and whimpered as dirt and debris pelted my already tender wings. My breathing became even more labored as I curled up under them.

"The sandstorm was destructive and blinding. Its high winds lifted an immense amount of sand rather quickly. In no time I was buried beneath it, weak and semi-conscious, trapped in my feathery cocoon until the storm passed.

"After what seemed an eternity, the howling stopped and the sands settled. I was entombed in the desert. I tried not to panic as I used my wings to dig my way out of the desert crypt.

"Breaking through to the surface, I clambered to my feet. I beat my wings to shake the sand off my face and body. The landscape was now vastly different. The shrill sound returned and I knew it would guide me. Thus, I maintained my course to traverse the sea of sand in the sweltering heat."

Lilith sighed. "Samael, you mentioned the Garden of Eden?" She stared at him eyebrows raised.

Samael reddened. "Forgive me, I thought you wished to know the entire account."

Satan scowled at her.

She touched her lips with her fingers. "Apologies, Samael, please continue."

"I-I dragged my feet for miles," Samael said. "My wings were causing me much agony and my mouth and throat were so parched it was difficult to swallow.

"In the distance, a generous patch of green captivated my eye. I hurried toward it. Since my arrival on this treacherous planet, I had seen only sand. A beautiful garden entryway beckoned with the welcoming colors of its adorning blooms. I nuzzled the flowers, taking in their magnificent fragrances. They smelled of relief, comfort, and safe haven. Within the garden, birds sang and chirped in melody, inviting me to enter. Peeking inside, I glimpsed a beautiful and intriguing garden, incongruous in the middle of the desert.

"I thought of how much I had suffered in the harsh environment of the lifeless, arid lands. Although I feared this beautiful place was not meant for one such as me, I desired more than anything to enter.

"I inched through the floral archway to find an awe-inspiring botanical paradise. The temperature in the garden was pleasant and comfortable, unlike the ferocious desert surrounding it.

"I shuffled farther in, stopping to inhale the fragrances emitted by the flowers and fruit trees. I was weary and winced with every step, for my feet were tender and blistered. The environment around me became even more soothing and delightful. The sun shone brightly, but it no longer singed my skin. A refreshing, gentle breeze, a blend of gratifying fragrances, and a medley of blissful sounds combined to calm and pleasure my senses and make me joyful. 'What place is this?' I whispered under my breath."

"Did no one try to stop you?" Lilith's wide eyes were fixed on him.

"Enough Lilith!" Satan frowned. She pressed her lips together. "Let Samael finish his account." Satan returned his attention to Samael. "Please go on."

"I strolled farther into the oasis," Samael said, "and a brilliant tree in the center of the garden caught my eye. It was dissimilar to anything I had seen during Creation. The tree yielded golden fruit irresistible to the senses. Its fragrance produced a feeling of euphoria. The sound of the wind slipping through its branches emulated Gabriel playing one of his wind instruments—beautiful and soothing.

"The fruit did not hang from branches by a stem, but rather were held in the clutches of the branches, as though they contained hands and fingers. The tree's trunk sparkled, and the tree's leaves twinkled with captured sunbeams when the breeze moved them. The leaves' colors changed with the direction of the wind. I could have stood there gazing at the marvelous tree for hours, enthralled by its beauty, like a beacon in the middle of the garden.

"I stepped toward the tree, squinting, for its brilliance was intense. I lifted my nose and took a whiff its aroma. But as I stood before it, I realized it was slowly draining the energy I had gained upon entering paradise.

"The tree's succulent fruits called to me. I reached for one. That is when Cam appeared before me, wielding his flaming sword."

Gadreel inhaled a sharp breath. Lilith leaned forward.

Satan stood tall, his eyes fierce nocturnal seas. He stepped forward with arms clasped behind his body. "Continue!"

"His red hair flickered and danced like the flames on his sword, and his vivid green eyes glared at me. Cam's large, powerful body was almost as brilliant as the tree he guarded, and his six large white wings were fully outstretched, as he loomed over me like a threatening storm.

"Cam pointed his blazing sword at me, and demanded I leave the Garden of Eden."

Lilith narrowed her eyes. Satan clenched his jaw and his hands balled into fists.

"He touched his blade here." Samael pointed to the black heart-shaped mark on his chest.

Lilith frowned. "I had often wondered where the mark had originated."

"My knees faltered and my legs collapsed beneath me. I did not have the strength to fight. I placed a hand over the painful area on my chest, stared at Cam and waited for my end.

"'You are in the Garden of Eden, and this is the Tree of Life. You are not worthy to eat of its fruit.' Cam's voice was commanding. 'Step away from the tree and be gone from this place, for you do not belong here.'

"I had no weapon." Samael licked his lips. "I did not have a shield against his mighty sword, so I hurried to my feet and moved away from the tree. Afraid to turn my sights from Cam, I thus stumbled, fell backward, hit my head on a rock, and lost consciousness."

Lilith opened her mouth to speak, but her eyes met Satan's, so she bit her lip instead and remained silent while Samael continued.

"When I opened my eyes, I saw the most fetching creature kneeling by my side. I gazed at her flawless, wingless, bare body and knew at once who she was. I heard the gurgling of flowing water. I raised my head and looked around. I was lying on the banks of a tranquil river."

"I asked her, 'Are you the one God calls Eve?'"

"Eve recoiled and stared at me with her big almond-shaped eyes, her head tilted to one side. 'Are you of this world?' she asked me in a silvery voice.

"I smiled and gradually sat upright, attempting not to frighten her. She was truly magnificent to look upon."

Lilith wore a sour expression.

"'I am known as Samael. I am from a place far beyond the eyes.' I stretched my arm toward the skies. Eve lifted her eyes toward Heaven. I explained how I once lived in Floraison, the lowermost realm of Heaven with God. 'I watched Him create you from the dust of the Earth, but now I live on Earth as you do,' I told her. She tried to smile at me, but it was as if the effort would injure her. She took me by the hand and pulled me into the river. She poured water over me, washing off the embedded sand particles. I submerged my entire body in the river, causing her to gasp. I emerged from the water and splashed her. She giggled and bit her lip.

"'You are a fascinating creature—you appear haggard, yet beautiful in a sad way.' Eve gazed at me.

"We shared a special attraction and bond I had never experienced with anyone else."

Lilith and Gadreel glimpsed at each other. Lilith turned away lips primed. Gadreel crossed her arms.

"Eve touched the small black symbol left on my skin by Cam's blazing sword. I had forgotten about it because it was healed, although a scar remained, in the same way my entire body was healed in this place.

"I desired her, so I pulled her close. She remained entranced by me. Her lips parted slightly and her bosoms heaved with quick, shallow breaths. We ogled each other and I leaned in and nuzzled my face against her neck and face. I sniffed her skin and hair. She smelled of frangipani blossoms, warm and comforting clove buds, spicy, sweet frankincense, and desire. I moved in to kiss her.

"'Release her at once,' a voice nearby cried, disconcerting both of us. Eve jolted. When I turned my head in the direction of the voice, I saw the man God called Adam advancing toward me. I stepped out of the river, feeling refreshed and invigorated.

'Move away from her and leave Eden at once!' Adam said. I outstretched my hideous black wings to intimidate him, but they terrified Eve as well. She screamed and ran into his arms as if I were a terrible beast." Samael ended his story with a downward glance.

"What happened afterward?" Satan asked.

"I flew away. Soon, I was soaring across a large expanse of desert. The shrill sound, which was somehow dimmed to a faint undertone in the Garden of Eden, pierced my mind like a lightning bolt, so I resumed my quest to its source.

"In flight, I stared at the desert and marveled at the russet, star-shaped dunes, but the marvelous landscape could not prevent thoughts of the beautiful, glowing creature Eve, and I wondered if I would ever see her again. And then I saw two winged figures in the desert, and I noticed that—"

"You spoke earlier of being weak, at the brink of death. How then were you able to fly?" Lilith did not want him to tell Satan about how she had abandoned Gadreel.

"As I mentioned earlier, I was feeble when I first entered Eden, near death. The garden rejuvenated me. Merely strolling through Eden restored me to full strength."

"If you were restored to full strength simply by being there—imagine the power you would have gained if you had eaten the fruits and drank the water from this place." Lilith's eyes widened. "We must go there!"

"Indeed!" Satan nodded. "We shall visit the Garden of Eden, but first things first. We shall journey now to find Beelzebub."

"Why not first refresh and strengthen ourselves in the river in Eden of which Samael spoke?" Lilith asked.

"No. Beelzebub needs us," Satan said.

"The journey to find him shall be long and arduous. Would it not be wise to feed and bathe in the Garden of Eden first? Who knows what powers we could gain and—"

"Enough!" Satan jutted his chin. "I have spoken."

Lilith turned away, gritting her teeth and clenching her fists in frustration.

Dagon and Fornues returned. Lilith inhaled a deep breath and blew it out slowly.

"Fornues and Dagon, you can head north and follow the coast around the landmass." Satan wasted no time. "We shall meet again on the northern shore. There, we shall head to the east."

"Your wish is our command," Dagon said.

"We have wasted enough time, we must be on our way at once." Satan took to the sky.

Lilith, Samael, and Gadreel flew after him. Fornues and Dagon returned to the depths of the ocean. At last, the journey to find Beelzebub was set in motion.

Chapter 24

DAGON'S SACRIFICE

Gadreel glided through the night sky. She grinned as the cool breeze caressed her face—happy she was no longer alone in the desert with Lilith. Although Lilith had always been mischievous and from time-to-time wicked, nothing could have prepared Gadreel for her conduct on Earth. Losing the war in Floraison changed her forever. She was now callous, wrathful, and unkind. She only sought one thing: revenge.

Gadreel feared her, for she believed there was little good left in her. Lilith was capable of committing any atrocity she set her mind to. Gadreel's flesh crawled contemplating it. She set her sights on Satan and inhaled a deep breath relieved to be in his company.

A large bird swooped past, jolting her. The bird returned and flew by her side. When she saw him, she gasped. "It is you! You are the bird from the beach. I recognize your brown plumage and the golden feathers adorning the back of your head and neck. Greetings, it is good to see you again." Gadreel communicated with the large bird in her mind. The bird whistled a high-pitched, soft sound in response. She gaped at the golden eagle and giggled. Lilith, who had been scrutinizing her since they left the beach, flew to her side.

"That bird has been flying by your side for quite a ways now," Lilith said. "It is a large bird and perhaps can feed us later."

Gadreel's mouth dropped open. The memory of Lilith and Samael devouring the little camel in the ice cave was still fresh in her mind.

"Go, my friend! Fly far away from here, now!" Gadreel shouted in her mind. The eagle immediately veered off and flew hastily in the opposite direction. Lilith's head swiveled to follow the bird, stunned by its sudden departure.

"What happened? Why did the bird fly away without warning?"

"How could I know the mind of a bird?" Gadreel gave her a one-sided shoulder shrug. "Perhaps it understood when you spoke about turning it into a meal."

Lilith narrowed her eyes and glanced at her sideways. "If you are concealing something from me, it is a mistake." Lilith glowered at her for a while and then returned to her place between Satan and Samael.

They flew by night and in the morning. By midday, when the sun rode high in the sky and swathed them in fiery radiance, the fallen angels dove to the seashore to feed and find shade. They strolled a strip of beach to a group of palm trees whose bluish-green fronds created a wide canopy.

Lilith spotted small brown fruits covering the ground beneath the palms. As she brought one to her nose, she found it was sticky and squishy between her fingers. Detecting a sweet quality, she ventured to take a bite.

She picked several of the dates from the ground, brushed off the sand, and offered a handful to Satan. He stared at the sticky brown fruit and furrowed his brow.

"What is this? It resembles bird droppings."

Gadreel chortled.

Lilith rolled her eyes upward. "Take a bite, it is sweet and sustaining, but be wary of a large, hard seed in the middle."

Satan took a small bite of the date. He grinned and nodded as he chewed. Upon seeing Satan's delighted expression, Samael and Gadreel began gathering fruit. They quickly consumed the dates scattered on the ground. Lilith cast her eyes at the palms' canopy, where fruit hung in bunches. She flew up, picked a few bunches off the tree, and tossed them to the ground. They ate until their bellies were full. Afterward, they accommodated themselves under the date palms to rest, avoiding the harshest hours of the day.

Gadreel strolled to the shore, as she often did, to contemplate the sea. Several days and nights had passed since they last saw Dagon and Fornues. She squeezed her brow together and stared out to sea.

All of a sudden, she hunched and cringed. A sensation of uneasiness and disquiet in her upper stomach made her legs falter. She fell to her knees, and the contents of her stomach were forcefully expelled onto the sand.

She pressed a hand to her throat. Wide-eyed she craned her neck to see past the palms to check the others for signs of ill health, but they slept at ease. "What is happening to me? Lately, I feel weak and tire so easily, but this has not happened before. Are my days on Earth numbered?" What would become of her if she could no longer keep any nourishment in her system? Gadreel grimaced with revulsion as she buried her vomitus. Its offensive, sweet rot smell caused her to gag yet again. She hung her head while on hands and knees. She crawled to shore and splashed water on her face. "Why is this happening to me?" Her lips quivered.

Gadreel got to her feet and entered further in the water, which splashed against her legs, cool and refreshing. Since it always made her feel better, she began to sing. Her voice was lyrical, and melodic. Soon several kinds of aquatic creatures surrounded her. A dolphin approached and nudged her on the leg. She chuckled. The dolphin chattered and invited her to come along, signaling with its head. She gazed at the mammal with a curious expression. The dolphin communicated using a combination of squeaks and chirrups. She decided to honor its invitation and go for a swim in the open sea.

Then it proceeded to put on a show for her. It leapt fifteen feet out of the ocean. The dolphin performed multiple flips, splashing her while she shook with laughter and clapped her hands. The sea mammal jumped and tail-walked across the surface of the water as she gasped in awe.

The dolphin approached her and kissed her on the cheek. It commenced a high-pitched clicking in rapid succession while moving away by beating its fluke back and forth.

"Goodbye my friend!" Gadreel waved. Soon the dolphin was gone, and she was alone in the middle of the ocean. The shoreline seemed miles away. It had been a mistake to swim so far. The sun parched her. She rubbed her weary eyes and swam toward the beach, but her arms and legs grew heavy.

An abrupt painful cramp in her leg muscles made her squeal. Despite her desperate efforts to stay afloat, she began to sink. She opened her mouth to scream, and water rushed in. She sank deeper. Her eyes were wide and staring and her body wilted, as if she had given up. As her eyes began to close, a pair of strong arms took hold of her and carried her to the surface.

Dagon kept her head and shoulders above the surface as he swam toward the coastline. She coughed and gasped, expelling water from her lungs. After several deep breaths, she moved her lips to speak, but could not form words.

"You do not need to speak," Dagon whispered. "I am pleased that Fornues perceived you were in danger, and we were nearby and able to come to your aid."

"Thank you, Fornues," Gadreel imparted with her mind.

She gazed into Dagon's piercing gray-blue eyes. "You are kind, unlike Samael who had left you to die. Thank you for saving me."

"Why were you so far from shore?"

"Several reasons. I have not been feeling well and have not been myself. I was also worried about you and Fornues. We have not seen you since we first began our journey to find Beelzebub."

"Fornues is king of the ocean, and I am with him. Thus, there is no need to fear for us."

She gazed up at him through her lashes.

"It has been awhile since I walked on two legs. I much desire to spend time with you." Dagon made eye contact with her. She put her arms around his neck and laid her head on his chest.

As Dagon swam toward the shoreline, Fornues asked, "Do you recall what it is like when you return to your fish form?"

"I remember hurting when I lost my legs to this fish tail, but spending time with Gadreel is well worth the pain."

"Do you recall what happened when you re-entered the sea after you had walked on land?"

"I drowned, as I did when I fell from Floraison."

"The like shall happen again if you walk the Earth," Fornues said. "Upon returning to sea, water shall flood your lungs until they burst. You shall drown once more, my friend. Surely being with Gadreel a few hours cannot be worth that."

"A few hours spent with her are worth that and more." Dagon swam ahead of Fornues.

Near the coast, Dagon willed his angel form and waded to shore, carrying Gadreel in his arms. He placed her on the sand and kissed her on the forehead. She caressed his face. He leaned forward, and they kissed on the lips.

"Thank you once again for saving my life," she said.

"I would do anything for you." His breaths quickened.

She took him by the hand and guided him to one of the date palms. She selected a date and presented it to him.

"Taste it. It is a sweet fruit."

He shook his head. "I satisfied my appetite with nourishment from the sea."

"Oh. I see." Gadreel poked out her bottom lip and tossed the date to the ground.

He grabbed her by the shoulders, pushed her against a palm, and began to kiss her with brute force. She squirmed and he pinned her to the tree.

"Stop!" she yelled. She shoved him away. "Please do not force yourself on me. If you continue to do so, I shall grow to despise you!"

He gaped at her and stepped back holding up his palms. "I do not desire your hate. I want you to feel what my heart feels for you."

"I know not if I shall ever feel as you do, but if you ignore my mind, surely hate shall flourish in my heart." Gadreel shambled away.

When Lilith heard Gadreel holler, she advanced toward her voice and hid behind a rock to watch. Thus, she observed and overheard everything occurring between them and watched Gadreel shuffle away.

"Greetings!" Lilith walked from behind the rock.

Dagon jolted, disconcerted. "Lilith—I did not see you there."

"I observed what transpired between you and Gadreel. If you desire to hear it, I have guidance, which may help you win her heart." If she aided Dagon in conquering Gadreel's heart, this would keep her away from Samael. This would please Lilith.

"Please tell me, for I long to gain her love." Dagon leaned toward her.

"Samael is a cherished sexual partner. He knows how to give pleasure to a female."

Dagon scowled. "What has that to do with me?"

"You are like an animal: rough, awkward, and crude. You hurt Gadreel physically and emotionally when you force yourself upon her. This is why she rejects you. If you desire to be a suitable lover, you must be mild, calm, use little force, and pay mind to what feels good to your companion. You must observe Samael. You can learn much from him."

"Observe him?" Dagon shook his head. "How am I supposed to do that?"

"There is no need for your abrasive tone. I can simply leave you to your predicament."

"No, no—do not leave." Dagon lowered his eyes.

"Come with me." Lilith took him by the hand and led him to a large rock.

"I shall bring Samael to this spot. We shall demonstrate to you how to please and satisfy Gadreel. Remain hidden behind the rock at all times. Do not allow him to see you."

She departed to find Samael, who slept under a small group of date palms. She shook him gently until he opened his eyes.

"Lilith? What is it? Is everything well?"

"Come with me, Samael. I crave you."

He flashed a toothy grin, jumped to his feet and followed her. She guided him near the large rock and glanced in the direction where Dagon hid to signal his lessons were about to begin.

Lilith began by kissing Samael. He curled his arm around her waist and tugged her close. Holding her against him he eased her gently to the ground.

Samael nuzzled her neck, inhaling, taking in her scent while she tilted her head back and moaned with pleasure. Dagon observed how he caressed her body with his hands and his mouth. He watched her writhe and groan as Samael used his tongue in sensitive places. During the sex act, he continued to kiss and caress her, remaining tender until the end.

Afterward, Lilith led Samael away. Dagon emerged from hiding, having learned a great deal about the art of making love. "My enemy instructs me with his skills of affection." Dagon shook his head and smirked.

Lilith and Samael strolled hand-in-hand until they approached the others. She let go of his hand and whispered in his ear, "No one is to know what happened between us."

Samael nodded in agreement and slouched away.

⋘

Gadreel slumped under a tree near the water. Her stomach had settled a bit, but she sensed the same would happen the following day. She stared at the water.

"Where is Dagon?" Fornues asked suddenly in her mind.

"I do not know." Gadreel wrapped her arms around herself.

"Dagon is quite fond of you. He left the waters to be with you."

"I did not ask him to do so."

"He shall suffer to a great extent when he returns to sea, and it shall all have been for nothing."

"What do you mean?" Gadreel leaned forward.

"Whenever Dagon leaves the ocean and walks on land, he must pay a price. He shall experience great pain as he attains his aquatic form once more. When he enters the water, he shall suffer a horrible drowning death before he is able to return to the sea once again. I believe today you got a glimpse of what it is like to drown."

Gadreel pressed her hands to her cheeks and jumped to her feet. "Does he not know these things shall happen to him?"

"Of course he does, but he said no amount of suffering would keep him from spending a few hours with you."

"His words make my heart swell with affection for him." She touched her bosom. "He left the waters knowing the agony that awaited him once he returned? To spend a moment with me?"

"Yes. He thinks you are extraordinary."

Slowly, a rosy color spread across her cheeks. Soon after, she departed in search of Dagon. She ran into him as he strolled toward the beach. She giggled and kissed him on the cheek. Her face flushed bright pink.

"Where are you going in such a hurry?" Dagon asked, his voice tender.

"My heart yearns for you, and my legs led me to you." She smiled the kind of smile that reaches places the sun cannot and warms your heart.

Dagon squinted at her as if her face was blurred. Gadreel leaned in and kissed him on the lips.

He slid his hands up and down her arms gently and gazed into her eyes with a concerned expression. "When I become aroused, a bony projection juts from my forehead. It is painful, but there is nothing I can do to stop it. In spite of this, I can assure you that I shall not hurt you."

Gadreel tucked a lock of hair behind his ear and caressed his face. He closed his eyes as she did so.

Dagon put his arms around her drawing her near. He kissed her softly on the face and nape of her neck. He set her on the ground, in the same way Samael did with Lilith. He continued to kiss her shoulders and nuzzle his face between her breasts. She panted and arched her neck and back. His horn broke out of his forehead. The pain was evanescent. She caressed his face and glided her fingers over the ridges at the base of his tusk. "I am not afraid," she said. He mimicked Samael's moves throughout their sexual encounter and she moaned and writhed in pleasure.

Lilith watched from behind a pomegranate shrub. Now that Gadreel has found a lover in Dagon, she would stay away from Samael. She strutted away with a satisfied grin.

Gadreel and Dagon continued to find pleasure in each other's arms until the sun began to grow dim.

He brushed her wild, golden curls off her face. "It is almost time for me to return to sea. Please do not look upon me when my transformation begins."

"Why not?" She scowled. "I am aware of what happens to you and I desire to be by your side when you change. Perhaps I can help alleviate your pain."

"Perhaps you can." Dagon closed his eyes and gently rubbed his face against hers. It was much better to be gentle and kind to your companion. Lilith was right and he was grateful.

"It is time to go!" Satan shouted.

"Let us go to the water." Gadreel extended her hand to him. "We can wait there until you have transformed. I shall be with you, and Fornues shall be there as well."

Dagon nodded.

They rushed to the water. The others were already there. Dagon advanced a few feet into the water. Gadreel sat next to him with her hand in his. Together they anticipated the transformation.

Lilith watched the sunset. Exquisite hues of purple, pink, and ruby colored the clouds as the radiance of the sun calmly diminished.

After watching the sun disappear behind the horizon, the fallen angels witnessed Dagon's agonizing change. He stared at Gadreel's glistening eyes during the transformation. Those dark russet eyes rimmed with thick, long, lashes that brushed her cheeks every time she closed her eyes. She caressed him as he tried to conceal his pain, but the agony was etched on his face.

After the transformation was complete, Dagon and Gadreel uttered their goodbyes. Samael sulked as he watched. Lilith peered at him with an insolent grin on her face.

"I shall see you in a few days," Dagon said. Gadreel pressed a hand to her bosom as he swam away. Fornues trailed behind.

Lilith strolled over to Gadreel and played with a lock of her hair. Gadreel was jarred by the unexpected gesture.

"This is why we must pursue our revenge," Lilith said. "Or perhaps you are at ease with Dagon's suffering whenever he leaves the waters to visit you?"

"Of course not. I suffer knowing of his agony, but vengeance shall not change anything." Gadreel hurried away. Lilith glared after her with a tightened jaw.

Chapter 25

GADREEL'S TUMBLE

Satan took to the skies. Lilith followed close behind.

"It is time to go, Gadreel!" Samael crossed his arms over his chest. Her eyes rested on the ocean and she ignored his bellowing. He gritted his teeth, flapped his wings and whooshed to the sky.

At the sound of rushing air, Gadreel lifted her eyes and saw her comrades soaring away. "I must hurry after them, but I feel so weak." She fluttered her wings with all her might and became airborne. "It is going to be a challenge to keep pace with them, but I need to make an effort."

Gadreel remained at the rear of the group. She preferred not to be too close to the others lest she become queasy. She did not have the strength to flap her wings nonstop, so she drifted through the air.

For a couple of weeks, they flew to the east by night and reposed by day. Every time they landed, Gadreel hurried to the shoreline. She had not seen Dagon since their last encounter at the beach with the date palms. Her eyes darted over the water as she stood on her tiptoes and searched for him. When she saw no sign of him she hung her head and dragged her feet to the nearest palm.

During their stops, she tried to nourish herself. It was vital she develop enough energy to proceed. Her bouts of nausea and vomiting had lessened in the last few days. She thought she might be getting better, although she still tired easily.

From the sky, Lilith and the other fallen angels viewed a monotonous landscape: sand and beaches punctuated by date palms and other desert trees and plants. Around the sixteenth day of their journey, Lilith spotted a river extending a considerable distance.

"Behold!" She pointed to the river. "There may be an abundance of food in and around that body of water!"

Satan and Samael aimed their sights in the direction she indicated. They all made a sweeping descent and landed near the river's bank, except for Gadreel.

She did not have the strength to control her landing. She plummeted from the sky, shrieking and whirling. She tumbled into the river, making a huge splash. Samael and Satan rushed to her aid.

Sunning on the riverbanks were numerous reptilian creatures, which moved about comically on four short, splayed legs. Several of the reptiles beat their long, powerful tails on the ground when they caught sight of the angels. Others slid into the river and rolled around, wetting their scaly hides. Lilith, Satan, and Samael watched in astonishment as small birds fed on meat scraps inside the gaping mouths of the crocodiles.

Samael decided to step through the hordes of crocodiles to enter the water. If diminutive birds have the courage to forage inside the beasts' mouths, he could certainly walk past them.

Gadreel floated in the water near the edge of the river. The largest of the reptiles swam around her. She appeared lifeless, yet the crocodiles did nothing to harm her. How was this so? They encircled her, as if forming a wall of protection.

Samael waded across the river toward her. Immediately, crocodiles lurking in the shallows surrounded him. The rough, massive creatures were submerged beneath the surface, except for their noses and yellowish-green eyes with vertical black slits, which peered at him.

Samael lifted his hands and his eyebrows joined in a frown. He expanded his wings and balled his hands to make fists, scanning from one beast to another. He continued inching closer to Gadreel until he got hold of her. As he attempted to fly off with her in his arms a crocodile gripped his leg with its massive jaws.

Samael howled in pain as the immense pressure of the beast's teeth pierced his flesh. He released Gadreel, who splashed into the water once more, still unconscious.

The massive animal dragged Samael deep into the river. At the bottom, the crocodile beat him against a rock. He flailed and wriggled, attempting to free himself from the crocodile's bite.

When Satan heard his cries, he transformed into the red beast. He whizzed in the air above the crocodiles and crashed into the river to rescue his ally. He caught the creature at the bottom of the river. The beast held Samael's leg locked in its jaws.

Satan attacked the crocodile with the sharp, pointed end of his tail. He stabbed it repeatedly on the head. As its life came to an end, the creature's mouth sprung open, releasing Samael's gnawed leg. The reptile's blood mingled with his and dispersed to cover the surface of the water.

When Lilith saw Satan spring into action, she too transformed into her alter ego, the powerful snake creature. She pulled Gadreel from the water, thrashing a few crocodiles along the way. She placed her limp body on the grass and waited until she regained consciousness.

Satan laid Samael alongside Gadreel. He pressed his lips together and grimaced in pain. Lilith examined the huge gash on his leg. She frowned.

"We must stop the vital life force from leaving his body." Lilith paced scanning every living thing around her as she searched for a way to help him. A curious plant caught her eye. She rushed to it. It exhibited hairy, dull green leaves and lovely little flowers. The odd plant beckoned her. She reached out to it cautiously, recalling the hostile vegetation in the forbidden forests.

When she handled one plant's hairy leaves, she suffered a painful sting. She recoiled and stared wide-eyed at her fingers. They were red and inflamed. She shook her fingers as they throbbed with pain.

Following her intuition she obtained a large leaf of another plant lying nearby and used it to gather a bunch of the stinging plants. She took them to Samael. Utilizing the sizeable leaf again, she crushed the stinging vegetation in her hands.

"This plant has a painful sting but it shall stop the bleeding." She demonstrated the mashed plant to Samael. "Do you trust me?"

Samael panted and trembled but he bobbed his head.

"This is one of the special talents I received from God. I am sure of it now. I have my visions and the knowledge and ability to cure others by using elements of the natural world." She applied the remedy to Samael's open wound.

Samael's eyes bulged as he experienced the excruciating, prickling pain of the plant's acid working on his wounded leg. He howled and squirmed gripping the ground in pain as Lilith continued to compress the stinging foliage into his gashes.

"Be still, Samael!" Lilith gestured for Satan to hold him down.

Samael opened and shut his mouth trying to form words. He shook his head, groaned and gnashed his teeth in agony.

Lilith exhaled in relief. "I have stopped the bleeding. Your leg shall heal quickly now."

"The pain is hard to bear," Samael said in a low, gruff voice.

"Your pain shall subside soon." She rubbed her hands together.

Satan released him and he closed his eyes and leaned back to rest.

Chapter 26

GRAVIDITY

After a long while, Gadreel opened her eyes to the scrutiny of Lilith, Satan, and Samael.

"What happened?" She glanced from one face to another, brows knit.

"You fell from the sky," Lilith said. "You plunged into the river. I saved you yet again."

Gadreel had a look of chagrin on her face when she learned of this rescue. "Oh—" She heaved a deep sigh. "I am grateful to you."

"What is happening to you?" Lilith peered at her. "I have seen you expel the contents of your stomach through your mouth. It weakens you. Why do you do this?" Gadreel had acted oddly before, but never like in past weeks. Lilith worried maybe their time on Earth was nearing its end, and she, being the weakest, would be the first to perish.

Samael cocked his head. "This behavior is most strange."

"I do not know what is happening to me, or why." She bit her lip and wrapped a curl around her finger in a pre-occupied way. "Food refuses to stay within me. I spew what I eat by force, like my body wished to expel something that did not belong. I feel weak and tired all the time. It took every-thing I had to follow you here."

"What is happening to your body?" Lilith pointed at her belly. "Your midsection is huge and round! I have seen you grow bigger by the day."

Gadreel gaped at her abdomen, which was much bigger than the last time they landed. Suddenly, her belly popped, becoming tight, hard, and spherical. She screamed. Samael and Lilith recoiled. Lilith stared at her wide-eyed. Samael shook his head in disbelief as he moved further away. After a short while, her belly softened again.

Gadreel panted and stared at her middle unable to move. "I think my life on this planet has come to an end."

"Perhaps you have consumed toxic vegetation? Have you eaten anything the rest of us have not?" Lilith asked. "In the South Forest in Floraison, there were many poisonous plants and seeds. They killed many of my troops. Perhaps on Earth, there are hostile seedlings as well."

Gadreel shook her head. "I have not consumed anything you have not."

"There is a parasite living inside you!" Samael exclaimed in a horrified tone. "Perhaps it crawled inside you while you slept. It depletes you of your substance and when it is done growing, it shall burst out of you!"

Gadreel shrieked and pressed her hands against her cheeks. Large drops fell from her eyelashes and splashed on her belly.

"Enough!" Satan shouted. Gadreel gawked at him.

He smiled with his mouth and his eyes and he stood with open arms. "There is something living inside you, for you are with child."

Gadreel gasped. She stared at her belly, stunned. Tears continued to drop from her eyes. "Are you certain of this?"

He raised his eyebrows. "As sure as the ocean is vast."

She covered her mouth with her hands and guffawed.

Satan looked at Lilith sideways. "How is it you did not know of Gadreel's condition? It is peculiar that by means of your visions and knowledge you did not know she was with child?"

Lilith looked away and lowered her sight to the ground. "I did have an inkling of suspicion, but I refused to believe that Gadreel would be the first of our kind to produce offspring." She reached out to pass her hand across Gadreel's belly, but she grabbed her wrist and stopped her. Lilith yanked her hand away. Her muscles grew tense and her eyes narrowed. "How could you be the first to procreate? It does not make sense."

Her nostrils flared. "Do you think carrying a child inside you makes you special? You are still the maladroit—Gadreel." Lilith leapt to her feet and stormed away.

Satan sucked air through his teeth and shook his head as he watched her go. "Indeed, you are unique, Gadreel." Satan turned to her. "You are the first of our kind to conceive. You have shown us that this is possible. Now, I shall spread my seed and fill this planet with my own kin." He cocked his head back and laughed.

Gadreel stared at him wild-eyed, as a damned soul on the edge of Heaven might look at the Power angel who shall push one to one's destiny. She smashed her eyes shut and shook her head as if she could shake loose those remembrances. She looked down at her belly and felt giddy once more. She was carrying a child. She would not die. Instead, she would soon bring a new life onto this planet.

Samael watched Lilith storm off. He hobbled after her, the wound made by the crocodile bite on his leg not fully healed. He found her sitting in a clearing.

"What is wrong?" Samael noted her expression of mixed sadness and anger. "Why does this new information upset you so?"

"It should have been me. I should have been the first. Why does Gadreel carry a progeny within her, while I do not?" Lilith looked at him wide-eyed.

"Perhaps it shall take a little more time for you to conceive."

"Perhaps Dagon's seed is the only one potent enough to create off-spring," Lilith scowled. Samael's lips tightened in contempt.

"I am certain that my seed is as potent as Dagon's!"

As she hoped, her malicious statement offended him. "Indeed? Why then am I not with child?" Lilith taunted him. "Perhaps I should lie with Dagon, so he may impregnate me. Seeing as there is no one else capable."

Lilith jumped to her feet and spun to leave, but he caught her by the arm and pulled her toward him.

"I shall spill my seed inside you, and you shall bear many sons with my likeness. This is my oath to you," he whispered as he nuzzled between her neck and ear. She pushed him away.

"We shall see." She flounced away.

Satan sat with Gadreel under a Ficus tree as they feasted on its large, dark purple fruit. To him, it was important she give birth to a healthy offspring. He figured if she could have strong progenies, Lilith would be able to do so as well.

He intended to have many broods to do his deeds. It would be the ultimate revenge. He knew nothing would make Lilith happier. Be fruitful and multiply. Were those not God's words? He would enjoy the freedoms here he was forbidden to experience in Floraison. Satan rubbed his chin, lost in thought.

Lilith returned and sat between them. Samael arrived soon thereafter. In silence they sat and ate the luscious fruit until they were satiated. The angels huddled together and slept for a while. Rest was good for Gadreel and her unborn child, and also for Samael's healing leg.

Gadreel sensed a gentle tug on her shoulder. She woke to find Dagon leaning over her.

"Dagon!" In her excitement she unintentionally woke the others. "I missed you so."

She embraced him. He picked her up off the ground and carried her away. Samael followed them with his narrowed eyes.

Dagon took her to a secluded place where they might be alone for a moment. "I do not have much time, but I desire to spend every bit of it on land with you in my arms." They lolled together in a shady area. He held her hand and kissed her fingertips one by one.

"I missed you so." Gadreel gazed at him and sat upright. "I have important news for you."

"Please tell me what new tidings you have."

"I am with child. Your progeny!" Gadreel waited with bright eager eyes for his reaction.

He tilted his head and creased his brow. "How is this possible?"

"I know not, but somehow it is so. I carry our offspring inside me."

"Are you sure about this?"

"Yes, I am without doubt. Satan assured me it is so." She placed his hand on her round belly. Something inside her shifted. He jolted, pulled his hand away and gawked at her middle. Her belly popped and he jumped. "That is remarkable! I did this?"

She nodded. "You have powerful seed. We are the first of our kind to conceive." Gadreel pulled him to her and kissed him. He made love to her once more, and it was gentle and sweet.

⊰

Satan returned to sleep after Dagon carried Gadreel away, but Lilith was restless and left his side. Samael rose to follow her.

Lilith found a small, opened area surrounded by bushes, trees, and flowers. She enjoyed the feel of the soft, dense grass beneath her feet, and the citrusy fragrance of the flowers. She spoke to Samael without turning around. "Lie with me here, and do not stop until you have spilled seed inside me."

Samael jerked. "Did you know all along that I was following you?"

Lilith spun to face him and smirked. She held out her arms and beckoned him to come to her. He proceeded to her like one who could not resist her and was willing to do all she desired.

After the deed was done, Lilith returned to Satan's side. She lay close to him and fell asleep. Samael sulked once more.

Chapter 27

REVELATIONS

Lilith sat upright and whisked her head toward the river. She jumped to her feet and dashed to the reptile-infested waters. When she reached the bank of the river, she stared ahead at the flowing water as though in a trance. She realized there were no crocodiles sunning on the banks of the river and it was no longer daytime.

How long had she been asleep? Where were the others? Why had no one woken her?

She walked to the edge of the water, but jolted at being suddenly surrounded by hairless, gray-colored mammals of tremendous size. They waddled and clomped about on four stubby legs in the fertile green valley.

Lilith observed the huge mammals with a quizzical expression. One of the beasts attacked her, knocking her to the ground as she walked toward the water. She made an attempt to transform into her snake form, but was unable to do so. She lay still, panting. "Fine, you do not wish me to enter the river."

On all fours, she crawled away from the water and rose to her feet. The hippopotamus stayed by her side, watching her every move, pointing its enormous head and broad muzzle at her. She intended to fly away, but her feet remained bonded to the ground. Night turned to day.

The sun bore on her head and shoulders without mercy. Yet she was unable to budge from where she stood. She closed her eyes. An earthy, green grass aroma emanated from the aggressive hippopotamus. The animal remained by her side, its huge belly hanging just above the ground, and grunted a warning.

Lilith opened her eyes and noticed an oily red substance oozing from the animal's skin. She gasped. "The creature oozes blood? If I continue to stand here will I too exude my life force through my pores?" She said in an undertone.

The mammals stopped feeding and formed a line to enter the river.

What force was keeping her frozen to this spot?

All of a sudden, she found herself below the surface of a great body of water. Surprisingly, she was able to breathe underwater. She saw trees, plants, and flowers, similar to what grew on land, as if the immense river had swallowed the solid earth.

She appeared to be standing in a river *within* the river. The water from this underwater stream was much denser than the water surrounding it, so it sank to the bottom, forming a clear separation. It appeared to be a channel of water flowing over the riverbed.

Lilith wished to follow this submerged waterway, and to her amazement she was able to move, so she followed it to a creature lying on the river bottom. She moved a few steps closer and became fixed to the spot once more.

The creature was bound in chains. For a brief moment, she was made to feel its pain and suffering, its loneliness, and its tremendous fury. She opened her mouth to scream, but could produce no sound. Physical pain overtook her entire body. A myriad of emotions threatened to drive her mad. A deep burning pain in the center of her core made it hard for her to breathe. The rage and torment experienced by this creature were too much for her to bear. She desired her own existence to end.

Soon, the intense suffering came to an end. Lilith's pulse beat fast and hard as if her heart was on the verge of bursting. The water that encompassed her pushed against her with great force, like a giant and powerful hand closing on her crushing her in its tight fist. Her eyelids stretched as far open as possible. She longed to escape the underwater prison, but was unable to move. She was compelled to watch as the pitiful creature lay restrained and was made to suffer. She was forced to listen to the being's painful screams and mournful laments, alternating with its soft, desperate, blubbering pleas and frightened whimpers. She had never experienced pain and suffering to such a degree. Why did this creature suffer so? She suffered but a moment of its torment, and had desired death. This creature's agonizing was infinite.

The creature was hideous, with blotchy greenish skin, seaweed-like hair, and pointed, brownish-green teeth. Its skin was covered in tooth-like scales and algae. Its arms and legs appeared gelatinous, punctuated by lumps of broken and calcified bone. It did not appear to have feet. Instead, long serpentine projections with transparent fins grew in their place.

The monstrosity's face was bloated and grotesquely malformed with a wide, large mouth. Its eyes were sometimes black, at other times red. They peeked through wisps of moldy diaphanous fabric. Its nose was flat with slits for nostrils. Small water creatures scurried in and out of its orifices. Its face was gruesome to look upon, and staring at it too long caused physical pain.

This ineffable creature was created from pain, misery, and rage.

At a distance, Lilith saw an underwater dust cloud. As the fog approached, she discerned a large bloat of hippopotamuses in its midst. The mammals trotted gracefully on the river floor.

The creature in chains lay in the path of the herd. Emotions deep inside Lilith were unchained—good in her that had long been buried arose and she suffered for this creature. She strained to move toward the creature. She wished to help it move away from the approaching pandemonium. Her mouth moved to warn the beast, but her efforts were in vain for she could not move or utter a sound.

Once again, Lilith was forced to watch as the chained creature thrashed desperately to release itself and escape from the oncoming stampede. The creature's efforts were to no purpose. The bloat of hippopotamuses trampled it, as if its existence was unknown.

Its screams were terrible—piercing and disturbing. She covered her ears, but even so she did not escape the agonizing wails of the creature in chains.

After the mammals rushed the creature, they continued on their way. Lilith raised her eyebrows high and her mouth slackened in horror. The pathetic creature survived and continued to groan and howl in agony. It was smashed, broken—even more revolting and deformed than before, but it went on living. Death would have been a mercy.

The creature wept and shrieked, pushing her to the edge of madness. The pain was too much to cope with and exhaustion infiltrated her bones.

The creature grew silent and swung its face toward her. Its gaze felt like an act of violence. She believed her eyes would bleed from witnessing such a stare but they seemed locked onto the monster's red gaze. Then came its chilling voice.

"Help me." She heard in her mind. "It is I, Beelzebub. Release me from these chains, so that I may escape this prison and walk freely on the surface with you and the others."

Her heart seemed to jump and become wedged in her throat.

"I have spent an eternity on my own and suffered much, and continue to endure unspeakable agony." His voice was low and raspy, but powerful enough to send chills through her body. In moments the voice boomed without a flinch and crashed like a surge through the water until the river was filled with only its voice.

Lilith trembled. What form of deception was this? How could this pathetic creature be her bright and joyous friend? She shook her head in disbelief.

"It is I, Beelzebub. I have not been bright or joyous in quite some time. Pain and suffering have distorted my appearance, and made me unrecognizable, but it is still I. Help me, for only you can."

Lilith beheld the repulsive life form claiming to be her ally. How could this be so? Had he been bound in chains this entire time? What good would his life be after what he had been through and after what he had become?

Lilith no longer wished to think, but her mind continued to form thoughts against her will. She reflected on Beelzebub—the amusing and gorgeous creature in Floraison. The splendor of his long, wavy, golden hair as it reflected the light of brillante. His large, deep-set eyes had been a shimmering green and always appeared to be laughing, even when he was not. His mischievous smile was contagious.

That image of Beelzebub was in stark contrast to the monstrosity before her. However, she saw changes in every fallen angel she had encountered. Perhaps being bound in chains, and suffering catastrophic physical and emotional distress, had indeed changed him into this grotesque monstrosity lying before her. Her body slumped and she covered her head with her hands. Tears flowed from her eyes, only to disperse and intermingle with the river's water.

She wished to help him and made efforts to move again, but it was impossible. Forced to only witness his suffering, she did nothing.

"I knew I would get no help from you!" Beelzebub's thunderous snarl made her head throb and her body trembled. "You and the others have betrayed me! My body is poisoned and twisted with the hate I feel for you. I detest you most of all, Lilith, for it was your plan that landed me in this watery prison. Someday I shall escape, and I shall have my revenge!"

Immense pressure began to build in Lilith's cranium. She no longer heard Beelzebub's words but he continued his harangue about how his allies had shunned him. She uttered soundless, desperate cries.

≶

"Lilith, please awaken!" Satan shook her as she squirmed and cried in her sleep.

She jolted upright and attempted to get to her feet, but her knees faltered. She grabbed Satan's shoulders. "Where are we? Why did you leave me? How many suns have set?"

"Lilith, please try to be calm." Gadreel stroked her hair. "What happened in your sleep that disturbed you so?"

Satan, Samael, and Dagon stared at her with puzzled faces. Lilith shifted her eyes toward the river. Reptiles still lay on its banks, and there were no large, gray mammals grazing there. The sun was beginning to set, and it was much cooler. Everything was as it should be.

"What happened?" Satan asked. "One moment you slept against this tree and the next you shook with sobs. Your shrieks were agonizing and awful. We took turns trying to wake you, but could not. Please tell us what transpired."

Lilith struggled with whether to tell them what she saw, or keep it to herself.

Perhaps if she told Satan what her vision revealed he would stop his relentless search for Beelzebub, and instead, they could begin their journey to the Garden of Eden. She finally decided to reveal everything to them.

"I have seen Beelzebub." There was a terrified expression on her wan face.

Satan puckered his brow and the others gasped in amazement at her words.

"I have traveled a ways from here to another river where our friend has been imprisoned since we were cast out of our celestial home."

The others glanced at one another with confused expressions.

"How is this possible?" Samael asked. "You have not moved from the spot where you sit."

"Perhaps my body has not moved, but my mind and spirit did travel. I saw Beelzebub lying at the bottom of a huge river, wrapped in chains."

Dagon nodded. "During my account, I did mention Beelzebub was bound in chains. I also heard Michael speak of a great river that would be prison to him and the other bound angels."

"Was he alive? Was he aware of your presence? Did he say anything?" Gadreel asked without taking a breath.

Satan raised a hand, gesturing for silence.

Lilith's lips quivered. "I shall relate to you what I saw. Beelzebub is no longer the happy, playful angel we remember fondly. He has transformed into a grotesque creature, one too agonizing to look upon."

Wearing a piteous expression they waited for Lilith to continue.

"His mind has been poisoned and corrupted by great physical and mental anguish, as well as loneliness. He threatened to annihilate us, for he blames us for his circumstances."

"Is he more hideous to look upon than I?" Fornues interjected from the shoreline, where he waited, listening to their words.

"Fornues, my friend, you have the appearance of a fierce and powerful warrior beast. You are not a monster," Dagon said.

"On the other hand, Beelzebub is horrifying and malformed. Catching a glimpse of him would make you wish to pluck your eyes from your head," Lilith said to Fornues and the others.

"Does this mean we shall no longer search for him?" Gadreel looked at Satan with doleful eyes.

"No." Satan scanned the faces of the others. "He is still one of us. We owe it to him to try and help him if we can."

Lilith frowned. "We are powerless to help him."

Satan shook his head. "I am not so sure. From what you have told us, he is infuriated with us. He thinks we abandoned him. The one thing I am certain of is that we must release him from his chains, so he may walk on dry land with us. If he has suffered great torment, loneliness, fear—we must help him, or end his miserable existence."

The others nodded in solemn agreement, except Lilith who gulped and slowly closed her eyelids.

"The sun shall soon hide," Satan said. "We should be on our way. I have seen such a river as Lilith described in my travels. Many large, gray mammals grazed on the lush grass of its banks. It is but a few days away."

After hearing Satan's orders, Gadreel accompanied Dagon to the shore where Fornues awaited.

"Hello, Fornues." Gadreel raised a hand in greeting. "Take good care of the father of my unborn child."

"I shall do as you say," Fornues said without speaking.

Dagon and Gadreel embraced each other awhile.

"Take good care of yourself and our small one." He rubbed her swollen belly.

Gadreel waved goodbye. "I assure you, I shall."

One of Fornues' tentacles wrapped around Dagon's torso and held him above the water until he changed into a merman. When his transformation was complete Fornues pulled him into the sea.

"It is time to go!" Satan called. Gadreel nodded and followed the others.

The fallen angels soared in the twilight sky once more, headed toward Beelzebub for the rescue attempt, with one great difference. Satan now knew his exact location.

Chapter 28

FORSAKEN

This time the journey was quite arduous for Gadreel. In his zeal to reach Beelzebub as soon as possible, Satan overlooked her delicate condition. He demanded they fly faster for longer periods of time, and when they finally stopped to rest, it was for shorter spells. She was exhausted, weak, and kept falling farther and farther behind.

"Samael!" Gadreel flew in a languorous manner. "Help me! I implore you. I know you can hear me."

Samael lowered his eyebrows and kept on flying. After a while, he groaned, rolled his eyes and turned back to her.

"Your pleas are like insects buzzing in my ears. What is it you want from me?"

Gadreel's face flushed bright pink. "I feel faint and weak. If you do not help me, I shall fall from the sky and lose my unborn child."

"What is that to me?"

Gadreel gasped. "I beg you, Samael, show me mercy. Is there nothing left of your former self?"

He pursed his lips and flew away to join the others, leaving her to fend for herself. Lilith and Satan flew ahead, and seemed to be oblivious to what was happening.

All color fled Gadreel's face. She

watched him fly away, leaving her and her unborn offspring to perish. As consciousness slipped away, she tried to call for Satan, but she was too debilitated to form words and he was too far away. She caressed her stomach and sobbed. "There is a fiery boulder in my chest and my mind overflows with regrets." She clutched her bosom. "Dagon, you shall lose us both, for I am weak. I beg you forgive me." Gadreel's eyes rolled to the back of her head. Her wings flopped and she plummeted to Earth. Meanwhile, the others flew at great speed, pulling farther away.

A large bird of prey soared above Gadreel, slowly circling on its broad wings, screaming, "Kee-eeeee-arr!" It swooped upon her, and with its hooked claws it clutched the shoulders of her wings and glided effortlessly above the Earth.

After making a sweeping descent to a sandy shore flanked by mountains, the giant golden eagle placed her on the beach and stayed by her side until she regained consciousness.

When she opened her eyes, a familiar face met them. It was the bird with the golden plumage.

Gadreel fixed her gaze on the bird. "Greetings again, my friend!"

The eagle expanded one of its massive wings and patted her on the head. She giggled and patted its massive head in return.

"One day I shall learn how to communicate with you better."

The eagle made a sharp cackling sound. Gadreel jolted and laughed.

"Are you the reason I still live?" Her voice was thick with emotion.

The eagle commenced a series of chattering squeaks. She sat upright and leaned forward. "You caught me in midair and flew me to safety." With tears flowing, she kissed the eagle on its beak. "I do not have the words to express how grateful I am. 'Thank you' does not suffice." The eagle shifted closer. It spread its foot across her belly, and she knew the bird would not harm her or the child within. The eagle emitted one last, loud, high-pitched squeak and flew away.

Gadreel waved. "Farewell, my friend. I shall always be grateful!"

She got to her feet and noted with relief she was near the sea. "We are alone now." She gazed at her ever-expanding belly while stroking it in circles.

She waddled about, certain she would find something to eat amongst the greenery surrounding her. She came across a large bush with bright red flowers, which also contained large fruits. The fruit was exquisite, beginning with its smooth, round shape and ruby color to its distinctive little crown.

She picked one and attempted to bite into it, but the skin was too thick. Recalling the coconut, she found a sharp-edged rock, scored the pomegranate, and broke it open. The berry contained many seeds surrounded by a deep red, water-laden pulp. She placed some seeds in her mouth and swished them around. She sucked the tasty pulp, which tasted sweet, refreshing, and a little tart.

When she had eaten, she searched for a source of fresh water. Nearby, she found a small waterfall.

"The great bird placed us here knowing there was food and water in close proximity," she told her belly.

She gathered water in her hands and drank her fill. She removed her green, leafy garments and went for a swim in the pool at the bottom of the waterfall. The water pouring over rocks created a peaceful, bubbling cascade.

After a while, she climbed from the water and found foliage to craft new garments. She strolled toward the seashore, but stopped abruptly when something fell out of her. She looked wide-eyed to the sand between her legs and saw a thick glob of stringy mucous with blood around the edges. She flinched and grimaced in disgust.

What did this indicate? Was she to lose her baby? She sat, rocking back and forth under a tree near the water, and began to sing. Singing always had a calming effect on her. She caressed her belly, feeling a great deal of movement from the baby.

Sitting with her feet in the surf, she sang a dulcet melody about an enormous, regal bird with brown plumage and a golden crown, and how it saved her and her unborn child from plummeting to their deaths.

Chapter 29

GADREEL'S SONG

Dagon and Fornues swam furiously in the sea to keep up with Satan, who flew full speed ahead above them. Without warning, Fornues came to a screeching halt. He hovered, wiggling his tentacles in a languid manner. Dagon stopped and stared at him, brow crumpled. Fornues appeared odd, in a hypnotic state.

"Fornues!" Dagon shouted in his mind. "We must move on."

He scanned his surroundings, expecting to see some strange, aquatic creature with the ability to control minds, but he saw no such thing. "Are you alright?"

"We must turn back," Fornues said.

"Turn back? What is your meaning? You mean retreat across the same ground?" He frowned and shook his head. "I see no need for this. If we fall too far behind, we may not be able to find the others. I do not wish to lose Gadreel."

Fornues' smooth, dark skin turned crimson and bumpy, as he pointed with an outstretched tentacle in the direction they had come. "Listen! Focus your senses and perceive the sound."

Dagon jolted and reacted when he saw Fornues' transformation and did as he was told. He puckered his brow and cocked his right ear in the direction Fornues pointed and heard Gadreel's enchanting song. Her voice was clear and mellifluous. "I do not understand how it went unnoticed before, but you are right, my friend, we must return. Her song comes not from ahead, but from waters left behind."

"Indeed, we must not delay."

They reversed their course and followed Gadreel's song. As they drew closer to her location, the song became purer, rhapsodic, and more gratifying. Near the coast, huge rocks separated an expanse of shallow coastal waters from the sea.

"This is as far as I am able to go. I shall remain here until you and Gadreel are ready to move on."

"I shall try to hurry."

Dagon swam past the massive, arched rocks and into the lagoon. He caught sight of Gadreel sitting on a smaller rock singing, while fish jumped and splashed, and dolphins danced over the water around her. He swam to her, mesmerized by her beauty and her exquisite voice.

"Gadreel!"

She stopped singing and turned her sights on Dagon, who clung to the rock she sat upon.

"My love! I sensed your presence nearby, but I thought it was wishful thinking. I am so happy to see you." She jumped into the water to greet him. She wept aloud as she embraced him, no longer offended by his fishy smell.

"Why do you weep, my darling?"

"I feared I would never see you again." She held him tighter.

Dagon chuckled and stroked her back. "As long as I draw breath, I shall always find you. Whenever you need me, your song shall lead me to you."

She kissed him on the lips. He looked at her middle. "I noticed your belly is larger, occupied by my burgeoning offspring. I am sure you carry a robust male child within you." He thrust his jaw forward with pride.

She kissed him again and again. He swam to shore with her in his arms.

"Stop. What do you intend to do?" She looked at him with a solemn expression.

"I miss the feel of the sand beneath my feet, the warmth of your body, and what it feels like to be inside you." Dagon waggled his eyebrows.

Gadreel remained earnest. "No, Dagon. That shall not happen today." She beheld his puzzled, disappointed face. "The sun shall set soon. There is no time, and if you want to catch up to the others you must leave now."

Dagon frowned and shook his head. "I shall not leave you. How is it that you are here alone? Why did the others continue without you?"

She tilted her head and pressed her lips together.

"I was weak. I could not keep up with them." She crossed her arms and looked down.

Dagon narrowed his eyes. "So they left you behind? Satan seemed interested in seeing the birth of our offspring. He told me he would look after you while I was away, and then he abandons you here?"

She lifted her hands. "No, Dagon, that is not what happened." Gadreel hung her head. "My middle has been growing quite fast. I shall give birth soon. I become weaker as our offspring grows, and I need more rest. This last flight was the hardest for me yet. I kept falling farther and farther behind."

Gadreel drew a long breath. She met his gaze, maintained eye contact and held out her arms.

"I called Samael to help me, for he was closest to me. I would have called Satan, but he was too far ahead with Lilith, and you know how she distracts him."

Dagon nodded.

"I begged Samael to help me. I told him I was unable to fly on my own. He refused to help and flew ahead to join the others."

Dagon clenched his jaw he lowered his brow and flushed crimson with fury.

"My wings grew heavy and I could no longer fly. As I plummeted to Earth, all I could think of was how I had failed you and our child. I lost consciousness. Next thing I remember, I was lying on the beach, and a magnificent bird stood nearby, protecting me. He caught me in midair and flew me to safety and did not leave my side until I was fully awake." Gadreel observed him, whose red face and enraged expression made her recall the angry mountain in her travels.

Dagon tilted his head back and released a thunderous bellow. Some sea creatures swam away in fear.

"I shall destroy him!" Fornues shouted. "I shall tear him apart with my tentacles and eat him while he still breathes!"

"No!" Dagon's tusk burst out of his forehead. "You leave him to me!"

"Stop, please, stop!" Gadreel's hands covered her ears.

Fornues stopped the shrill tone. Dagon peered at her, his chest heaving.

Gadreel said in a soft voice, "There shall come a moment when retaliation against Samael shall be permissible, but now is not that time. At present, he is untouchable, for he is close to Satan and Lilith. We must be patient. His time shall come, I assure you."

Dagon stared ahead with a sardonic grin. "Perhaps his time shall come, sooner rather than later, for I know things about him that shall turn Satan against him forever."

"What do you know? That Samael and Lilith are lovers?"

He looked at her slack-mouthed. "How do you know this?"

"Have you forgotten that I spent many days and nights with them before we found you and the others? They engaged in all manner of sex acts without giving a second thought that I was a witness to their betrayal."

"We have both witnessed their treachery. Why not go to Satan now with this?"

"It is not the right time, Dagon."

"When then? When shall it be the right time?" He turned away and gave an exasperated sigh.

"When the proper moment presents itself, we shall know it." Gadreel turned his head in her direction and caressed his cheek. His face twitched, and she glanced at him sideways. "Are you fighting a smile?" She dragged her fingertips up and down his sides and danced her fingernails gently on his waist and middle until he laughed.

"Very well, I shall heed your suggestion and wait, but leaving you here is unthinkable. You shall travel by sea with Fornues and me."

Her breath quickened. "You and Fornues travel in the black depths of the ocean during the midday hours. I cannot go to such depths, and I shall require shade during such hours." She raked her fingers through her hair for the third time.

Dagon took her and wrapped her in a warm embrace.

Right then, a large dolphin approached. It began to whistle, along with a loud series of clicks and Gadreel nodded and beamed.

"You are willing to transport me to where I need to go?"

The dolphin bobbed its head and whistled in response.

"I am grateful for your help."

The dolphin positioned itself, and she mounted its slippery back. Dagon watched Gadreel's interaction with the dolphin, mouth gaping.

"This creature shall take me where we need to go and bring me to shore during the midday sun, so I may feed and rest in the shade." Gadreel patted the dolphin's head.

Dagon looked at the dolphin and stroked the nape of his neck.

"Very well. If you are certain it is safe."

The dolphin bobbed its head and made burst-pulsed sounds and clicks. Gadreel giggled as she sat astride the dolphin. The other members of its pod performed acrobatic displays—leaping and spinning above the water's surface. Both Gadreel and Dagon indulged in a hearty guffaw at their amusing ways.

The dolphin carried Gadreel beyond the lagoon. In the open sea they met Fornues, and the dolphin came to a sudden standstill. Gadreel lurched and almost fell into the water. The mammal refused to go on. It trembled and stared at the enormous creature.

"Do not fear. Fornues shall not harm you." She kissed the dolphin on the side of its head. It shook its head and again communicated with whistle-like sounds.

"Fornues, please make a vow that you shall never harm this creature or any like him. Do this, I implore you, for they are my friends." Gadreel looked at Fornues with imploring eyes.

"This I swear: I shall never intentionally harm such a creature, no matter what the circumstance." Fornues lowered his massive head so that Gadreel and the dolphin may look at his solemn eyes. The dolphin nodded and turned to glance at the members of his pod. The intelligent sea mammal communicated to them with short, sharp sounds.

"Let us be on our way!" Gadreel leaned forward and held on. Fornues led the way. Dagon swam alongside the dolphin, and the rest of the pod followed them closely. They traveled through the night and part of the next day. Later, the sun grew stronger and beamed hard on them.

"It's time I go ashore to seek shelter from the sun." A deep flush spread across Gadreel's face.

Dagon nodded. "You are right, for I, too, feel the grueling effects of the sun's rays."

Gadreel leaned toward the dolphin's ear holes. "Take me as close to shore as possible." The dolphin obeyed.

Dagon followed her and the dolphin until the mammal stopped and she climbed off its back.

Dagon embraced her and kissed her forehead. "I must go to the depths to feed now before I walk on land, for I shall be no good to you in this weakened state. You shall be fine on your own awhile?"

Gadreel gazed at his sweet concerned expression. "I shall be fine. You go and nourish yourself. I can see this beach shall provide me with plenty of shade and nourishment."

"I shan't be long." Dagon kissed her on the lips, tapped her belly, and dove into the sea.

"Farewell," Fornues said in her mind, although she could no longer see him. The dolphin also needed to feed, but communicated that it too would return for her. She waded to the beach and found a shady tree heavily laden with fruit. She ate her fill and curled under it to nap until her love returned.

Chapter 30

FALSEHOODS

As he flew, Satan's attention turned away from Lilith for a brief moment. He looked over his shoulder to check on Gadreel, whom he had not seen or heard in a while. He turned, stopped in mid-flight and lingered, but there was no sign of her.

"Where is Gadreel?" Satan stared at Samael.

"She was far behind, the last time I saw her." Samael licked his lips and shoved his hair away from his face.

Satan scowled. "How long ago was that?"

"It was quite a while now." Samael's voice was unsteady.

"You fool!" Satan yelled. "Did I not ask that you look after her?"

"Yes. I-I beg your pardon, but I do not know her whereabouts." Samael gulped and bit his lip.

"It is not his fault. He is not Gadreel's keeper," Lilith said.

Satan glared at her. "Silence! I did not ask for your opinion in this matter."

Lilith clinched her jaw but then had a sudden change in demeanor. "Perhaps we should delay our search for Beelzebub, and go search for Gadreel instead." There was a sarcastic tone in her voice and she shrugged and scratched her nose.

"Yes!" Satan said.

Lilith's eyes widened and she lifted a hand. "Wait—what?"

"You are right," Satan said. "We must turn around at once and find Gadreel. She and her unborn child may be hurt and in need of our help."

Lilith gasped. "Are you sure this is what you desire? You seemed eager to rescue Beelzebub."

She had come to terms with the search for him. After all, she could always manipulate him any way she wished, monster or no. She was certain he would not be angry with her for long. Then she desired to go to the Garden of Eden to claim what was rightfully theirs, and finally take her revenge on God. But now, her plans would be delayed because of that maladroit—Gadreel.

"Gadreel and her offspring must come first! We shall return now from whence we came." Satan raised his eyebrows. "I hope it is not too late."

Lilith smacked her palm against her forehead, shook her head and followed Satan and Samael as they turned back to find Gadreel.

Gadreel had become rather significant to Satan. "I must put an end to this," she said under her breath.

Samael clenched his hands to stop them from shaking. His jaw closed tight and his teeth chattered. If they found Gadreel alive, she would divulge what really took place. Satan would be furious with him, and who knew what punishment he would bestow for his disobedience. His eyes opened wide as he stared ahead.

Lilith scrutinized his facial expressions and body language. His face was pale and he seemed uneasy and terrified. What did he do? Lilith did not wish for Satan's rage to fall upon him. It would put her plans to conceive Samael's child at risk.

"The sun is at its harshest, my prince," Lilith said in her most appealing voice. "Perhaps we should land and rest in the shade. We can delay our quest for Gadreel for a short while."

"Not possible. It may be too late already."

Satan did not respond as usual to her use of the word 'prince'. Though she raged inwardly, she wore a mask of complacency. "As you wish, my prince."

They maintained flight under the mighty midday sun. As their skin began to singe, Lilith and Samael moaned and flinched in pain. Satan transformed into the red fiend. His tough crimson skin was better able to withstand the sun's fiery heat. The clothing Lilith fashioned from the small camel's hide and fur offered some protection, but it did not cover much of her.

Finally, Satan stopped. "I sense Gadreel's presence." He aimed his sights on a small cove separated from the deep sea by a barrier of hills jutting from the water.

"We shall land there." Satan pointed to the cove's beach.

Lilith exhaled a sigh of relief.

Satan's tracking skills were becoming more precise. They landed mere yards from where Gadreel slept.

"Eat in silence and get some rest," Satan whispered, staring at her as he spoke. Lilith stormed away to feed and find her own resting place, followed by Samael.

Satan ate his fill of fruit and sat next to Gadreel. His eyes fixed on her belly, which bunched and became lumpy as the unborn offspring shifted within her. He placed his hand on her belly and felt the baby's rolls and kicks. He chuckled.

Gadreel jolted out of a deep slumber. She caught sight of a large, clawed hand grasping her belly. Her partially closed eyes sprang open, and she screamed.

Satan withdrew his talons. "Apologies! I did not mean to frighten you. I saw the shifting of your unborn child, and I was compelled to feel its movements." Satan transformed into his handsome angel form.

Gadreel scanned the area in search of Lilith and Samael.

"How did you find me?" Her heart still lodged in her throat.

"I was able to sense your presence and thereby track your location."

"Where are Lilith and Samael?"

"We are right here." Lilith approached from a short distance away.

Samael trailed behind. He gazed at Gadreel with imploring eyes.

"Now that we are all present, please tell us what happened to you," Satan said. "I was not aware you were gone. When I glanced behind me, you had vanished, but here you are in good health, and without so much as a scratch. What transpired?"

Gadreel gazed at Samael whose eyes were like sunlight shining through amber. She covered her face with her hands. "I am close to giving birth now, so I tire easily. As a consequence, flying and keeping up with you was very difficult."

As Gadreel spoke, Samael trembled. What would Satan do to him once he discovered the truth? He swallowed hard and held his breath.

"When Samael approached me, I felt lightheaded, but I never thought I would lose consciousness."

Samael's knees began to falter.

"He offered to assist me, but I refused his help. I blame my pride. He insisted, but I persuaded him to rejoin you and Lilith. I told him I was well and wished to be on my own. He believed me. A while later, I lost consciousness and fell out of the sky." She looked at the ground while scratching her neck. If Satan would one day destroy Samael, it would not be because of her. It would be because of his treachery with Lilith. In addition, despite his cruelty, Gadreel was not prepared to never set eyes on him again.

Samael stared at her wide-eyed and openmouthed.

"Not possible!" Lilith squinted and creased her brow. Gadreel recoiled. "You would have never survived such a fall."

"We were able to survive an even greater fall when we were cast down from Floraison." Gadreel wrapped her arms around herself.

"We possessed much of our angelic strength then, and bore none of the weaknesses that now afflict us."

"You are right, but here I am safe and undamaged. Perhaps I am stronger than you think."

Lilith opened her eyes wide and glowered at her. Could it be that Gadreel had divine guidance on Earth, while the rest of them were in constant threat of annihilation? Or perhaps she feigns weakness and was much more powerful than they thought.

Satan chuckled. "The important thing is that you and your unborn child are not hurt, and we are once again united. Get some rest, for we leave soon."

Satan grabbed Lilith by the arm and took her away to a hidden area to have his way with her.

Samael treaded softly to Gadreel. She withdrew from him.

"Do not fear. I shall not hurt you or your unborn child. I appreciate what you did for me: omitting the truth of what really happened. Why did you do it?"

Gadreel avoided his eyes, fidgeted and bit her lip.

He held her face in his hands, gazed at her lips and leaned in to kiss her.

"Move away from her!" Dagon charged him with his forehead tusk.

Gadreel jolted out of her stupor. "No!"

Dagon knocked him to the ground, straddled him, and placed his massive hands around his neck.

"Aargh, awk, awk, gak!" Samael shook and clutched at Dagon's hands, which squeezed his windpipe.

Gadreel jumped to her feet and hurried to them. She yanked at Dagon. "Stop! I implore you!" He released his grasp and punched Samael in the face.

Samael turned on his stomach and crawled toward the coast. He managed to climb to his feet. Unable to catch his breath, he staggered to the water and fell to his knees. He wheezed while splashing water on his reddened face.

Gadreel gaped at him and rocked from side to side. She scowled at Dagon.

"What did we have words about earlier?"

He held her. "I know we discussed this, but when I saw him so close to you, something inside me shattered."

She glanced at Samael lying on the sand and noted his breathing was easier. She sighed with relief. "I do not wish for Satan's wrath to fall upon you."

She took Dagon by the hand and led him to a remote area where they could be alone. On the way, they passed by Lilith and Satan. She lay lifeless on the ground, her eyes glazed over and staring into nothingness, as Satan in his grotesque fiend form assaulted her. Gadreel shuddered. She was almost sorry for her as they tiptoed past. Dagon recalled her enjoying the act much more with Samael.

Chapter 31

PRIMORDIAL

When Dagon and Gadreel arrived at their secluded space, they put the disturbing image of the crimson monster upon Lilith behind them. Lying on a patch of lush grass, they held each other, kissed and caressed. In an abrupt gesture, she flinched and pushed him away. Her face twisted and contorted in pain.

"Gadreel, what is wrong?"

"I am having a stretching sensation in my middle," she said breathless. "I have never experienced anything like this." She groaned while clutching her belly and jumped to her feet.

Dagon sat hunched over on the grass speechless, following her with his eyes, as she paced back and forth.

She screamed and panted. "Something inside me snapped!" She stopped, a gush of warm water pour out of her. At the sight of liquid running along her legs, she shrieked.

Dagon hopped to his feet and scrambled to her.

"What is happening to me?" She asked in a wobbly voice.

"It must be time for our offspring to be born." He furrowed his brow and his hands trembled as he stroked her back.

"Bring Satan and Lilith to me. Please make haste!" Gadreel panted and grimaced in pain.

Dagon rushed to where he last saw them. He found them sleeping. He sighed with relief when he saw Satan had resumed his angel form.

"Wake up! I believe it is time for my progeny to arrive on this planet." He shook them from their slumber.

Lilith and Satan rose, and they followed Dagon to Gadreel. She sat reclining against a tree, grasping her belly with both arms. Her cheeks inflated she puffed again and again, staring ahead.

"What is happening? What do you feel?" Lilith asked, more from curiosity than concern.

"My lower back hurts. It seems like my insides are being ripped apart." Gadreel groaned and opened her legs wide. She instinctively began to push. She closed her eyes, and shrieked as she attempted to thrust her offspring into the world.

Her ruby face was wet with tears and perspiration. Dagon held her hand as she wailed in agony. Her abdomen became hard. She howled and clenched her fists, crushing his hand. Her belly became soft again. She puffed and experienced a slight relief. She released Dagon's hand and then her middle became rigid once more. "I am experiencing a dull ache in my back and lower belly. There's a lot of pressure. I am going to burst!" Gadreel squealed in pain.

Satan drew nearer and glanced between her legs. "I see the child's head!"

Dagon knelt before her. Satan held one of her legs and Lilith the other, and together they spread her legs wide.

"Push, Gadreel!" Lilith shouted. "Thrust the babe unto the earth!"

Big drops fell from Gadreel's eyes, mingling with the moisture seeping from her nose. Her eyes opened wide. She gripped Satan's forearm and released a booming scream as the baby's head and shoulders finally became visible. Those around her stared in awe as they witnessed the first of their kind being born.

"Grasp the infant by the shoulders, and draw it from her with care, Dagon," Lilith said. Dagon gripped the baby and pulled it from Gadreel. The baby began to cry at once, as if it did not wish to emerge into the hostile environment.

Samael heard the commotion and came to stand by Lilith and Satan. All three gawked at the baby. Lilith's hand flew to cover her mouth and stifle a scream.

Dagon almost dropped the infant when he drew it from its mother and saw it in its entirety.

Gadreel gaped at the newborn in his arms. She gripped her hair, shook her head nonstop, and bawled.

The baby possessed the head and upper torso of an infant, and the lower body of a fish.

A birth cord connected the infant to Gadreel.

"You must cut the conduit between the newborn and Gadreel," Lilith told Dagon.

"How?" Dagon asked. "I do not want to harm my offspring."

"Simply cut it!" Lilith yelled. Dagon looked perplexed.

Satan transformed into his red form and sliced the cord with one of his talons.

Gadreel's labor pains intensified once more. She was not yet done giving birth. She felt the urge to push again, but as she did so, she screamed in agony. Another head presented between her legs. She bore down and strained until her face turned a deep crimson and forced another infant from her insides.

Dagon grabbed his second child. It too had the head and torso of an infant, but the scaly lower body of a fish.

Lilith fixed her gaze on the babes. "Gadreel has given birth to twins, and to the Earth's first mermaids." Her voice was low and dripping with disdain.

Satan, Lilith and Samael snuck away quietly to give the new parents time alone with their offspring. Dagon held them, while Gadreel rocked back and forth, her body racked with sobs.

"Embrace your little ones." He extended one of them to her, but she shook her head and blubbered.

"You do not love our offspring because they have fish tails?" Dagon's lips trembled and his body slumped.

She hung her head. "I do not even know if they are male or female."

She stared at the ground away from his gaze and blinked away teardrops stuck to her eyelashes.

"They are both female."

"Forgive me. I was wrong to despair." She buried her face in her hands. "I am ashamed of my behavior."

He leaned forward. "All is forgiven. Embrace your little ones, for they shall soon need to go to sea."

"What?" Gadreel asked in a brittle voice. "They shall not stay with me?"

"No, they are bound to the sea like me, when I am in my aquatic form."

"Oh no, how shall I ever know them?" She whimpered, her glittery eyes filled with sorrow.

"They shall remain with Fornues and me. We shall provide for them and protect them. You shall see them whenever you desire. Sing, and your songs shall guide us to you."

Gadreel held out her arms, and he handed her the infants. She stared at them. "I watch my newborns peer through brand new eyes at what must be a strange world after life inside of me." She giggled. "These are new beings, and I am already filling up with love for them." She glanced at Dagon eyes wide.

One of the mermaids was born with her father's intense gray-blue eyes. The other possessed Gadreel's big, almond-shaped, and hooded brown eyes. They were both fair-haired.

The little mermaids smiled at Gadreel, wiggled in her arms, and gurgled. She hugged them and kissed them. Dagon looked at his family and beamed. He put his arm around her and allowed her to enjoy their newborns a little while longer, but soon he would have to take them away. They had to go to the ocean or they would not survive.

"Gadreel, it is almost time to take our daughters to sea," he said in a gentle manner.

She was hoarse from the screaming. "But there is still at least an hour of sunlight left."

"They are not land and sea creatures to my knowledge. I believe they are purely aquatic beings. They are beginning to appear uneasy out of the water."

She gazed at her babies. Their little faces seemed pale and feeble. "I love you. I shall never leave you." She handed one of the babies to Dagon, and they hurried to shore.

As they approached the beach, Lilith rushed to them. "May I carry one of them?"

Gadreel held tightly onto her infant, but before she could pronounce a word, Dagon handed the baby he held to Lilith. She held her breath as Lilith grasped her other daughter.

"We have only a moment, for they need to go to sea." Gadreel slowly raised her heels.

"Oh, she is not *so* hideous." Lilith sneered. She held the newborn to the sky.

"Be careful!" Gadreel blurted, standing on the tip of her toes.

"Be calm. I shall not harm her." Lilith squinted at her.

"How did you know the infant is female?" Gadreel asked.

"I just knew. Somehow, this area indicated it to me." She pointed to a small black spot under the mermaid's tail. Lilith rocked the infant in her arms. The innocent darling smiled, causing her to grin.

Dagon came forward. He removed his child from her arms. "It is time we take them to the water."

Gadreel exhaled with relief once he had the child in his arms. She waded waist deep into the ocean and held both infants, while Dagon began his painful transformation into a merman. Then he reclaimed the little ones and gently placed them in the water. Their little tails smacked and spattered about. Gadreel watched, holding both arms outstretched in case she needed to intervene. The small mermaids began to swim around on their own. They wiggled their little fish tails and jumped in and out of the water. She tittered. "I am relieved. They appear happy and comfortable in their new environment."

"They are beautiful!" Fornues said.

"Thank you!" Dagon and Gadreel replied in chorus, causing laughter among them.

Lilith peered at the happy family as they played in the water. Her eyes glinted with resentment toward Gadreel. She was deep in thought when Satan and Samael approached her. They watched the blissful couple and their little mermaids from the shoreline. Satan and Samael wore smiles on their faces. Lilith looked at them and narrowed her eyes as an awful idea came to mind.

What if Satan impregnates her? What if instead of having beautiful offspring, she had little red monsters? That was quite possible, since Gadreel gave birth to sea creatures in Dagon's cursed image. No—it must be Samael who impregnates her.

Lilith's chest heaved. She glanced at Satan, grimaced, and dashed away. He followed her with his eyes until she was beyond his sight.

She meandered about until she found a beautiful lake and waterfall. She swam awhile and stood under the cascade, as she remembered doing when she first landed on Earth. She left the water and lay on the lush green grass surrounding the lake. She closed her eyes, desiring to daydream about her future child. Instead she fell asleep and had an epiphany about Beelzebub.

Chapter 32

THE MAKING OF PURE EVIL

Beelzebub remembered a time before the creation of Earth or human beings: an era before the angels were ranked, and the mood in Floraison was not so solemn. He reminisced of running through green meadows in the exquisite brillante of Heaven, hiding behind fragrant flowering bushes while playing games with friends, swimming in the crystalline waters of Lake Serena, and watching the thrilling sparring matches in Guidance Park. These recollections sustained him for a while, but his memories were becoming hazier. Even the ones of his cherished Gabriel sitting by the golden double doors leading to the portal to Meta Heaven, singing God's praises, were now obscure remnants in his mind.

His warm and cozy nostalgia—embracing Gabriel, playing with his lush curls, listening to his songs, music or poetry in the cheerful and picturesque Triumph Gardens—were slowly exchanged for bitter, cold thoughts of vengeance. Beelzebub hated God. He despised everyone he once called friend, especially Lilith, as well as his once true love Gabriel, and even himself.

He endured the gloomy darkness of the Euphrates River, feeling alone and abandoned by everyone he once loved. He lay bound in chains, unable to move or defend against the relentless torture of the river monsters.

The only taste on his tongue was of the moldy cloth Jetrel had stuffed in his mouth to quiet him. The taste was pungent, bitter, and rancid. The decomposing material oozed into his throat like putrid slime. The rotting fabric did not, however, satisfy the intense hunger pangs in his stomach.

His keen eyesight enabled him to see around him, even in the murky depths of the river, and as the river's current slowly pushed him to shallower depths, where the sun's rays penetrated the water, he was able to see even more. He knew this, too, was a curse, for he believed he lost his eyes when he first plunged into the depths of the waterway. An explosion had occurred behind the blindfolds Jetrel placed on them, yet he was still able to see. The band once covering his eyes was now diaphanous and torn, barely obstructing his view. Beelzebub would have preferred his eyes plucked rather than having to witness the terrors that surrounded him.

A giant, brown, disk-shaped fish swam above him, increasing the darkness around him with the shadow of its large form. It floated undulating its ovoid fins and lingered over him.

The stingray peered at him with its tiny yellowish eyes and brought its mouth closer. Beelzebub flinched, expecting the creature to bite him, but the flat fish swam past him, its long, black, whip-like tail trailing behind. He shook with fear as he noticed the end of the creature's tail was a menacing spine, constructed with serrated edges and a sharp point.

The creature swam past him, flapping its sides like wings. Then without warning, it returned. It raised its tail, and stabbed him again and again with its serrated spike. The barb pierced and mashed the bones in his legs. Beelzebub wailed in agony. No one could hear the howling in his head. He continued to suffer long after the creature departed.

Even after Beelzebub ceased his muffled cries, the pain persisted, worsening with time. He burst into laughing fits. Why? Why must I suffer so? I am so alone!

Before long, he spotted a predatory fish approaching in the near distance, accompanied by four others identical to it. They looked aggressive. Beelzebub squirmed and burst into high-pitched laughter. "No more pain, no more!" he shouted in his mind, but suffering appeared to be his destiny.

The silver fish flaunted muscular bodies with black horizontal stripes.

They displayed interlocking, razor-sharp teeth. Having bodies built for speed, the fish whooshed to him when they caught sight of him.

In a wild fury they attacked his bare feet, head, face, and any areas they could get to between the chains. "No more! No more!" Beelzebub screamed.

The water was tainted red with his blood. The immense pain contorted his face and his body convulsed. He lost consciousness. When the ferocious fish were done, portions of flesh were torn from his face, neck, and body. His feet were no more, having been devoured by the creatures. Pointy stubs at the end of his misshapen legs remained in their place.

Beelzebub awoke to ineffable agony and disappointment. "Why did the creatures not end my miserable existence? I wish I had never survived the fall from Floraison. I have ruminated about the bad things that have happened but cannot make sense of them. I long for death."

Days turned into nights. Time passed, and whether there was light or darkness he was able to see in every direction as though his mind wore eyes.

He had a deep, burning hole of hunger where his stomach should be. He was starving, but he was cursed to live. Swathed in gloom and oblivion, he no longer remembered the beauty of Floraison's radiance.

Tiny sea leeches with elongated, tube-like bodies slithered on him like snakes. They carried sturdy spines on their fins, which clawed and scratched Beelzebub as they moved across his body. This became intolerable when they tore through injured areas of his body. He shrieked, slowly losing his mind. Despite the pain, he shook his body, trying to get them off. It was of no use.

"Go away! Why must you torment me? Leave me be!" He attempted to speak but the rotting cloth in his mouth stifled his cries. An abundance of putrefied slime flowed sluggishly into his throat. He gagged and retched. Bile, acid, and slime erupted from his stomach into his throat and mouth. Having nowhere to go, it slid back into his stomach and the repulsive taste lingered in his mouth.

"You must not utter words. No one can hear you. Even if they did, they would not stop. You were meant to suffer." Beelzebub's alter ego communicated in his mind.

The small, spiny fish continued to crawl on him. One dug a home in his ear canal, scratching and scraping the delicate structures within while Beelzebub wobbled his head, gnashing his teeth. Two others tore into his nostrils, deeply embedding their spikes. He blew out his nose, trying to eject them, but only managed to make them angry. They burrowed through the septum dividing his nostrils, collapsing his nose. Afterward, the spiny fish moved to his sinuses, lodging their sharp spines there. Large drops floated from Beelzebub's black globes and mingled with the river water.

He feared the little fiends would crawl into his mouth if he opened it, so he continued to clench his jaw, only shrieking on the inside.

Yet another spiny fish forced itself into his urethra, tearing the tube along its path. He tightened his hands into fists until his knuckles turned white. Blood vessel after blood vessel burst as he squealed in anguish and torment. Wheezing and hacking, he underwent convulsive attacks, which caused him more pain as the chains bit into his flesh. The miniature creatures buried their spikes deeper into him when he moved, but the fits were involuntary. Thus, his torture, both physical and mental, was constant.

More days and nights went by and the malevolent change began. Pain became second nature to him. The creatures in the river seemed to hold but one function—to punish him in some way.

Dismayed, broken, and contorted by torture and mutilation, Beelzebub was transformed into a grotesque and evil monstrosity. His skin took on a fungus-green tone and barnacles attached to his head and face. His eyes were large, spherical, protruding globules that glowed red, with black vertical slits in its center.

He was a vile creature, bred by hatred, loneliness and pain. He lay seething in the depths of the Euphrates River, waiting for the day he would be set free to bring torment and chaos to Earth.

Lilith's eyes snapped wide open and her mouth gaped. She inhaled a sharp, screeching breath and grasped her neck as she tried to catch her breath. Her eyes darted in every direction. She heard the gurgling of the waterfall and exhaled in relief. "I am by the pretty lake." Her breathing became less labored. "It was another vision." Her shoulders relaxed feeling relieved but then she clenched her arms. "My vision indicates that Beelzebub has become pure evil, and he despises me above everyone else."

Chapter 33

EVIL OMEN

Lilith hastened to inform Satan and the others of her revelation. Before long, the sunset would announce it was time to resume their journey.

"It is time we were on our way," Satan said. "I sense we are close to finding Beelzebub. I shall not rest while our friend yet lies in bondage."

Lilith approached. "Please remain a moment longer."

"Of course, we shall not leave you behind." Satan chuckled. "I was about to instruct Samael to—"

"I mean we must discontinue our search for him!" Lilith bowed her head as she interrupted.

"Suspend our search?" Satan frowned and eyed her askance. "That is absurd. I shall not stop until we find him."

"You do not understand. I had another vision." Lilith's lips quivered. "Beelzebub has become pure evil. There is no part of our friend left in this monster. He feels nothing but hatred and rage."

"How do you know your vision has come to pass?" Satan asked. "In Floraison, you had visions of the future of mankind. Perhaps your vision was Beelzebub's future if we do not rescue him now."

Lilith stared at him with imploring

eyes, but he turned his back on her and faced the others. "Prepare to resume our journey."

What if Satan was right? Perhaps what she saw was the monster Beelzebub could become. If this was so, perhaps she could sway him to become this monster for her cause, and use him to exact her revenge on God. On the other hand, she feared for her existence if he harbored half the hate for her that she experienced in her vision.

Either way, Lilith had no choice but to go along with Satan's plan. The fallen angels departed. Fornues, Dagon, and the twin mermaids voyaged by sea. The rest of them journeyed by air.

After giving birth, Gadreel regained her strength and endurance and kept up with the others. Her wings beat the air as if it took no effort. She swooped and twirled, laughing and humming against the cerulean-kissed skies. With each burst of giggles, Lilith glared at her with a suffocating stare, but Gadreel took no notice of her.

"Sing us a song, Gadreel." Satan beamed at her. Lilith shook her head and massaged her temples.

Gadreel sang about the joys of being a mother, of seeing Dagon again, and of their journey. Samael beamed and performed acrobatic feats in the air. Satan soared with his giant wingspan. Lilith watched them through eyes crinkled by frustration.

They traveled three days and nights before spotting a large river.

"We should land near that body of water." Lilith pointed at the Euphrates River from the sky. "I recognize it to be the same river I saw in my vision."

Satan nodded. "Somewhere in its depths, our friend lies in chains."

Lilith stared at Satan and trembled. "I hope you are right and my vision depicts a possible future and not reality."

They landed near the riverbank.

"There are many creatures inhabiting this river." Gadreel stared wide-eyed at the jackals, hippos, and mongooses along the river. "How shall we get close enough to search for Beelzebub?"

"We shall not find him by simply scanning the surface of the water," Satan said. "As told to us by both Dagon and Lilith, he is lying on the riverbed. We must submerge ourselves and search for him underwater."

Gadreel gasped and shook her head. "That is impossible. We cannot breathe underwater like Fornues and Dagon. Our insides shall fill with water!"

Lilith rolled her eyes. "How would you have knowledge of this?"

"I have acquired this understanding through experience." Gadreel wrapped her arms around herself. "Not long ago, I swam too far into the ocean without realizing. My body became fatigued in my pregnant state, and I was unable to return to shore. Since treading water weakened me so, I began to sink. Water rushed into my body by way of my mouth. I was almost in death's grasp. Dagon snatched me from the deep at that precise moment, saving my life, and unknowingly, that of our unborn children. We cannot do what you are requesting, Satan."

"Shall we all perish striving to rescue Beelzebub?" Samael ran a hand through his hair.

Satan sucked air through his teeth and waggled his head side to side. "We must not attempt to breathe underwater, for we are incapable of doing so. We, however, have the ability to hold our breath below the water's surface for long periods of time. Our bodies can also withstand the pressures of the deep. I have already tested this concept." He turned to Gadreel. "You nearly drowned because you made an attempt to breathe while submerged. Instead of air, you inhaled water. If you would have held your breath, you would have been fine."

Gadreel lowered her head. "Apologies, for I should have known better than to doubt you."

Satan heaved an exasperated sigh and gave a dismissive wave of his hand.

"We shall proceed to the coast by foot since it is not far, and wait for Fornues and Dagon to arrive. Thence, we shall return to the river and begin our underwater search."

Chapter 34

POSSESSION

Upon returning to the coast Gadreel hurried to the water and stood knee-deep, singing.

"Do you sing to lure your lover and lost offspring to shore?" Lilith curled her upper lip as she sneered.

Gadreel kept her eyes on the rolling waves. "If by lure, you mean persuading, then yes. I am guiding Dagon and my little ones to me, for I miss them so."

"I am certain your singing is not necessary. If Dagon desires your company, he shall come without the enticement. If he loves you, he would desire to make you happy, thereby fetching your offspring for you. He would make haste, finding it unbearable to be without you."

"What does a serpent know of love?" Gadreel dove farther into the ocean, the saltwater washing away the sorrow and uncertainty flowing from her eyes, and when she was far enough from Lilith she began to sing again.

Lilith stood frozen staring ahead with wide eyes and raised eyebrows, as if Gadreel's reply pierced her heart like a blade. She abandoned the beach in search of Samael.

Gadreel's voice was sublime and haunting, it surged with the ocean currents to Dagon's ears. He advanced at full speed toward the shoreline, and Fornues followed as close as his immense size allowed.

"I cannot go any further, my friend," Fornues communicated. "I shall wait here. Go to her, follow her song, for I feel the presence of her voice, and it is the most delightful sound on Earth."

Her song guided Dagon and his little mermaids to the beach where she stood. Her eyes were closed, her head tilted to the sky as she uttered her enticing vibrations.

"My love, we are here, anxious to be by your side." Dagon's smile crinkled his eyes and nose.

Gadreel opened her eyes. She screamed and jumped with excitement upon seeing him and their girls once again. She waded to them. She embraced him and gaped at her twins, who were already toddlers.

"They have grown so fast." Her voice had a tinge of sadness. "I have missed much of their growing." She hugged them both and kissed them over and over again. "Do they yet utter words?"

"No, I have not heard words emerge from them as yet," Dagon said. "You may spend some time with them now. After a while, I must take them to Fornues so he may look after them while we devote time to each other."

She hugged and kissed her girls again. They swam around and splashed in the water together. Dolphins, turtles, and manta rays swam around them, joining in their play.

"It is time for me to take the little ones to Fornues." He wore a doleful expression and held out his arms. "I value our moments alone and do not want our time to expire."

Gadreel held her young in her arms and continued to kiss them while whimpering her goodbyes. He gently removed them from her. Fornues was expecting them and welcomed them with open tentacles. Dagon thanked him and returned to embrace Gadreel, who was still sobbing.

"When we finally rescue Beelzebub, we shall find a home for us, and then you shall spend every day with them. But for now, it must be this way." He wiped away her tears. She nodded and kissed him.

∽

Lilith watched as Dagon and Gadreel ran to each other's arms when he arrived. She observed her frolicking cheerfully with her darlings, as he gazed upon them with loving eyes. She gagged as a wave of nausea hit her. Her face fell into a sour expression and she turned her shoulders and crossed her arms. She retched and tasted something vile in her mouth.

"What does a serpent know of love?" Lilith repeated Gadreel's words under her breath. She clenched her teeth. Her eyes stung with gathering tears. She would have her vengeance against God by making Eden her home. She would give birth many times and fill the garden with her off-spring. Gadreel would have to live on a beach somewhere to be near her brood, whilst she would run on lush, green grasses and swim in crystalline rivers in delight with her progeny. She would be happy living in paradise.

"Lilith, I shall have words." Satan approached her.

She turned away and wiped her tears as fast as she could, and then set her sights on him again. "Yes, my prince?" her tone was sarcastic.

Satan furrowed his brow. "Your eyes betray recent lament."

She kissed him on the lips. He slipped his tongue between her lips and curled his arm around her waist, tugging her close to him. His male organ grew and hardened against her. She pushed away from him. "Stop," she said with a petulant toss of her head.

Satan tilted his head and puckered his brow. "Why do you turn from me?"

"Apologies, my love, but I cannot face the red fiend. Not at this moment. I shall not!" She bolted from him.

Satan sagged against a tree and hung his head. Hours passed. Darkness conquered the day again. Satan continued to idle under the tree, brooding. Gadreel and Dagon strolled over to him.

"Satan, the hour grows late. I shall accompany Dagon—" Gadreel's words drifted off as she noticed his demeanor. "What has come to pass?" Her eyes were wide with alarm, for she had never seen him look so defeated.

"I feel as though a fire has erupted in my chest and my heart grows heavy with sorrow. For the first time, I am at a loss to remedy a situation. I do not know how to satisfy Lilith, and more than anything I aspire to make her happy." Tears welled in his blue eyes.

Gadreel gave him a pitying look. "You are the best among us. You are a great and powerful being with no equal. Why do you pursue one that has the heart of a serpent?" Dagon yanked her arm and gestured to her to stop speaking.

Satan gazed at her with eyes withered with crying and exhaustion. "We do not decide to love. Love claims each of us as it desires."

She lowered her head, recognizing the truth in his words. "You may one day find your love in the arms of another, for she is not devoted to you." Gadreel gasped and clapped a hand over her mouth.

Dagon pulled her back and stepped in front of her to face Satan's retaliation in her stead.

Satan flushed a deep scarlet and sprang to his feet. Wild-eyed, he dashed in the direction he had seen Lilith go when she left him. He found her in a small open meadow surrounded by fragrant flower bushes. She lay on her back on the soft, verdant grass with her arms and legs wrapped around Samael's torso. Satan watched from behind a bush their naked bodies entangled in a lover's embrace. They moved as one, and they uttered sounds of extreme pleasure and bliss.

Satan stood motionless and stared with wide eyes and raised eyebrows. He buried his hands in his hair. "I should be enraged by what I see." His voice was but a breath. "Instead, all I feel is fear—fear of losing her." His shoulders hunched and he covered his head with his hands and snapped his eyes shut. "More than anything I desire to be Samael, so that she can experience such ecstasy with me."

Suddenly, Satan was on top of Lilith. Her arms held him close, and her long legs wrapped around his torso. He gazed into her half-closed eyes, his brow knit tightly in confusion. She leered at him as she arched her back and gyrated beneath him. He kissed her face and neck, and she returned his kisses.

He narrowed his eyes still mystified, but he groaned with pleasure. He glanced down at his body. Although he was making love to her, he had not changed into the red fiend she so detested. He inspected his chest. He gasped and stopped moving.

"Who am I?" Satan asked in a tight voice.

"The one and only Samael, of course!" Lilith giggled at his antics.

Satan jumped out of Samael's body, landing beside her. While yet on top of her, Samael howled in pain. She gasped and pushed him off and watched in fear as he wriggled in pain on the grass.

"You were inside Samael's body?" Her bosom heaved and she trembled as she stared wide-eyed at Satan.

"Indeed, I had possession of him." Satan scowled.

Lilith's eyes zipped back and forth between both of them. She was immobilized by fear.

"I sensed your presence inside me, but I was a prisoner in my own body," Samael told Satan in a gruff voice. "I experienced immense pain, as if I were covered in flames, all the while you seized my body. There was no longer pleasure, only physical torment and fear."

Lilith cringed and trembled.

Satan crouched before Lilith and ran a knuckle down her cheek. "If Samael is the lover you desire, I shall make love to you using his body as my vessel."

Lilith's lips quivered and she glanced at Samael.

Giant tears fell from Samael's eyes. He wrapped his arms around himself and rocked side to side. He dared not speak a word in contradiction to Satan's plans for fear of further retribution.

With no warning, Satan took possession of his body again. He leered at Lilith "It gives me great satisfaction to know I shall experience immense pleasure, while Samael shall suffer unspeakable agony." He made love again and again to Lilith in his ally's form.

When done, he left his friend's body. Once more, Samael writhed on the ground, his body racked with pain. Lilith gave him a pitying glance.

She strolled away, holding Satan's hand and left Samael behind to suffer alone the consequences of their actions.

❧

Gadreel sat on a rock a few feet into the ocean. Dagon, in his merman form, was submerged waist deep in the water. She gasped and bit her lip as she watched Satan and Lilith saunter hand-in-hand toward the beach. "My plans to turn Satan against Lilith has backfired it seems, and now I fear suffering their wrath."

When Dagon caught sight of Satan and Lilith strolling toward them together, he moved closer to Gadreel. He lowered his eyebrows, his hands tightened into fists and he spread his arms out.

"The hour grows late," Satan shouted to them from the shoreline. "We shall rest this night, and at first light, we shall search for Beelzebub in the depths of the river. We shall submerge together, for we are stronger in numbers. We do not know what manner of mayhem we shall stumble upon in the deep." He and Lilith found an area to sleep and nestled against each other.

Gadreel twisted her mouth and her eyes rolled skyward in disbelief. "What happened between the time I revealed Lilith's betrayal to Satan, and now? What brought on such a change in him?" She looked at Dagon with a perplexed look on her face. "How did that acid-tongued serpent convince him that what she did was acceptable?"

Dagon threw his hands in the air and shook his head.

They uttered their goodbyes and he swam to Fornues and his daughters. She swam to the beach, dug a trench near the water, and slept within it.

Fornues converted empty shells of a large clam into beds for the mermaids. They slept comfortably, while he kept watch.

Dagon gazed at him with affection, opened his arms and met Fornues' eyes. "I want you to know that I am grateful for everything you do. I appreciate you."

Fornues gave him a nod. "If I were smaller I would join foreheads with you."

Dagon chuckled. "Satan requires us to rest this night. Tomorrow, we shall search for Beelzebub in the light of day. The water shall protect us from the sun's rays."

"How can I be of use? I cannot come any closer to shore, for my size prevents it."

"Satan is wise. He shall think of a way to use you in this effort. Do not fret and get some rest."

"I do not require sleep." Fornues dropped the last two words to a grumble. "Go now, and sleep with your babes. I shall be your guardian."

"Thank you, my friend." Dagon flung himself onto the sea floor between his daughters' cradles and fell asleep.

Chapter 35

IN FORNUES' HULK

The next morning Dagon awoke and proceeded to shore. Gadreel ran to him, and they embraced. Samael inched his way up to Lilith and Satan. She glanced his way, but swiftly turned her face away. Satan did not acknowledge his presence.

Everyone consumed his or her fill of the abundant nutriment obtained. Afterward, they congregated under a grouping of shady trees.

"The time has come to release our ally, Beelzebub, from bondage. We shall grant him freedom from the river that imprisons him." Satan stood tall, chest out and shoulders back.

Fornues turned a stark white hue. "I am afraid I shall be useless in this endeavor, for there is a stretch of land between the ocean where I now dwell and the river that holds our friend."

Satan peered at the ocean, admiring how the sun's vivid light sparkled and danced over the surface of the water, knowing Fornues' large form drifted beneath it. He focused his unblinking stare at the others. "Take refuge on high ground!"

Gadreel gasped and without hesitation took Dagon's hand and flew him to high ground.

Lilith pulled Samael by the hair. "Come, we must take cover!"

Samael glowered at her. They took to the sky and joined the others.

"Fornues, make yourself ready." Satan peered at the dark water.

Lilith and the others watched from a nearby cliff overlooking the ocean, waiting to see what Satan planned to do. As they looked at Satan, he disappeared.

Lilith stood slack-mouthed, her gaze fixed on the area where he had stood, unable to move. Gadreel gasped and pressed her hands over her mouth. Samael hurried to the edge of the cliff and search for Satan his eyes flashing in every direction. Dagon appeared to be in a stupor.

Their attention turned to the ocean, which began to stir violently. Large waves smashed into the rocky shore. Coastal birds squawked and zoomed and whooshed, as they flew to take cover. Gadreel covered her sensitive ears from the cacophony.

The fallen angels watched in awe as Fornues hauled himself out of the ocean and onto dry land. For the first time, they saw him out of the water.

Through Fornues, Satan spoke into the angels' minds. "Follow me to the river, and we shall begin our quest."

"Satan, is that you in Fornues' bulk?" Lilith gaped at the large beast.

"Indeed. I have taken possession of Fornues' body. I shall remain within him until his body is submerged in the large river."

Lilith stared wide-eyed and openmouthed pressing a palm to her forehead.

Fornues had changed to his original shiny black color, and the angels observed his immense bulk, under Satan's domination, lurch onto the beach and crawl across dry land.

A breeze wafted Fornues' powerful aroma into the angels' nostrils. It was the combined fragrance of the ocean—salt, fish, algae, and seaweed. Lilith covered her nose. Gadreel turned pale and wrinkled her nose. Samael scowled and pinched his nose.

"I need to move at a rapid pace to prevent Fornues from desiccating in the sweltering sun," Satan said.

Gadreel, holding Dagon, dove off the cliff to the beach. Dagon hurried to Fornues, and she scuttled by his side.

"I fret for our friend, and for our daughters whom we left to fend for themselves in the ocean." Dagon rubbed the nape of his neck, his chest heaving with rapid breaths.

Gadreel wrapped a curl around her finger and bit her lip. She looked over her shoulder at the sea. "Oh, please be safe and stay near the coast."

Fornues was trapped in his own body. An immense, hot pressure built in his head, making it difficult for him to have an orderly thought. He saw his friends and the land around him, although everything appeared hazy, but he held no control over his body. He trembled with fear, never having left the ocean since he was cast from Floraison.

Samael strolled alongside Lilith. "I yet suffer the after effects of Satan's possession. My skin is tender to the touch, and I struggle to take a deep breath."

Lilith glanced at him and sighed. "This is not a good moment to speak of this. We are on a quest to rescue our friend Beelzebub. I know you agonize on account of what we did, but do you not prefer to be the one made to suffer in my stead? I—I would take your place if I could." She touched her lip, gave him a one-sided shoulder shrug and walked ahead without making eye contact.

Samael's body drooped. He shoved his hair back away from his face and clasped his hands over his head. He gaped at the giant creature. "Fornues, are you suffering as I did when Satan occupied my body?"

Satan lacked the skill to maneuver Fornues' large hulk, so he advanced awkwardly, dragging his eight muscular arms. As he scooted across the rough terrain, Fornues' suction pads took a dangerous thrashing.

Gadreel pointed at a large smear left behind by the giant. "What is that cerulean fluid trailing Fornues?"

Dagon lowered his head. "He leaves behind a stream of his blue blood."

Fornues' color changed from black to gray.

Gadreel pressed her hands against her cheeks. "He is losing a great deal of body fluid."

Gnashing his teeth, Dagon confronted Lilith. "Fornues shall die. Will Satan sacrifice one life for another?"

"I am certain that Satan is well aware of what is happening. Fornues shall be fine." Lilith used a honeyed voice to assure them. Dagon glanced at her sideways, closed his eyes briefly, and then moved on.

Gadreel took his hand and kissed it. They walked hand-in-hand. Samael stared at them and sulked.

Satan and his followers neared the river. Gadreel gasped and pointed. "Behold! There is an abundance of wildlife along the river banks." A large clan of spotted hyenas cackled outside their dens near the waterway, while jackals barked and engaged in aggressive play. Wolves howled. A pride of lions reposed along the riverfront with their cubs, and a bloat of hippopotamuses, some partially submerged in the river and others patrolling the banks.

Gadreel gawked at the animals. "It appears it shall be quite a challenge to get near the river. I cannot imagine what perils awaits us beneath the surface." She rushed to Dagon's arms and he embraced her and kissed the top of her head.

Satan maintained his gradual advancement, determined to get Fornues' large form into the river before it was too late.

When the pride of lions caught sight of the large beast they stood before their cubs and roared as if they perceived Fornues was a threat to them and their litter. Hence, they pounced on his tentacles, scratching, biting, and tearing off chunks of flesh with their sharp teeth. Satan cringed and howled, suffering every painful blow delivered by the animals. Fornues would remain oblivious to the injuries until he abandoned his body.

"Satan!" Lilith rushed forward. Samael caught her by the shoulders, wrapped his arms around her pressing her against him and pinning her arms by her sides.

"Release me! I must help him!" She struggled to escape from his grasp. Who would ensure she would make it to the Garden of Eden if Satan were gone?

Samael lowered his eyebrows and pushed her away. "Go then!" He ran his hands through his hair in an aggressive manner. "Satan is a powerful being. These beasts are no matches for him. Much less now that he occupies Fornues' immense bulk." Lilith frowned and crossed her arms but she did not take another step.

Dagon approached her. "If you go to him, you shall put him at a disadvantage, for then his focus shall be on you instead of the animals."

Lilith lowered her head and looked away from them. "You are both right."

Satan retaliated. He waved Fornues' powerful tentacles, striking the lionesses with great force. He killed several of them and knocked others dazed. The surviving lionesses rushed to their cubs.

A pack of wolves surrounded his bleeding body. They growled, exposing huge canines, erect ears pointing forward and tails held high. Satan slapped one, smashing its skull and knocking it down. He grabbed another, wrapping a tentacle around it. The wolf yipped. Satan crushed its body, tasting its blood, and then tossed it aside. He pitched three others into the river.

Hyenas whooped and growled over the lifeless bodies of the wolves, whose skin and bones they had begun devouring. The surviving wolves howled and barked. Gadreel covered her ears. "There is no sound as haunting as a wolf's howl," she whispered. As pack members fought off hyenas and dragged away their dead, her eyes glistened with accumulating tears. "There is so much death and destruction."

Satan opened Fornues' large mouth. A loud piercing shrill tone filled the ears of the surrounding animals, as well as the fallen angels. The jackals yelped and whimpered.

Lilith ran to him. "Cease the shrill noise, I implore you!" Lilith's hands covered her ears as she screamed. Satan noticed her and ended the piercing sound at once.

"Are you well?" He asked in her mind. She nodded, so he proceeded to the river. He stopped on the riverbank. "I shall hold each of you in one of Fornues' tentacles. When I provide the signal, take a long, deep breath. Then, together we shall go below the surface."

Satan grasped the angels one by one. When he held them all, he ordered, "Inhale a deep breath and hold it. We shall submerge."

Lilith, Gadreel and Samael inhaled and Satan entered the river.

Dagon willed the transformation to his merman form. The others watched in horror as he suffered the drowning process before he was able to breathe underwater again.

Satan swam many fathoms at great speed with his allies wrapped in Fornues' tentacles. At the bottom of the river, he released them.

"I sense we are close to the area where I saw Beelzebub in my vision," Lilith communicated to them mentally. "He is no longer at the greatest depth. We can disperse and initiate our search for him from this point. There is a stream that flows over the riverbed. If you find it, follow it, for it shall lead you to him."

"Do as Lilith has instructed," Satan said. "We shall not rest until we find him."

Lilith and Samael proceeded in separate directions. Satan used Fornues' eight sucker-lined arms to move about on the river floor. Dagon and Gadreel left together and soon found the enigmatic underwater river Lilith described, and followed it as she instructed.

Chapter 36

THE BATTLE FOR BEELZEBUB

Beelzebub sensed the presence of Lilith and the others. His eyes darted in every direction. At a distance, he saw a strange creature, one he had never seen, part man and part fish, swimming in his direction. His body trembled and rocked from side to side—but then he caught sight of Gadreel. Her long golden blonde hair was like a small piece of the sun whose rays rolled and undulated in the murky waters.

"Gadreel!" Beelzebub bellowed in her mind.

She came to an abrupt halt. Her wide eyes scanned her surroundings.

Dagon stopped and stared at her with a quizzical expression. "Why did you stop?" He saw how she trembled. "What frightens you so?"

Gadreel remained as if in a trance.

"You are near. Draw closer to me." Beelzebub's voice summoned.

She exploded out of her daze and blasted in his direction, followed by a bewildered Dagon. Before long, they encountered the chained leviathan.

When they saw the creature lying in chains, Dagon froze and stared with broad eyes and eyebrows raised high. Gadreel inhaled a sharp breath in shock, allowing water to rush into her system. More water squeezed into her lungs. She bobbed languidly, head thrown back, and arms at her sides.

Dagon woke from his stupor and leaped into action. He tugged her close and pressed his mouth over hers, pumping the water out of her and passing it over his gills. He then extracted oxygen from the water and passed it to her. She held her breath once more. She peeked at Beelzebub, winced, squeezed her eyes shut, and pressed her face against Dagon's chest. He pushed her away gently and swam closer to him. He stared at him.

"Dagon, it is I, Beelzebub."

"It is difficult to believe what you have become. A creature hideous and painful to perceive," Dagon said. Beelzebub turned his head away from them.

"Satan, is that you?" he asked. Dagon and Gadreel turned to see Satan in Fornues' form approaching.

"Yes, it is I." Satan continued to crawl over the riverbed.

"Have you come to free me from these chains?" Beelzebub asked.

"Indeed, my friend. We have finally found you, and we mean to set you free."

Lilith arrived and cringed, appalled by Beelzebub's appearance. She did not have a future vision. Everything was as in her dream.

A short time later, Samael arrived. When he saw Beelzebub, he pressed the heels of his hands into his eyes.

"Are you going to hover and stare, or are you going to rescue me?" The creature said in their minds, and they got a taste of the old Beelzebub they knew and loved.

"I shall wrap my tentacles around you and take you to the surface. Once on dry land, we shall find a way to release you from those chains." Satan began to coil his limbs around him.

Beelzebub cringed and wailed one moment and grinned, showing his greenish, pointed teeth the next.

Lilith raised an eyebrow and looked at him sideways. She suspected he was conjuring up ways he would make them suffer once he was freed. She remembered the threats he had uttered in her vision.

Satan finished wrapping his muscular appendages around his disfigured body and with great care and effort he began to lift him off the riverbed.

"Leave the water and clear a path on the riverbank for us," Satan told the others.

Dagon took Gadreel's hand once again and swam to the surface. Lilith and Samael trailed behind them. They surfaced and swam for the banks, but as before, they had a myriad of animals to manage.

Lilith took the lead and changed into her snake form. She thrashed aggressive hippos and cleared a path for the others. Dagon summoned his legs and waded out of the river. Gadreel and Samael took flight, arriving first at the riverbank. They came together and waited for Satan to emerge from the water with Beelzebub.

The unusual rise of water along the riverbanks made the angels and animals nearby seek shelter on higher ground. The hippos and other animals in the water scrambled for cover as Fornues ascended.

Fornues heaved his hulk from the water, carrying in his four front tentacles Beelzebub's chained body. Whilst Satan lowered Beelzebub to place him on the grass near the bank, five luminous beings appeared in the sky above him.

Satan stared at the remarkable beings. The glowing creatures were not part of the natural environment. They were Heaven sent. His breaths quickened.

Lilith glanced at the others and saw fear etched on their faces. Peering at the spherical entities in the sky, she saw the outline of five celestial beings.

She stepped forward. "Show your true form, so that we may look upon you and know your true identity. Cease veiling yourselves behind the resplendent light."

Raphael stood in front, glowing like a star. His radiance painted the four angels behind him with brightness. Upon hearing Lilith's words, he dimmed his glow allowing her and the others to see him and the holy angels accompanying him.

Michael came forward, dressed in his green and gold general's uniform and carrying his golden spear. The weapon symbolized the downfall of the dark forces in the war in Floraison. Like Raphael, Michael's six large white wings were expanded in battle formation. Jetrel advanced and stood by his side, holding in her powerful hand the silver lance God fashioned for her.

Hashmal and Esar followed suit. Soon they were side-by-side, hovering above the fallen angels.

"You must return Beelzebub from whence he came, Satan," Michael said in an orotund voice. Satan gasped, shocked by Michael's knowledge of his possession. He defied his orders by placing Beelzebub on the grass before his followers.

"The leviathan must remain imprisoned in this river, until the end of days." Michael lifted his head.

Lilith's body stiffened at the remark. "This creature was once our friend Beelzebub."

Beelzebub's eyes rolled languorously to Lilith.

"He is no longer Beelzebub. At present, he is pure evil. If he is liberated, he shall wreak chaos upon this planet."

Lilith knew Michael spoke the truth, but she continued to defy him nevertheless, blinded by hatred for him. "Return to your celestial home and leave us be."

"If he is released, his hostility would have no bounds. It would be aimed at God, the angels, and human beings," Raphael told them in his usual mild manner. "His hatred shall be aimed at your kind as well."

"Yet, it was not always so." Lilith scowled and crossed her arms. "He is a monster because of the severe punishments inflicted upon him. Perhaps he shall change once he is freed."

"He merits the punishments he received for his depravities and misdeeds!" Jetrel moved forward pointing her weapon at her. "He has always been weak and easily led astray. He was always going to be evil. There is no changing him!"

Lilith tightened her hands to fists. "Let us decide what to do with him. We are the rulers of this planet—not you!"

Michael observed Lilith with a pitying expression. "I have been watching you— For a long time I had hoped that you would repent and ask forgiveness for your wrongs. Instead every decision made by you has been an act of defiance against God. You believe that you and your followers rule on earth?" He shook his head. "You and your allies are merely crepuscular insects amongst the lowest forms of life on this planet. Rulers you are not."

Lilith snarled, brandishing her fist. She curled her viper's tail over her head in a menacing stance. "I hate you Michael! I hate you! Come down and face me on the ground."

"Enough! We are here to implement God's commands!" Hashmal emitted from his mouth a powerful beam of fire setting ablaze the trees surrounding the fallen angels. The animals nearby fled, leaving them to stand-alone.

Gadreel winced and screamed as the heat from the blaze singed her. Dagon picked her up and whisked her away from the flaming trees. Lilith and Samael also ran from the firestorm.

"We shall return Beelzebub to his watery prison where he shall remain until God orders his release. Now stand aside or perish!" Michael's voice was like a thunderous boom.

Gadreel, Dagon, and Samael huddled together, afraid to challenge Michael and those standing with him. Lilith stood alone, defiant—glowering at him. She looked at Satan, anticipating his next move.

Watching his followers shrink in the presence of Michael enraged Satan. "Beelzebub shall remain here, on dry land with us."

"Defiant to the end." Michael shook his head, staring first at Lilith and then at Satan. "Very well." With a mere glance, he conveyed orders to Hashmal.

Hashmal flew to Lilith, hovered before her, and spit a fireball, which caught her hair on fire. She collapsed to the ground, wailing as the fire burned her hair and consumed her skin.

Gadreel and Dagon hurried to her and threw dirt over her to snuff the blaze. Samael dawdled behind. It took a long time to smother the flames. Lilith's long hair was completely incinerated by the fire. Her scalp, wings and the skin on her face, neck, and upper body were burned. She shrieked and tried to touch her face, but Gadreel held her hand back. The three of them pulled her away from the ensuing battle.

Hashmal emitted flaming breath aimed at Fornues' bulk. Satan lifted Fornues' tentacles to protect his eyes and withstood the flames. Hashmal moved in closer. The fallen angels watched in horror as Satan, endured a firestorm of attacks from the fiery angel. Satan extended Fornues' muscular arm and grabbed Hashmal in a tight grip.

Esar advanced, transforming into a poisonous creature equal to

Fornues in size and fierceness. Like Fornues, he possessed eight muscular arms, but unlike him, he was nimble and able to fly.

Esar flew swiftly around Fornues. He lashed at him from every angle. Before Satan could maneuver his gigantic form, Esar attacked him from behind, injecting him with his paralyzing saliva.

Satan could no longer maneuver his body. He stood immobile and defenseless, so he abandoned Fornues' body, leaving him to fend for himself, and jumped into Samael's.

The holy angels moved in to finish Satan, not yet realizing he had abandoned Fornues' body. Fornues stood vulnerable against them who rained down upon him. He knew Satan abandoned his body, but he was paralyzed by Esar's venom, he could not move to defend himself. He now experienced the damage inflicted to him by Satan's possession, his travels on land, the animal attacks, Hashmal's firebombs, and at present, the thrashings he endured from Esar and the rest of the heavenly warriors. His body turned white with fear.

Fornues was made sightless by Jetrel's relentless attacks to his eyes with her lance. A sensation of falling into a dark pit conquered all other feelings in his consciousness. He fell deeper and further into the dark void. His life was slipping away. He could do naught to stop his ensuing death. He collapsed on the banks of the river, and with his eyes fixed on his dark brethren, he drew his last breath.

"Satan!" Lilith screamed. If he was dead, what would become of her? She would be free, no longer in fear of his mistreatments, but she needed him to occupy Eden and exact her revenge, which she desired now more than ever. She needed to see if he was truly dead.

Satan, now in Samael's body, grabbed her arm and prevented her from running to Fornues' carcass.

Gadreel's body shook with sobs. Dagon held her, his own face wet and contorted with grief. "Fornues, my dear friend, you shall be missed."

The holy angels ceased their attack on Fornues. Esar, in his giant, monstrous form, hoisted Beelzebub to deliver him to his watery prison once again.

Beelzebub, who had watched everything unfold in silence, now shrieked at the thought of being laid at the bottom of the river once more.

"No! No, I implore you!" Beelzebub yelled in the minds of the fallen. "I cannot endure anymore pain and suffering, I beseech you, fight for me!"

However, Lilith, Satan and the others realized it would be futile to resume fighting. They were too few and their powers were diminished in the presence of Michael and those alongside him.

"I knew you would abandon me. You, who call yourselves my friends, I despise you all! Beelzebub raged in their heads. Lilith looked away and Satan in Samael's body closed his eyes and tucked his chin into his neck.

Michael winged toward the dark angels, but none of the holy angels ever touched ground.

"You yet draw breath for a lone reason—because God has deemed it so. Be gone from this place at once. Do not make another attempt to free Beelzebub, for next time God may not show such mercy." Michael glared at Samael. When he was done, he joined the other holy angels higher in the sky.

Raphael emanated his intense radiance once more, and the celestial beings disappeared in the light of the sun.

Chapter 37

BURIAL AT SEA

As soon as the celestial beings vanished from sight, the dark angels went to their lifeless friend.

Lilith dropped to her knees and wept large briny tears that stung her injured face. "Satan, why have you forsaken me? You vowed you would always be by my side. Now that you no longer draw breath I shall be forlorn." She turned away. Who would make sure her bidding got done? Would the others follow her now that Satan was gone? Or would they try to go their separate ways? Surely Gadreel and Dagon would try to follow their own path. What of Samael? How could she exact her revenge on God without allies?

Samael knelt beside her and whispered in her ear, "I yet draw breath, my treasure." She whirled her head around and gazed into his eyes. Samael was finally pledging his love and commitment to her? He would be her new vessel. With his aid she could go where she needed to go and get the revenge she craved. She embraced him and kissed him while the others yet stared in disbelief at Fornues' corpse.

Fornues' eyes remained open. Dagon closed them. Gadreel leaned against Fornues' white hulk and caressed his bumpy skin. Dagon held her, and they grieved in each other's arms.

"Who shall protect you and

our daughters at sea, now that Fornues is gone, my love?" Gadreel asked between sobs.

Dagon lifted his head and pushed his chest out. "I need not protection, and our daughters shall be secure by my side. I shall keep them out of harm's way."

Fornues' immense carcass was already desiccating in the intensifying sun. The odor released by his corpse enveloped them. He reeked of acrid, colorless despair. They stiffened and their eyes watered.

"The cloying, sweet smell of death is in the air, never to be forgotten, for never before has an angel perished on Earth." Gadreel's gaze was fixed on Fornues. The others wore a stunned look on their faces.

Satan released Samael's body and reappeared before their eyes. Lilith jolted and stared at him, wide-eyed and openmouthed. Satan scowled at her. Gadreel and Dagon gasped. Samael collapsed to the ground, his arms wrapped around his body, whimpering. Steam emerged from his ears, nose, and mouth as though he had been in an inferno. Lilith panted, staring at him and Satan.

Dagon stood motionless and slacked-mouth. Gadreel gazed at Samael with pity, and hurried to him and placed an arm around his shoulders. The heat coming off his skin singed her. She ran her hand through his hair and kissed his face. Dagon looked at them sideways, arms crossed, his eyes narrowed to crumpled slits. His lips set in a grim line.

Lilith also frowned at them. She sensed Satan's gaze upon her and quickly changed her manner. She embraced him and closed her eyes. It had been Satan. Samael never pledged his devotion to her. It seemed she must endure life with Satan until her deeds were done.

"We must depart from this place," Satan said. "First, I wish to move Fornues from this site and return to shore so we may lay him to rest in the water. I am unable to possess his body any longer since there is no life left within it. Thus, we must all do our share to transport his remains to sea."

Gadreel helped Samael to his feet and returned to Dagon's side. Dagon and Samael glared at each other before embarking on the task of hauling Fornues to sea.

"Are you able to do your part?" Satan stared at the huge blisters forming on Lilith's burnt face and body. "You are injured."

"I am in much pain, but I could still do my part."

Satan shifted into the red fiend. They each grabbed hold of one of Fornues' limbs. The others did the same, including Samael in his weakened state. They hauled the enormous corpse to the shoreline. Once there, they slid him into the sea.

"I must change into my aquatic form to ensure he comes to rest in a suitable place." Dagon caressed Gadreel's cheek. "I must also find our daughters and ensure their safety."

"A great part of the day has gone by, and the sun has begun to diminish. I know it is time for you to leave me, but I need you so at this moment." Gadreel embraced him. They spoke their farewells, and he disappeared into the ocean.

After Dagon underwent his transformation, he scanned for Fornues' drifting form. When he found it, he took hold of one of his tentacles. He came across a coral reef, which was alive and vibrant. He admired the many rocks encrusted with assorted thriving and strange marine plant life. As he swam about admiring the different corals, seahorses, eels, and many other species living on the reef it occurred to him that this diverse and exquisite marine habitat would be an excellent resting place for his friend.

"You shall rest here, my friend, and someday, you shall become part of this delightful seascape." Dagon's tears dissolved in the seawater. After devoting a moment longer to his dear comrade, he surged through the water in search of his little mermaids.

He found them at once, for they, too, had come across the coral reef and loved it, not venturing too far from it. They had grown even more by feeding on shrimps, crabs, and lobsters. Dagon was delighted to see they were able to fend for themselves. When the twins saw their father, they swam to him and greeted him with warm embraces.

"We missed you, Father," the mermaids uttered in unison inside his mind. He beamed, surprised at their communicating with words.

"Where is Fornues, for we missed him as well?" They stared with eyes sparkling with innocence.

"It is with sadness I say to you that our beloved Fornues draws breath no more." Dagon lowered his head, feeling certain the news of his demise would break their little hearts.

The twins glanced at each other, scrunching their little brows, and then stared at him with blank expressions. He realized their confusion. He noticed one of them, the one whose wild, curly blonde hair and big brown eyes resembled their mother, held in her hand the husk of a lobster.

He pointed at the useless outer shell of the crustacean and asked his girls, "Do you see the lifeless creature you hold in your hand?" The mermaids glanced at the dead lobster and nodded.

"It is void of life, but it was not always so, for once it lived, swam and ate. Fornues is like this creature at present, a lifeless carcass."

Understanding bloomed on their little faces. Their eyes opened wide, and they moved about fitfully. They embraced each other, pouring out grief for the first time in their short lives. Dagon put his arms around them and held them for a long time. Afterward, he accompanied them to see Fornues for the final time.

Chapter 38

THE HEARTLESS SERPENT

The fallen angels sat on the beach together, listening to Gadreel's melodious songs and watching the sunset. When the sun disappeared below the horizon and day became night, Gadreel stopped singing and waded into the black sea. "I shall not see my daughters on this day. I miss them so." She pressed her hand against her bosom.

Satan got to his feet. He shuffled away, engrossed in his thoughts, leaving Lilith and Samael sitting together on the beach. Samael rubbed the nape of his neck and stared at the ground. Lilith looked away and squirmed.

After a long silence, Lilith spoke in a honeyed voice. "Samael, I am miserable you have suffered so because of me." She pressed a finger against her lower lip.

"I do not blame you. It was not your doing; we both did things that led to my suffering. There is, however, something you can do on my behalf." Samael stared at her blackened and blistered flesh. Her bald head was charred and areas of her skull were exposed. He lowered his eyes and crinkled his nose.

Lilith peered at him. "What is it you would have me do?"

"When Satan takes possession of my body, it causes me great pain and anguish. At first, the force of his body constricts me, suffocating me. Thenceforth, there is great pain. The agony begins in my head and spreads to the rest of my body. It is as if I had fallen into a pit of fire. I experience my flesh being consumed by flames, as though my skin is melting off my bones!" Samael's words jolted her, and she turned away. He turned her head in his direction and lock eyes with her.

"You can request Satan never take possession of my body again."

Lilith looked past him, crossed her arms and shook her head side to side in a languid manner.

"Is it too much to ask that you help cease my suffering?" Samael stared at her wide-eyed and creased his brow.

She nodded. "No."

"Then turn the words in his ears!"

"We narrowly escaped Satan's wrath. I—" Lilith's words were strangled by Samael's cries.

"I did not escape his wrath!" He massaged his temples. "He punishes me every time he takes possession of me. Do you not understand?"

Lilith shook her head. "Yes." She gave a half shrug. "Fault lies with us for grieving him. We must give him sufficient time to get over our betrayal." She shifted her eyes to the ground.

Samael clasped his hands over his head and gawked at her. "You have experienced what it is like to burn, although in a small portion of your body, and we were able to extinguish the fire before it had consumed you wholly. Imagine your entire body burning unceasingly!"

Lilith shook her head and avoided his piteous stare.

"We both betrayed Satan, yet I am the only one who suffers. How is this reasonable to you?" Samael's voice was thick with emotion. He gazed at Lilith's expressionless face. He tried to blink away gathering tears. She remained silent.

"Thus, I should go on agonizing, while you revel in the gains of Satan's control of me?" His tone was flat.

"What is your meaning?" Lilith gulped.

"You get to have us both, your chances of having offspring have multiplied, and the red fiend need never show its ugly face again."

Lilith stared at the ground once more eluding Samael's imploring gaze.

"Satan longs to please you. If you wished to end my suffering you have but to whisper."

Lilith finally looked at him. She tilted her head and pressed her mouth together in thought. "I cannot help you."

Immobilized, he stared at her with wide eyes and raised eyebrows. He smacked his palm against his forehead and shook his head. "You have turned my heart as black as the mark left by Cam's blade. At this moment my love for you has turned to hate."

Lilith moved away and pursed her lips.

He ran his hands through his hair. "I should have known I would get no sympathy from a deceitful snake! You have a cold and unfeeling nature and have wounded me more deeply than any injury Satan could ever inflict on me. Although you can shift in and out of your serpent form, you shall always be a legless reptile in my eyes." Samael jumped to his feet and left her side.

Lilith rubbed her throat. Her eyes shifted to the ground and became glazed with a glittery layer of tears. She folded her legs close to her body and hugged her knees and wept as the magnitude of Samael's words swept over her. She no longer heard the sounds of the world, only a haunting ringing in her ears. Her body convulsed with sobs.

Gadreel sat on a flat rock in the water. She heard Lilith's desperate cries and thought Satan's punishment had finally come. She waded to the beach and saw her weeping.

"What is the matter?" Gadreel's forehead puckered. "You have never allowed anyone to see you in a vulnerable state. Are you mourning the loss of your hair?" Gadreel leaned in and touched her shoulder. "You know if you burrow underground overnight, you shall heal and your hair shall grow back."

Lilith stared ahead. "Satan has seen Samael and I engaged in sexual acts." Her voice was hoarse. She turned and glanced at her. Gadreel blinked a long blink through tousled curls.

Lilith cocked her head and frowned. "You do not seem surprised by this. Why not?"

"I knew sooner or later Satan would discover the two of you."

"Indeed? And you are pleased, are you not?" Lilith sprang to her feet and stepped toward her. Gadreel recoiled in fear. "You are becoming bold. Do you think me weak because of my injuries?"

"What was Satan's reaction seeing you in Samael's arms?"

"We did not see Satan coming. We were making love and suddenly, Samael asked me who he was. When I told him, Satan released his body. Only then, I understood that Satan had possessed him."

Gadreel moved away and crossed her arms. "I know Samael's punishment, for he has told me how he suffers under Satan's control, but what retribution does Satan have planned against you?"

Lilith glared at her and then quickly changed her demeanor. She shrugged and looked at the sand. "My punishment is knowing that when Satan makes love to me in possession of Samael's body, my good friend shall be in agony."

Lilith glanced up and looked right into Gadreel's eyes, the smile she still wore dripping with a silent threat. "Do you know what is good about this arrangement?"

Speechless, Gadreel shook her head.

"I no longer have to fret about having offspring that resemble little red fiends. Samael is gorgeous and he does not have an alternate form. My offspring shall be beautiful!"

"Oh Lilith." Gadreel chuckled and looked up. "You have forgotten about your alternate form. And although Satan takes possession of Samael's body, do not believe for a moment that he shall not affect your offspring. It may end with your young hatching out of an egg."

Rage bloomed on Lilith's face. She snarled and shifted into the snake creature. Using her tail she knocked Gadreel to the ground and pounded her with it. Gadreel held up her hands and wailed, writhing on the sand, as she received blow after bone-crushing blow.

Satan ran toward them. "Cease this attack at once!"

Lilith stopped, her tail dripped with Gadreel's blood. Her claws were spread wide, fangs exposed and her bosom heaved with rapid breaths.

When he heard Gadreel's screams, Samael dashed to the beach. He stopped short when he saw her lying in her own blood.

He stared at Lilith, crinkled his nose and curled his lip with disgust. "You must control your revolting beast, for she is heartless, and dangerous."

Gadreel lay unconscious on the beach, her blood still spilling onto the sand.

Satan glared at Lilith. "You must save her. We cannot lose any more of our own."

Lilith returned to her angel form. Panting, she approached Gadreel's body. She looked at her with a slight frown and pressed lips. She knelt beside her, searched her body for open wounds and created patches of sand to stop the bleeding.

"Dig a trench and put her in it. Let her rest the night. She shall be fine come sunrise." Lilith left her side.

Samael and Satan dug a large ditch. They placed Gadreel's limp body in it and Samael laid by her side.

"I shall stay with her this night to ensure no more harm comes to her." Samael looked at her with woeful eyes. He put his arms around her motionless body and slept.

Satan seized Lilith's arm and dragged her away. He returned to the small meadow where he had discovered her with Samael.

"Do not assume that I have overlooked your infidelity. I shall soon think of a punishment befitting your transgressions." With these words, he transformed into the red fiend. He shoved her to the ground. He grabbed hold of one of her wings' shoulders and stomped on it, breaking its bony frame and then did the same to the other. He clawed her face, head and back ripping off pieces of her charred skin. She squirmed and groaned in pain, but he continued punching and kicking her, all the while snarling in rage. Afterward, he violated her again and again while she shrieked and wailed, knowing no one would come to her rescue.

After the deed was done, Satan turned over and fell asleep. Lilith lay motionless, paralyzed by pain, for a long while. Then she crawled, wracked with pain to an area of hollow ground and burrowed underground for the night. She lay very still in her hole, for the slightest movement was agony. "I shall fill my heart with hate until there is no room for any other weak emotion. I shall be strong, and make myself emotionless, uncaring, hard like a stone." She clamped her eyes shut. "I shall remain focused on my one true goal. Revenge."

Chapter 39

MISJUDGMENT

The following morning Gadreel woke to find Samael lying by her side asleep with his arms around her, and Dagon looming over the ditch where they slept. He glowered at her, his chest heaved with rapid breaths and his nostrils flared. He pivoted on his heel and rushed toward the ocean. She scrambled to get out of the ditch, but she was yet in a great deal of pain. She finally clambered out of the trench and crawled a distance before struggling to her feet.

She staggered after Dagon. "Wait! Please stop!"

He stopped, his feet already in the water. He turned to face her, his teeth gnashing. "Say what you must." His manner was curt.

"You have misconstrued the situation. Nothing took place between Samael and I," she said.

"Yet there he was with his arms around you, sleeping the restful sleep of a gratified male." Dagon pointed toward Samael the blood vessels in his neck throbbing.

"No!" Gadreel shook her head eyes wide. "I cannot explain why he was by my side, for I do not know, but—"

"Do not deny what is clear to my eyes!" Dagon turned away, jumped into the water and disappeared into the sea, taking their daughters.

"No!" She screamed, sagged to the sand her body shaking with sobs.

Samael awoke. "What is the matter? Did Lilith try to hurt you again?"

She gazed at him her eyes red and wilted from weeping and shook her head. "Dagon saw you lying by my side and misjudged the situation. He is gone now and with him, my daughters. I shall never see them again." Gadreel curled into a fetal position and buried her face in her hands. "Oh Samael, how shall I live without them?" She glanced up at him with doleful eyes her face colorless, like the snow on the tall mountain they landed on long ago.

Samael sat by her side with slumped shoulders, looking down and away. "You have always been good to me. I apologize for the way I have treated you in the past." He looked at her, maintaining eye contact. "I vow to be kinder, and I shall do everything I can to reunite you with your little ones."

Gadreel looked into his golden amber, wolf-like eyes for a long moment and then nodded. She sat upright and struggled to get to her feet. Samael helped her stand and held her arm as they ambled together to the coast-line. She stared at the vast ocean with him by her side, holding her steady.

Satan and Lilith joined them.

"We shall rest this day." Satan heaved a deep breath and blew out slowly. "I must decide our course of action. We must also provide time to all those needing to recover." He returned to the area lined with trees to sit under one and form thoughts.

Gadreel quivered and glanced wide-eyed at Lilith, who stood nude and silent by her side. Gadreel gasped. Lilith's head hung low, shoulders hunched. Her burns had healed noticeably and her hair had grown to just below her jawline. It was a jumbled mess and hung covering most of her face. Although the burn-marks were faded, her body showed bumps, bruises, and abrasions. She lifted her head in an abrupt manner and stared at them. Gadreel stepped back and pressed a hand over her mouth.

Samael gasped, crinkled his nose and turned away. "Your face is—difficult to look at. You are grotesque."

Lilith could not open one of her eyes, for large, black blisters compressed her eyelids shut. Her other eyeball was swollen, bloodshot, and bulged from its socket. Her nose was puffy and crooked, and her bottom lip was split and twice its size. There was swelling and deep bruises around her throat. Spherical clotted pits replaced her nipples, as if they had been bitten off. Large bite marks, welts, and claw marks covered her body. She opened and closed her mouth but could not emit words.

That morning after she crawled out of her burrow, almost fully restored from her burn injuries, Satan had thrashed her and violated her once more. She cleared her throat. "Satan desires to show you that I shall suffer for my betrayal," she said in a soft hoarse voice. She rubbed her throat as she spoke. "He also requires that I remain unclothed—like an animal."

Gadreel leaned in to hear her words because they were barely audible.

Samael grimaced. "I am unsure whether to feel pity for you, or rejoice in the fact that now you understand what it is to truly suffer."

Gadreel frowned, grasped his arm and shook her head lightly. "Be kind, for this is only the beginning of her torture."

Many days gave way to nights. They stayed on the coast where Fornues was released. Lilith remained silent and reclusive. Night after night, the red fiend tortured and ravaged her, but she suffered in silence. She would not give the others the pleasure of listening to her agony. She ceased paying mind to Satan's actions. Instead, she escaped to a different place in her mind where she focused on vengeance against God, and on her new quest to destroy those who betrayed her and caused her pain.

After what seemed an eternity to Lilith, Satan's anger over her affair with Samael began to abate. While he continued to lie with her in the form of the red fiend, the instances became few and far between, and he finally stopped the beatings.

Although her body's wounds healed, her heart was blackened and bursting with hate. Her mind was occupied with thoughts of vengeance. She desired revenge on God for not giving her a rightful place in the hierarchy of angels and casting her from Floraison. She sought retaliation against Satan for the way he had mistreated her, and against Gadreel and Samael for turning their backs on her. She would never recover from the damages inflicted to her heart and mind. She was forever changed.

Though many lunar months came to pass, Gadreel never set eyes on Dagon or her little mermaids. She spent many moments staring out to sea. "I fear I shall never see Dagon or my daughters again," she whispered to the fish that surrounded her. "I miss them with all my heart." She lowered her head.

Samael kept his promise. He was kind toward her while she was mending from her injuries, and long after she had recovered from them.

Chapter 40

BIRTH OF THE INEVITABLE

Time continued on and they lingered on the beach. Lilith began to feel unwell and was unable to keep food within her. Every morning she became ill and expelled the contents of her stomach onto the beach. Her middle began to swell and her breasts engorged. She knew she was with child, and so did everyone else.

Once she had believed it would be a joyous occasion when this finally happened, but she detested the thing growing inside her. She huddled in hidden corners away from the others and wept. "Why do you go on living and growing inside of me?" She snarled and slammed her fists on her pregnant belly again and again. "I loathe you and I wish for your death!" Her body shook with sobs. She stopped, all of a sudden, wiped her face and changed her demeanor. "I must conceal my feelings." She hurried and raked her fingers through her hair in an aggressive manner and sauntered to shore.

One day, Lilith bent over in terrible pain. Blood gushed from her. She was alone gathering figs when the intense aches began. She fell to her knees, screaming and clutching her belly. No one came to her aid. She struggled to her feet and waddled to where the others were gathered and stood before them, blood streaming down her legs.

Gadreel gasped and scrambled to her side. Samael grimaced, turned his face and continued what he was doing. Satan strolled to her.

He placed his hand on her burgeoning stomach. "My offspring is not yet ready to be born." His voice was chilling. Lilith stared at him with wide eyes and Gadreel helped her sit under a tree.

Lilith groaned and writhed in convulsions of pain for days. The thing inside her clawed and kicked, stretching and expanding her belly. Gadreel held her hand and sang softly to her attempting to ease her pain while Satan and Samael ignored her.

Finally, the day arrived for the birth. Satan paced to and fro, unable to remain still. He grinned and laughed and tilted his head back and yelled, "My son is coming!" Samael shook with laughter and clapped his hands. Gadreel furrowed her brow and observed her.

Lilith lay sprawled, shrieking and beating on the ground in intolerable pain. She looked ashen and feeble. Her squinted eyes were bloodshot, and there were dark gray circles under them, since she had not rested in days.

Satan propped her against a tree and positioned himself between her legs.

"Hold her legs apart! My offspring shall be born." He grinned at the others and they rushed and did as he instructed.

Lilith sensed an overwhelming urge to push. She exerted several times under immense pressure and pain. At last, they saw a head crowning between her legs. It was large and gleaming red. It tore its way through her. She screamed through her teeth and clutched Gadreel and Samael's arms.

All eyes were fixed on the creature exiting her womb. As she feared and Gadreel predicted, the infant was the very likeness of its father's red alter ego, with one exception: it had a serpent's tail like its mother.

Gadreel stifled a scream. Samael recoiled with revulsion.

The small being was hairless and red. Two small, bony nubs protruded from its head. It was born with small, sharp claws on its hands. Two dark, bone-like lumps jutting out of its back indicated the creature would sprout wings in time. Its head and torso resembled theirs, but instead of legs, it carried a scaly serpent's tail. The male infant slithered through Lilith's opening and began to bawl.

Lilith whimpered, fearful Satan would discover her loathing of their newborn. She looked to Samael and Gadreel for sympathy, but she saw nothing but disgust and fear in their faces.

Satan took the infant and placed it upon her torso. The newborn slithered toward her head, led by its long, black tongue, which split into two prongs at the tip. The baby used its tongue to smell the milk in Lilith's breasts.

"Feed our offspring, for I sense his hunger." Satan raised his chin. She shook her head and scrunched her nose, but the small being reached her breast and began to suckle. She clenched her hands into fists so tight, her knuckles turned white and her nails cut into her palms. Blood from her hands dripped to the ground.

There was compassion on Gadreel's face, but Samael's face revealed only disgust. They left her side. "I cannot go on witnessing this horror," Samael told Gadreel in an undertone.

"Stay, please do not abandon me." Lilith trembled.

Gadreel glanced over her shoulder at her, but Samael pulled her away. Lilith's eyes burned with hatred as she watched them walk away.

Satan jerked her head in his direction. "I see how your face contorts with revulsion for our son." He glared at her clenching his jaw. "There are worse ways to suffer."

She shuddered and stared at him silently.

"This is my firstborn," Satan said, standing straighter jutting his chin. "Be certain he grows healthy and strong. Should any harm come to him, your own life shall be forfeit."

Lilith bobbed her head.

"His name shall be Dracul!" Satan lumbered away, abandoning her, like the others, to her motherly duties.

She wilted against the tree, and paid languid attention to her newborn. The nursling stopped suckling and fell asleep on top of her. She placed him on the ground by her side.

Lilith glared at the infant and shook her head. "I shall take suitable care of you, for your father demands it be so. You shall grow big and strong as he wishes, for my life depends on it, but I shall never love you."

Chapter 41

LILITH'S ILLUSIVE DESIGN

Themselves... The fallen angels witnessed many grand pas de deux performed by the sun and the moon. Gadreel and Samael grew closer with each passing day. "Since the day Lilith injured you, Satan has not taken possession of me," Samael said.

"That makes me very happy," Gadreel said in a flat tone.

Samael narrowed his eyes. "You do not look pleased."

Gadreel looked at him. "Oh no, I am happy for you, but my mind is occupied with thoughts of Dagon and my little mermaids. I have lost hope of ever seeing them again." She hung her head. Samael moved closer and place an arm around her shoulders.

Lilith took good care of her infant, not because she loved him, or because she had any maternal instincts, but simply because the quality of her life was directly related to the wellbeing of the child. If anything happened to him, his father promised her a fate worse than death. So Dracul grew into a strong, healthy boy.

Lilith's relationship with Satan became even more tense, cold, and unpleasant. She feared he no longer treasured her as he once did, which meant she might not be able to bring her plans of revenge to fruition. This was a great burden in her mind, as her thirst for vengeance grew with each passing day.

It had been a long time since Satan attacked her in the form of the red fiend, and she did not know if it might be to ensure she was well to care for his son, or whether she no longer appealed to him.

One morning as she sat feeding her child, she noticed Samael and Gadreel sneaking away together.

"You stay here under this tree, Dracul. I shall return as soon as possible." The child smiled and nodded.

She followed them to a small grotto they had been using as a love nest. She hid from their sight and watched as they engaged in sexual feats. They seemed blissful in each other's arms. Lilith's eyes narrowed as she witnessed the lovers. "They experience great pleasure and happiness while I suffer." She watched them with a sour expression and crossed her arms. "I am consumed with desire to see harm befall those who have wronged me."

She stormed to the beach and began to think of ways to put herself in control once again. It was her thirst for vengeance that willed her to go on living. While her son built objects in the sand, she hatched a plan. Her scheme would change everything.

That night as her son slept, Lilith minced her way up to Satan, her mind fixed on a plan.

"My prince." It had been quite some time since she called him such. "It has been too long since we lay together. I miss you."

Satan cocked his head and narrowed his eyes. "You wish to lay with me?"

"I yearn for it," she told him with bated breath.

"You know what I shall become if we do this."

"I no longer care." She looked down and shrugged. "The red being is part of who you are, and I desire to embrace every part of you. I love you. The love I feel for our son has taught me this."

He tilted his head to the side and smiled in return. "I have never stopped loving you. You are as beautiful and desirable as ever." He gazed into her eyes. "It also pleases me to know how much you cherish our son." She stroked his arm as she listened.

"Has he not grown big and strong?" She beamed. "Only a mother's love can ensure that."

Satan took her into his arms and embraced her. As her head lay on his chest she wore a sardonic grin.

She pushed away and gazed up at him through her lashes. "We must forget the unpleasant things that have transpired between us in the past. Let this be a new beginning for our sakes and for that of our beloved Dracul." She licked her lips.

He smiled a smile that crinkled his eyes and nose and then he cocked his head back and laughed. He kissed her tenderly and it was simple to see that he believed all of her deceits.

He made love to her in the form of the red fiend, and she moaned, stretched, and gyrated playing the part of happy and satisfied lover. She often turned her face and grimaced in disgust and displeasure but her need for justice was great. She believed she was validated in her indignation and her need to retaliate for hurts to her body, mind and sense of identity. She had lay dormant for too long; now, she would do whatever was necessary.

Afterward, she lay in Satan's arms, caressing and kissing him as she had always done to his angel form—only he had not transformed yet and was still the red fiend. He looked content and relaxed. She devised her next move.

"My darling prince, I believe it is time we left this beach. What say you?" She widened her smile, which in her experience could open more hearts than a dagger.

"I must admit, I have been thinking of moving on for quite some time." He ogled her. "Where should we go?"

Lilith caressed his red face and stared into the black hollows that were his eyes, and tried not to tremble. "You mentioned once you desired to find the Garden of Eden—a grand and flawless plan. Samael has already been there and can indicate the way."

Satan frowned.

"If you are concerned about our son, you need not fret," Lilith said. "He is robust and intelligent like his father. He shall only grow stronger and wiser with this journey. Imagine the life we could give him if paradise was our home."

"The Garden of Eden is protected," Satan said in a tight voice.

"Samael spoke of strolling into the garden without difficulties. He only mentioned Cam as the protector of the garden. Cam is strong, but he is but one, whereas we are four." She leaned forward.

Satan cocked his head left and rolled his eyes to right corner of the sky. "What of the humans inhabiting the garden? They shall not freely give up the home God provided them."

"No, my prince, but if seduced and corrupted by us, they shall feel compelled to leave." Lilith kissed Satan's face as he pondered her scheme. "If not, we shall expel them ourselves. Once they have sinned against God, they would no longer have his protection or that of the holy angels."

Satan grinned and nodded. "When the next day gives way to night, we shall begin our journey to the Garden of Eden."

She leapt into his arms, kissing him and laughing with delight. He chuckled.

Lilith embraced him. Soon her plans would come to pass and she would have her vengeance.

The next morning, she was up with the sun, anxious to tell their plans to Samael and Gadreel. She found them asleep in each other's arms in their trench near the water.

"Rise, my friends! I have wonderful tidings for you," Lilith shouted.

Gadreel jolted awake. Lilith loomed over her, standing in front of the sun, which outlined her form with radiance. Her face was alive with joy. Her long hair floated in the sea breeze. Rarely had she seen her so cheerful.

Gadreel nudged Samael and he awakened.

"Tell us your joyous news." Gadreel rubbed her eyes.

"Satan has decided we shall leave this coming night in search of the Garden of Eden." Lilith's tone was cheerful.

Gadreel and Samael glanced at each other, their eyes teeming with dread.

"We are happy here." Gadreel tilted her head and furrowed her brow. "Why would we leave this place?"

"You are merely comfortable with familiar surroundings. Think of how much happier we would be living in paradise," Lilith said.

"Although we are not far from the Garden of Eden, the journey shall still be arduous, and when we arrive, we shall not be welcomed." Samael frowned, and bit his lip.

Lilith rolled her eyes skyward. "We have grown lazy and complacent on this beach, but we do not belong here. We merit much more than the humans. We deserve to live in paradise." Lilith's demeanor was sweet, but assertive. "Do not concern yourself about the journey's toil. We have been through much worse. As for my son, he is powerful like his father."

Samael threw his hands up in the air, his arguments spent.

Gadreel wrapped her arms around herself. "By entering the Garden of Eden and attempting to occupy it, we would once again disobey God and challenge the holy angels."

Lilith waved a dismissive hand. Gadreel lowered her head. Lilith was again in power.

"Prepare for the journey, for as I told you, we leave this night," Lilith said with a honeyed voice before proceeding to her son.

She woke Dracul, fed him and took him to the shore. She had a feeling Satan would be observing her every move over the next few days to ensure things were truly set right between them.

So Lilith built sand figures with her son, frolicked in the ocean with him, and lavished him with cuddles and kisses. Everything expected of a loving mother, she did for Satan's eyes. When the midday sun grew strong, she took Dracul and Satan to Gadreel and Samael's secret grotto, pretending to have discovered it. She lay her son down and when Dracul fell asleep, she seduced Satan and made love to him again and again to fortify her dominance over him.

When her son awoke, she tended to his every need. Lilith put on a great show for Satan and the others. As the night grew closer, the fallen angels gathered coconuts, figs, dates and water to bring with them on their journey. They also made sunshades out of enormous leaves. They held on to the large, thick leafstalk, and the leaf lamina shielded them from the sun's rays. When the sand ceased to glitter like thousands of tiny crystals, and touches of pink and purple covered the sky, they began their journey to the Garden of Eden.

Chapter 42

SCHEMES SET IN MOTION

They traveled inland for many moons, heading northeast through the desert. They flew above mountains, resting only during the midday sun to feed Satan's son. Dracul had grown significantly since the onset of their quest.

"Are you certain we are headed in the right direction, Samael?" Lilith appeared weary of travel.

"Indeed, I did say the journey would be arduous." Samael licked his lips.

"Yes, but you also spoke of the Garden being close at hand." Lilith scowled at him.

"We are close now," Samael said to the others' sounds of relief.

Satan grinned at his son, who did not seem burdened by the demanding trek. Dracul was no longer a small child, but a strong boy. The horns on his head were beginning to curve back like his father's. His small, pointy teeth had developed into fangs. His canines were predominantly larger, longer, and sharper than the rest. His nails grew into sharp claws, which Lilith filed down with rocks on a daily basis so he would not accidentally hurt her. His snake tail grew long and strong, boasting an assortment of colors like the pale blue of the late morning sky and the rich azure of twilight. His tail also displayed the yellows and gold of the setting sun, the intense green of emerald crystals, and the shade of fresh blood.

Coconut milk and figs no longer satisfied Dracul. He and his father hunted rabbits and other small animals whose blood gratified Dracul, and whose flesh was shared amongst Satan, Lilith and Samael. Gadreel still refused to consume animal flesh.

Dracul was cunning and intelligent like his mother and strong and majestic like his father. He was also becoming an eloquent speaker.

"We are fortunate, Lilith," Satan said, "for we have not encountered any of the dangers you, Gadreel, or Samael suffered when you traveled through the desert and over the mountains."

"Fortune and chance have played no part in this, my love. We are simply better prepared this time, since we now know what to expect." Lilith arched a sly brow. "We have brought along plenty to eat and drink to keep us strong. We have fashioned sunshades to cover us. We know what to do when the sun is at its most fierce. We also recognize which areas to avoid and fly over, thus this knowledge has kept us safe."

"You are wise as you are beautiful, my treasure." Satan kissed her hand.

Gadreel rolled her eyes and shook her head.

"I wish to fly, Father, now that the sun is mild," Dracul said.

Satan stroked his son's head. Together, they took flight. Lilith and the others followed.

Dracul's black, leathery wings boasted twice the span of his small body. He was able to fly at great speeds, his long multi-colored tail moved sinuously behind him. From the sky, Samael saw a familiar sight in the distance.

"We have arrived in paradise!" Samael indicated the verdant patch. "There! The green cover in the distance with the four rivers flowing beyond it in four distinct directions."

"What do we do now?" Lilith looked at Samael. "We cannot just land in the garden."

Samael shook his head. "We should land a short distance from the garden and walk inside as I did beforehand."

The fallen angels landed as he advised, a brief walk from the entrance to the Garden.

"I glimpsed a large, dense growth of trees from the sky. It is right beyond the Garden. Perhaps we should camp there until we have a plan," Lilith said.

Satan nodded. "That is an inspired suggestion. We must have a plan of action."

The angels moved by foot to the nearby forest.

Gadreel stopped short of the woodland's entrance. "Have you forgotten the forests surrounding Guidance Park in Floraison? They were dangerous, dark places, bursting with hostile vegetation. What if this wilderness is equally perilous?"

Lilith heaved an exasperated sigh. "Everywhere we turn, we run risk of pain and death. This planet does not care about any of us. We are but bits of dust passing through. We were banished from Floraison to suffer on Earth, while God's humans live in paradise, oblivious to pain, sadness, and suffering. This is God's design, but we shall ruin His perfect plans with our own."

The others stood silently listening as she spewed venom.

"My prince," she said. "I think we should venture into the Garden together. You can spy on Adam, while I observe Eve. I am certain that together we can devise a plan to corrupt God's prized creations."

Satan nodded with raised eyebrows. "Your words are wise, and I shall heed your plan. Gadreel and Samael, you stay hidden in the forest. Lilith and I shall enter the garden. I leave you responsible for my son." Satan directed his fierce gaze at Samael, who gulped.

Lilith and Satan proceeded toward the Garden of Eden. Gadreel and Samael took Dracul by the hand, and entered the forest.

"Gadreel, why do you squeeze my hand so?" Dracul creased his small brow.

"Apologies, little one. It was not my intention." Gadreel twisted her face in fear.

"Do not be frightened." Dracul stood straighter and pushed out his chest. "I shall protect you." Gadreel patted his head. Samael chuckled.

She pointed to a small cave not too deep into the woods. "Perhaps we could wait in this small cavern. It appears to be harmless."

They entered the hollow and settled in.

It was not long before Samael and Gadreel became involved with each other, and Dracul grew bored. Distracted by their sexual spree, they did not notice Satan's son exiting the cave.

Chapter 43

TAINTED INNOCENCE

L ilith and Satan proceeded into the Garden of Eden. As they stepped
across the threshold, they experienced feelings that were difficult to
put into words—a joyous tranquility, as if a heavy load had been
lifted. The lighting was unique to any they had seen on Earth and closer
to the magnificent light of Floraison and the temperature was perfect. The
unique hues and effects of trees and flowers captivated them.

"Behold! Some blossoms seem to glow, while others shimmer." Lilith
stared openmouthed.

Trees possessed a life of their own: some bore enticing fruit, while others
had leaves that produced mellifluous melodies as they quivered in the soft
breeze.

Satan grinned. "Strolling on this lush, soft grass is like walking on air."

Lilith stared wide-eyed at the exceptional scenery. "I have never
beheld such sights. It is a shame this place has been wasted on
humans all this time."

"We should now go on separate pathways," Satan
whispered. "I shall locate Adam. You find Eve."

They parted ways, but quickly rejoined when
they found Adam and Eve together near a

beautiful lake, not unlike Floraison's own Lake Serena. They hid behind plants with large leaves to observe them.

"Your beauty rivals that of any flower," Adam told Eve. She kissed him ever so softly on the lips.

As Lilith observed the pair through narrowed eyes, she took notice of their blissful innocence, especially Eve's. She was overwhelmed by a desire to soil her essence.

Adam left Eve's side to tend to another area of the Garden, followed by Satan. Lilith stayed behind to continue to watch Eve, who lay on her stomach, admiring her own reflection in the lake's still waters.

Lilith hurried to find Satan. When she found him she smiled, the kind of smile that shows all of your teeth. "The human woman is simple and vain. I shall use this knowledge to bring about her disgrace."

"I also gathered much information about the man. He sings many songs about Eve as he tends the garden. Adam's love for Eve is pure. To bring shame on him, one simply has to taint her first, and he would certainly follow."

"Consent to leave this place, for we have much to discuss and conspire," Lilith said, as she licked her lips.

Satan nodded, and they headed for the forest.

When Gadreel and Samael finished their lustful deeds, they realized Dracul was nowhere to be found. Gadreel scurried around in circles within the small cave, trying to find him. She gawked at Samael, and nibbled at her fingers.

"Satan shall destroy us if we fail to find his son."

Samael took hold of her upper arms. "Do not fear. He cannot be far. I shall search the forest and find him. You stay here in case he returns to the cave."

In the woods, Samael ran into Lilith and Satan.

"Where are Gadreel and Dracul?" Satan scowled.

"They are together in a safe place." Samael lowered his head.

"We should return to the Garden of Eden with Samael." Lilith's eyes glinted with eagerness.

"To what purpose?" Satan looked askance at her. "We only departed the Garden but a moment ago."

"I recalled Samael's narrative of his chance encounter with Eve." She turned to Samael. "Did you not express that there was a mutual attraction between you and the woman?"

Samael smirked. "Yes, there was an undeniable attraction between us."

"This is perfect for my—our plans. Do you not see?" she said. "Samael shall be the vessel we use to corrupt Eve and rid her of her purity and innocence, thereby forfeiting her right to live in paradise. Thus, as we were cast out of Floraison for breaking the rules, so shall she be expelled from the Garden, and surely Adam shall follow her. Hence, the Garden of Eden shall become our home, and I—we get our vengeance against God by ruining his prized creation."

Satan and Samael glanced at each other nodding.

"Let us take leave of the forest and return to the Garden at once." Lilith's bosom heaved with rapid breaths.

"Indeed, I shall do all that is required of me." Samael exhaled and relaxed since the subject of Dracul's whereabouts had been dropped. He hoped the young one would make his way back to the cave before they returned.

The three of them slipped back into the Garden of Eden. They remained unseen, and found Eve alone once more, marveling at the fruits of an unusual tree.

"Go on. Approach her in silence and be at your most charming." Lilith coaxed Samael.

While in hiding, Lilith and Satan watched his every move.

"Another chance encounter, beautiful Eve," Samael whispered, trying not to startle her with his presence.

Eve gasped. "You should not be in this place." She pivoted on her heel and fled, then skidded to an abrupt halt when he spoke again. She looked over her shoulder and peered at him.

"I am aware of the danger this place holds for me, but I could not stay away any longer." Samael shoved his hair back away from his face. "I needed to set eyes on your exquisite face once more before I perish."

Eve's eyes widened and she turned to face him slowly. "Perish? Why do you utter such things?"

"Your beauty has sealed my fate. I cannot forget the curves of your face, the outline of your roseate lips, or the radiance of your eyes as they caress me the way they do now." He took a couple steps toward her. "You haunt my thoughts. I was compelled to look upon you once more—even under the penalty of death."

Eve placed her hands over her heart and her bosom heaved with rapid breaths. "Stranger, you risk much for a mere glimpse of my face." Her eyes remained fixed on him as he swaggered toward her.

Samael maintained eye contact and he moved closer still. "Please do not fear me. I would give my life to protect you."

She flushed bright pink. "I do not understand the changes occurring in my body."

"Do you feel a heat rising inside of you?" A smiled dangled on the corner of his lips.

She nodded and gazed up at him through her long lashes.

"That warm, pulsating feeling is natural." He tucked a lock of hair behind her ear and gently brushed her neck.

She stared at him in awe. His warm gold irises were strikingly wolf-like and alluring. She allowed him to caress her face. She closed her eyes and he leaned forward and breathed in the scent of her hair. He nuzzled his nose and mouth against her neck, giving her soft kisses and inhaling the aroma of her skin.

She inhaled a sharp breath and moved away a little. "What are you doing?"

Samael leaned forward and whispered against her ear, "Certainly you shall not let me draw my last breath without ever having tasted the sweet nectar of your lips?"

Eve's lips parted slightly and she quivered. He kissed her on the lips and curled his arms around her, drew her body close, and after a few delicate touches of his warm lips on her lips, neck, and bosom her resistance crumbled. She arched her neck and moaned, wholly captivated by his tender, yet animalistic, ways.

Eve did not fully understand the consequences of their actions. Her eyes glazed over and stared into space overwhelmed by feelings of elation and profound pleasure that she had never felt with Adam.

Samael, in one fluid motion lowered her to the grass and continued kissing her. Every kiss carried electric tingles and she groaned and arched her neck. He flashed heat in his eyes, his body, poised the perfect blend of relaxation and tension. She was ensnared by the delight he bestowed upon her. He slipped inside of her, and they were both in ecstasy.

Lilith and Satan watched, concealed behind foliage as Samael had his way with Eve. Lilith closed her eyes and a monstrous grin distorted her face. She gave a low, strained humorless laugh and opened her eyes to look at Satan.

His eyes were fixed on Samael and Eve. "I must be a part of this—the downfall of God's most valued creatures."

Lilith twisted her mouth and raised the eyebrow over her blue eye. "Go on, my prince. Finish what Samael has begun. Spill seed in her so our kind may multiply on this planet, and God's plan may be ruined."

Satan leapt into Samael's body and copulated with Eve until he burst forth semen within her. Afterward, he released Samael, who rolled off her to the ground by her side howling and twitching in anguish. Steam discharged from his ears and out of his nostrils. His face was a deep scarlet and he smelled of burnt pyres.

Eve jumped to her feet and stared at him with a terrified expression. "What is happening to you?" She stepped back. Samael could not form words as his face contorted in agony. She cringed and ran away.

Eve ran to the Tree of Knowledge of Good and Evil. She prostrated herself before it as primal tears fell from her eyes.

Lilith changed into her snake form and followed her. She hid behind the extraordinary tree to watch her for a moment. The look of confusion and fear on Eve's face aroused her.

"Why do you weep?" Lilith asked in an ingratiating tone.

"Who are you?" Eve's lips quivered.

Lilith tilted her head and smiled the kind of smile one reserves for special friends. "I am someone who means you no harm. I wish to help you." Her voice was sweet as ripened grapes. She hid her serpent tail behind the tree, and kept her wings tucked, so that Eve only saw her agreeable face and torso.

Lilith heard a rustling of leaves above her. She lifted her eyes to see her son amongst the tree's many branches and for a moment, she was distracted from her purpose.

What was Dracul doing in the Garden? And why did he perch on the branches of this peculiar tree?

Dracul plucked a fruit from the tree and swooped down from the branch where he sat. Eve shuddered when she saw him. He landed before the woman and offered her the fruit. Eve shook her head gaping at the little red fiend.

"We must not partake of the fruit this tree bears." Eve held up her hands and leaned back while waggling her palms. "This is the Tree of the Knowledge of Good and Evil. We are forbidden to eat of it."

Lilith cocked her head and raised her brow. Tree of Knowledge of Good and Evil. If Eve eats of this tree, her eyes shall be opened to her betrayal of Adam with Samael, and she shall be innocent no more.

Dracul slunk closer to Eve and dropped the forbidden fruit by her side. He then slithered to his mother.

"Eat of the fruit." Lilith attempted to wheedle her to disobey God. "We are the keepers of this tree. If you eat of it, you shall gain wisdom. Soon after your first bite, you shall understand everything that perplexes you. Adam would be most impressed by you. And only then shall he forgive you for your acts against him." Eve frowned. "Eat the fruit. It is the only way you can redeem yourself in his eyes. God shall not be angry, for you shall become his equal."

Eve was gullible and vain. She aspired to be great in Adam's eyes and to please him, but most of all she enjoyed the concept of being wise and sagacious. She reached for the fruit and held it in her hand.

Lilith leaned forward watching her with steady eye contact and raised eyebrows. Go on—eat of the fruit. One bite is all it shall take to disgrace you further. She licked her lips as the tip of her tail rattled.

Eve ate several bites of the fruit. Her head cocked back in an abrupt movement and a powerful beam of light flashed from her eyes. She inhaled a long, loud breath, as her eyes were unsealed. Her eyes opened wide and she trembled. Wise to every wrong she had committed, she buried her face in her hands, rocking back and forth on the ground, gasping and sobbing.

Lilith looked upon her with disdain. "This is only the beginning."

Eve lifted her head and stared at Lilith, her eyes widening with recognition. The color drained from her face, as she understood the cruel deception.

After a while, Satan and Samael joined Lilith. At the sight of Dracul, Samael's eyebrows rose high.

"What is my son doing here?" Satan frowned. Samael looked to the ground.

"I know not, but he has been of great help to us," Lilith said, unable to peel her eyes away from Eve. Satan stroked the little one's bald red head with affection.

"You claimed my son was safe with Gadreel in the forest." Satan scowled at Samael.

"Apologies." Samael ran his hands through his hair and avoided Satan's gaze. "He was safe with Gadreel in a small cave we found. He must have slipped away without notice and followed me when I left the cave."

Lilith waved a dismissive hand. "It is of no importance. Our son is safe and with us now. He has served me well."

Eve lay crumpled on the ground, an inconsolable wretch. Her face was crimson with distress and fear. Samael stared at her looking shamefaced, and crossed his arms.

Eve lifted her haunting gaze to him. "You are the greatest liar of all." She looked as if she wanted to say more, but was unable to find the words. She hung her head.

"It is done?" Satan asked Lilith.

"It is done, but we must not leave this place until we know Adam has met Eve's fate," Lilith said in an undertone. Satan nodded.

"We must remain here. It shall not be long before Adam misses his woman.

He shall return to find her," Samael said in a gruff voice, breathless, still suffering the impacts of Satan's possession.

"He speaks out of turn, yet verity escapes his mouth," Satan told Lilith with a sardonic tone, as he glared at Samael.

Samael bowed his head. "I recognize you are still angered by my betrayal. Know that I would do anything to ascend in your eyes once again."

Satan stood straighter, shoulders back and chest pushed forward. "Waiting in secret for Adam is a sound idea." Hence, they hid and waited.

Chapter 44

CONSUMED FOR LOVE

Adam was tending the Garden when Gabriel appeared before him. Adam jumped and recoiled. At first Gabriel was no more than a shimmer of mist. Through him the edges of the trees and bushes became blurred. It was not until he spoke that he congealed into a form, an angel with brilliant white eyes and silvery skin, and a horn dangling from one hand.

"Do not fear me, for I am a messenger of God," Gabriel said. "You and Eve are not alone in the Garden of Eden this day. I sense malevolent beings roaming this place, and your woman is in great danger. Find her before it is too late." Having delivered his warning, Gabriel vanished.

Adam gasped, dropped the crops he carried and ran in search of Eve.

"Eve!" he yelled. "Where are you?"

When he finally found her. She lay on the ground before the Tree of Knowledge of Good and Evil, looking like a wilted flower. Adam tilted his head and stared at her with a confused expression.

"Eve, I have been searching for you. Did you not hear my calls?"

She shook her head, having learned to be deceitful.

"An angel appeared to me. He spoke of creatures in the Garden that mean to do us harm." Adam scrutinized her. Sorrow was etched on her face and her downcast eyes made him apprehensive. Her face flushed. He looked at the tree and then at the ground where a half-eaten fruit rested. He trembled.

"Please assure me you did not eat of this tree!"

She avoided his pleading gaze. "I did not eat of this tree, for I know it is forbidden."

Adam blew his cheeks out, knelt beside her and embraced her.

The sound of a horn jolted them. Its timbre was complex and poetic and it was heard throughout the garden. Adam looked around. The resonance of the horn imbued their senses once more. Eve began to spasm and jerk in his arms, soft whimpering sounds escaped her lips, and her eyes again became cascades.

"What troubles you, my love?" Adam asked whilst the bright, insistent sound of Gabriel's Horn of Truth filled their ears.

"I ate the fruit of the Tree of Knowledge of Good and Evil!" Eve covered her ears. "I have done horrid things for which I shall never be forgiven by you or by God."

Adam stared at her and moved away shaking his head.

"Why would you do such a thing?" He touched his eyes and stared at his fingers wet with tears. He clambered to his feet and his body drooped.

"I was deceived." Eve wept into her hands.

"She sought to gain knowledge." Lilith stepped from behind the bushes to reveal her angel form. "She shall be taken from you now."

"No! I shall never leave her side, for she is my companion, and I love her above all else." Adam stood straighter.

"The choice shall not be your own," Lilith said.

Adam clasped his hands over his head and paced side to side. Lilith strolled to him and placed a hand over his heart. He froze and stared with puckered brow.

"Your heart flutters like the wings of a bird caught in a spider web." She turned away. "There is but one way you can remain with your woman. You must join her in her disobedience to God. You must also eat of the fruit of this tree." She gave a half shrug. "It is the only way you can remain together."

Adam looked at Eve's expression, which was frantic with fear, and made his choice. Lilith picked a fruit from the Tree of Knowledge of Good and Evil and sashayed to him.

She placed the fruit in his hand. "Savor the taste of awareness." She walked around him. "This fruit shall nourish your body and give you godlike wisdom."

Adam held the cold fruit in his hand. Lilith watched him with a fixed stare and passed her tongue over her lips. He glanced at Eve's woeful face once more, and took a reluctant bite.

Lilith threw her head back and shook with laughter. It was a cold, shrill cackle, piercing the air. She had damaged God's prized beings. Her vengeance would soon be complete.

Adam finished the fruit, and like Eve, his eyes were opened. He ogled his wife's gorgeous naked body through different eyes. He heaved quick, shallow breaths. "A swarming heat surges through my body." He took Eve's hand and led her away from Lilith's presence to a delightful lagoon. He tugged his wife closer. "I am unable to control my urges." He kissed her with fervor, and they had lustful sex in the Garden.

"You are a changed man, and I too am a different woman." She gazed at him, and the tormented look on his face made her tremble. "Fear creeps into my soul and overwhelms my body, making it weary. We disobeyed God."

Adam wrapped his arms around her and they wept together. He whispered against her ear in a somber tone that was frightening. "We must hide."

Chapter 45

FRUIT OF WISDOM

"We can leave this place, for we have succeeded at what we embarked on." Lilith jutted her chin. "We shall return once God has expelled the humans from the Garden. Thenceforth, we shall make this paradise our home."

"Perhaps we, too, should partake of this tree, Father," Dracul said. "I am hungry, and I, too, desire to be wise like God."

Satan chuckled. He plucked a fruit from the tree, and as he passed the fruit to Dracul, it became sand in his hand and slipped through his fingers. Satan inhaled a sharp breath and grabbed another fruit, but it too disintegrated into sand in his hand. He made several more attempts, but each time the fruit crumbled. He stepped back.

Lilith narrowed her eyes and plucked a fruit from the tree. Without hesitation, she bit into it. The fruit turned to sand in her mouth. She coughed and gagged and spit, trying to rid herself of the gritty silt in her mouth.

Before long, the entire tree began to disintegrate, becoming sand, mixing with the soil on the ground. Satan picked Dracul from the ground and stared openmouthed as the Tree of Knowledge of Good and Evil ceased to exist.

The fallen angels gaped at the area where it once stood.

"There is yet another tree far greater than this one," Samael revealed with an audible tremor in his voice. "It is located in the center of the Garden. It is called the Tree of Life. This tree can give us amazing powers. We can gain immortality and wisdom upon eating of its fruit."

"Let us partake of the fruit of this tree and become gods." Lilith bobbed her head.

"Will the fruit from the Tree of Life not also become sand in our hands?" Dracul creased his little brow.

"We have no way of knowing that, my son, but that should not deter us from trying." Satan put him down.

"There is but one obstacle." Samael gulped and rubbed the back of his neck. "The Tree of Life is guarded by Cam and his flaming sword."

"Cam is but one, and we are three!" Lilith clenched her fists. "Besides, the fact that this tree is guarded indicates that the fruit may indeed be eaten by us."

"Lilith's logic is undeniable," Satan said. "We shall leave the Garden, reunite with Gadreel, and form a strategy, thus we shall have a better chance of succeeding."

"Why do we need Gadreel?" Lilith put her hands on her hips.

"Four against one is better than three against one. Is it not?" Satan said.

"Yes, you are wise." Lilith turned her face and rolled her eyes skyward.

Satan took her by the hand. Dracul flew to Satan's shoulders and rode with his tail wrapped around his neck. Samael followed them. They departed the Garden of Eden, forsaking Adam and Eve to suffer their disobedience and face God's wrath alone.

Chapter 46

GADREEL'S PENITENCE

They entered the forest near the Garden and quickly found the cave. Gadreel sat, back curved, legs bent and drawn up to her torso. Head bowed as she hugged her knees and rocked.

"Gadreel," Samael said in a blasé voice. "We are back."

Upon seeing Dracul riding on Satan's shoulders, she jumped up and danced around. "Dracul! You are safe!"

Samael opened his eyes wide at her and pressed a finger to his lips without letting the others see. "Of course, he is safe, why would he not be?"

Heat bloomed across Gadreel's face, painting her skin a shade of rose. "I am happy to see him."

Dracul swooped off his father's shoulder to hug her. She kissed his shiny red head, and they all laughed. Samael took a deep breath relieved their incompetence was not revealed.

Lilith tilted her head back and yelled, "Triumph!" She chuckled and looked at Gadreel. "Our task in the Garden of Eden is almost done. God's prized creations are tainted. Adam and Eve are no longer pure or perfect as God intended."

Gadreel froze and stared with wide eyes and raised eyebrows.

"We returned from the Garden for one purpose only," Lilith said. "To form a plan to defeat Cam, who guards a sacred tree that can give us godlike immortality."

Gadreel's shoulders slumped and she stared at the ground with an agonized expression. Another day amongst them seemed unbearable and she missed Dagon and her daughters. She must flee, but how? Unsure of what to do next, she remained silent and listened to their schemes.

Lilith glanced at her sideways.

"We must forge weapons from raw materials that the forest shall provide. We must not enter the Garden empty-handed," Satan said. Lilith and Samael nodded and left in search of objects to be shaped into weapons. Gadreel remained seated, staring at the cave floor.

"Have you ceased to believe in our cause?" Satan raised his eyebrows.

Gadreel rose to her feet and moved about, inspecting her fingernails. "I—I thought I would stay behind with the little prince." She shifted her weight to the balls of her feet.

"Very well, but be certain this time he remains in the cave," Satan said in a somber tone.

"I shall take good care of him." She scratched her nose and avoided his eyes.

With a deep sigh, Satan hurried to join the others. As soon as he was gone, Gadreel planned her escape.

"Dracul, you are an intelligent little being, thus, I shall not fret to leave you on your own." She held on to his shoulders.

"Why must you leave me?" Dracul's eyes were large and doleful.

She passed her hand over his hairless head. "This may be difficult for you to understand but unlike Lilith, Satan and Samael, I yet wish to return to God's good graces, and I am unable to obtain pleasure from destroying other beings. I am determined to never again allow Lilith to manipulate me into situations that make me feel unworthy of God's love. There is good in you, Dracul. Remember that. Hold on to it despite what you see happening around you." She kissed the top of his head. "Besides, I, too, have little ones like you. I miss them. I need to find them, for it has been too long since I have held them in my arms."

"I shall go with you and help you find them."

She kissed him again. "No, Dracul. If you follow me, I shall be punished. You must vow to stay in the cave until your father and mother return. Stay, I implore you. Otherwise my life shall be forfeit."

Dracul nodded, wearing a frown. "I shall stay in the cave until my father returns."

When his words of promise reached her ears, she took flight. She flew at full speed toward the beach where she last saw Dagon and her little mermaids.

Dracul followed her with his eyes until he could no longer see her. He lowered his head and sniffed, holding back tears.

When the others returned, they found him alone entertaining himself with a bat pup he found hanging upside down in the cave.

"Where is Gadreel?" Lilith scowled as she looked about the cave.

"She fled." Dracul said. "But she made me promise to remain in the cave until you and my father returned."

"What do you mean, she fled?" Lilith's face flushed a raging red.

"She said she needed to find her little ones—like me." Dracul looked as innocent as a daisy. His pet bat now hung from one of his horns and he giggled.

"And you allowed her to leave?" Lilith yelled, making him jump.

"Enough! Do not yell at our son! He is an innocent," Satan said. "It is not his doing that Gadreel abandoned us."

"I seek retribution for her betrayal!" Lilith's nostrils flared and her eyes glinted in anger.

Samael's face slackened, he shrunk back against the cave wall. "Gadreel, what have you done?" he said, under his breath.

"Another time, perhaps. We have more pressing matters now," Satan said.

"No! We shall leave now before she gets too far out of our reach." Her face contorted in an all-consuming rage. Dracul jolted. Satan glowered at her. He shifted into the red fiend and clenched his jaw.

"I have already spoken on the matter." He grasped her neck with a clawed hand. "Raise your voice to me again, and I shall quiet you for an eternity." When he released her, she gasped for air and collapsed to her knees, coughing and rubbing her throat. His fingers left stinging scorch marks on her skin.

Satan turned his sights on Dracul, who was curled into a ball, wide-eyed and trembling. "Do not fear, my son, for no harm shall ever come to you."

Lilith glared at Satan and watched him through eyes burning with hatred as he strolled away, carrying his beloved son on his shoulders. Samael glanced at her, but looked away when their eyes met. He followed Satan, out of the cave.

For all the ways Satan had made her suffer, she would take away that which was most precious to him, inflicting equal wounding. Her revenge was almost complete.

Day gave way to night as Satan and Samael worked hard to construct weapons worthy of fighting Cam. Using wood, bones, horns, bark, and other materials found in the forest, they made spears, lances, and knives. "I have decided it would be best if we return to the Garden of Eden in the light of day. In the Garden, the debilitating effects of the sun do not affect us. We must rest this night, so we may be revitalized and strong in the morning." Satan sighed and made himself comfortable next to Lilith, but she turned away from him. Dracul slept at his side.

Samael slumbered alone in a dark corner of the cave. "Why would Gadreel abandon me?" He placed a hand over the black, heart-shaped mark Cam had inflicted over his own heart. "I shall never give my heart to another."

Chapter 47

LILITH'S NURTURING WAYS

The sun introduced a new day, although inside the cave it was yet dark. Lilith's body alerted her it was morning, and she rose in the darkness. She strolled from the cave and looked to the east. Slivers of sunlight peeked through the trees. She returned to the cave to wake the others.

"Wake up, for the sun rises in the sky." She nudged Satan.

"It is yet dark." He shifted.

"Only in this forest," she said, and jostled Samael awake with her foot.

Satan sat upright, and woke his son. "Today is the day we shall acquire everything that is due us."

Samael nodded. Lilith wore a smirk.

"Is it time to go?" Dracul's eyelids were heavy.

Lilith portrayed the nurturing mother. "We shall eat first, my son."

They hunted in the forest and caught several small animals. Satan allowed Dracul to first drain the animals of their blood while they yet lived. Later, they shared the flesh.

Lilith observed her son with loathing whilst he drained the animals of their life force. She noticed how he sank his fangs into an animal's neck, creating two holes from which he drew its blood.

Her son grew taller and stronger by the day, and his father taught him to be an efficient hunter. Soon he would be able to overpower her. She must act quickly if her plans were to come to pass. While rubbing the blistering burn marks Satan left on her neck after nearly strangling her to death, she conceived a plan.

"Satan, my prince, I have growing concerns." Lilith frowned.

"What troubles you, my treasure?" Satan furrowed his brow. She slid her hand along her throat as she spoke to remind him of what he had done.

"I have a foreboding regarding our son." She brooded. "I fear he shall not fare well if he goes into the Garden of Eden with us. He must remain here, but I dare not leave him alone as the callous Gadreel did. I shall stay behind to protect him."

"Did you see this in one of your visions?" Satan asked.

"Yes, but my vision was unclear." Lilith trembled, terrified he would read her thoughts.

He took her hand and kissed it. "You fret so for our son. You tremble and I also see fear in your eyes. Your great love for our son moves me. If I hurt you, it is not what I desired."

"It is of no consequence now," Lilith said. Satan kissed her on the lips. When he turned to look at his son, she grimaced and wiped her mouth, for his kiss had long ago ceased being dulcet, and left a bitter taste in her mouth.

He stood straighter and jutted his chin. "Very well, Samael and I shall confront Cam without you. When we defeat him, we shall partake of the Tree of Life. We shall return for you and Dracul, so the two of you can gain immortality as well. Thenceforth, we shall reign on this planet as gods."

Lilith smiled while the corners of her mouth fought to fall and reveal her true self, but she could not expose herself yet, so her rage sat behind the facade and waited for the right moment. She placed her arm around her son and kissed his head. Dracul winced, for he seldom received her affection.

Satan and Samael uttered their farewells and began their course to the Garden. Lilith wasted no time. As soon as they were out of sight, she took Dracul by the hand and dragged him deep into the forest.

"Where are we going, mother?"

"I wish to show you something." Lilith flashed him a lackluster smile. "Do not fret, for you shall enjoy what I shall demonstrate to you."

Dracul slithered through the jungle, looking eager to see his mother's surprise. Lilith transformed into her snake form, and he beamed. "Now you look similar to me. We both have tails." Lilith glanced at him and nodded once.

When she reached a river, she stopped. "Behold! You have never seen or bathed in a waterway like this one before. Go on! Take a closer look, my son."

Dracul tilted his head and narrowed his eyes with confusion at her dour expression. He slithered with caution toward the river. He panted and looked at her with a worried grimace.

"Why do you look at me that way? Why are you moving at the pace of a salamander?"

Dracul stopped and stared at her with woeful eyes.

She growled and rushed him, knocking him to the ground. Her pulse beat loudly in her ears, drowning her son's screams. She wrapped her massive tail around his body and pinned him down.

He trembled and stared at her with a stunned expression. She ignored his terrified face, grasped his small head with her clawed hand, and exposed his neck. She penetrated his neck with her large, sharp fangs, creating two large holes. Bright red blood spurted from the puncture wounds. Lilith placed her lips over the openings, allowing the arterial spray to fill her mouth with warm blood. She began imbibing his life force. While she drank his blood, he struggled, gurgling, and thrashing his tail.

She heard her son's heart pulsating, at first robust and then feeble. After a while, Dracul's heart ceased beating and he lay lifeless and ashen on the wet soil. Lilith stared at what she had done. Sorrow and remorse tried to creep into her heart, but she disposed of them, and made her heart a rock once again.

She carried his limp body to the cave.

"Goodbye, my son." She muttered the words with scorn. "My only regret is that I shall not see your father's face when he finds you sprawled on the cold ground, forfeit of life."

Afterward, she desired to slip into the Garden of Eden. She craved the fruit of the Tree of Life. She would gain godlike immortality and fly to the cave Satan raved about when they first reunited. She would wait there a while, amongst the cave dwelling animals, where no one would find her until the Garden of Eden became hers to take. Lilith continued to scheme while her son's blood yet dripped from the corners of her mouth.

She took a final glance at the small lifeless body and screamed. After emitting several piercing shrieks, she flew to a nearby tree and hid within its branches. When she saw Satan and Samael run through the forest in the direction of the cave, she began to fly from tree to tree, using them as cover until she reached the edge of the forest.

Still in her snake form, she slithered to the Garden's entrance and sneaked inside without hesitation. She hid behind a bush decorated with large, exquisite flowers possessing the color and glow of the setting sun.

"Where art thou?"

God's voice was like thunder. Lilith's body stiffened. She cowered behind the flower bush. Her lips quivered and she was about to show herself when she heard Adam's voice as he confessed to hiding from Him.

She puffed with relief realizing that God addressed Adam and Eve, not her. They would soon inform Him of her deceit, but He had not acknowledged her presence in the Garden as yet. Perhaps because of her serpent form, he mistook her for an animal? She peeked around the bush and saw the humans look up to God's light as he reprimanded them. They were at a great distance from the Tree of Life. She seized the chance and rushed to the tree as fast as possible, taking the risk of being noticed by God. She also chanced a confrontation with Cam.

She arrived at the tree and froze before it, marveling at its brilliance. Coiling her tail around its base, she slid to a branch, and plucked one of its blushing fruit. Recalling what happened when she bit into the fruit from the other tree she stared at it, reluctant to put it in her mouth.

The fruit was like none she had ever seen, draped in shiny reddish-gold. It was cold and smooth in her hand. She placed her mouth over the fruit and sank her bloodstained teeth into its crisp, delicious flesh. The fruit squirted its sweet, succulent juice into her mouth. The scent swathed her like a dip in a pool of warm water, conjuring images of Floraison's light and bathing in the River of Life. The aroma was bright, cheerful, and more fragrant than any flower in the celestial Triumph Gardens.

Upon finishing the magnificent fruit, she began to undergo a transformation. She grew stronger, full of energy and vitality. The eyes on her wings gained the power of sight, having been of no use in the past. Now she saw in every direction at once, except directly behind her. The feathers became lustrous and able to withstand extreme temperatures. The inner frame of her wings became stronger, capable of enduring powerful impacts. Her tail grew longer and robust. The colors of her lower half were dazzling. She spread her arms wide, tilted her head back and closed her eyes. "I am becoming godlike."

Blinding flashes of lightning sliced through the sky. Thunder, which followed closely, shook the ground. As the wind grew stronger, the numerous trees in the Garden began to disintegrate one by one. The dust left behind by the crumbling trees blew to and fro in the increasing wind. Flowers and greeneries no longer crooned melodies. The vegetation wailed and screeched as it ceased to exist.

Lilith scanned her surroundings. The colors of the Garden were gone, and only dreariness remained as it all turned to sand. She released the Tree of Life and leapt to the ground before it, too, dissolved. She lifted her eyes to the sky, now an ominous dark gray. A jagged bolt of lightning struck nearby; she jerked. Overhead thunder continued to rumble, boom, and clash. Her hands flew to her ears to cover them. She slithered ahead, leaning into the wind. Dirt and debris whizzed by her, whipping her face. She pressed her eyelids together against the sting of the violent wind. A heavy, humid smell spread through the air. The Garden of Eden was in turmoil. If she did not exit soon, she would suffer the wrath of God.

She flapped her wings. Thick, turbulent winds attacked her from every direction, making it difficult for her to take flight. She beat her powerful wings faster and began to lift herself off the ground. She moved through the dense, forceful atmosphere, and finally escaped. Had she not eaten from the Tree of Life and gained supernatural powers, she would have perished. Once more, she headed to the cover of the forest. She settled on the tallest tree where she could overlook the destruction of paradise.

She watched Adam and Eve scurrying away in fear. They were no longer naked, but dressed in natural fibers, such as hibiscus and palm. Shortly after, she witnessed two powerful holy angels descend from Heaven. Each boasted four large, white wings. They stood guard at the entrance to the Garden of Eden. Both Cherubim held impressive weapons, which she was certain were fashioned by God's own hands.

God means to restore the Garden. Why else would he go to such lengths to secure it? Satan and Samael shall never enter the Garden of Eden while God's holy angels guard its entrance. They shall not taste the fruit of the Tree of Life as she has. "They have failed, whereas I am a goddess." Lilith cocked her head and laughed a cruel, mocking cackle that echoed through the forest.

She lingered on the treetop, waiting to see Satan and Samael approach the holy angels and attempt to enter the Garden of Eden. She desired to be a spectator to their devastation.

Chapter 48

THE LIFE FORCE

Satan and Samael were at the edge of the forest when they heard Lilith's terrible shrieks. They hurried through the woods toward the cavern where they left her and Dracul.

When they arrived at the cave, they caught sight of Dracul's pale, limp body, slumped on the dirt. Satan's face twisted and contorted, reflecting the pain and dismay in his heart. He winced as his flesh became fiery red, and he transformed into the red fiend. He clutched his upper body, experiencing intense physical pain at the sight of his son void of life.

His legs faltered, and he collapsed to his knees. He rocked back and forth, burying his head in his hands. Streams of blood originating from his eyes stained his cheeks. He groaned and shook his head. "I cannot endure the agony of losing my only son."

Samael scanned the cave for Lilith, but did not see her anywhere, and he did not know what to make of her absence. He staggered away from Satan and pressed his body against the cave's wall in the shadows, trying to vanish.

Satan spilled his grief over the body of his son for a stretch of time. Some of his blood-tears fell on Dracul's face and entered his mouth.

Satan ceased his sobbing. "Losing blood this way has weakened me."

His voice was frail and low. He gazed at his son and grimace in pain covering his head with his arms and shook with sobs once more. After a while, he wiped the blood from his eyes and gasped when his son's eyes snapped open and stared sightlessly.

"Dracul, my son, do you yet live?" Satan peered at him.

Dracul's eyes rolled languidly toward him and he moved his lips. Satan only heard a faded, voiceless breathing of words, so he lowered his head. Dracul whispered a second time, but again his words were inaudible. Once more Satan moved his ear closer to his son's mouth.

In a swift motion, Satan suffered the hot, painful sting of Dracul's bite on his neck. The sensation was both terrible and delightful. His body became slack with feebleness. He pulled away and gaped at his son, whose lips dripped with his blood.

"More." Dracul looked at his father. "If I am to live, I need more living body fluid."

"I understand. You need more blood since your own supply has been depleted?" Dracul nodded.

"Samael! Come to me." He beckoned him.

Samael toddled toward Satan and Dracul. "You have summoned me?"

"Fall to your knees beside my son's body."

"Why must I do this?" Samael licked his lips.

"My son yet lives, but he is frail. He requires some of your life force to sustain him." Satan rose to his feet.

"If I offer him my blood, what then shall sustain me?" Samael trembled.

"I am not requesting that you give him all your blood, only some, as I did." Satan glared at him. "Besides, I request merely as a formality, my friend, for I can possess you with ease and allow my son to drain you dry."

Samael shoved his hair back away from his face and knelt by Dracul's body. He lowered his head, placing his neck close to the small one's lips, closed his eyes and grimaced in anticipation of what was to come.

Satan propped Dracul's head so he could easily reach Samael's neck. Without hesitation, the little red fiend sank his fangs into his flesh. Dracul's lips were ice cold. Samael inhaled a long, audible breath as pain shot through his body. At the edge of the pain was a slight feeling of ecstasy. He sensed wetness drip down his neck as Dracul greedily drank of his blood.

Samael grew pallid. His mouth moved soundlessly. His eyes rolled to the back of his head, and he fainted. Satan clutched his long hair and held him so his son could continue feeding. He stopped Dracul just short of killing him.

Dracul's blood-red color returned to his face and body—he was once again strong and healthy. Satan laughed and hugged his son.

Dracul licked his lips and pushed Samael aside to get upright on his tail. Samael tumbled limply to the cave floor.

"Dracul, I am overjoyed that you are once again in this world, but I am at a loss to understand what occurred here. Where is your mother? Did she flee into the forest to acquire our help?"

He stared at his father with a blank expression. He furrowed his brow in confusion. "I cannot recall anything that happened." His young mind was unable to interpret the horror of what his mother did to him, so it hid the memory of all things Lilith deep inside.

"How could you forget your mother's whereabouts?"

Dracul gaped at Satan with vacant eyes. He shrugged and shook his head.

"I cannot imagine your mother left you alone and injured." Satan leaned against the cave wall and looked up.

Satan sought answers his son could not give him. He would not be at ease until he knew what happened to Lilith. Since he could not recall past events, Dracul fabricated a story to relieve his father's mind.

"Father, the very creature that attacked me must have attacked my mother and dragged her body away to feast on her flesh." Dracul placed his fingers over his mouth.

"Are you certain she has met this fate?"

Dracul shook his head. "Yes, father." He watched his weary, pallid father pound on his chest with his fists and howl as he grieved his mother.

"I shall never look again upon your sweet face. Your striking gaze, alluring smile, warm embraces and kisses shall be forever lost to me." Satan once again shed blood tears.

Whilst Satan mourned Lilith's death, and Samael lay unconscious on the ground, Dracul slipped out of the cave. He returned quickly with several hares, which he had already drained. He threw a couple on the ground by Satan, who was yet wailing.

"You must eat to regain your strength!" Dracul yelled over his father's mournful howls.

Satan stopped grieving. He gazed at his son with love in his bloodshot eyes. Samael was finally regaining consciousness.

"Eat!" Dracul tossed him a hare as well.

The corners of Satan's mouth raised a touch as he looked at his son. "You are so much like your mother." Satan was certain she had lost her life fighting for her son.

They ate greedily. When they were full, they fell asleep. Satan and Samael regained much of their strength while they slept.

The next morning they were up with the sun.

"We must make another attempt to enter the Garden of Eden and consume the fruit of the Tree of Life." Satan looked at his son, who smiled innocently and nodded. "We must take back what is ours and make a good home for ourselves. It is what Lilith desired above all."

Satan and Samael gathered their weapons once more and proceeded through the forest toward the Garden. This time, Dracul moved along with them.

Chapter 49

GADREEL'S SONG OF LAMENT

G adreel flew in darkness and in light, only stopping to eat and rest. She did not fear Lilith's certain retaliation for her desertion. Her mind was focused: she wished to reunite with her little mermaids. She was liberated, no longer dominated by Lilith, whose only thought was to seek revenge on God.

After some time, she arrived at the beach where Fornues was laid to rest, and where she last saw Dagon and her daughters. She tiptoed to the edge of the water and stared to sea. The azure, never-ending ocean was calm and untroubled. It sparkled under the sun, but she saw no sign of Dagon or her children.

Gadreel entered the water. She waded to a nearby flat rock jutting from the ocean. She sat on its surface with folded legs. The ocean breeze played with her curly hair, the color of desert sand in the late afternoon sunlight. Once comfortable, she gazed across the ocean once more certain somewhere underneath the surface her little mermaids swam with their father. She began to sing:

The Fall Of Lilith

Keenly, I watched my infants' eyes,
dreading the stares, and soft sighs,
I'm blinded by what they surmise.
They mesmerize; they mesmerize.

Extraordinary off-springs,
Like new exotic samplings,
Shown with Dagon's unique offerings,
They're my blessings; They're my blessings.

Soon there dawned an epiphany;
Daughters of our love's symphony,
Scintillas of our harmony.
True synchrony! True synchrony!

We shared moments evanescent,
When they flourished luminescent.
Now where fishes float florescent,
Is their descent, is their descent.

My heart was lilt in their gaze,
Wilts now in their absence and blaze
Deprived of their love, is to faze
As in a daze, as in a daze.

Emptiness is all fills my core.
My soul burns with hunger once more.

My daughters, I long to adore,
Come to the shore! Come to the shore!

I fear I shall starve, o'er my babes,
Lest their dulcet gaze meet my face.
With time, I'll be part of this place,
Singing their praise! Singing their praise!

Oh, bring back my mermaids, love-charm!
Come now, or I'll make loud alarm,
Until my last breath suffers harm!
Cold rocks, no warmth! Cold rocks, no warmth!

"I shall continue to sing," Gadreel whispered to herself, "and with time become part of this rock, lingering for my little mermaids to be in my arms once more—Or until I utter my last breath in song."

Gadreel sang all day and night, unwavering in her purpose.

Chapter 50

MASS OF FLESH

Lilith grew weary and bored waiting for Satan and Samael to return to the Garden of Eden. Perhaps the cowards decided to abandon their purpose. She wore a sardonic smirk. She prepared to take flight when she heard footfalls in the forest. Peering through the dense trees she squinted, distinguishing Satan and Samael. However, she did not see Dracul. She waited once more for them to step from the forest and make their useless attempt to enter the lost paradise.

When they reached the edge of the forest, they looked toward the Garden. "Wait! I see changes," Samael said. "There are two large Cherubim with divine weaponry guarding the entrance to Eden."

Satan took a look at the guardians and their weapons and then glanced at the weapons he and Samael held and frowned. He immediately understood they were no match. However, knowing his son's eyes were upon him, he did not wish to admit defeat.

"My son, I desire you remain hidden within these trees," Satan said.

"But father—"

Satan lifted his hand before him and strangled his words. "Listen to what I tell you." Satan placed a hand on his son's shoulder. "You must not allow the holy angels guarding the Garden's entrance to become aware of you. You must remain in the forest, hidden from view, no matter what happens. Heed my words, my son, and know I am most proud of you. You have been my greatest triumph since I was banished from Floraison."

Dracul gazed into his father's despairing eyes. He saw love and pain in them, but he was baffled by his wish for him to remain behind, shrouded by the trees of the forest. However, he understood it was important for him to agree to his father's request.

"Very well, Father, I shall follow your command. I vow not reveal myself. No matter what happens, I shall remain hidden in the forest."

Satan embraced his son and kissed him on the forehead. He then glanced at Samael and with his eyes, communicated for him to follow.

Samael looked confused and taken aback. "I assumed after seeing the guards, you would renounce your plan of attack."

"We shall march together toward our objective, and break words away from young ears." Satan led Samael away from his son and toward the Garden's entrance.

"We are incapable of being victorious against the guardians of Eden," Samael whispered to Satan.

"Perhaps, but we shall try nonetheless." Satan's tone was dispirited. "Since we were cast out of Floraison, nothing has gone our way." Now he had lost his one true love. How was he to go on without her? "We must try to conquer the Garden of Eden because it was Lilith's utmost desire that her son live in paradise. We shall do this for her."

Samael noted Satan's dejection and was certain they marched to their defeat. Even so, as his one true friend and servant in all his undertakings, he believed he must share his doom. Crestfallen, he followed without another word.

Meanwhile, Lilith saw them reach the edge of the forest. "What is taking them so long?" She tried to get a better look, but trees and branches obstructed her view.

At last, she watched Satan in his angel form and Samael leave the forest. Together they advanced toward the entrance to Eden. She watched them with wide eyes, rubbing her hands together, unable to sit still.

They marched to the floral archway adorning the entrance and confronted the Cherubim guards.

"Is this where we shall meet our end?" Samael whispered as they approached the entrance.

"I would not deem it so." Satan wore a veneer of confidence and strut like a peacock.

"Halt!" the Cherub on the right said, his voice booming. "Take another step forward, and it shall be your last."

"We desire entry into the Garden," Satan said.

"Yet here we stand in your way, ensuring neither you nor any of your kind ever gain admittance into Eden, for God commands it so," the Cherub on the left spoke in a ringing voice.

"Why would God deny me access?" Satan looked at them askance. "It is no longer occupied by his humans."

"Enough, Satan!" Michael descended toward him. "God and all of Heaven have grown weary of your arrogance and pride." Raphael and Jetrel accompanied him on one side, and Esar and Hashmal on the other.

Satan and Samael lifted their weapons, threatening the holy angels, but their trembling hands betrayed their fear.

"Even now, you are defiant in the face of annihilation! Who are you to question the will of God?" Michael pointed his golden spear. "You do not deserve entry into the Garden of Eden, and you are even less deserving to partake of the Tree of Life. It is time you and your followers be given proper punishment for all of God's deeds you have undone!"

Samael's legs faltered and he collapsed. Jetrel swooped down and hovered over him, pointing her silver lance at him, lest he try to escape, but he trembled and held up his hands.

Satan made an attempt to flee. However, Raphael skillfully flung his net over him, knocking him to the ground and paralyzing him before he could take flight. The others swooped toward him. They tied his wrists and ankles. Jetrel bound Samael the same way.

Esar shifted into a giant green behemoth with shimmering scales and an enormous wingspan. The beast's sharp teeth were as long as javelins, and its massive, powerful tail was swathed in serrated spikes. The fearsome creature carried a heavy metal chain in its sharp clutches.

Michael and Raphael hauled Satan's rigid, paralyzed body. Jetrel and Hashmal carried Samael. The holy angels placed them together on their feet, back to back. Satan's breaths quickened. Samael shuddered. In the form of the massive beast, Esar once again received the task of wrapping the chain around the fallen ones.

When they were bound, Hashmal stood before them. "To ensure you are bound together for eternity, I shall consummate this rite with fire."

Flames shot from his mouth, burning Satan and Samael. The fallen angels howled in pain. Samael gagged at the sweet, acrid smell of his own burning flesh. Satan grimaced and wailed in torment, as his skin blistered and popped, the odor of his sizzling skin so strong he could taste it. Their hair caught fire. The sharp, jarring stench bombarded their nostrils and left a bitter taste on their tongues. The chain heated to ineffable temperatures. Roasting metal links melted into their flesh—joining them forever. When Hashmal was done breathing fire, Esar grabbed the mass of igneous flesh and took flight.

The others followed the beast to a land covered in ice and snow. Amid this frozen land was an enormous mountain. The beast halted prior to reaching its summit.

"Remain here," Esar told the holy angels. "Do not come any closer, for this mountain presents great danger, even for us. I shall place the fallen ones inside, where they shall remain imprisoned until the end of days."

He proceeded into the mouth of the mountain. He placed Satan and Samael standing near the bottom of the volcano's inner crater at the edge of a large magma lake. Although the weather was freezing cold outside the mountain, inside by the lake of fire was a raging inferno.

The magma lake boiled and erupted, spewing lava, which scorched and ate away at the prisoners' flesh. Satan and Samael wailed in agony and horror. This would be their eternity, and this knowledge brought them close to madness.

Esar was unwilling to bear the terrible heat and gases from the magma lake a moment longer. He soared from the volcano to meet the other holy angels, leaving behind the tortured cries of the condemned.

"Let us be gone from this cursed place," Esar said upon reuniting with the others. He shifted to his angel form, and they departed the cold, desolate location and returned to their celestial home.

Chapter 51

THE BEGINNING OF
THE END

Dracul remained motionless, dominated by terror as he watched his father's capture. Trapped under Raphael's net like an animal, Satan used his last bit of strength to glance in his son's direction. Their eyes met, and in his father's eyes Dracul saw a reminder of his wish for him to remain hidden in the forest.

What could he do? He did not have the strength to save his father and Samael. Dracul lifted his drenched eyes to the sky. He squinted, focused, and saw a figure within the trees. The feminine creature hiding amongst the branches sported a tail similar to his. She appeared to be a powerful being. He thought to call upon her, but his instincts quickly warned him against it, although he did not know why.

What was she doing hiding amongst the trees? Why would she not try to help his father? She was one of them. Was that a smile he saw on her face?

Dracul looked askance at the creature and shook his head. He curled up into a quivering bundle on the ground. Every sound, no matter how minute, made him jolt. He placed his cold, clammy hand over his heart as he sought to understand.

His father and Samael were captured by celestial beings. He watched them being burned alive by a fire-breathing angel and taken away by a large and terrible beast, while a fallen companion watched delighted, hidden within the trees of this forest. "I have no one to care for me," he whispered hidden between trees and overgrown shrubs. He was alone in the woods.

His mind seemed to unravel as he stared into oblivion. How much can a young, fragile mind endure?

✦

Lilith witnessed Esar, in the form of an enormous monster, carry in its clutches Satan and Samael, burnt and bound together in chains, away to share a fate similar to Beelzebub's.

"Things could not have come to pass any better." Lilith shook with laughter and clapped her hands. "Now that my deeds here are done, I shall leave this wretched place and find a dwelling suitable for a goddess."

She flew out of the trees in her snake form. As she tore through the sky, she spotted Adam and Eve. "It looks like the humans are establishing a new beginning on lush grounds near a large river." She planned to continue on her way, leaving them in her past, but when she saw Eve stroll away from Adam, she could not resist having one last exchange with her.

She swooped down and landed behind a large plant. In silence, she slithered to the tree where Eve was picking fruit.

"Greetings." Lilith stepped from behind the tree in angel form.

Eve jumped and dropped the fruit she carried. "You! What are you doing here?"

"Why do you ask? Are you not happy to see me?" With a sardonic grin, Lilith picked a fruit from the ground, and took a bite.

Eve staggered away from her. "Why do you torment me so? Have you not done enough?"

"I merely assisted you in doing what you desired all along." Lilith savored the fruit.

"Since you misled us, Adam and I were banished from the Garden of Eden to live among dangers unimaginable."

Lilith chuckled and then noticed Eve's rounded midsection. She tossed the fruit to the ground and hurried to her. She touched Eve's belly. Eve recoiled.

"You are with child!" Lilith clapped her hands.

Eve swallowed hard and looked away. "I am aware of my gravid state."

"I was not the only one who misled you, was I?" Lilith sauntered around her examining every inch of her. Eve shook her head wearing a wounded expression.

Lilith poked her lip out to mock her. "His name is Samael or Satan, whichever you choose, for they are one and the same in this matter." Lilith was delighted to see realization dawn in Eve's honey-colored eyes.

"You carry his offspring." Lilith looked at her with a sour expression.

Eve flinched and shook her head vigorously.

"Yes! The seed you carry is only part human. It is a powerful and malevolent creature you tow."

Eve trembled staring at the ground.

"Adam need never know," Lilith said. "You never told him of your shameful acts with Samael, so why confess now?"

Eve stared wide-eyed at her, tears of anguish meandering over the curves of her face. She passed her hands across her belly.

"It would not be wise to disclose this information to him now." Lilith waved her pointing finger from side to side as she spoke. "Only harm can come to you and your unborn child."

Eve buried her face in her hands and whimpered.

"Adam shall never know." Lilith glared at her middle. "Your son shall be beautiful. He shall grow big and strong, and make you proud to be his mother."

Eve gazed at Lilith's sulking, resentful face, and almost pitied her for her pain. Lilith caught a glimpse of sympathy from her and pounced, straddling her on the ground.

"How dare you pity me?" Lilith's chest heaved with rage. "I am a powerful godlike creature! You are a pathetic being of no significance!"

"I do not pity you! You have ruined my life!" Eve muffled a scream.

Lilith leapt to her feet. She clutched Eve by her hair and lifted her. Eve bit her lip as she sobbed, not wishing Adam to hear her cries.

"You carry perdition in your womb," Lilith whispered in her ear before releasing her hair and shoving her. "But you shall love him nonetheless, for he is a small innocent creature, and it is by no fault of his that he was conceived."

Eve slammed her eyes shut and pressed both hands over her mouth.

"I speak only the truth," Lilith said in a honeyed tone.

"Please, leave us be. I implore you." Eve sobbed. "You have brought enough havoc into our lives."

"I shall be on my way, but rest assured that the damage I have caused shall forever grow, rippling across the planet until the entire earth is touched by the devastation of my deeds." Below Lilith's unmoving eyes was a grin that showed almost every tooth and stretched her lips thin.

She expanded her wings in preparation to leave. Eve saw the plethora of eyes glaring at her—judging her. She gasped, her knees faltered, and she tumbled to the ground.

Lilith pointed to her belly. "You shall name your son Cain, which means *spear,* for just like Michael's golden spear struck Satan's chest and marked the beginning of his end, so shall your son be the spear that shall mark the beginning of the end for mankind."

Eve trembled before the piercing eyes in the face and wings of her accuser. She threw herself face down on the ground. Her body shook with sobs.

"When you gaze into your son's eyes, Satan shall forever be reflected there." Lilith took flight; laughing, satisfied she had finally delivered her vengeance.

Made in the USA
Monee, IL
21 October 2020